PRAISE FOR EMMA'S DRAGON

Best Fantasy Novel – Royal Dragonfly Award
IPPY Award Winner
Foreword INDIES Finalist

"M. Verant's colorful worldbuilding, nuanced characters, and suspenseful plot made for another enthralling read right to the very last tantalizing page. This is Gaslamp fantasy at its best and I can heartily recommend it to Austen lovers, dragon fantasy fans, or those who like an exciting historical with fantasy elements." – *Sophia Rose, Books of My Heart*

"5+. Intense. Riveting. Enthralling. Downright Amazing! There is no way my review can do justice to all that this book encompasses. Elizabeth's role was a tour de force and one that still leaves me in wonder. But Emma's journey, along with the others, is far from over... it is just beginning." – *Carole in Canada*

"Dark and beautiful. Profound and consuming. With a still flawed but actually sympathetic Emma, a Harriet who has a backbone, a Mr. Knightly who is a character in his own right, and a fully realized Georgina Darcy and Mary Bennet, this volume deals with racism, homophobia, the restricted role of women, class struggle, the Napoleonic Wars, and dragons. Like the first book— and for heaven's sake read that book first—it is at times very very dark, but shot through with hope and wonder." – *Hope E. Ring*

"The writing was detailed, lush with description and drew the reader into the tale. The continuation of Lizzy and Darcy's story is seamlessly woven into Emma Woodhouse's. Containing brilliant world building and compelling characters, the second title in the 'Jane Austen Fantasy' series scintillates as it entrances the reader." – *Kylie Clayton, NetGalley*

"The book is not 'Emma with dragons,' nor is it a lighthearted gaslamp fantasy. It feels more like Naomi Novik's Temeraire series, as the draca are enlisted in the

Napoleonic War. We recommend this book if you enjoy serious gaslamp fantasy." – *Plot Trysts*

"Dragons and Regency—need more be said? In *Emma's Dragon: London and Pemberley*, M. Verant's storytelling is richly detailed—filled with Regency manners, romance, mystery, intrigue and dragons." – *Llynnya, BookBub*

"The story unfolds in London, with dark forces kidnapping wyves and dosing them with crawler venom. The cast of characters runs from Royalty to orphans, with a mix of races as befits a story which addresses both racial and class prejudice. *Emma's Dragon* is a fast-paced and exciting read, and it is sure to please fans of both Jane Austen and fantasy fiction." – *My JAFF Obsession*

"*Emma's Dragon* combines all your favorite Jane Austen characters and draws you into a world of dragons and powers. You don't want to miss this amazing book!" – *Odette Swan, Goodreads*

"Alongside the 'draca' are a myriad of other themes. Female power in a patriarchal society. Radical evangelism. Slavery. Choice and free will. The nature of true evil/psychopathy vs madness. Heavy stuff, but woven seamlessly into the plot. The storytelling itself was impeccable." – *Megami, Vine Voice*

Emma's DRAGON

LONDON AND PEMBERLEY
JANE AUSTEN FANTASY - BOOK 2

M. VERANT

ACERBIC

First edition: March 2023
Acerbic Press www.acerbicpress.com

ISBNs: 978-1-7366629-4-6 (paperback), 978-1-7366629-3-9 (ebook), 978-1-7366629-5-3 (audiobook), 979-8387996764 (hardcover)

Publisher's Cataloging-in-Publication Data

Names: Verant, M., author.
Title: Emma's dragon : London and Pemberley / M. Verant.
Description: California: Acerbic Press, 2023. | Series: Jane Austen Fantasy, bk. 2.
Identifiers: ISBN 9781736662946 (paperback) | ISBN 9781736662939 (ebook) | ISBN 9781736662953 (audiobook) | ISBN 9798387996764 (hardcover)
Subjects: GSAFD: Fantasy fiction. | BISAC: FICTION / Fantasy / Historical. | FICTION / Fantasy / Romance. | FICTION / Adaptations & Pastiche.
Classification: LCC PS3622.E731 E46 2023 | DDC 813/.6–dc23

BREEDS OF DRACA

Bound breeds, from greatest to least social prestige:

Wyvern: A winged, two-legged draca. Near the size of an English foxhound (60-75 lb).
Firedrake (drake): A winged, two-legged draca the size of a large goose or eagle (16-18 lb).
Lindworm: A draca with a heavy build like a bulldog or badger (20-25 lb).
Tykeworm (tyke): A draca the size of a Yorkshire terrier (5-7 lb). Does not throw fire. Unusually affectionate with their bound wyfe.
Roseworm: A draca the size of a rabbit. Distinguished by red or rose scales on its belly.
Broccworm: A tunneling draca with powerful front legs. Rather like a small badger.
Ferretworm: A tunneling draca, long and thin like a ferret.
Tunnelworm: A nocturnal, palm-sized draca that burrows and prefers to be underground.

Unbound breeds:

Song draca: Robin-sized. Scaled muzzles and heads; feathered wings and swallow-like tails.
Needledrac: The size of a dragonfly. Two-legged and clawed like a miniature firedrake.

CAST OF CHARACTERS

Woodhouses, Knightleys, and acquaintances:
Miss Emma Woodhouse: Mistress of Hartfield estate.
Miss Harriet Smith: Emma's friend.
Mr. George Knightley: A gentleman musician.
Isabella and John: Emma's sister and her husband.
Miss Taylor: Emma's childhood nanny.
Mr. Elton: Vicar of Highbury.

Bennets, Bingleys, and acquaintances:
Mrs. Elizabeth Darcy (Lizzy): The second-eldest Bennet sister.
Miss Mary Bennet: The middle Bennet sister.
Miss Kitty Bennet: The next-to-youngest Bennet sister.
Mrs. Lydia Wickham: The youngest Bennet sister, deceased.
Mrs. Jane Bingley: The eldest Bennet sister. Married to Charles Bingley.
Mrs. Bennet: Mother of the Bennet sisters.
Miss Caroline Bingley: The younger of Charles Bingley's two sisters.

Darcys and acquaintances:
Mr. Fitzwilliam Darcy (Fitz): Lizzy's husband.
Miss Georgiana Darcy: Mr. Darcy's sister.
Mrs. Reynolds: The Darcys' housekeeper.
Lucy: Lizzy's lady's maid.
Lady Catherine de Bourgh: Mr. Darcy's aunt and mistress of Rosings Park.
Mr. Digweed: Headman of the Pemberley Briton clans.
Mr. Rabb: The Pemberley gamekeeper, deceased.

London:
Mr. Tinsdale: A member of Parliament.
Lord Castlehurst: The Secretary of War.
Lord Wellington: Leader of England's armies in the Peninsular war.
Dr. Davenport: A physician teaching medicine to Mary Bennet.
Mr. Needham: Teaches harness making at the Martin school.

Nessy: A young student at the Martin school.
Miss Bathurst: An abducted wyfe.
Miss Rees, Miss Spoon: Mary's friends and members of the "Marys."
Mrs. Hickinbottom: A widowed innkeeper in London.
Mr. Debrett: Publisher of *Debrett's Dracal Lineage*.
Prince George: The Prince Regent, son of King George III.

Draca:
Yuánchi / 元气 : The scarlet dragon bound to Lizzy.
Fènnù / 愤怒

The wedding ritual that binds draca, an offering of marriage gold blessed by the Church, is central to aristocratic Englishness. Yet, in this Enlightened era, we cannot deny the evidence of binding in cultures different from our own.

— DEBRETT'S DRACAL LINEAGE. 8TH ED, 1812

The empowerment of binding is a female right, independent of religion, class, or love.

— MARY WOLLSTONECRAFT BENNET. ARGYLL STREET PROTEST, JULY 1812

I shall not give you any advice.

— EMMA WOODHOUSE

PART I

LONDON

EMMA WOODHOUSE

EMMA

I am Emma Woodhouse. I have three secrets.

Our coach rattled over the cobblestones of London. The city's unfamiliar clamor had grown: shouts and whistles, thudding hooves, and traces straining above the clatter of wheels. The coach windows were shut, tightly latched and curtains drawn, but the sound crept through.

"Miss Woodhouse..." Harriet's voice had a concerned wobble.

My gaze was trapped by the pearl button that snugged the wrist of my glove. Twelve loops of perfect thread wrapped the button shank—my defense against the miasma. It took all my courage to look up.

Even pinched with worry, Harriet's black eyes were pretty, framed by slightly plump cheeks, charcoal brows, and umber skin. I told her often that was more attractive than my winter-pale face and blonde ringlets.

"Are you certain I should bind a draca?" Harriet said.

I reached across the carriage to take her hand, the crook of my wrist almost blue beside the warmth of her brown fingers. "Dear Harriet. I am certain you are a lady, and ladies bind when they marry." She shook her head nervously, so I added, "Let me show you London."

Emma Woodhouse, comfortable and clever, does not fear a city.

I trapped a breath in my lungs, summoned the memory of my glove's pearl button, then drew the curtain from the coach window.

"Oh my." Harriet gawked out the window. "It is grand. You must look, too!"

My eyes were locked on the coach's pleated red cushions. "I have seen London before."

After Papa's death, I met his lawyer here. The lawyer clutched my hand as I left, reciting condolences and advice. Then a strange man staggered against me and sprawled in the gutter, wracked with cough.

That fear, vivid as life, seized my mind.

Harriet turned from the window, and her smiling lips moved as if speaking, but her skin became ashen and mottled. The colorless miasma of illness swirled around her, and she gasped and choked for air—

No. That is false. Harriet is not ill. It is an evil fancy.

I found my glove's button and counted perfect loops of thread. Harriet's cheerful voice resumed, describing a milliner's window.

Here is my first secret. False thoughts slip into my mind. These evil images of sickness are so terrible that I visited a famous physician for a private opinion. The doctor wore fine tweed, but his watch chain dangled, unfastened. I do not remember what he said.

I summoned a smile for Harriet, unfolded *The Times*, and reread the announcement:

For Ladies:
A Musical Salon and Social Discourse upon Feminine Power, the Right of
All Women to Bind, and other Topics.

By invitation.
Misses Mary Bennet and Georgiana Darcy.

Miss Bennet's reply to my letter was folded in my reticule. Emma Woodhouse, handsome and rich, was welcome at their London salon.

The miasma slipped putrid tendrils under the seams of the carriage door. *No.* That is false.

My gloved fingers were trembling. I willed them still. Since the illness and death of my dear father, these false thoughts have pressed harder and harder. But I have a tool to master them.

"Come, Harriet," I said. "Let us have you looking nice." I smoothed her collar, like I had smoothed her life, perfecting her rise into society.

Perfection is proof against illness.

I aligned a point of lace on her shoulder, and serenity filled me. The miasma skulked and hid below our seats.

LONDON'S VAPOR of coal smoke stung my eyes as I stepped down from the carriage. The street swarmed with gentlemen, ladies, energetic children, and an astonishing range of carriages and cabs.

One passing coach had an iron travel cage strapped atop. A small, sleek draca was inside—a dark brown ferretworm as long as my forearm, and not much thicker. Her black eyes met mine before the coach vanished around the corner. An echo of brown woodland-earth flickered in my mind.

I looked for the building named on the invitation. The doorway was down the street, but the path was blocked by a dozen working men shouting and waving hand-drawn signs. One sign faced me: "Of the Heathen, Ye Shall Buy Bondmen and Bondmaids."

The man holding the sign saw my attention. He grinned, stretching skin that was rough with stubble. His gaze crawled down my yellow silk gown.

Harriet stepped from the coach. She looked around, her raven curls swiveling, then she saw the men. Her hand caught my arm. "We should go another way."

"Another way?" I said. "Why?"

She leaned close. "They are pro-slavers."

"Oh." I recognized the sign now, a Bible verse that slavers cited as divine proof of their cause.

Slavery was outlawed in England, but the slave industry and its horrors still flourished in the colonies. The pro-slavers sought to repeal the government embargo on transporting slaves aboard English ships. They claimed it cost jobs.

Unexpectedly, the opposition to slavery was led by women. Ladies Societies throughout England had organized the movement for full abolition. Of course, the encroachment of ladies into politics only fanned the fury of the pro-slavers. That made a lady with Harriet's coloring twice a target.

The man's coarse grin was now an angry sneer at Harriet.

I linked my arm through Harriet's and clasped my hand on her puffy muslin sleeve. "Come, Harriet. You are a lady, and ladies are above such people."

I strode forward, and Harriet fell into stride with me, although stiffly. Two paces short of the men, I stopped and stared at the stubbly man. He shuffled aside with a mutter and a glare. The group parted, most of the rest touching a hat or forelock. When the path was clear, we proceeded, and I felt Harriet's arm relax.

"I have seen their kind twenty times," I said to her. "They cannot impede proper ladies."

"You have seen their kind." Harriet's voice was somber. "You have not seen what they do." Fiercely, she added, "I am glad you have not."

We entered a quiet, elegant lobby. A note in a lady's hand gave directions to a salon on the next floor. There, a dour maid asked to see our invitation and admitted us.

The salon was a good-sized room, about twenty by forty feet, with windows overlooking the street. It was furnished like a lady's sitting room but excessively bland, with beige fringed curtains, plain cushioned chairs around small tables, and undersized, dull watercolors hung on the walls. This was a space for hire, not one decorated to an owner's taste. The sole unusual item was a tremendous grand pianoforte of gleaming mahogany.

At one side of the room, the hostesses were buried in a bustle of chattering ladies. Around them were draca.

A broccworm, wingless and quadruped like most draca breeds, sat at the edge of the crowd. Broccworms are one of the larger draca, and this was no exception, at least fifteen pounds and solidly muscled under armored brown scales. In a farther corner a pretty roseworm lazed, no bigger than a rabbit, her belly scales streaked with pink.

The invitation had suggested that wyves bring their bound draca, but seeing them in the room was remarkable. Draca are rarely together. A gentry couple bind a single draca on their wedding night, and the beasts themselves lead solitary lives. Even seeing a broccworm or roseworm indoors was exceptional, as they can throw fire. Flamers were usually kept outside in stone draca houses, away from wooden structures.

A third draca, a tykeworm, waited by a lady observing from the far wall. I encouraged Harriet to mingle with the crowd—it would be good practice—then crossed the room. The lady watched me with lively eyes, her curly chestnut hair barely restrained in a chignon and an amused quirk on her lips. She wore light blue muslin, simple but finely tailored, and practical, slightly scuffed shoes. The tykeworm sat alertly at her feet, a few pounds of puppyish energy sheathed in nutmeg-brown scales that became carrot orange at his toes.

"Have you attended the salon before?" I said.

"This is my first visit." She offered her hand. "Mrs. Elizabeth Darcy."

"Miss Emma Woodhouse." We shook hands.

The binding to her draca crackled up my arm and flooded my mind, a blinding flash of scarlet, numbingly potent even through gloves.

Shaken, I missed Mrs. Darcy's next words. Her dark brown eyes became puzzled—waiting for a reply.

I guessed, a talent I had mastered to hide my distractions. "One of the hosts is your sister?"

She smiled, relieved our conversation was on track. "Both hosts are my sisters. Georgiana Darcy by marriage, and I was Elizabeth Bennet before."

"How delightful that your sisters share their project with you."

"Share?" Her eyebrows narrowed.

I unfolded the program included with my invitation and touched her name on the list of speakers: *Mrs. Darcy, against social prohibitions to binding*. This was why I had brought Harriet to London—to ensure she would be allowed to bind. No gentleman would marry a woman forbidden to bind draca.

Mrs. Darcy folded her arms and glared at the knot of ladies. "Mary neglected to inform me that I shared her project. I may spend our afternoon delighted by one fewer sister."

I laughed at that and found I quite enjoyed Mrs. Darcy. "Please forgive your sister. I have learned that sisters are precious."

She became still. She did not look away, but a pair of glistening tears pooled on her lower lashes.

"I am sorry," I said. "I have upset you."

"You could not know. I lost a sister this year." She touched my hand. I was prepared this time, but the scarlet of her binding hammered my wrist like a giant pulse. "Please call me Lizzy."

"Of course. I am Emma."

I introduced Harriet Smith, who had returned to report on the styles of the London ladies. Lizzy listened with great amusement, and I was pleased to see Harriet at ease in city society.

While they spoke, I studied the tykeworm, who had padded close to investigate the lace trim of my petticoat. Lizzy's scarlet binding could not be with this tyke. The color I sensed from a binding was the color of the draca themselves, and the tyke was brown and orange. To my knowledge, no draca were scarlet.

I addressed the tyke, mock serious. "Which wyfe is yours?" Gleaming black eyes turned up to consider me. I felt the stirring of his binding, but weak. Distant.

"He is bound to my aunt," Lizzy answered, and the tyke switched his attention to her. "Today he is my companion. My aunt's legs tire, and he is high-spirited, so when I come to London, I take him out." She bent to him. "You are my loyal guardian." He sat back on his haunches, chest flung out and for all the world appearing proud. All three ladies laughed.

Although the event was for ladies, two gentlemen entered. One was dark skinned, and my gaze caught on him. Black men were common in port cities like London, often sailors from the Caribbean who had settled, and Black gentlemen were mentioned in the society papers, but I had never met one. Our small Surrey village of Highbury had only a Black farmer and Harriet.

This man was elegant and poised, his charcoal coat fitted to a strong, tapered torso. He wore no gloves and gestured while he spoke. His hands were strikingly expressive. I wondered if he had passed the men shouting that England should resume the slave trade.

"Who is that?" I asked Lizzy as the man bowed to a pair of fashionable young ladies.

"Mr. Knightley. He is prominent in the London musical establishment. I have been looking forward to meeting him."

A cough echoed through the room.

I spun, unsure where it had been. Lizzy gave me a surprised look. I grasped for an excuse. "Such a pretty salon."

Who coughed? The compulsion bit like a demon, curling my fingers.

I dragged a smile onto my lips. "Harriet, if I may..." I smoothed the ribbon on her collar, explaining, "Harriet will warn you. It is my favorite project to keep my friends' clothes neat."

The ladies laughed. But the ribbon had not been enough. Pestilent, colorless miasma curled around our feet. My fingers crooked.

"I have a challenge for your clothing project," Lizzy said. Her friendly smile became intimate as she took the hand of an approaching gentleman—the fair skinned one, although he also had dark hair. He was very tall. "Mr. Darcy, may I introduce my new acquaintances, Miss Woodhouse and Miss Smith."

I shook hands, relieved by the distraction. When Mr. Darcy's glove touched mine, the Darcys' scarlet binding flashed. It was rare to sense anything from a husband, and this was strong, like touching a wyfe, although nothing to the raw power when I had touched Lizzy.

Beside me, Harriet managed a wordless bob, her eyes wide at Mr. Darcy's bearing and social consequence, or perhaps his broad shoulders.

"Do you see your challenge, Emma?" Lizzy said, an eyebrow cocked in amusement.

At first, I hardly heard her. My eyes were searching his clothes, my fingers itching. Men's clothes were better—concealing, snugly buttoned—but also worse because touching required elaborate contrivance.

But the compulsion faded. I recalled now: the miasma was a fancy of my mind. It was not real.

"He is perfect," I said, then laughed and corrected myself, "Your clothes, Mr. Darcy, are quite perfect." Relief left me giddy.

"It is his most annoying habit," Lizzy said. "I am overmatched in any dressing contest."

"My habit is in remembrance of my mother," Mr. Darcy said. He had a resonant baritone that suited his height.

"What?" Lizzy said, turning to him. "I did not know that."

"My mother was distressed by imperfect clothing," Mr. Darcy said. His eyes had not left me. Attention from gentlemen was familiar, but this felt odd. Was he suspicious? Impossible. I was too practiced at concealment.

The other draca in the room were a roseworm and a broccworm. To sense the Darcys' binding so strongly, one draca must be theirs. Bindings were stronger when the bound draca was near. Could a roseworm feel scarlet? That seemed unlikely.

"Which is your bound draca?" I asked.

Silence.

Mr. Darcy replied, "Regrettably, my wyfe and I were unable to bind."

He had lied. I felt their binding.

I offered the traditional, vacant sympathies. Lizzy stared at the floor as if shamed by their failure—deserved or not, blame fell on the wyfe—but her pose was unconvincing after her frank grief for her deceased sister. Mystified, I braced myself and grazed her gloved hand again. Her binding flashed scarlet in my mind.

Why would a bound wyfe pretend she had failed to bind?

Here is my second secret. I sense the bindings between wyves and draca. This secret is not illusion; bindings are real. But only I can sense them. It is a strange skill, and harmless, but I conceal it. A gentleman and wyfe bind draca through the passion of their marriage night. That makes curiosity about binding improper, but my skill is even more troubling—too much like the powers claimed by sinful crones who peddle binding charms to desperate brides.

These first two secrets are a dangerous pair. One senses truth but must be concealed. The other fills me with false terrors I must ignore or be declared a madwoman.

Hand-in-hand, the pair of fashionable ladies left the larger group and crossed the room to join us. The remainder of the group quieted, every eye following. These were the salon hosts and influential in London society.

"Mary!" Lizzy said as they arrived. "Imagine my surprise when I discovered my name printed in your program."

Miss Mary Bennet was an intense young woman in an unremittingly black gown, her only jewelry circular gold spectacles and a delicate gold musical note hanging on a hair-thin necklace. Her brown hair fell straight to her shoulders, a peculiar style but one shared by several guests. Some trending London fashion.

"The male aristocracy has conspired to restrict binding to gentry," Mary replied, her words so rapid they were almost staccato. "You should be the speaker, as you made me aware of it." When Lizzy seemed taken aback, Mary adjusted her spectacles—inexpertly; they must be new—and added in painstaking tones, "Our *theme* is society's conventions that disempower women."

"I did not intend to give a public speech on the matter," Lizzy protested.

Mary squinted through her spectacles. "Why not?"

"Did you not even *ask* her?" said the woman beside her. She was younger yet but blooming into a beauty, black-haired with ocean-blue eyes, although slim as a reed. She wore an unembellished, exquisite blue watered-silk gown. Around her neck hung a twin to Mary's musical note necklace.

The three women launched into overlapping claims and counterclaims, all delivered with the happy annoyance of loving family. Harriet and I exchanged an amused look.

Mr. Darcy's powerful voice intervened. "Miss Woodhouse, Miss Smith. May I present my sister, Miss Georgiana Darcy, and my wyfe's sister, Miss Mary Bennet."

Miss Darcy was the young beauty. She greeted us with unselfconscious grace, her hand elegant as a duchess and her voice a song. Behind her back, Miss Mary Bennet traded sisterly scowls with Lizzy before shaking my hand distractedly.

While Harriet listened to the ladies debate the merits of public speech, I stole a glance at Mr. Darcy. He no longer watched me. His gaze hung on his wyfe, enthralled. They were very obviously in love. That was by no means the rule for a gentry marriage.

I examined his snow-white waistcoat. It fastened with a single column of seven oyster-shell buttons. Each button had grooves dividing it in quarters. All the buttons were oriented identically, one groove precisely vertical. I exhaled a long breath as the last crawling twinges of my panic cooled.

This could be a good day. A day with no need for deception. London might be more tolerable than I thought.

A sharp motion drew my gaze to the salon's doorway. The dour maid had her arm extended, blocking the entrance of two rough men in leather cloaks. I recognized the stubbly man from the protest on the street.

One man grabbed the maid and dragged her aside, his hand stifling her mouth. The other man strode into the unaware crowd.

"Mrs. Elizabeth Darcy!" he shouted. "Where is she?"

Shocked faces turned to him, but also to Lizzy. The man's gaze followed, and his eyes narrowed. He drew his hand from his coat pocket. Steel and brass gleamed as he pointed his arm at Lizzy. He held a pistol.

Mr. Darcy wrapped his wyfe in an embrace that drove her against me. We stumbled sideways in a tangle. The pistol flashed dirty-orange with an ear-thump of sound, blowing a ragged hole in the wall a foot from my shoulder. Plaster dust stung my face. Settled on my eyelashes.

Mr. Knightley charged at the gunman. They collided with a yell, then pushed across the room to slam the wall. A painting fell, and they fell on top of it, wrestling and shouting. Mr. Darcy ran to help.

Like a choir after a synchronized breath, a chorus of ladies' screams sounded. Pastel and print dresses retreated to press walls and chairs. The center of the room emptied other than the sulfurous smoke from the pistol shot.

The second man stood unnoticed by the entrance, the silenced maid struggling in his arms. He shoved her viciously, banging her head into the doorframe, and she collapsed, skirts askew. He strode across the room, his eyes on Lizzy.

Lizzy was beside me, her gaze on her scuffling husband. I shouted, "Lizzy! Run!"

Her eyes turned to me, then she saw the other man. Her empty hand rose, a finger outstretched as if to point.

Authority hammered my awareness. Command drove the air from my lungs. I had never felt this. I did not understand what I felt.

The man reached the abandoned center of the room. He pulled his cloak aside and reached for a huge pistol on his belt. The barrel was flared like the blunderbusses favored by coach drivers.

The broccworm ran forward and gaped its jaws, throwing a raging wall of blue flame between the man and us—inches from the man's hands and so hot that it scalded my face a half-dozen yards away. The man fell backward, his arms flailing. The edge of his cloak swung through the flame, and the heavy leather crisped and blew away like paper in a bonfire.

The man sprawled hard onto the floor, and the broccworm's fiery breath stopped. The ceiling above flashed into a sheet of orange fire, then extinguished itself to oily smoke.

Lizzy walked forward to stand over the man. Smoldering curls of burned paint fell around her like black snowflakes tipped with sparks. They alighted on her hair and dress, cooling and staining her shoulders with ash.

The broccworm jumped onto the man's chest, snarling. Unnatural blue flame flickered with each growl.

The man drew his pistol, but the tykeworm ran from Lizzy's side to catch the man's wrist in obsidian-black teeth. The tyke was small, no bigger than a Yorkshire terrier, but even the smallest draca has teeth sharper than razors and harder than steel.

"If you wish to keep your hand," Lizzy said, "you should drop that."

The man splayed his fingers, and the pistol clattered to the floor.

Even the scuffling men by the wall had frozen at the spectacle. Now, Mr. Darcy rolled their cowed opponent onto his belly. Mr. Knightley produced a coil of peculiarly fine string from his pocket and wound it around the man's hands.

Mr. Darcy joined his wyfe. He kicked the discarded pistol across the floor. The broccworm, tyke, and roseworm spaced themselves around the terrified man's head.

"Are you hurt?" Mr. Darcy asked, his voice tight with concern.

Lizzy looked up. She seemed impossibly calm. "I am unhurt, but..." She turned to a window. To the north. "Yuánchi heard me. He comes. I must stop him."

Scarlet flared and faded in my mind. This time, I felt the thread of their binding stretching far, far to the north. How could a distant draca feel so powerful? And there was something more... a vitality in the binding that tugged at my soul. A familiarity that drew me.

Roiling, acrid smoke swirled through the room. Women coughed and sobbed. Harriet was comforting a crying woman beside me.

I remembered the maid at the door. I had seen her injured. I saw her fall.

I ran to the entrance. The miasma flooded the floor, clutching at my shoes with every step. The maid, a woman of forty or fifty, was a senseless heap in the doorway. I knelt by her, my hands trembling.

I had to help her. Save her. I placed my gloved fingers on her unconscious brow, as useless as when I had comforted Papa.

But here, the Darcys' scarlet binding glimmered around Lizzy, tantalizing and potent. My soul reached for it, but it was ungraspable. Claimed by another.

The miasma surged, colorless pestilence that drowned the world. Awareness fled.

2

ELIZABETH DARCY

LIZZY

"Elizabeth," my husband said in my ear. "I must speak with the constable."

I nodded, and Darcy crossed to the constable, joining Mr. Knightley, who had helped subdue the attackers. One attacker had been taken away, but the other lay tied at the constable's feet. Behind the men, the chill autumn wind gusted through the windows, thrown wide to clear the smoke.

Memories of the attack clicked through my mind as if I were watching a reenactment. The gunmen brought their weapons to bear so slowly. They were fools. I had an eternity to act.

But that was a strange way to think of it. I knew nothing of weapons, other than profoundly disliking them.

My recollection froze at the moment I had commanded the three draca to attack. The sensation hung, bitter in the back of my throat. I had not commanded a draca since I forced the Longbourn drake to stay after Papa's death. The concept of command repelled me—compelling any creature was wrong—but beneath that, a rawer emotion lurked. Exhilaration.

Why had this happened?

I crossed the room and sank to my heels by the man who shot at me. He lay on his side, glaring at me with an uneven squint.

Above us, the gentlemen's conversation fell silent. Three pairs of trousered legs and polished shoes turned in my direction.

"Why did you try to kill me?" I said.

"That bleedin' Negro got 'is hands all over me!" The man launched a spittle-spewing tirade, although at Mr. Knightley, not me. Five months ago, I would have known few of the words, and fled blushing from those. Now I had sterner standards from my visits to the slums of London. The desperate poor were usually polite, even starving in a wealthy city, but the men who earned enough for drink were unpredictable, some admirable, others as vile as this one.

"You might want to take your lady away," the constable suggested to Darcy above my head.

"Mrs. Darcy is resilient," Darcy said. He offered me his hand with a lift of his eyebrow, and I rose, very satisfied with my choice of husband.

Mr. Knightley gave me a refined bow at odds with his disheveled collars from tussling on the floor. He frowned at the man by our feet. "This fellow has consumed my entire reserve of string."

"String?" I asked, looking at the fine coils around the man's wrists.

"Mr. Knightley is a violinist," Darcy explained. Mr. Knightley's and my introduction had been rather rushed. "He is a founder of the Royal Philharmonic Society."

"I know these two ruffians," Mr. Knightley said. "They have caused trouble at meetings of the Freedom Society."

"What is the Freedom Society?" I asked. It did not sound musical.

"We assist refugees from slavery who wish to settle in England," Mr. Knightley answered.

"Would you be an abolitionist, ma'am?" asked the constable. "These two were with those pro-slavers. That might be the cause."

"I support abolition, but not in a public manner." If they wished to hurt an abolitionist, Mary would be their target. She was positively strident. I cast a worried glance to where she stood by the pianoforte, speaking to Georgiana. She seemed unshaken. Mary had become very steadfast in the past year.

Darcy indicated a vacant corner, and he and I moved to speak privately.

"That man sought you by name," he said. "It is not hard to guess his motive. You are bound to a creature that could destroy the French army. Napoleon sought to raise a legendary dragon and failed. An informer could have reported that you succeeded."

I snorted. "Except the Council of War insists we keep Yuánchi secret."

After Lord Wellington told the Council that Yuánchi had risen, they sent a delegation to Pemberley. Three pompous cabinet ministers had lectured a bemused Darcy, saying that dragons did not exist and he had likely seen a distant wyvern—which reached seventy pounds or so. They thoroughly ignored me.

I led them to the shore of Pemberley lake where Yuánchi's arrival shook the stone beneath our feet. One minister, blanched and trembling, extended a gold-sealed proclamation. Yuánchi nosed the ribbon, informed me silently he was as unimpressed as I, then departed in a storm of wind.

I noticed Darcy was developing a frustrated glower. To head him off, I added, "Whether Yuánchi is secret or not, I have no intention of being drawn into the war."

"The French do not know that."

"You are being dramatic. I cannot imagine an emperor sending a man to kill me. Even if I am bound to a dragon."

Darcy took my hand. "Elizabeth, you wield power that Napoleon covets. You are dangerous to his empire. More dangerous than Lord Wellington, for all the armies he commands. And you are far more vulnerable."

"I am not so vulnerable." I flicked at the ash on my shoulder but only ground it into the light blue cloth.

"Any idiot can aim a pistol at a person's back. Prime Minister Perceval was killed this spring."

Mary and Georgiana had crossed the room to join us, and they heard our last exchange. Georgiana looked alarmed, Mary thoughtful. Both knew of Yuánchi. Georgiana was present when he destroyed Wickham's rebel army and killed Wickham, and Mary was so close to Georgiana that excluding her would be silly.

Darcy's explanation did not sit right. "Then why have a pro-slaver attack me? Why not a French spy? Any well-dressed man could approach me on the street without raising an iota of alarm."

"I do not know," Darcy admitted. "I cannot even understand how they knew you would attend today."

"*That* I understand," I said, casting a glance at Mary, author of provocative programs. She looked abashed.

"I am concerned for Miss Woodhouse," Darcy said abruptly.

The salon was almost empty, the excited ladies having reluctantly departed at the urging of the constables. But Emma remained, sitting on the floor, her back propped against a wall and her arms hugging her knees. Her friend Harriet was kneeling beside her, evidently worried.

"Was she hurt?" I asked.

"She fainted," Darcy said, and he strode in her direction. I followed, surprised by his attention. They had barely spoken.

Even in a crowd of London ladies, Emma had shone with her coiled gold hair and a bright gown and bonnet of saffron silk. With the room emptied and darkened by smoke and soot, her clothes were even more striking, but her pose was fragile. She sat curled and staring at the ash-stained floor. The hems of her gown and petticoat formed immaculate curves on the floor, each point of lace precise. Fastidious. I thought of her habit of straightening her friends' clothes.

"Miss Woodhouse," Darcy said, bending stiffly to address her on the floor. "Are you well?"

"She is hurt. She is hurt." Emma whispered the words to her knees. Her fingers hugged her shins so tightly that her arms quivered.

"She is very worried about the maid, sir," Harriet said. "The one who hit her head."

"I am sure she will be well," I said.

That was the accepted response in matters of health, but it seemed the wrong thing to say.

"No!" Emma gasped, twisting. "She is hurt!" She began panting with distress.

I opened my mouth to offer more reassurances but stopped when Darcy crouched beside Emma, the tails of his coat brushing the floor.

"Miss Woodhouse," he said. "The maid has been taken to a physician. If her injury is serious, she will be treated. Whether that succeeds or not, her health is out of your hands. There is nothing for you to do."

That seemed a strange sort of comfort, but Emma looked at him and nodded, her eyes wide. One hand released her knees and reached out. Her fingers fumbled at his waistcoat buttons.

"*What?*" I said. Darcy caught my eye and gave a reassuring nod.

Mystified, I watched as her shaking fingers touched each of his buttons in turn.

Mary's head cocked. She knelt by Emma's other side and laid two fingers on Emma's wrist, then untied Emma's gold bonnet, touched her temples, and

M. VERANT

probed gently in her hair. All that time, Emma's fingertips traced Darcy's waist-coat buttons.

"There is no evident injury," Mary said. "I wondered if she struck her head." Mary had been studying medicine for several months, as much as was possible for a lady. She assisted a prominent and suitably radical London physician.

Emma's fingers had reached Darcy's bottom button. She began again from the top. "A scarlet draca," she murmured. That was strange. Yuánchi was scarlet, but regular draca were not.

The room's door had been left open for the constables. From the stairway beyond, voices rose in disagreement. I heard a shouted question.

"That is a reporter for *The Morning Post*," Mary said in an aggrieved tone. She must know from the protests she organized. "He will gain admittance."

Darcy said to Harriet, "Miss Woodhouse would not wish her presence reported in the papers. I am sure you share her concern."

"If you say so, sir," Harriet answered uncertainly. Despite her friendship with elegant Emma, she seemed unaware of how damaging it was for a lady's name to appear in print. Perhaps Harriet was not gentry.

"The constables are finishing," Darcy said. "I suggest we depart. Where are you staying in London?"

"Miss Woodhouse did not say," Harriet said, sounding stricken. "We talked of returning to Surrey this evening."

"That is hours in a coach," Mary protested. "That would be unwise."

The voices outside were becoming more distinct.

"Miss Woodhouse," Darcy said to Emma. "We must leave this place. Would you honor us by accepting an invitation to Chathford House?"

"*Chathford?*" I said, surprised. "Is it ready?" Chathford House was the Darcys' London home. I had never seen it, as it had been shuttered since the death of Darcy's parents. Darcy had spoken vaguely of reopening it now that Georgiana and I were spending time in London.

"Mrs. Reynolds has some rooms open." His smile was rueful. "I had planned to surprise you."

Emma had not answered him. Her fingers continued their ritual pattern. Muscles worked along Darcy's jaw, then he turned to Harriet. "May I have your permission to assist your friend?"

"Of course, sir," Harriet said, awestruck. Darcy glanced for my nod before he gathered Emma in his arms and stood.

"Oh. He does that so easily," Harriet whispered to me as Darcy strode to the

18

door, Emma's skirts hanging gracefully. They looked like an illustration in a scandalous novel.

"He does," I said, vaguely proud that I felt not a flicker of jealousy.

My curiosity, however, was raging. I knew my husband. He would not sweep a strange woman into his arms unless she was in graver danger than an encounter with a reporter.

3

THE COUNCIL OF WAR

LIZZY

Mary led us briskly down a servants' stair, out a plain pine door, and onto a narrow and chilly side street. Mr. Knightley came also, talking with Georgiana and carrying a beautiful instrument case of lustrous cherrywood—a violin, from the scrollwork designs. He tucked the case under his arm and jogged to the corner to hail a coach.

I stepped close to Darcy, who was so composed one would think gentlemen regularly strolled through London with ladies draped in their arms.

"You and I cannot accompany them," I whispered. "Our other engagement..."

"Of course." He grimaced. "I had forgotten."

Forgotten a meeting with the Secretary of War?

Mr. Knightley returned leading a large hackney coach, the horses prancing skittishly in the tight space. Darcy and Harriet settled Emma into a seat. Emma did not answer when Harriet spoke to her.

Darcy jumped down so Mary could step in. He stopped Georgiana before she followed, and said to Mr. Knightley, "Sir, I have another engagement. Would you accompany my sister to ensure that Miss Woodhouse and Miss Smith remain safe at Chathford?"

Mr. Knightley nodded. "I would be honored."

"*Safe?*" Georgiana's brunette brows arched over her ocean eyes. "I thought to offer them tea and summon a doctor. Is that safe enough?"

"Call it 'private,' then," Darcy replied. "I do not recommend a doctor if Miss Woodhouse recovers soon. I think she will. I hope to speak with her then. Convey that, please."

Georgiana considered him. For a reed-thin girl of seventeen, she had a tough spine. Georgiana had her own extraordinary abilities with draca, so she had been pressed into difficult situations before. Last year, and against Darcy's advice, the military had attempted to use bound draca in battle. Georgiana had been called by her brother to settle maddened draca in the disastrous aftermath.

The driver of a smaller coach caught behind ours shouted to clear the street. Georgiana gave a rushed, unsatisfied nod to her brother, then accepted Mr. Knightley's hand to take her seat.

I closed my eyes, found the tykeworm's bright awareness, and imagined Georgiana as she appeared to draca senses—her lithe posture and the golden aura that surrounded her. This was suggestion, not the brute force of command, but the tyke scrambled happily into the coach to follow her.

The large coach pulled away. Behind, the other driver clucked his tongue to start his horses but reined in when Darcy hailed him. Darcy helped me up, then gave directions before closing the door.

In the privacy of the coach, my curiosity came to a boil. "I trust you appreciate that only an exceptionally tolerant wyfe would stand meekly while you pay such attention to Miss Woodhouse."

The corner of Darcy's lip twitched. "I do not recall marrying you on a blessed Beltane eve for your exceptional tolerance. But you are right that she has my attention. I am curious about Miss Woodhouse's ailment."

"I see that. I am wondering why."

The tip of his thumb brushed my cheek, then traced the crescent of my ear, the fine weave of his glove trailing a tingling frisson. His fingers landed lightly on the nape of my neck.

"You are distracting me," I said sternly while fighting a blush.

Darcy had been smiling, but his smile faded. His hand cupped my neck in a far more businesslike manner. "You are very warm. Are you well?"

I pulled his hand away. "You are *still* distracting me. What of Emma?"

Now I was distracting him. Bursts of fever had struck me several times in the last few weeks. This latest one had crept in unnoticed, pricking a damp line up my spine. But the attacks left me energetic, not ill, so the last thing I needed was my over-protective husband worrying.

Darcy's gaze was thoughtful. "I have seen an ailment like Miss Woodhouse's before. I may have advice on treatment. Does that satisfy you, for now?"

I nodded and assumed the dutiful expression of a generous and understanding wyfe.

Darcy laughed out loud. He took my hand. "Elizabeth, the Secretary of War awaits. Do not exhaust your exceptional tolerance on your husband. You may require it soon."

The coach swayed and bounced over London's rough streets while fever prickled my neck.

THE CARRIAGE LET us out on Margaret's Street. While Darcy paid the driver, I walked past the cab, then stopped short.

Westminster Palace sprawled before me, home to the House of Lords and House of Commons. I had seen engravings in *The Times*, but in life, it filled one's eyes—a vast mass of rambling gray stone streaked with black soot from London's smoky rain. The structure ranged from three to five stories with no discernable plan and fronted at least two hundred yards of the Thames. The lack of planning extended to the jumbled architecture. Crenelated towers suited for a ruined Scottish castle abutted modern, sloped roofs and shining glass windows. Still, the effects combined to create an air of age and importance.

"The seat of governance for Great Britain," I said as Darcy joined me. "How remarkable."

"Do not be overly impressed," he said. "It is notorious for mice and rotting sills."

"Which of us is intolerant?" I asked innocently and took his arm.

The large yard in front of the building was hidden behind a twenty-foot stone wall. We followed the perimeter to an iron-railed gate where a guard dispatched a runner to announce Mr. Darcy. Then he stared down his nose at me. "Have you arranged for the lady to wait?"

"Mrs. Darcy will accompany us," Darcy said before I could open my mouth.

The guard's pointy chin thrust forward, then left and right before settling dubiously in the center.

Was it unexpected for a lady to enter, or improper? There had been a tremendous scandal when Lady Caroline Lamb stole into the Commons gallery to observe her husband's speech, achieving her feat by dressing as a teenage boy. Of course, the London newspapers implied that Lady Caroline performed many outrageous feats, usually accompanied by Lord Byron, who was not her husband.

With relief, I recognized a figure striding across the yard in a scarlet coat and shining gold epaulets. Darcy greeted him with a bow. "Lord Wellington."

Lord Wellington shook Darcy's hand warmly. "Save your 'Lords' for when I thrash you in our next bout." My husband and Lord Wellington were fencing partners, a discovery I still found bemusing. Lord Wellington commanded England's forces in the long-running war with France. There was hardly a more famous or admired figure in the kingdom.

My hand was swept up next, and with not much more formality. "Mrs. Darcy. I am delighted that a charming wyfe is visiting this dreary pile of stone. Do you not agree, Hicks?" he added, directing the last to the guard.

The guard, who had assumed the rigidity of a flagpole when Lord Wellington appeared, inclined his head a half inch.

We crossed the yard to enter a set of broad doors, climbed a wide staircase with fading red carpet, then wound through a series of dark-paneled rooms. A scent of stale tobacco and spilled port grew. Darcy and Lord Wellington seemed comfortable and chatted cordially, but I found it off-putting, as if I had stumbled into the gentlemen's parlor after dinner.

We stopped outside a heavy, elaborately carved oak door.

"This meeting is, of course, unprecedented," Lord Wellington said, speaking in a soft voice that would not penetrate the closed door. "This has become more urgent, and more secret, in the last week. Only two members of the Council will join us." He hesitated, his eyes on mine. "The Council of War has voted to implement the policy described in my letter."

Darcy opened his mouth, but this time, I was quicker. "That sounds very settled. You proposed using Yuánchi in war. My reply expressed my reservations. I should say, my disagreement. How did the Council respond?"

"The Council addressed their request to Mr. Darcy," Lord Wellington said. "I judged it unwise to present a reply penned by his wyfe." I drew a big breath, but he raised a finger and continued, "Instead, I insisted that you be invited to this meeting. I have respected your privacy about the events at Pemberley, but my discretion has left the gentlemen of the Council with... conventional expectations."

Lord Wellington had witnessed me controlling draca and summoning Yuánchi—and the destruction that followed. Afterward, Darcy extracted his promise to conceal my abilities. Darcy feared they would be irresistibly tempting to the military.

However, pretending to be a wide-eyed innocent was irritating in situations like this. I plucked a fold of my skirt. "I should think the 'conventional expectation' is that the *wyfe* who bound a dragon is *Mrs.* Darcy."

Lord Wellington studied me with no hint of humor, but a glint in his eye. He almost seemed pleased. Then he knocked twice and opened the door.

We entered an office like a large gentleman's study. The walls were panels of quarter-sawn oak dulled by decades of beeswax polish. A rack of shelves held thick legal volumes. A square window faced the walled yard. The sill had a hole, mouse-sized and distinctly nibbled.

A massive walnut desk dominated the room, each chunky leg carved with a lion's head and clawed foot. One corner held cut-glass decanters of whisky and port. Beside a pen and blotter, an empty glass tumbler weighed down several sheets of paper. Four armchairs upholstered in ruby velvet formed an arc in front.

Two gentlemen were waiting. They rose as we entered.

Lord Wellington introduced the man behind the desk, War Secretary Lord Henry Castlehurst, a viscount. He was an older man with short, gray hair and a mustache so thin it could have been cut from a strip of felt. His full title was Secretary of State for War and the Colonies, a powerful role that consolidated England's foreign interests.

I curtsied, and he bowed, then turned to greet Darcy.

The other gentleman rose from an armchair. He was about forty, robust, tall and barrel-chested with a confident stance. He greeted Lord Wellington with a chuckle about some prior disagreement, then met me with a genuine smile.

"Mrs. Darcy." He bowed over my hand, his straw hair thick and wavy. "Mr. Tinsdale, at your service. It is an honor to meet such an exceptional lady and wyfe. You have done England proud with your binding. Who would have thought a modern wyfe could raise a dragon—a true creature of legend."

The War Secretary flicked a hand toward the armchairs.

Silently, Darcy adjusted my chair, then sat precisely in the adjacent seat. When Darcy conducted business at Pemberley, he was decisive, friendly, and matter-of-fact. Here, he had answered the introductions with formality and the barest minimum of words. I recognized this stiff, taciturn Darcy from when we first met in Hertfordshire—my husband in an unfamiliar setting with unknown rules.

Darcy caught my eye, and he gave a nod, his eyes alert. Taciturn, but not intimidated.

The War Secretary began. "Mr. Darcy. Mrs. Darcy. I second Tinsdale's congratulation." He said that grudgingly, as if anything uttered by Mr. Tinsdale was suspect. "You have secured a great treasure for England. King and country are grateful." To Darcy, he added, "I knew George Darcy, your father. An honorable man. Fate chose a worthy house for this service."

I answered that. "Draca choose the wyfe they bind. I do not believe in fate."

The War Secretary eyed me. "Wellington, this meeting was your idea. I suggest you explain."

Lord Wellington nodded. The silence lengthened before he spoke.

"Six days ago, the HMS *Dapper*, a fourteen-gun brig, was patrolling the blockade off the French coast. Their lookout spotted a schooner several miles distant. It did not match their guns and they had the wind, so the captain was not alarmed. Then the lookout saw a large bird approaching—a bird with the wingspan of an albatross, ribbed wings, and shining bronze scales."

"A firedrake," I said, stunned. My mother and father had bound a drake when they married—a point of pride for Mamma, as drakes were one of the few winged breeds of draca. There were fewer than three dozen bound drakes in all of England.

Lord Wellington nodded. "The lookout was an ordinary seaman. He had never seen a winged draca, but he learned soon enough. The creature threw blue flame as it passed, setting a topsail afire.

"The crew cut down the burning sail, and the captain improvised a defense. He issued muskets, and they loaded the deck swivel cannons with grapeshot. When the drake circled back, they fired a fusillade. The drake was struck—visibly jarred in midair. It fell."

I breathed an involuntary, dismayed gasp. Draca are protected by their scales, so they are rarely hurt, let alone killed. But drakes are few and long-lived, so the loss was a terrible thing.

The War Secretary frowned at my reaction. Lord Wellington hesitated before he resumed.

"Whatever injury the drake took, it was not disabled. It caught itself before striking the water—the lookout heard the snap of its wings opening, like a sail filling. Then he saw that the first assault was only a probe. The drake attacked ferociously, weaving and spinning. The deck was raked repeatedly with flame. The lookout leaped from the burning foremast into the sea, then the ship's powder magazine exploded. The *Dapper* was lost with fifty men. The lookout, clinging to a piece of flotsam, was the sole survivor."

Lord Wellington stopped. The War Secretary exhaled a long breath.

Darcy spoke. "How could the French have a firedrake? There are no draca in France."

"We think the drake was English. Last month, in Lowestoft, a newly wed wyfe went missing. Her cloak was recovered on a beach, so she was presumed drowned by a sudden wave. Especially since her bound draca, a firedrake, vanished."

Draca depart if their bound wyfe dies, so the drake's disappearance would seem confirmation of her death.

"You think she was abducted?" I said.

"Abducted, or a traitor, or she was killed, and her drake taken."

I shook my head. "A newly married wyfe turned traitor seems unlikely."

Lord Wellington gave me a level stare, and I realized how foolish I sounded. My own dead sister, Lydia, had been precisely that. Although Lydia had been manipulated and drugged. And mad.

But Lydia was no random wyfe. She had extraordinary power over draca.

"Whether the wyfe lived or not," I said, "the mystery is why the drake attacked. Draca cannot be trained to fight. They are not war horses or hounds."

The War Secretary's eyes narrowed, and he gave an annoyed grunt. I was not sure if that was due to my words or because I had dared to speak at all. I folded my arms and stared back.

Lord Wellington resumed. "Grim as this news is, it grows worse. After the *Dapper* was lost, the enemy sailed close. The lookout saw two flags. One was French. The other was unfamiliar to him—blue with a white crescent. We know that flag. It is raised by privateers who smuggle African slaves to the plantations of Spanish Florida and Texas."

"A slave ship?" Darcy said. "Why would slavers visit France?"

Mr. Tinsdale answered, each word deliberate. "Nine years ago, when Bonaparte needed funds for his war, he attempted to reacquire Louisiana for French slave plantations. Nelson foiled that plan by routing the French navy at Trafalgar. Now, Bonaparte has allied directly with the American slave states. They provide ships for France's war, and the French territories pay in slaves."

"An evil alliance," Darcy said and caught my eye. Napoleon allied with slavers, like the men who tried to kill me.

"A *powerful* alliance," the War Secretary said. "One that shifts the balance of the war. The American cutters are light ships, but fast. And, somehow, this pact has enabled our enemies to field an English draca as a weapon. We must strike before there are greater losses. The time has come for England to bring her great power to bear. The Darcy dragon must join the war."

"No!" I exclaimed. Yuánchi had fought for me once, and dozens had died. The scars of his fury still stained a meadow above Pemberley.

The War Secretary dismissed me with an insulting sniff and addressed my husband. "*Mr.* Darcy. This is not a matter for debate. This is a matter of duty."

"Darcy, you must see—" began Lord Wellington.

"Mr. Darcy has no *duty*," Mr. Tinsdale boomed. He cleared his throat and continued more mildly. "There is nothing he *must* do. Mr. Darcy, understand that the Council is not unanimous in this request. I oppose this escalation. The loss of the *Dapper* is tragic, but she was caught unawares, and she was a small vessel, not a ship-of-the-line. We are discussing the response to a single firedrake. Bonaparte is a dangerous and capable man. Send a dragon to burn his ships, and what horrors will he unleash in return?"

Darcy was so still that I suspended my anger and turned to him. His hands were gripping the arms of his chair.

When he did not speak, I said, "I quite agree with Mr. Tinsdale."

"Bonaparte will not hesitate to perform *any* horror," Lord Wellington said. "Our restraint will not slow him."

"I care less for his horrors than ours," I said, "I do not support war."

The War Secretary's face flushed. "Mrs. Darcy, when Lord Wellington insisted on your presence—"

"How did they convince the drake to attack?" I interrupted. "*That* should be our concern. Draca do not fight on command."

The War Secretary barked a frustrated laugh. "Mr. Darcy, *you* are very quiet. It was you who advised this Council not to attempt the use of draca in war. You declared it impossible to command draca."

Darcy finally spoke. "I did."

"And then, your new wyfe bound an extraordinary draca thought to be legend. Has that altered your opinion?" Darcy did not answer. The War Secretary jabbed his finger into the papers on his desk, crumpling them against the tumbler. "When the *Dapper* was sunk, Lord Wellington sent me this report. I have read it, and I am no longer surprised that a dragon was bound at Pemberley."

Darcy stiffened in his seat. "I know nothing of his report. But Lord Wellington himself informed the Council of Mrs. Darcy's binding. We did not conceal it."

"Your wyfe is not the subject of this report," the War Secretary said. "It discusses your young sister, Miss Georgiana Darcy."

Darcy's chair skidded as he rose to face Lord Wellington. "What have you done?"

From his chair, Lord Wellington raised an eyebrow. "Last year, Miss Darcy demonstrated her ability to control draca in a room full of soldiers. I gathered those soldiers' testimony for the Secretary."

"Georgiana saved wyves and draca," Darcy said. "I asked for her help, and she trusted my discretion. *You* asked no permission, even though you swore to respect our privacy. You have contrived to avoid your oath." His lip curled. "That is ungentlemanly."

Lord Wellington's calm vanished. He shot to his feet, a slighter man than Darcy and inches shorter, but whip-taut and dangerous. "Watch your words."

Mr. Tinsdale stood and landed a beefy hand on each man's back. "Gentlemen. We are all honorable men—and women," he added, glancing at me. "Do not quarrel over actions in defense of England."

The tension stretched, then Lord Wellington nodded. He settled into his chair, crossing one polished Hussar boot over his trousered knee.

Darcy did not sit. He stood with fists clenched. I grasped his wrist and tugged, then harder. At last, he sat, his shoulders square.

It was time for a cooler head. Unexpectedly, that appeared to be me.

"Whatever skills Miss Darcy has, they do not include commanding draca to fight," I said. Darcy's hand caught my forearm, but I ignored him. "Georgiana is a gentle soul, not even married and bound. It is not her you want."

"Then who?" Lord Wellington said, his gray eyes bright. Perhaps this had been his ploy all along—the master strategist forcing Darcy to reveal either Georgiana or me without breaking the letter of his promise.

"I am the one who commands draca," I said. "If you are gathering 'testimony,' your agents will tell you soon enough. I did so before a room of witnesses, no more than an hour ago. I am a great wyfe. My skills far outstrip Miss Darcy's."

That last part was flatly untrue, as Miss Darcy was a great wyfe in her own, different way. But her skills were certainly unsuited to war.

Lord Wellington slapped his boot with a fierce grin. "Mrs. Darcy, your country will thank you."

"Thanks are premature," I said. "I will not assist a war."

The War Secretary had watched with relief. "So it is Mrs. Darcy that we require? *Only* her?"

"Yes," Lord Wellington said.

"Well, that is much better. A pair of ladies seemed like trouble." The War Secretary gave me an encouraging smile. "Overcome your feminine anxiety, Mrs. Darcy. You need only deliver the dragon and ensure it is compliant. Wellington will manage the messy part."

"Compliant?" I laughed in disbelief. "Your arrogance is astonishing. First, the dragon has a *name*—"

Darcy rose, abruptly as poised and disciplined as an ambassador at a royal ball. "Mrs. Darcy will not assist a war because I have forbidden it." He offered me his hand. After a moment of surprise, I put my fingers in his and rose as well.

Darcy gave a slight bow to the War Secretary. "Your trust in sharing this information is appreciated. In turn, you may trust that any information I withheld was in service to solemn vows. I have never compromised England's security, nor will I do so while I draw breath. I swear this on my honor."

"Well, certainly." The War Secretary was flustered. "I thought nothing else."

"The situation is grave," Darcy continued. "I must study your request. Three days would suffice."

Lord Wellington's eyes narrowed, but the War Secretary nodded. "Of course."

Darcy bowed deeply, and I curtsied. We turned to go, but Mr. Tinsdale's solid hand caught mine, and he bowed to me. "Mrs. Darcy. Your counsel was heard today. And valued."

I nodded silently, then Darcy and I left.

"WHY THREE DAYS?" I whispered as we hurried toward the exit. I was trotting to keep up with his long strides, but the motion was a relief. I blazed with energy.

"I wished to speak with you," he said as he held the door to the yard. "And it is better that I deny the Council than you. Women have few rights under the law. The choice of three days was arbitrary."

"Arbitrary? What has happened to my precise husband?"

Darcy stopped in the center of the yard. He took my hands and pulled me close. I had to throw back my head to look into his eyes.

"Elizabeth, do not joke. When you bound Yuánchi, he... challenged you."

"I have not forgotten," I said. "He asked if I was the wyfe of war."

"More than asked. He threatened. He said he could not bind the wyfe of war."

"But we do not even know what 'wyfe of war' means. And if that is your concern, there is no need. I refuse to be involved in war."

His fingers tightened. "What if England's survival were at stake?"

I laughed. "You cannot be serious. Lord Wellington is handily winning the war."

"You know this from the newspapers?"

"Well. Yes. I suppose so."

"The papers print what they are told." His jaw worked. "I know Wellington. He manipulated you—and me—to reveal your ability to the Council. He has a soldier's pragmatism, but even so, he would not do that lightly. He is worried." Darcy exhaled through pursed lips. "I wish he had spoken to me instead. Asked."

"Love, this will shock you, but your friends find you difficult to influence." Darcy smiled crookedly, and I continued, "I am glad the Council knows. It will end the ridiculous secrecy about Yuánchi."

"You wish that? You will become 'the lady with the dragon.'"

"I *am* the lady with the dragon. Pemberley's staff knows, and half of Lambton town. For all their discretion, word will spread. Secrecy is hopeless and frustrating."

Darcy's lips compressed thoughtfully. Then he looked up at the sky.

The air had chilled. Sparse flakes of snow danced around us, so weightless they might have been ash rising or snow falling. Then the wind hushed, and their dance died. Ice from the darkening clouds kissed my cheek, deliciously cold.

4

CHATHFORD HOUSE

EMMA

lackness fell away to reveal golden wood wainscoting and white plaster. I
was lying on my back, suspended in space. My knees, bent and draped
in yellow silk, hung level with my eyes.

I floated up a hallway—a stairway. Slanted rectangles of winter light passed
on the wall. The ceiling was a fresco, a spiral of serpentine seraphim that were
winged and fiery. They spun as I turned on a landing, seeming to ascend to
Heaven. The hem of my dress tugged on a banister, then pulled free. I rose again
in steady steps.

When my father died, I collapsed for a day and a night. When I woke, there
had been this same calm. Freedom from the false images that overran my mind.
Freedom from the itch of compulsion.

With some surprise, I realized I was floating because I was in a man's arms.
His ebony chin was inches from my nose, close shaven and framed by a starched
white neckcloth. Mr. Knightley, the Black gentleman from the salon.

Politely, I said, "Were we introduced?"

His eyes went wide. He took two driving steps—we fairly leaped up the
stairs—then I was dropped on my feet. Rather suddenly and solidly.

The landing filled as Harriet, Mary Bennet, and Georgiana Darcy rushed
up. Harriet took a two-handed grip on my upper arm while the other ladies
peered with concern.

The gentleman had backed to the far banister. He raised his hands, fingers spread in tense apology.

"I beg your pardon, madam," he said in a roughened tenor. "Miss Smith and Miss Bennet insisted we bring you inside. I asked several times, but you did not answer."

"Have I given you a fright? I fear the excitement made me faint." I produced a delicate laugh while I looked around. How long was I unaware? "May I ask where we are?"

"This is Chathford, our London house," Georgiana said. "It was closed six years ago. It is as new to me as to you, almost. I have... forgotten it." Her voice faltered at the end.

"Are you better?" Harriet asked me.

"I feel perfectly well," I said. Her grip on my arm eased a fraction.

The gentleman maintained his exaggerated, unthreatening pose. His fingers were very long and elegant.

Harriet whispered in my ear, "Some ladies are offended if a man of color touches them."

Oh. "I am very thankful, sir," I told him. "Is it Mr. Knightley?"

"It is. At your service, madam." He bowed, one arm sketching a subtle flourish. Like an actor might bow, if an actor had good taste.

"I am Miss Emma Woodhouse," I said and offered my hand. When he did not move, I added, "Mr. Knightley, you have already carried me"—I looked over the banister—"*two* flights of stairs! I think we may shake hands."

His bare, dark fingers lifted mine in their white satin. After sensing the strange binding of the Darcys, I half expected something peculiar would occur. But it was merely a handshake. A firm one.

"That is better," I said. "I feel we have known each other our entire lives."

"You honor me." He smiled at last, an unreserved smile that crinkled his eyes.

"Oh, it is just a feeling. But I am decided about such things." The frightening events of the day skittered through my memory. But buttons did not wrench my gaze. No miasma lurked in the corners. I floated on relief. "This is a handsome stairway. Were we going somewhere interesting?"

Georgiana answered. "Mrs. Reynolds is showing us to the afternoon sitting room." She nodded to an older woman in black watching from the top of the stairs. The housekeeper.

After further are-you-well's and yes-I-truly-am's, we began a winding tour.

The house was being reopened, overseen by the severely clad but friendly Mrs. Reynolds. In an aside, she told me Georgiana had not entered the house since she was a girl of eleven "when her dear father and mother passed."

We saw several rooms partially refurbished, then climbed a stair to an arched entry carved like weeping willow branches. Inside, the furniture and paintings were draped in linen. The curved outer wall held a tremendous window—twenty panes side-by-side. Three or four stories below, the sweep of the Thames caught remnants of chilly silver light, shining wide and cold.

Georgiana had stopped on the room's threshold. "I remember this," she said in a little voice. "I called it 'the river window.'" She thrust out her arm to point, and her childish pose and slender frame could have been that younger girl. Then she ran to a delicate porcelain ornament on a mantle. "This was Mamma's favorite." She burst into tears.

Mary was with her in two swift steps, embracing her while Georgiana buried her head and sobbed. Mrs. Reynolds circled them, distraught and proffering handkerchiefs.

Harriet and I exchanged a sympathetic look and slipped into the next room. A drawing room, I thought. It was hard to judge with the furniture hidden.

Mr. Knightley joined us. "I think Miss Bennet is her best comfort now."

"I am sure you are right," I said. "They seem very close."

"Mary has been good for Georgiana." He strolled to a pianoforte hidden under yellowing linen. His fingertip flicked a fold of cloth. A puff of dust rose.

"What is your connection to the salon?" I asked.

"On occasion, I have the honor of performing with Miss Darcy."

"Music, you mean?" He nodded. "I have never met a gentleman who performs. Do you sing?"

"I am a violinist."

Harriet looked over at that. "We have a man who plays violin in Highbury. He plays reels at the assemblies! Oh, I love to dance a reel. Can you play reels?"

"I can," Mr. Knightley answered with a smile that was friendly but a shade too considerate.

"I believe Mr. Knightley performs serious music," I said.

He appraised me. He had a thoughtful way of moving, as if the choice of where to place one's head or hand was significant. "What would serious music be?"

I gave a careless smile. "I always fail to apply myself to one subject for long. So, I am not a sufficiently serious musician to answer."

He laughed with a flash of strong teeth. He was really quite handsome. And a gentleman. I looked between him and Harriet, considering. But a performing musician did not seem a very *secure* sort of gentleman. I had already hurt poor Harriet when I attempted to make a match between her and Mr. Elton, our vicar in Highbury. Who I now knew was a profoundly cruel man.

I would not meddle again. Harriet must choose her own way.

With a brilliant smile, Harriet stepped close to Mr. Knightley. "You were so brave today. Fighting that horrible man!"

It seemed Harriet could meddle on her own behalf. Irritated, I walked to the window, arms crossed and satin fingertips dug into yellow silk.

Across the room, Mr. Knightley replied, "I have encountered my share of horrible men. Fortunately, the others did not hold pistols." He lifted a corner of the linen, wafting more dust and exposing an octave of keyboard. "I may be able to cheer Miss Darcy after all."

He played a chord. The notes grated on strings horrendously out of tune. He tapped out a few discordant notes—the melody of a reel—and nodded to Harriet, who clapped her hands with a laugh.

Georgiana, her eyes reddened and cheeks wet, rushed into the room. "What have they *done* to the pianoforte?" Mr. Knightley bowed gravely and stepped aside, but he was smiling as she pulled the linen cover off.

That launched a billowing cloud of dust, and Harriet began coughing. An image of pestilence stirred in the back of my skull. I fixed my eyes on the cold light of the Thames and jammed my crossed wrists against each other, drawing my gloves snug. The image faded.

Georgiana struck a sour note and uttered a dismayed cry. She played a chromatic scale, every note from bottom to top, her hand roaring up the keys at jaw-dropping speed. Mrs. Reynolds arrived as Georgiana finished and exclaimed, "This instrument has not been tuned *once* in all these years!"

The abandonment of a pianoforte was, apparently, a great sin. Miss Darcy began dictating atonement. A particular sort of hammer felt was required, and a German provider of wire strings. Bowls of water must be placed to prevent the freshly warmed air from drying the soundboard. Mrs. Reynolds nodded as the instructions mounted.

Mary Bennet entered the room and joined me by the window. We watched together.

"For all the terror of this afternoon," I said, "I regret the salon performances were canceled. I should have liked to hear Georgiana play."

"She lives in her art," Mary said. "There is emotion in every note that she plays. And in every memory she recalls." Mary's eyebrows knitted as if that were foolish, but her lips parted in wondering admiration.

"I would find that exhausting," I said.

Mary gave a short laugh. "The music was not the only event canceled. We had planned to protest the aristocracy's restrictions on binding. Your letter was on this subject." She closed her eyes and quoted: "*My dear friend Harriet, through no fault but uncertain parentage, is assumed unable to bind—condemned as inferior by a cruel gentleman.*"

"That is why I wished to attend," I said, disconcerted that she could recite words I had written months ago. I had been very open with my thoughts. "In my enthusiasm to help Harriet, I may have shared her situation too freely."

"Many women come to us for help. Their wellbeing is at risk. We hold secrets close." There was a pause. "You did not say that Harriet is Black."

That was an unexpected comment from so liberal a lady. "Surely that is irrelevant."

"In a moral world, it is irrelevant. In this world, her position is more precarious."

"Oh." I laughed. "I have solved *that*."

Mary's spectacles glinted as she turned, golden circles around her light brown eyes. "How?"

"I have elevated her in society. We are the best of friends."

"That is a solution?"

"If we are together, she can hardly be turned aside." Mary's eyebrows arched to match her round lenses, so I added, "All that remains is overcoming the silly perception that, because Harriet's parents are unknown, she will fail to bind. When that is done, she can marry a suitable gentleman. We could not continue our friendship if she marries poorly."

"You speak of her like she is a project!"

"Yes," I said, pleased she understood. "Some years ago, I made an excellent match for my dear friend Miss Taylor. This is a better challenge."

"A challenge?" Mary's voice was tight. "Do you comprehend the issues she encounters? The prejudice?"

Perhaps she did not understand after all. "I am opposing prejudice."

"With no experience of it. What if—"

Mary was cut off as a footman announced, "The master and mistress have arrived."

WE DESCENDED to the main floor and joined Mr. Darcy and Lizzy in a sitting room. The windows again overlooked the Thames, but now through autumn-bare branches. We strolled the room in pairs or threes, the tone formal and too bright. The violence of the day hovered unsaid.

This room was fully reopened, missing only carpets. The narrow floorboards gleamed, inlaid with ruby patterns of rosewood or cherry. The chairs and end tables were delicate Rococo curves awash in gilded filigree—a beautiful style, although out of fashion. The war discouraged French influence.

Harriet's eyes were agog. Hartfield, my family home, had a comfortable country style that was the peak of fashion in Highbury, but it was far less shiny than this.

Mr. Darcy and Mr. Knightley strolled to the far window, their hands clasped behind their backs while they discussed whatever gentlemen discuss when ladies are out of hearing. Shooting. Horses. The near-murder of a wyfe.

The ladies gathered. I complimented the room's restoration, and Georgiana agreed happily; she seemed recovered from the emotion of homecoming. Then she said, "My brother asked me to give you a message when you woke. I had forgotten until now."

"He must tell me himself," I said.

"He wishes to speak with you," she said earnestly. "I am sure he will do so."

"You make it seem serious!"

Lizzy, Mary, and Georgiana exchanged glances that did seem serious. But it had been a serious day.

Gingerly, I cast my mind back to the fears of the salon.

The injured maid had caused my collapse. The way she fell in a tumble of skirts, still as death. That image alone made me seek the defense of perfection. I pressed a gloved fingertip against the Rococo swirls of a chair and traced a soothing spiral of carved flower petals.

So, the cause was no surprise. But the scarlet potency surrounding me had been different. Even in memory, it vibrated and beckoned. As if I could grasp it and—

"Emma?" Lizzy said quizzically.

Blankly, I looked into her staring eyes. I tried to pull an echo of her question from my ears, but it was lost.

"Chathford House is beautiful," I said. Compliments were safe. "And a large house, for London."

"Is it?" Georgiana asked in a surprised tone. Her slender neck craned as she looked about, searching for an overlooked wing.

"*Very* large," Mary said tightly, frowning at the raised gilt scrolls of the chair I was stroking.

"Oh." A blush spread on Georgiana's cheeks. "You think it excessive. I am sorry."

"No! I did not... that is..." Mary bit her lip. The two women stared at each other. They seemed very distraught for such a modest disagreement.

"It is larger than I expected," Lizzy said matter-of-factly. "But the space will go to good use. We need rooms for the school."

"What a wonderful idea!" exclaimed Georgiana. She beamed a relieved smile at her friend.

"You have a school?" I asked Lizzy.

"My husband is a patron of education for those who cannot afford other teaching. I have added my own project, instruction for practical trades. There will be tremendous opportunities as mechanization grows. But practical trades require space, and the London school is overfull."

"How wonderful to improve a life so profoundly," I said. "Perhaps I could help a school in Surrey."

Mary gave an annoyed snort. Lizzy shot her a quelling look.

"What are practical trades?" Harriet asked.

"Some are apprenticed trades," Lizzy said. "Smithing. Coopering. But teaching those requires permission from the guilds. They are jealous of their exclusivity. Still, a visit from a lady disconcerts them enough that I make headway."

"Trades for boys." Harriet seemed disappointed.

"Not just boys. I am only unsure what is most helpful for the girls. Eventually, mechanization will reduce the need for brute strength, but girls without families need livelihoods now. I should hate to fall back on sewing. The wages are working poverty. Harness making is more promising. It is like sewing, just with leather, punches, and heavy needles. The wages are far higher."

"The wages are higher because the wages are paid to men," Mary said in a biting tone.

"I would like harness making!" Harriet exclaimed. "I adore horses. Miss

Woodhouse's groom always complains that he cannot find properly made harnesses."

I blinked at that. He had never said a word to me.

Lizzy smiled. "Well, if you wish to learn, I have a harness maker who will teach ladies. But you should not make harnesses." Harriet looked hurt, so Lizzy explained, "Teaching would be more valuable."

"Teaching?" Harriet said in astonishment.

"Certainly. If you were willing to teach a practical trade, I would hire you in a moment. Few women are willing to instruct anything but a governess's subjects."

Harriet's lips opened in stunned amazement.

"It is an amusing idea," I interposed, disliking her reaction. "But no lady would teach, and Harriet is a lady."

There was a breath before Lizzy said, "Of course. But I think ladies should not refuse to teach. I may teach, myself. Perhaps mechanized production... I am intrigued by the disagreement on threading for bolts. Only the pettiness of men could prolong such confusion. I certainly need an activity. Darcy has such competent estate managers that our household requires far less attention than Longbourn. There is only so much one can care about how well the silver is polished."

"Oh, teaching would be so exciting!" Harriet said. "I help the young children at Mrs. Goddard's with their reading! That is the school. Mrs. Goddard's, that is. Where I live!"

"Harriet!" I exclaimed, laughing at her enthusiasm.

"Does your school have a name?" Harriet said. "Where is it?"

"It is the Martin School," Lizzy said. "Only two miles from here."

This was becoming alarmingly specific. "Harriet!" I said more firmly. "You must not lead Mrs. Darcy on. She requires serious applicants. You are marrying a gentleman."

Lizzy beamed. "Goodness! What wonderful news."

"If one will have me," Harriet said in a distressed tone. Lizzy's smile became confused.

A nudge on my toe made me look down. The tykeworm sat on his haunches by my feet. Most draca are disinterested in people, but tykes are an exception, affectionate with their bound wyves and, because they do not throw fire, safe indoors. A bound tyke was a prize in high society.

This tyke's nutmeg-brown head lolled while he considered me, panting happily through black teeth edged like knives. The lamps reflected pinpricks in his inky eyes.

"He has followed you since he arrived," Mary said She was eyeing me narrowly. I had irritated her, but I was not sure how.

"We have only three bound draca in Highbury," I said, testing a smile. "Perhaps he sees I am curious."

"You may have an affinity for draca," Georgiana said enthusiastically. "Mary has researched binding. Affinity varies among wyves, you know."

"It varies greatly," came Mr. Darcy's voice behind me. He and Mr. Knightley had rejoined us. Mr. Knightley, though, had arrived only to make apologies for departing and say his farewells. He bowed elegantly to each lady. I raised an eyebrow, so he laughed and shook my hand.

Mr. Darcy saw him off with sincere courtesy but a noticeable sense of impatience. Then he turned to me and gave his own stiff bow.

"May we resume your tour of Chathford? I wish your opinion on a work of art."

5

THE GREAT WYVES

EMMA

We passed through several rooms, halting once so Lizzy could ask questions about a boathouse she spotted through a window. Then we entered a hall with a half-dozen paintings on the undecorated, white walls.

Mr. Darcy led us to a faded triptych, a painting with three wooden panels hinged so they could close like shutters. The center panel was about fifteen inches square, the two side panels half that width. It looked very old. The wooden frame had splits and stains, and the paint was damaged.

The left panel was unevenly faded and crazed with cracks. It depicted a queen in the fashions of two or three centuries ago—a voluminous black gown trimmed with gold and a pearl-edged French hood that covered the back of her hair. Her hand was outstretched to a golden wyvern as large as a hunting dog. A bearded king stood behind her. Around them, courtiers and ladies had fallen to their knees in awe.

"This was commissioned by Queen Mary the first," Mr. Darcy said. "She was the sole surviving child of Katherine of Aragon, who was herself a powerful wyfe. Katherine bound a firedrake when she wed Henry the eighth. But Queen Mary surpassed her mother. In 1554, she married and bound a 'tremendous wyvern of shining gold.' Mary was the first queen regnant—a female monarch ruling England and Ireland. Her binding secured her claim to the throne, for a time. It proved her divine right to rule." His formality softened, and he smiled at Lizzy. "Historians thought the gold color was embellishment until your sister bound a gold wyvern."

They were *that* Bennet family. The binding of a golden wyvern by Mrs. Jane Bingley, née Bennet, had been the talk of society.

Mr. Darcy turned to me. He seemed to expect a response. I nodded, and he gestured to the center panel.

This image was better preserved. The queen was seated on a throne, resting her hands on the sides of a kneeling child's neck. The child was bent and sickly, his cheeks flushed.

The rendering of the queen's robes was extraordinary, far more detailed than any other part of the panel. Every fold of cloth, every embroidered accent, every fastening was flawless. Yet it had the realism of life, not the flat perfection of a dressmaker's illustration.

I took a step. I bent close. Each sewn pearl was a miracle. There were hundreds, faultlessly distinct. I could count the center decorations of her gown... eighteen. And—

"Miss Woodhouse," Mr. Darcy said. "Do you admire the queen's clothes?"

I started, unnerved by the precision of his question. "They are painted very finely."

"The painter's commission required that the queen's robes be exact. The artist, likely eager to keep his head, complied."

"What is she doing?" Lizzy asked.

"The queen is performing the Royal Touch. She is healing the boy."

Georgiana's head snapped around to her brother. "*Healing* him."

Mr. Darcy nodded. "The Royal Touch was performed by kings and queens until a century ago when enlightened science began to question its efficacy. But Queen Mary's healings are significant. They created our custom of offering marriage gold to bind draca. Mary gave each cured person a freshly minted piece of gold, called a *touch piece*. Brides believed these were blessed and would help them bind on their wedding night. Later, when Queen Elizabeth assumed the throne, her famed virginity joined the tradition. Now, Church doctrine states that binding requires both virginity and marriage gold."

"You are saying Queen Mary was a great wyfe of healing," Georgiana said eagerly. "Like Mamma."

"The other important aspect of Queen Mary's cures is that they succeeded. Not always, but often. She saved lives." Mr. Darcy's eyes met mine. "The precision of this painting is no accident. Before Queen Mary married and bound, she was subject to mental fits. Accounts of these were destroyed when she ascended the throne, but we know the queen was obsessed with illness and injury. She found solace in certain habits. Precise clothing was one."

Air fled my lungs. He *knew*.

"I cannot imagine how this is relevant to me," I said.

"My mother, Lady Anne Darcy, fought the same evils of the mind. An obsession with illness. Comfort in a compulsive search for perfection of clothing. Her struggle and her gift matched those of a queen centuries before."

Lizzy was studying the third panel. "What is this?" Her voice was disturbed.

Mr. Darcy turned away from me to answer. A held breath escaped my lips. I felt like a rabbit saved when the fox leaps the wrong way.

"The third panel is *The Immolation*," he said. "Queen Mary's mania returned as she ruled. Her obsession with perfection drove her to condemn Protestants as heretics. She executed them with the symbol of her divine rule, her wyvern. That earned her other name in history. Bloody Mary."

In the rightmost image, the queen's hand was raised in imperious judgment. Dismembered bodies heaped the ground. Her wyvern, wings spread and claws clotted with red pigment, was breathing sky-blue fire. The color would seem pleasant if not for a screaming monk tied to a stake.

"I know the story," Lizzy said dismissively. "What is *this*?"

Her finger pointed to a dagger in the queen's lower hand. The blade was slightly curved and painted pitch black except one edge where glistening flakes like black glass had been embedded in the paint.

Lizzy's fingertip touched the black flakes. The ever-present hint of her scarlet binding flared like flame in my mind, then it was blotted out by a presence monstrously huge and dark.

I backed away, my shoulder knocking someone so violently they gasped. Then I was running, through a shrouded room, a hallway, a door, a kitchen. A cook and scullery maid looked up as I fell against the rough outer door. I fumbled at the latch, pounded it with my fist, then something jarred free and I was through.

Fresh snow crunched under my boots. The world had transformed; it was dusted in crystalline white. The slippery footing and shock of cold stopped me. I grasped an iron railing with both hands. Freezing wet soaked my gloves. They felt dirty and isolating, so I pulled them off and threw them into a snow-topped hedge.

The day was ending, the sky tarnished to darkest pewter. Warm light from the open kitchen door carried my shadow across the snow. The outline shifted as a figure rushed out.

"Miss Woodhouse," Harriet said breathlessly. "What is wrong?"

I moved my lips to say, *Nothing*. No breath sounded my voice.

Tiny, bounding steps crunched the snow. The tyke pawed at my ankle, his scales gleaming. I bent down and rested my bare fingers on his sides. He leaned into my hands, warm and caring, so I picked him up. He curled against my chest, his breath puffing clouds of steam.

Lizzy was speaking urgently. Her fingers touched my bare forearm. Without the shield of gloves, her scarlet power swarmed up my arm and slammed my mind, blinding and overwhelming. Painfully desirable, but locked away. Jealously defended.

Shuddering, I pulled away. My head rang and reeled. "Too bright! Your binding is too bright."

"You see my *binding*?" she said. She closed her eyes. Her arms relaxed. Her head tilted back as if contemplating the sky.

The scarlet potency swirled into existence, ribbons of power that stretched to the north. Awareness flickered like an unseen moth in the night. The tyke squirmed in my arms to peer up at my face. Lizzy's awareness hung within his black eyes, seeing me.

"In the tyke's vision, she shines," Lizzy whispered. "She has the aura of a great wyfe."

"Leave me alone!" I cried, dropping the tyke. Panic squeezed my ribs. I turned to the white shadows, hunting a path to run, but a lithe hand caught my bare palm. A woman's hand, fine-boned but with fingers sure as steel.

Georgiana lifted our clasped hands high between our eyes. Drawing me near. "I have faced what you face," she whispered. Then she sang, so soft that only I could hear. "I am not bound. I am not bright. You are not alone."

That scarlet power faded behind layers of music, foundations of strength and perfection. My panic became wonder.

I touched my other palm to the back of her hand, and she added hers behind mine.

6

THE BOATHOUSE

LIZZY

I watched Darcy pull his chair closer to Emma. She listened seriously as he explained, her hazel eyes wide, her elbows hugging her sides from her chill. A damp handkerchief twisted in her hands.

Harriet and Georgiana had helped her into the house, where she shrank onto a sofa. A few hours earlier, Emma had met us at Chathford House with an exuberant smile. Now, she was compressed, a shivering, frightened woman.

Harriet sat at her left, her pretty features screwed up in determined support. Georgiana sat on her other side, occasionally quieting Emma's restless hands with a touch of her finger. Outside, I had felt Georgiana's power rise—the great wyfe of song ordering whatever forces governed the world of draca. More than emotional support passed between them.

When I touched Emma outside, she cringed and cried out. So, I stood on the far side of the sitting room. Mary stood beside me, her arms locked across her breast.

I wondered about the painting. The image of Queen Mary's dagger had felt unpleasant—a murky chill through my hand. And dissatisfying, like a hint of flavor too faint to name. That was when Emma fled.

Emma's shoulders rose and fell. Her voice strengthened enough to cross the room. "What do you mean, 'great wyfe'?"

Darcy frowned, his black eyebrows drawn. He was always more handsome when intense. "Throughout history, wyves have risen with powerful affinity to draca. The Scots have the most recent account, but even that is centuries old. Their songs name the three great wyves. From your sensitivities, I believe you are the great wyfe of healing."

He recited:

> *"To sound our claim,*
> *the three wyves came:*
> *Of healing, wise.*
> *Of song, who cries.*
> *Of war. Arise."*

I nudged Mary's stiff elbow and whispered, "He told me the same verse. Then I accused him of attempting to collect a set of great wyves—his mother, his sister, and me. That was when I refused his first proposal."

"They have their set," Mary said. Her tone was caustic. "Lady Anne Darcy, the beloved and mourned mother, will be played by tragic Emma Woodhouse wearing tear-soaked silk."

I turned and studied Mary until, reluctantly, she met my gaze.

"Why do you dislike her?" I said. "*I* should be the one irritated. It is my husband obsessing over her."

"Her relationship with Harriet is arrogant. Dangerous for Harriet."

"They seem good friends to me." Mary's lips thinned, so I added, "Georgiana likes her."

Mary made a sound low in her throat, like a small bird trapped and fluttering. Finally, she whispered, "I am mundane."

I remembered Mary upset and ignored at a ball, long ago. It seemed another world. "That is ridiculous. Did you not see the ladies at your salon? They mimic your clothes. They straighten their hair. They even call themselves 'Marys'! One morning, I will butter my toast and spot you leading a parade of black-clad Marys to tear down the patriarchy."

Mary gave a hollow laugh. "They are debutantes playing at rebellion."

I pressed her elbow with mine. "Mary. What is wrong?"

"I... it cannot be spoken. I cannot."

"Will you tell me later?" When she did not answer, I added, "I will return soon. I wish to examine the boathouse. For the school." Mary gave one puzzled blink before I slipped out of the room.

45

While I sped down the hall, I wondered why I was not worried by Darcy's attention to Emma. I had comforted wyves infuriated or frightened by wandering husbands. Reprehensible behavior was terribly common in London.

Part of my faith was simple trust. I could visit Longbourn and leave Darcy and Emma at Chathford without a thought. Darcy's character—his life—was a construct of honor. It made him rigid at times, but there were benefits.

And we were in love. Passionately, as I was gathering from the delicate curiosity of other, possibly envious, wyves. I remembered our trip in the coach, and the shell of my ear heated.

The cook, a stick-thin woman kneading dough and dabbed head to toe with flour, met me with a bob. My feet had retraced Emma's flight to the kitchen. I lit a lamp and walked into the night.

Each breath became a puff of cloud. I had brought no coat, and the cold felt glorious. I lifted my free hand to the sky, a slick of perspiration cooling my wrist. The stars were obscured, but it was not utterly dark. The house windows glowed, and a third of the sky glistened palely—moonlight scattered through unfallen snow.

The boathouse was a void in the watery reflections of lights from the far shore. A snow-dusted path led to a buckled door. It opened with a hard shove from my shoulder.

The interior was long and empty, the roof beams shadows fifteen feet above my head. Four carriages could have fit along the length. The floor was packed clay. At the far end, a ramp descended to lapping water. A wooden gate on ropes and pulleys closed the river entrance, the gate's bottom a foot or two above the water's surface.

Darcy had mentioned a disreputable history under a prior owner—smuggling of some sort. That had given me an idea.

I set the lamp on a shelf and turned the flame high, then closed my eyes. I inhaled and emptied my lungs. Petty distractions faded from my mind.

The world of draca opened. The tyke's awareness was a spark of bubbling energy in the house behind me. In front of me, the Thames was dark. I had wondered about that, as draca live half their lives in a fish-like form. Perhaps this part of the Thames was fouled with waste. On land, feral draca preferred the country; they did not roam London like stray cats. Water-borne draca might be the same.

For all that binding was a linchpin of social standing, most wyves considered their bound draca to be no more than a permanent, dangerous, and rather disengaged pet. However, I was a great wyfe. I could sense draca minds over a large distance. Most of London. But in the intensity of the salon, I had done something I thought impossible. I had spoken with Yuánchi while he was at Pemberley, two days' travel by coach.

My binding to Yuánchi was a silver thread vanishing to the north. I focused on it and cast my mind outward.

Do you hear me?

There was no sense of connection. But the remnants of Georgiana's song lingered, melody visible as shifting, interleaved colors. The tones sang, clarifying my thoughts.

Do you hear me? I tried again, and the words were tuned and harmonious.

You are far. Yuánchi's silent response rumbled in my mind like distant thunder.

I am in London. And you are at Pemberley. How remarkable.

I left Pemberley.

"What?" I said aloud.

You were in danger, so I wished to be closer. I crossed half the distance. No one saw. It has been miserably wet. I flew above the clouds.

Well, I could hardly scold him given why I was here. *My principal danger is frustration. I met the War Secretary today. He is an irritating man.*

You go to war. Yuánchi's tone was tense.

What? No.

There was no response.

The chill had penetrated my skin. I rubbed my hands, then thought, *He cannot command us. But I miss you. Perhaps you can visit while I argue sense into his head. I have found an empty boathouse. Would you fit?*

Fit inside a house? Yuánchi's tone was amused. I imagined the huffing snort he used for laughter.

It is more a hall than a house. At least twenty yards long. The response was puzzlement. A dragon did not measure yards. But Georgiana's power still hummed, strengthening my own. *I can see through your eyes when you let me. Can you see through mine?*

I have never done that. With any wyfe.

Try, I thought.

I opened my eyes. The lantern's flame was sharply bright, the boathouse a flickering cavern that faded to black by the water. I threw my mind open, like throwing my arms wide for an embrace.

Something caught hold. My interest tugged, making me look up at the rafters, then down at the floor. It was not unpleasant, but it was... strange.

I see. Yuánchi's thought was astonished. Then it became concerned. *It is blurry. What is wrong with your eyes?*

I laughed. *My eyes are quite healthy. This is how humans see. Our eyes are inferior to draca.*

Your sight is dim as well. Show me the length.

I picked up the lantern and walked to the far end.

It is long enough, he mused. *I could turn without dipping my tail.*

An important consideration, I agreed.

It would be comfortable, for a time. I would like to be near. Shall I come?

Draca saw perfectly well in the dark. He could fly here before dawn. A dragon in the center of London.

I must make preparations, I thought. *There is more to comfort than a dry tail. Food. You cannot hunt deer.* I nibbled my lip. *I suppose I should ask Darcy as well.*

After all, trust went both ways. This seemed the sort of thing a wyfe would discuss with her husband.

He will do what you wish, Yuánchi thought. *You are a great wyfe.*

I crouched down by the water, considering. Yuánchi might hide for a few days, but not forever. Revealing a dragon would shake the world. Would the Council's desire to use Yuánchi rise or fall? Perhaps publicity would intimidate the French. End their experiments with draca.

Yuánchi's curiosity tugged my eyes to the smeared lights reflecting under the gate. I was not sure how long he had slept at the bottom of Pemberley lake, but it was many centuries. Even the Scottish legends did not include a dragon. What would he think of London? Had he ever seen a city?

I swept a fingertip through the frigid water, shattering the city's light to sparks.

My vision turned black. I plunged to another world.

I KNELT *in a long silk robe beside a river as deep and ponderous as a lake. The night air was sticky-hot. The shore was tepid mud, soaking the delicate cloth under my knees.*

My fingers, bronze-skinned and shriveled with age, nudged a paper lantern into the current. The paper was brushed with symbols in a Far Eastern script, but I knew them: the names of my husband, and my son, and my son's family.

This was how I mourned.

The lantern spun downstream, attracting fluttering moths. A fish rose, and the candle wobbled. Behind me, the executioner stood with his sword held high, waiting to end my duty as a noble wife.

But the words of acquiescence stuck in my throat. They were caught on my anger. Treachery had killed my family. Only the perversity of respect postponed my death, an old woman disempowered and unthreatening. Unable to exact justice.

A silver thread tore through my heart. Fury.

The river exploded in mist and spray. A shadow rose, dark as char and black as pitch. Huge enough to enfold the world. Violent as the fall of an iron hammer.

I WAS CROUCHED in the boathouse, my fingers sunk in freezing mud.

"What happened?" I gasped.

I am coming to you.

"No. Wait."

I saw. I am coming. I will not wait. Yuánchi's thoughts were inhumanly potent, piling in my mind like a fall of boulders. My vision flickered. I saw forest streaking below, lit in the peculiar violet that draca saw under a night sky.

"What did I see?" I said aloud.

It is old. The memory of a first wyfe binding. But I do not know her.

Old? Yuánchi called nothing old. Not the gnarled oaks. Not even the druids' ruins. "Should you know her?"

I know the first wyfe I bound. This is another.

"Then how do I remember?"

I sensed rushing wind. *Who was with you, before? A great wyfe touched me.*

"Georgiana?" I said. Foolishly. I knew that was not the answer.

I know the wyfe of song. It was another... Yuánchi sounded wistful.

"Her name is Emma."

Silence. Speed.

"What did I see?" I said sharply. "*Who* did I see? You know more than you have said."

You saw the binding of a first wyfe. The first wyfe of war.

7

LOVE AND SONGBIRDS

LIZZY

"**M**a'am? Mrs. Darcy?" a girl's voice whispered.

Light tickled my eyelids. I was cozy in bed. Well, not so cozy. The sheets were soaked. I felt cold, and yet... I touched my forehead. Sheened with sweat.

A maid of thirteen or perhaps fourteen was grinning at me. I wiped a sticky curl out of my eyes and whispered, "Good morning, Lucy. Do not wake Mr. Darcy." His shoulder was pressing my back, but for once I was not trapped under one of his immovable arms.

I felt under the quilt for my nightgown, then searched with my toes. Nothing.

Lucy's grin tilted mischievously. She lifted a length of gauzy muslin from the floor. "Lost something?" she whispered.

I pulled it over my head while she innocently studied the ceiling. The fabric clung unpleasantly to my wet spine and breasts. I pinched a fold and fanned it to dry off.

I whispered, "Was the fire high last night?"

"Don't know, ma'am. Mrs. Reynolds had a coach for me at the hotel this morning. Brought your things."

We tiptoed out, leaving Darcy sprawled across most of the bed. Really, it was a good thing I was small. In the dressing room, Lucy tugged my damp curls into a mass that could be tied while she prattled about what she had packed. Then she *tsked* and held up a petticoat I had worn yesterday. "How'd you get so muddy?"

"Oh," I said.

The door to the bedroom was ajar. I leaned to peer through. Darcy's hand and wrist were sticking off the side of the bed. Sound asleep.

When I returned from my trip to the boathouse, the house had been in a tizzy. Mrs. Reynolds had every servant running one way or another. It had been decided that our party would stay the night even though rooms had not been made up.

Amid the fuss, I had not a second alone with Darcy until we shut our bedroom door. And then I barely drew breath before... Well, he had been distracting.

Lucy was watching expectantly.

"I am infamous for muddy petticoats," I said. "Consider it training as a lady's maid. Will you take it down and see if Mrs. Reynolds has a laundress?"

"Now?"

"Please. I should hate for it to stain."

Lucy tripped off. I heard her shoes tap down the stairs.

I laid my palms flat on the dressing table, still empty despite Lucy's arrival. There was mud under my fingernails. I closed my eyes.

You are awake, Yuánchi thought. *Good. I am hungry.*

"Oh," I said again. I opened my eyes.

Who first, Yuánchi or Darcy?

Yuánchi. I had used the pulleys to open the boathouse gate before I left. Presumably, the rump of a dragon was now on display for any passing boat.

Darcy swung the dressing room door wide, yawning within a thick maroon robe. "Good morning."

"Oh," I said, mentally reordering my conversations.

"I have been considering our meeting with the War Secretary." Darcy grimaced and rubbed his unshaven chin. "Wellington's goals are straightforward enough. But the Secretary is a politician. How does one influence a politician?"

I thought about it. "Other politicians? Or important personages. Perhaps we should host a ball." That last was a joke, as Darcy abhorred large social events.

He ran a finger under the thin muslin covering my shoulder, and I touched his wrist, watching our wedding bands gleam in the looking glass. I wore a gold fede ring with interlocked knots to honor our Beltane ceremony. Darcy wore the posy ring my father had worn, plain gold but inscribed inside with verse.

"A ball seems drastic," he said. "Our London acquaintances are already curious. They would poke into every nook and cranny."

"Nooks and crannies?" I said, not understanding.

"A ball at Chathford."

I held up a warning finger. "No. *Not* at Chathford!" Darcy looked surprised, so I summoned my well-crafted reasons for stuffing a dragon into our boathouse. "Last night—"

Lucy popped in the other door. "No laundress yet, but we put it in to soak. I'm to tell you that the cook is sorry, but it will be a half hour before you can bathe. The stove is not drawing properly, so there's no warm water."

"The trials of a new home," Darcy said cheerfully. "I will walk the grounds first."

"Yuánchi is here!" I cried.

"He looks bigger," Lucy said.

"It is an illusion," I said uncertainly, while fastening a button on the thick pelisse I had thrown on. "I think. From being inside."

The peak of Yuánchi's back, sheathed in neatly folded wings, was a few feet shy of the boathouse rafters—certainly taller than the gate. The air roiled with a vital scent like cooking cloves. His faceted eyes, each larger than my fist, gleamed gold, green, and blue from a shadowy mound of neck and shoulders. It was difficult to tell what connected to what.

Like wyverns and firedrakes, Yuánchi was two-winged and two-legged, although his sinuous shape was more reminiscent of the smaller firedrake. But, sinuous or not, the question was…

"How did you *fit?*" I exclaimed.

I curl up to sleep.

Scales chimed and flashed scarlet in the dusty light as his torso straightened and lowered… slightly. His long neck unwound until his nose was a foot from mine.

"Well, it is good you managed," I said. Then I remembered something. "May I see your teeth?"

Yuánchi's head cocked in human-like bemusement. Then his jaws stretched wide. Heat deep in his gullet lit my skin as if a hearth had opened. Lucy hastily stepped back.

His obsidian-dark teeth were four or five inches long and slightly back-curved. The front of each was rounded and a half-inch thick. The backs were knife-edged with gleaming serrations. His tongue was also black and had sharp scales pointing down his throat like barbs. I had not known that.

I wiggled the tip of a tooth between two fingers. "Do you ever lose them?"

His head withdrew a yard. The jaws closed with a snap that blew my curls back.

No.

There was a clatter from the far end of the boathouse. Darcy had closed the gate. His silhouette returned through the narrow passage between Yuánchi's torso and the boathouse wall.

"No one could see," Darcy said as he reached us, knocking dust off his palms. "It is bright outside and dark in here. I would have to come within twenty yards to make him out."

"What about boats?" I asked. The Thames was busy from dawn.

"The river froze in the night," Darcy said. "There is ice from shore to shore. This winter will be one for the books."

No one saw when I came, Yuánchi thought. *I was careful.*

"I am glad someone was," Darcy said dryly. He could hear Yuánchi through our binding, at least when Yuánchi wished.

"I meant to tell you," I said. "It was a confused evening."

"I think it's grand," Lucy said, sidling up next to me. "I've never seen him so close. He sparkles."

"He will touch you, if you wish," I said with a smile.

Hesitantly, she reached out a hand. Yuánchi pressed his nose against her palm and puffed a rumbling snort. Her jaw dropped, and she stepped back, eyes wide.

She is brave, he thought. *She will bind well.*

I thought of Mary's campaign for the rights of women to bind. Why not a housemaid bound to a draca? I chuckled, tugged his nose closer, and rubbed the smooth scales under his jaw.

You are very warm, he thought in a fussy tone. I stole a glance at Darcy, but it seemed Yuánchi had shared that thought only with me.

That is an amusing comment from a dragon, I thought.

GEORGIANA, Emma, and Harriet had left by the time Darcy and I arrived for breakfast. Darcy spotted Mrs. Reynolds in the hall and went in pursuit, muttering "sides of beef." I presumed that was a menu for Yuánchi, not a ball. I liked my idea of hosting a ball, but Darcy would require persuasion.

Mary sat alone in the breakfast parlor, poking a ragged slice of cold toast with a bare butter spreader.

I sat beside her. "Are you not hungry?" Her head shook a slow *No*, her face lowered over her dented toast. All I saw was hanging hair and glints of her spectacles. "Why did you not accompany the ladies to the salon?"

"I am meeting Dr. Davenport. He advises outside exercise for health, so we walk to discuss cases." That was the doctor Mary studied with, a commitment that had grown until she was often gone at unexpected hours.

"May I walk with you?" I asked. She nodded, her loose brown hair swaying.

We set out, dressed for the cold and leaving the tyke snoozing by the fire. The day was silvery-bright, overcast but dry. I chose a practical bonnet and checked I had coins for a coach if the weather turned. Mary wore her customary black, fashionably cut despite the intimidating hue.

I had barely noticed Chathford's exterior when we arrived in the snow, so Mary and I stopped to inspect it from the circular drive. We had exited the front, which faced the river. The main entrance was recessed between a pair of octagonal towers that fronted the main house. The walls were variegated red-brown brick and decorated with inset busts of anonymous figures. It was handsome and elaborate and far more conventional than Pemberley. Several acres of park surrounded us, fenced by a stone wall. In the Darcy tradition, there were few groomed gardens. Most was wilderness—chestnut, oak, and birch, their bare branches capped with thin snow.

Two footmen bundled in brown wool stood beside the iron gate. I did not know them, but they greeted me by name.

"Mrs. Reynolds described you, ma'am," one explained with a bob of his head. "We was brought on yesterday. We're to watch for miscreants."

Darcy had hired guards against French assassins. He was nothing if not efficient. But they had been told to watch the property, not me, so they cheerfully pulled the gate wide for Mary and me to leave.

Mary studied the skyline, then set out parallel to the Thames, her pace determined and wordless. We passed two other estates, then a shipping warehouse. It was certainly a different neighborhood than the country. But that would lessen the outrage when we converted a floor or two for the school.

After another silent minute, I said, "Tell me of Dr. Davenport. You speak of his work, but I know little of the man."

That got a smile. "He is a brilliant physician. I am fortunate to assist him. He even attends our marches in support of women's rights."

"Another radical, then."

"We agree that disease must be addressed by prevention as well as treatment of acute cases. Even a cursory study shows social risks to health. That is all too apparent in London." Her stride lengthened energetically. "Any ethical doctor must advocate social change."

"I have seen the risk. The London school serves poor families. We lose children to illness." I puffed a sigh, wondering what to say next. This was important, but not why I had asked to walk with her.

We entered a small public park. A seawall abutted the river. Couples wandered arm-in-arm. I gathered my courage.

"Let us sit for a moment," I said and dropped on a bench so suddenly that Mary overshot by several paces. She returned and sat by me.

I squeezed her gloved hand. "In our conversation last night, you said you could not tell me what was wrong. You are no happier today." Mary eyed me warily. "Do you remember the ball when you accused me of being complacent?"

"Lizzy. I was angry."

"You were *right*. You are never complacent. I admire that about you." She smiled hesitantly, and I took a breath. "My complacency affected my relationships. My... romances. I was blind to other people's feelings. So, I am resolved to do better. To see others more clearly. I have rejoiced to see you joyful these last months. When you are suddenly so sad, I can guess why."

After a silence, Mary gave a shaky half-laugh. "I am not brave enough for this discussion."

"You and I have overcome trials before. My loyalty is to my sister, no matter the circumstances." I tightened my grip on her hand. "But it is a serious situation. I know that Dr. Davenport is married."

Mary stared at me with the most perfectly stunned disbelief I had ever witnessed. Then she burst into laughter.

"What?" I said.

"Oh, Lizzy." She hooted through a hand clapped on her mouth. "Oh my."

"What is so amusing?" I said uncertainly.

"The irony. Or the relief." She pulled off her spectacles and wiped her eyes. "Dear Lizzy. You do see clearly. I am in love." Her cheeks flushed, and she became still. "I have never said that. To anyone."

"Evidently, you are not in love with Dr. *Davenport*," I said, then hoped that had not sounded cross. I was dismayed I had been so mistaken.

"No."

"Well, who then?" I ran through acquaintances in my mind. Mary rarely discussed men. The few she mentioned, she knew through Georgiana, like Mr. Knightley.

Mary settled her spectacles in place. "Unexpectedly, this has been profoundly clarifying. I think it is wrong for me to tell you before I have... before I say all I can to the person I care for." She sighed. "More likely, I am a coward."

"You are the bravest woman I know." It felt good to speak from my heart and not puzzle with my brain.

She hugged me and whispered, "You may see the truth before I am brave enough to speak." She threw her head back and took several huge breaths. "It is beautiful here."

The park was a small square with skeletons of rose bushes, bedraggled hedges, and snow stomped into mud. Across the street, a row of run-down tenements bustled as men set out to their jobs. The day had grown colder, the silver of the sky darkening a shade.

I patted her gloved hand. My sister was in love. "Yes," I said.

A songbird swooped to a deft landing at Mary's feet. It had gorgeous blue feathers with aquamarine edges, iridescent as a peacock. But its beak was strange —a tiny muzzle covered with sapphire scales. Its entire face was a jeweled mask. I checked the feet. Ebony claws, wickedly hooked. "That is a draca. A *feathered* draca."

"Yes," Mary said. "Georgiana and I have seen him before. He lands at the window when we compose. Listen." She whistled three notes. The draca's head flicked back and forth, then he sang the notes, sounding rather woodwind and revealing needle-like teeth.

"I have never heard of a feathered draca," I said.

"I found references in a Chinese scroll."

I looked at her in surprise. "You read *Chinese* now?"

"Georgiana taught me the characters she knows, but that is a few dozen. It was the drawing I recognized." She whistled another pattern, and the draca repeated it. "He is drawn to the wyfe of song."

"He is drawn to *you*," I said. His attention had been on Mary the entire time.

Mary opened her mouth to argue, then closed it. She could hardly disagree when Georgiana was not present.

"You see?" I said. "Mary Bennet is far from mundane."

8

A SCARLET CALM

EMMA

I am Emma Woodhouse. Two of my secrets are revealed. I imagine false illness, and I see bindings. One secret remains.

Today, Harriet and I planned to tour the Darcys' school, but we started our outing by accompanying Georgiana to her music salon. She wished to inspect it. Specifically, it appeared, the instrument.

The salon air had the stale, charred odor of an uncleaned fireplace. Harriet and I watched Georgiana prowl around the massive mahogany pianoforte. Already, the cuff of her sleeve had a half-inch sooty smudge.

Harriet touched my arm. "I keep thinking of those horrible visions you had. They must be so frightening."

"They are frightening while I see them," I admitted. It was strange to be so open, even with Harriet. I pictured the miasma flooding the world. "I lose my sense of what is impossible. You would laugh if I described what I see. It would sound like a silly dream."

"Why did you not tell me before?" Harriet's tone had no hint of accusation, only concern.

I smiled brightly. "I prefer happy topics."

Harriet hesitated, then grinned. "We are staying in London! That is happy."

The Darcys had invited us to stay the week.

Yesterday, I rode to London, fearful outside the shield of Hartfield's walls.

Today, I woke in a borrowed nightgown, and an unfamiliar maid fastened my dress and bemoaned the weather. I had been tipped into a foreign sea, but I had not sunk.

"I shall take you shopping," I decided. "This trip will be your coming out as a lady. You need finer things for London." I had written a letter asking for clothes to be sent, but Harriet's wardrobe was dictated by Mrs. Goddard's boarding school and very dull.

"I did not think of clothes when I asked to visit the school. Is my dress good enough?"

I gave a little sigh. The school was already a tiresome topic. "Your dress is more than sufficient for a school. It is society where you must present yourself with perfection."

Harriet's hands twisted. "The children at Mrs. Goddard's do not notice my clothes. They do not care how I look."

I patted her reassuringly. "That is exactly my point. You are wasted on children." Her fingers wiggled. I patted more firmly.

Georgiana's head was upside-down to see beneath the pianoforte's lid. She straightened, tucked a fallen raven lock behind her alabaster ear, then sat and played a thundering excerpt of something jarringly modern. Beethoven, perhaps. Serious music.

As if summoned, Mr. Knightley appeared in the doorway, puffing and laughing. His coat was sprayed with snow like a child after a snowball fight. I fought an urge to rush over and sweep it off.

"Oh!" Harriet said. "Mr. Knightley is here." She crossed the room, her steps a natural chassé. Mr. Knightley bowed to her extravagantly, and she clapped in delight. Then he caught my eye and mimed a handshake with a glove caked in snow. A laugh tumbled through my lips, surprising me.

Georgiana joined me with a satisfied sigh. "At least there is no damage."

I looked up. My borrowed maid had enjoyed the novelty of yellow hair, so I peered through exorbitant curls. Blackened paint and broken plaster dangled from the ruined ceiling. "That appears damaged."

"*That* does not matter." Georgiana flicked her fingers ceilingward. "Fitz will pay the landlord if he makes a fuss. More likely, Fitz will scowl tremendously, and the landlord will pay *him*. But the instrument is a treasure."

"Fitz?"

She beamed. "My brother is Fitzwilliam. I am an indulged sister, so I call him Fitz."

"Your brother is quite intense." Our long conversation at Chathford filled my mind.

"He is a good brother." She glanced at me. "How are you today?"

I wore my dress from yesterday, although it had been ironed and freshened. My fingers were pinching a pleat to align the crease.

I forced my hand still. Putrid illness did not erupt from the floor.

Georgiana watched my fingers hover above the cloth, then said, "I was a girl when my parents died. My grief suffocated me like a choking blanket. I could only breathe if I made music, so I played day and night. Then my affinity with draca revealed itself, and it became easier."

"If I have an affinity, it is no comfort."

Her head tilted encouragingly. "Perhaps your affinity is not yet revealed."

"When you sang last night, outside Chathford, I felt things change. What did you do?"

"I make music. Draca hear it. They trust me. If they are hurt or distressed, they are soothed. Lizzy says it is power—amplification—but it is only melody. Last night, the world of draca was discordant around you, so I... found the harmony."

"At least you sound like a wyfe of song," I said. "Your brother says I am the wyfe of healing, but I obsess over seams and buttons. I should be the wyfe of sewing."

"Mamma straightened my seams, but she was a healer. I was eight when she died. I remember no miracles or magic. She was like a country healer, brewing herbs for tea and ointments. She said the herbs spoke to her."

I remembered the verse Mr. Darcy quoted. "There are three great wyves. Does that mean Lizzy is the wyfe of war?"

"None of us believe that. Least of all, Lizzy." Her brow wrinkled. "Fitz says my powers will change when I marry and bind. But I do not intend to marry."

"That is very sensible," I said. "I cannot imagine marrying."

Her eyes darted to me, then fixed on the floor. "Why not?"

"I know precisely how I like things. It would be irritating to be in thrall to a gentleman." I watched Mr. Knightley illustrate some point for Harriet with a swirl of his fingers. "Even a handsome one. Papa was very clear that I should keep Hartfield. Independence is a rare gift for a lady."

"Yes," Georgiana said pensively.

"Does your... affinity... show the scarlet around your brother?"

Georgiana did not answer. I turned and met her gaze, serious and still.

"Scarlet?" she said.

"Both your brother and Lizzy surge with scarlet. I thought it was a binding. I *sense* bindings, in the color of the bound draca. But they did not bind, and there are no scarlet draca. Besides, it is too strong. With Lizzy, it is blinding."

"And with my brother?"

"With him it is... different." The word that came to mind was "enticing," but that was inappropriate.

Georgiana pursed her lips. "You must ask Lizzy. This is hers to tell." Her tone became amused. "You should start your outing. Harriet has had her chance. Mr. Knightley must have a crick in his neck from stealing glances at you."

"Do not joke," I said, feeling the warmth of a flush.

MR. DARCY ARRIVED, then Lizzy. We set forth, leaving Georgiana happily cranking the pianoforte's tuning pins.

It was good walking weather. The air was cold, but the sun was spilling between the clouds. The grime of London's streets sparkled under crystals of ice and snow.

Lizzy was anonymous in a concealing coat and wool bonnet. She and I made a great contrast. I had dressed for the cold with long woolen gloves, extra petticoats, and knit stockings, so only the shoulders of my bright dress were covered with a shawl.

"Darcy and I are meeting Mr. Tinsdale at the school," Lizzy told me. "He is a politician, and we needed a discreet location. That should be brief, then we can do our tour." She lingered until Mr. Darcy, Mr. Knightley, and Harriet were a dozen steps ahead of us, then said seriously, "I am unsure how near to approach you."

I remembered pulling away when she touched my bare arm.

"I can manage if we both have gloves." I stretched out my hand. Cautiously, she touched my fingers, glove to glove. Scarlet writhed, powerful to the point of pain, but it was locked away—walled behind immense strength. That was the difference from touching Mr. Darcy. Then the scarlet shone, available and open.

"Do you sense something when we touch?" I said.

She shook her head. "No."

"I sense scarlet. It is stronger today than yesterday. Nearer. Georgiana said to ask you."

Her cheeks blushed rosier in the cold. "I misled you when we met. Darcy and I are bound. It is a secret. You sense that binding." She set out at a brisk walk. "If apologies are due for last night, they are owed to you. Darcy gave you little choice about revealing your secret. It is fair that we share ours. I will show you when we are back at Chathford." After a few steps, she added, "My husband was close to his mother. He blames himself for her death. He is determined to save you."

I cocked an eyebrow. "I do not require saving. But I am excited to remind gentlemen of their mothers. That is a fine accomplishment." Lizzy laughed merrily, and I remembered how much I had enjoyed her before... everything.

We followed as our party turned onto a street that hugged the Thames. This was a shipping district. Burly men shouted orders, slinging sacks or rolling barrels to a queue of horse-drawn carts. Skiffs and barges sat motionless at the river's edge, trapped by the freeze. The main channel was deserted, the ice so thin it was dark and glasslike. A few feet of wispy fog hung above the surface.

The gentlemen and Harriet abruptly stopped. As Lizzy and I caught up, Mr. Knightley said, "I should escort Miss Smith by another route." Ahead, a group of rough-looking men were milling, holding signs and shouting. Pro-slavers, all with cropped hair and belted black coats. An equal number of men in sailors and soldiers' uniforms shouted back, many of them dark skinned.

"We encountered pro-slavers before," I said, squinting to make out their signs. They had not been dressed alike, though. "We simply walked past."

"That would distress Miss Smith," Mr. Knightley said. He offered his arm to Harriet. She accepted, and her posture straightened nicely.

"After yesterday, we should be cautious—" Mr. Darcy began.

Ribbed bronze wings that spanned six feet whooshed low over our heads. The taloned feet barely cleared Mr. Darcy's hat. We all ducked, rather too late.

"A drake," Lizzy said, turning to watch. The firedrake veered upward, soaring toward the river.

The bronze glow of his binding filled me, but with it, suffering. Pain. "His bound wyfe is hurt!"

The bronze glow pointed toward the river. I followed it and spotted her at the end of a short dock, a simple walkway of floated planks extending a dozen feet into the river. She stood hunched in a dirty blanket, an invisible sliver of London's poor. Her eyes were sunken, her hair filthy, her skin pallid.

The urge to help—and the race to preempt the miasma—filled me. I ran toward her. She saw me and thrust out her hand, clutching something small. "Stay away!" She had a lady's diction, but her voice was excruciatingly hoarse.

I stopped at the riverbank. Mr. Knightley pounded to a halt beside me, then Lizzy and Mr. Darcy on my other side.

The woman pointed her clenched hand at Lizzy, waving her fist like she held a weapon. She backed from the planks onto the frozen river. "He ordered me to kill you. But I could not. Now he will punish me." The blanket fell from her shoulders, leaving only a thin chemise streaked with dirt.

A pendant hung from her neck, incongruously bright with gold and emeralds.

Mr. Knightley uttered a soft oath when her blanket fell. He shucked his coat onto his arm and held out his hand. "Come back. The ice is not safe."

A crowd was gathering, and there were concerned gasps and ribald jokes. A rude man shouted, "Get that Negro away!"

"Let me help," I said and stepped past Mr. Knightley onto the ice. The patch under my feet sank slightly with a woodish creak that made me hold still.

The woman backed farther. She was ten yards from shore. Dangerously deep if the ice broke. Shouted warnings joined the catcalls from the crowd.

"I am the lightest," Lizzy said and stepped off the dock.

Like her touch was a stone thrown into a pond, a ripple rushed outward from her foot. Instead of diminishing, it strengthened as it crossed the river, making the ice look fluid but trailing ominous crackles and hisses.

The river groaned, a grumble I felt through my shoes. The crowd gasped and fell deathly quiet, anticipating disaster.

The wisps of fog hugging the ice sank and turned to silver hoarfrost on the glassy surface, the filigrees and feathers lengthening before our eyes. There was another creaking groan, but not in fracture. The ice was thickening. I felt it rise and harden beneath me. The dark glass turned opaque, then whitish-blue. Ridges pushed up, inches thick with strange, cold steam that trickled down their raised edges.

Amazed cries rose from the crowd, but frightened shouts also.

Lizzy's pose softened, then she sank to her knees. Mr. Darcy rushed to her and helped her to the dock where she sat weakly. She shook her head. "I am fine! Go help her."

In her ruined voice, the woman cried, "You are what they said! The Darcy witch!" Her tone was triumphant—joyous—but the crowd echoed "witch" with fear.

The woman turned and began a broken run across the river. The back of her chemise was ripped, exposing skin crisscrossed with ugly red lines. Mr. Knightley bellowed a furious, wordless sound—a shouted gasp—and I saw the red lines were crusted, ragged cuts.

The terrible wounds wrenched my mind.

Miasma erupted, flooding from the moored skiffs until it poured over the gunwales in a deluge of colorless sickness. Lizzy, groggy on the boards, spoke to her kneeling husband, but her words were a wracking cough. Her shoulders hunched and her back distorted, matching the woman's injuries.

My vision darkened. I was fainting, like at the salon. But this time, the scarlet strength was close. I dragged at my left glove, yanking until the long sleeve fell away.

Mr. Darcy was kneeling by his wyfe. My bare hand landed on his collar, and scarlet threw the miasma back like a hissing animal. His head turned, astonished, as I pushed my bare fingers against the skin of his throat. Scarlet flooded me, unfettered by cloth. The miasma flickered, became ephemeral, and vanished.

The woman's pain crystalized in my awareness, every horror revealed. Her back had been torn and re-torn, her throat crushed. Her mind was a wreck of terror and despair. But she could be saved.

"Let me help you," I called. I began walking across the thickened ice toward her. My hand floated free of Mr. Darcy, leaving me brimming with strength.

The woman turned to me, wide-eyed, backing away. "The pain is gone." She croaked a laugh. "You are too late. He has crept inside!" She thumped her skull with her fist. "I must drive him out." Her hand tipped to her lips, then she flung a small object that skittered past my feet. A vial.

I sensed a darkness spread in her body, an evil.

"Emma!" Lizzy shouted. "Get away! She is corrupted. Addicted! She will kill you!"

The woman stretched her arms in the cold air, reaching for an unseen lover. "I free myself!"

Command hammered my consciousness, the same sensation I had felt at the salon before the draca fought for Lizzy.

With a wailing cry, the bronze firedrake swept past me, wingtips skimming the ice. His flaming blue breath roared out and enveloped the woman. Glowing, sky-like radiance wreathed her, then it blossomed ugly orange. The clean blue became a searing inferno.

Her pain swept through the bronze of her binding to envelop me in a fiery ocean, but the scarlet calm swathed us both in a blanket. It was the thought of pain, not pain itself. It sputtered, faded, vanished. Her form darkened to a flaming charcoal statue kneeling in a steaming pool of melted ice. The pendant was a splash of molten gold down the chest.

The drake soared upward with an endless mourning shriek. He rose high, high, then his wings furled, and he fell. Like a stone. Like a lance. He slammed into the ice beside the woman's body, the elegant lines of his head and sinuous neck crushing like eggshell.

The melting ice cracked. Slow as an overloaded boat, a six-foot chunk tipped. The smoldering shape of the woman fell through with a sizzle and gout of steam. The drake's body, limp and gleaming, slipped after her and vanished into the dark water.

9

ROYAL JEWELS

EMMA

"Miss Woodhouse. It is not safe here." Mr. Knightley's hand touched my forearm.

I did not want to look away from where the woman died. The sole remnant of her presence was a sheen of water on the ice, already vanishing as it froze. But his hand drew me, insistent, so I turned.

The shore was thirty yards distant. The river was abandoned. We stood alone, actors on a blue-white stage.

Ashore was chaos. People ran and fell. Arms flailed—men struck each other. Scattered cries reached me, filled with slurs of race. What had this to do with a dead woman?

Harriet was running with the Darcys. She waved frantically, and I raised my hand. They ducked around a squall of men in belted black coats and vanished in the confusion.

"We will meet them," Mr. Knightley said. "I told them to take Miss Smith while I came for you. It is better that she does not wait among these louts."

"Thank you," I said. We began walking. The ice was so cold it felt gritty, not slick. By the time we reached the dock, the chill was biting through the soles of my boots.

Mr. Knightley pulled me to a half-run along the planks. One of the cropped-hair men rushed out of the crowd, his thin face dangling reddened jowls. "Get the witch!" he shouted, his hand stretching for my face. Mr. Knightley stepped between us, grabbed a fistful of the man's collar, and turned, bending so their hips collided hard. The man flew over Mr. Knightley and crashed to the dock, shaking the planks and sprawling onto the ice. Mr. Knightley's arm had already retaken mine. In three steps, we were among the crowd, his touch leading me, ducking low and stepping fast, then waiting tall and firm while a knot of bodies swirled past.

We turned into a quieter alley. He asked, "Can you continue this pace?"

"Of course," I said. "No, wait!" I lifted my hands between us, shocked by dissymmetry—one was gloved, one bare. My breath caught, braced for terrors, but Mr. Knightley's face did not swell with pustules. Miasma did not flood the ground. I gritted my teeth, then pulled the lone glove off and dropped it behind me, out of sight. "I am ready."

We hurried down one street, then a second. "Where are we going?" I asked.

"The school."

The Martin School. Would Harriet still insist on her tour? Surely I could dissuade her after this.

I thought of the man rushing toward me. "Does your musical training include sending men flying head-over-heels?"

Mr. Knightley's lips were a grim line. "I believe I mentioned that I have encountered horrible men."

"*I* have encountered horrible men." My skin crawled at the memory. "My last encounter with Mr. Elton was vile. That does not mean"—we reached a large wooden building, and Mr. Knightley opened the door for me—"that I can toss him over my shoulder."

The Darcys looked up, and Harriet, red-eyed, rushed over. We embraced. Without gloves, the wool of her borrowed coat was scratchy against my palms. I rarely touched her clothes directly. It seemed profoundly intimate.

"Are you well?" Lizzy asked me. "We were worried that you would... react poorly to what we saw."

"I see horrors every day," I said. "I recover."

"You see false horrors," Mr. Darcy said.

"They are real to me." Of course, their reality was in the moment, like nightmares. Afterward, I could comfort myself they were illusion. Today, a woman had truly died. My throat caught. Then I remembered something else. "Lizzy, were you hurt?"

"No," she said dismissively. "Just... affected. A tremendous power stirred."

I looked at Mr. Darcy and found him watching me. He looked quickly away. I remembered touching him and felt a blush rise.

We were in a modestly sized, empty schoolroom. Ten small chairs and desks formed two loose ovals. Papers with childish script were tacked on the wall, titled "When I Bind" and decorated with pencil drawings of fantastic draca.

Mr. Knightley strode down the aisle between the chairs, then back, his motion furious and his jaw corded. "That woman was *whipped*," he burst forth. "I attend the Freedom Society. I have seen the scars on escaped slaves. Their healing wounds. What barbarians do such acts?"

"She was no slave," I said. "She was white."

"Yes." Mr. Knightley's mouth twisted. "When I saw her injuries, that shocked me. Am I so despicable that I expect my kin to be beaten but am dismayed when a white woman is hurt?"

Mr. Darcy stepped into Mr. Knightley's path and caught his shoulders so they faced each other. "I have seen you challenge injustice many times. You are only surprised because this was unexpected. Your anger has never depended on the color of a person's skin." Mr. Knightley sucked air through his teeth, then clasped Mr. Darcy's shoulders in return. He nodded, and his furious tension diminished.

I heard voices in the next room, then a knock at the door. A woman in a good, practical dress, like a governess, stuck her head through. "Mr. Darcy, Mr. Tinsdale is here."

A barrel-chested gentleman in a charcoal tailcoat and waistcoat rushed in. He had an aura of importance, somewhat undermined by overgrown eyebrows and a shock of disordered, straw hair.

His eyes went round when he saw Lizzy. "Mrs. Darcy! I heard a wyfe was burned. You cannot imagine my relief." His gaze scanned the room and fixed on me, curious.

Mr. Darcy stepped forward. "Miss Woodhouse, may I present the Honorable Mr. Tinsdale. A member of Parliament."

"At your service, madam," Mr. Tinsdale said, his solid hand swallowing mine as he bowed. My curtsy was sober and suited for mourning.

Mr. Tinsdale rose quickly from his bow and gave his coat an agitated tug. "I cannot stay long. There is a riot at the docks and stories of witches battling with draca. The Darcy name is circulating. When the Council of War hears that another dangerous event occurred in Mrs. Darcy's presence, they will call an emergency meeting. I must hurry there to prevent reckless decisions." He dug his fingernails into his bushy eyebrows. "*Were* you there?"

"Yes," Mr. Darcy said. "It was another attempt at assassination. By a wyfe bound to a bronze firedrake."

Mr. Tinsdale drew a sharp breath. "The wyfe who sank the *Dapper*."

"I believe so. She was coerced. She had been terribly abused." Mr. Darcy turned to Lizzy. "She said she could not kill you."

"I heard her," Lizzy said. "Despite her fear, she refused to attack me with her drake."

"Perhaps," Mr. Darcy said. "Or perhaps she *could* not attack. Draca perceive great wyves. Her drake may have rebelled. You were not alone. You stood with"—his eyes flicked between me and Mr. Tinsdale, then he finished—"all of us."

"It was her choice," Lizzy said. "She defied her captors and saved her true weapon to take her own life." Lizzy lifted a small vial between her thumb and forefinger. "She drank from this. It reeks of sour orange and bitter almond. Crawler venom. I felt the filth of its potency. Her control of her drake became absolute... until she died, leaving her draca in an agony of remorse."

"Crawler venom?" I said. "Would that not just kill her?" Foul crawlers were small, dangerous pests, like armored, multi-legged worms with stingers—a sting that was lethal.

Mr. Darcy answered, "A powerful wyfe can tolerate small doses of venom. It strengthens her control of draca. It also addicts her and destroys her mind. But this explains how she was able to compel her drake to attack the HMS *Dapper*."

Lizzy bent and carefully placed the vial on the floor by her feet. "I could have found her."

"You must not blame yourself," Mr. Tinsdale said. "No one could find one woman concealed in London."

"A wyfe bound to a *drake*?" Lizzy gave a rough laugh. "I could find every drake in London within minutes. I needed only to *try!*" She stomped her boot, smashing the vial. Mr. Tinsdale looked very taken aback.

"You had no reason to suspect she was in London," Mr. Darcy said.

Mr. Tinsdale cleared his throat. "Mrs. Darcy, I suggested that we meet because we agree it is inadvisable to escalate our war with the French. But the Council will insist that you be kept safe."

"I wore a long coat and plain bonnet. I thought myself unrecognizable." Her lips twisted. "One woman concealed in London..."

"Your husband is well known," Mr. Tinsdale pointed out. "And rather apparent, even in a crowd."

Lizzy looked up from the smashed vial, but she watched me, not Mr. Tinsdale. "I will be more observant. Assure the Council that I will protect myself."

Mr. Tinsdale seemed dissatisfied. "I can arrange guards."

Lizzy's answer was a whisper. "I will summon guards."

"What of that brutalized woman?" Mr. Knightley broke in. "Who did this? We cannot allow such conduct on English soil. It is an abomination!"

Mr. Tinsdale gave him a cool look. He made no move to introduce himself. That was an oversight for the higher ranked gentleman, bordering on rude. Or had they met before?

"Did you see the woman's pendant?" I said. "She wore rags, but that was jewelry fit for a queen. A gold wyvern with a flaming breath of huge sapphires."

Mr. Tinsdale's fluffy eyebrows rose. "The Pendant of Fiery Justice! That *is* royal jewelry, made for the first Queen Mary to celebrate her binding. But it is a dragon, not a wyvern." He shrugged, abruptly self-conscious. "I am rather an aficionado of Tudor history."

"I have read of the pendant," Mr. Darcy said. "Some claim it gave Queen Mary mastery of draca."

"Like the crawler venom you described," Mr. Tinsdale mused. "We must recover the pendant."

"The sapphires, perhaps," Mr. Darcy said. "It was melted."

"Oh," Mr. Tinsdale said. Solemnly, he added, "What a loss."

"There were worse losses," Mr. Knightley said pointedly.

Mr. Tinsdale frowned but nodded. "You must be fatigued. I will leave you to recover while I attend to the Council." He bowed and hurried out.

Immediately when the door closed, Lizzy said, "Emma. Why did you touch Darcy?"

Mr. Darcy stiffened, and his face whitened. I could not guess his emotion. Outrage? Embarrassment? My own feelings were more obvious. My cheeks were heating.

"I beg both of your pardons," I said. "With the panic, it was an... impulse. I intended no impropriety. It will not happen again."

She shook her head. "I am not accusing you. Or asking you to apologize. When you touched him, I sensed a... change. What did you feel?"

I pinched the seam of my sleeve, drawing my fingers to the cuff while the silk whispered. "I thought I would faint. Then a scarlet strength drew me. It was like it spoke. It filled me when I... made contact."

"It is imperative that you return with me to Chathford," Lizzy said.

Harriet had recovered enough to fold away her handkerchief. "What about the *river*?" she exclaimed. "The water froze. Like magic! Was that woman a witch, after all?"

Lizzy shook her head. "There is no such thing."

I thought of how the river froze when Lizzy's feet touched the ice.

10

A SIGNIFICANT MEETING

LIZZY

We left the school, and Darcy hailed a pair of coaches. He returned to stand beside me, stiff and chagrined.

It was early afternoon, not even two, but the light was dwindling faster than nightfall. Cold, yellowish fog rolled up from the river like a rising tide. The low clouds had the same peculiar hue, churning through brass, then bronze, then corroded copper.

Mr. Knightley took the first coach. He would meet Georgiana at the salon and escort her to Chathford.

The second coach pulled up, and Harriet found a seat. Emma followed her friend, her pale lashes lowered and a blush locked high on her cheeks.

Darcy gave directions to the driver, then offered his hand to me, somehow managing to be simultaneously rigid and cringing, and I decided to put an end to this nonsense.

I drew him away from the coach door and laid my palm on his heart. "Love, you are indulging in vanity." His surprised dark hazel eyes met mine as I continued, "Only a silly wyfe would think a touch is betrayal. I hope I am not that. But you are behaving like a penitent nun and unjustly embarrassing Emma. A woman *died*. If that is not sufficient perspective, I felt the strength that surrounded us on that river. Emma was a scarf blown in a gale." I looked up at the stormy, orange sky. My sense of the draca world seemed to tremble with the chilling air. "I think we all are."

His shoulders straightened. "You are right. I will apologize to her."

"Go in. I require a minute." Darcy entered the coach and pulled the door just shy of latching.

The driver called down, "Are you not comin', ma'am?"

"I will. I am greeting a guest." I had sent a summons, and the answer approached.

A lindworm, the heaviest of quadruped draca, was loping down the street and drawing stares—draca in London usually lolled out-of-sight in their draca houses. She settled eagerly at my feet, twenty-five pounds of stout muscle, wide-chested as a bulldog but equipped with a squat, lizard-ish tail and sheathed in moss-brown scales.

I bent, staring into her black eyes and wondering how to express the future tense. My affinity let me share the silent mental speech of wyverns and dragons, but other draca breeds communicated more simply, with images and emotions.

I spoke aloud for focus and concentrated on images to convey my words.

"Men wish me harm. Your strength would be welcome. If you travel with us, I will ensure you are returned to your home."

The lindworm nodded her head in a sneezy *huff* that left a smoky odor, then looked up at the top of the coach. I had pictured her seated there, having no other inspiration for a draca traveling by coach.

She tensed, powerful muscles bunching in her hips and legs. "Do not—" I began, but she had already leaped an astonishing eight feet up and was scrabbling into the spare seat beside the driver.

"Bloody hell!" the man shouted and jumped clean off the far side of the coach, which was almost as impressive.

"Wait!" I called, running around the back of the coach. "She will not hurt you." The lindworm trotted across the driver's bench to peer down at the driver, who was spouting excited oaths. *Wait*, I thought to her as well. If she jumped after him, I would be chasing the two of them across half of London.

Ignoring Darcy's shouted "What was that?" from the window, I finished circling the coach and affixed a smile. The driver had a teen's wispy beard, but his arms were burly—a young man who had driven horse teams for years. He propped his fists on his hips and gaped up at the draca occupying his seat.

"She is quite tame," I said. "Here, for your trouble." I opened the drawstring on my reticule and held out a shilling. "There will be another if you bring her back to this street after."

"Back? *Her?*"

"Yes. Her home is there." I pointed to a stone draca house outside a terrace home on the next street.

He exhaled the long, doubtful sigh of a tradesperson indulging insanity, then took the shilling. "All right, then." He climbed up, and the lindworm made room, turning a dog-like full circle before settling on her side of the bench. Perhaps she was admiring the view.

I climbed into the coach. Emma looked exhausted but no longer mortified. Harriet was watching Darcy with ill-concealed awe. Darcy himself looked slightly smug. Doubtless he had enjoyed a dramatic speech brimming with ethics and remorse.

Gravely, he turned to me and drew a preparatory breath. I raised a restraining hand—gently, I hoped. "My pulse has raced enough. Tell me when I have had a cup of tea."

AT CHATHFORD, we joined a line of three coaches waiting to discharge passengers. Darcy banged on the roof and called up, "Find out what is happening."

There were curt, professional shouts, then the driver called down, "Music, sir."

I watched ladies disembark from the coaches before us, then we climbed down. The driver took his extra shilling and rolled off, the lindworm beside him and peering at every passing sight.

Inside, Mrs. Reynolds curtsied to us, then waved a despairing hand—high drama by her standard. "A dozen guests already! And the footmen are missing. Madam, I must ask Lucy to help serve."

"Of course," I said. "But whose guests?"

"Miss Bennet. She is mad with music!"

Mary. I tended to forget that she led a prominent London society. "Please see Miss Woodhouse and Miss Smith to a quiet room. They have had a trying day. I will look for Mary."

Darcy and I followed excited echoes up two flights of stairs and found at least fifteen ladies chatting while poring over sheets of music spread on tables and the lid of a pianoforte. The missing footmen were here as well, being directed by Mary as they settled a four-foot-long wooden box on a table.

"Gently!" Mary cried when the wood clunked. "You will throw the tuning —" She saw me and gave a radiant smile. "Lizzy! We have moved the salon to Chathford. Come meet the society. Here is Jane Savage. It is her virginal we are unpacking."

I greeted a gray-haired, pleasantly matronly woman. "Mrs. Rolleston," she clarified. "But we use our musical names. I publish under my maiden name. Better for sales if they imagine a doe-eyed maid penning music in a gothic attic."

I managed a fleeting "I see" before I was whirled through more introductions: Maria Parke, whom I had heard sing at the Argyll Rooms; Harriet Browne, a confident girl no more than fifteen; and Sophia Dussek, a happy Scot with long, wavy hair and a ferocious brogue who ran a music school.

"Mary, slow down!" I said. "I shall not remember. Are they all composers?"

"Of course," Mary said, as if nothing could be more natural in a room full of ladies. "Wait and see who attends next month. We are having an international gathering. Maria Mozart—she is like royalty. I cannot understand why people fuss over her dead brother instead. The Baroness de Bawr will stage her *Suite d'Un Bal Masque*. And I am corresponding with Charlotta Seuerling, who is the fashion in Sweden, but she is blind which complicates travel."

"I suppose," I said, looking around the room. Darcy was conversing with two well-dressed wyves. Perhaps he knew them. Georgiana was celebrated as a performer, and the Darcys had moved in musical circles for years. To my chagrin, I had not even known that Mary composed until Georgiana informed me at Jane's wedding.

"Mary, could I take you from your salon for a few minutes?" I said. "I have serious news."

We moved to another room, and I described the events at the river.

"That is sad and highly disturbing," she said when I was done. Her eyes roamed behind her round lenses as she thought. "The wyfe was alone?"

"Yes, alone but terrified. I do not think she understood she could escape."

"There is more evil here than crawler venom. Venom creates dependency and induces mania, but her captors must have thought their control absolute if they trusted her with the pendant."

"You think the pendant important?"

"I think *they* thought it important. But they were foolish. It is superstition to believe metal and gems are magic because a jeweler gives them a pretty shape.

And they were reckless as well. It was a royal artifact. We can discover who owned it."

I LEFT Mary to her salon. After such a disturbing day, we scattered to private activities—that is, until several large wardrobe chests arrived from Surrey. Then I joined a suspenseful unpacking as Emma and Harriet discovered what clothes had been sent by Emma's Hartfield maids. The ladies' happy smiles and mock despair lightened everyone's mood.

That evening, we served Chathford's first supper in six years—only for family, Emma, and Harriet, as the salon members had finally departed, swishing embroidered hems and hauling decorated albums filled with supportive notes and copied music. Dinner was winter fare: roast duck, onions in mustard, shepherd's pie, and a hearty dish of pumpkin and beans because Mary did not eat meat. That practice had become a fad with health-obsessed, wealthy Londoners, which was a trial for Mary as she had to balance philosophical support against disdain for their motives. She considered this a matter of ethics.

Harriet became happily talkative, telling stories of her life at Mrs. Goddard's. We compared memories of the shopkeepers in Highbury village and Meryton, finding amusing quirks shared by the two distant towns.

When Darcy excused himself, the ladies moved to a drawing room. Harriet and Emma had dressed in simpler white muslin for dinner, although Emma's was beautifully worked, lace-edged and accompanied by a spencer that covered her shoulders with scalloped fringes and cords. When she stood by the fireplace, a jade shawl draped behind her arms, she was eerily perfect, even the shawl hanging symmetrically.

I smoothed my own sleeves—either self-conscious or considerate, I was not sure which—and joined her.

"I said I would share the secret of Darcy's and my binding," I said. "Will you walk outside with me? It is cold, but the dark is better for privacy. And he must be let out for the night." I smiled at that. It sounded like I was caring for a poodle.

"Will I be astonished?" she said seriously.

"You are meeting him, and he is meeting you," I said. "I feel both are significant."

I put on a coat and mittens. Lucy retrieved Emma's long pelisse, ruby-red and fur-trimmed at the collar and cuffs. We went out the side entrance carrying a lantern.

The sky was the sullen black of thick cloud at night. The air bit my nose and eyelids, and smelled of frozen leaves. I closed my eyes, casting my mind toward the river and finding a brilliant but diffuse awareness. "He is asleep. Perhaps that is good for a first glimpse. He is very large." Emma did not reply. I was not sure why I did not say "Come see a dragon," but my tongue tied at the thought. I gave an encouraging smile instead, and we walked side-by-side to the boathouse, sharing the light.

Emma's steps slowed. Five paces short, she stopped and whispered, "I am afloat in a sea of scarlet."

I lifted the lamp enough to see her face. Her eyes were wide, her pupils huge in the dark. "Should we go back?" I asked. She shook her head. "Wait here." I went and opened the door, repaired and level on new hinges, then held the lamp past the threshold to illuminate the interior. "This is Yuánchi. A dragon."

Emma's hand, gloved in red leather that matched her coat, grazed her cheek, her fingers spread in wonder. She walked through the door. I followed and set the lamp on a shelf.

Yuánchi's breath was rumbling through an endless exhalation. He lay on his side, blanketed by a folded scarlet wing that could have hidden a carriage, his ankles protruding and crossed so the higher foot dangled, relaxed as a cat's paw —if that cat had ankles thick as tree trunks and ten-inch claws like ebony pickaxes. We were facing his chest and the muscled trunk of his neck. The rest of his neck curled away from us. His head lay by his feet, and the tip of his tail was draped rather comically over his nose.

"Do you sense anything?" I whispered.

"Life," she said slowly. "Vitality. Like a forest in a summer rain."

"Our skills are certainly different. I sense his mind shining. An awareness." Yuánchi's chest began to fill, and his scales seemed to roll in the lamp's reflection. Emma took a step toward him. She was four or five feet away. I took a breath to say "Do not touch him," then stayed quiet. I was not sure why I wanted to speak, or why I did not.

Yuánchi shuddered in his sleep. His claws snapped closed, grating across each other like crossed swords while muscles bulged in his calves. Impressive as draca teeth were, claws were the real weapons of flying draca, black scythes that struck from the sky. And their fire, of course.

Louder, I said, "Yuánchi." He shuddered again. The coil of his tail rubbed the side of the boathouse. Wood groaned, and dust fell from the rafters, thin streams in the lamplight.

This was strange. He should have heard us and woken before we reached the door. It was like he was trapped in a dream.

I closed my eyes, concentrating, and reached through the silver thread of our binding. *Yuánchi. We are here with you. Emma and I.*

There was a thunderous snort. He scrambled and rolled onto his belly, his two massive legs crouched like gnarled stumps, his wings tensing until they brushed the walls. His head lifted to face Emma, their noses two feet apart.

Emma's lips were open as if caught mid-gasp. Yuánchi was still as stone. Only his eyes seemed to move, their facets shining ruby, citrine, and topaz as the lamp's flame flickered.

He had not answered. I thought again, *This is Emma.*

Slowly, as if mesmerized, Emma raised her gloved hand. Yuánchi made a noise, high pitched and uncertain—he was *whining*. Her hand moved an inch closer, and he exploded into motion, scrambling backward through the boathouse on his huge legs. With a surprisingly inconsequential *snap*, the gate flew off its mountings, and he surged out into the night.

"Yuánchi!" I cried. I grabbed the lantern and ran after him, then turned back to Emma, not wanting to abandon her in the dark. "Come!" She blinked as if dazed, then ran toward me.

The last few feet of the boathouse floor descended to ice, but each wall had a walkway over the water. I trod carefully along the foot-wide ledge, then clutched the wall while stepping to shore. Emma followed me.

"Where has he gone?" she said, sounding disappointed and quite unastonished.

"In the air." I could sense him high above and hear his wings, the slow strokes like storm gusts. "There is some effect between you and him. On the ice, when you touched Darcy, I felt it through my binding."

I thought, *Yuánchi.*

I am here. I see you. Both of you.

I spoke aloud so Emma could hear. "We wish to understand what disturbed you. Will you come down?"

In answer, the wing beats ceased. I sensed him descending in a wide arc. "Do not be alarmed when he lands. He can see us perfectly in the dark. But it will be windy."

The first hint of his coming was a spreading void, darker even than the black sky. Then the lantern caught sheets of ruby as his wings cupped a storm of wind, driving us to the side of the boathouse until his claws grasped the earth. No longer crouched, his head, neck, and chest were higher than our heads and barely lit by the lantern, darkening his color to the red of old coals.

"I should have woken you before we approached," I said. "I am sorry."

I dreamed of you. Yuánchi's rumbled thought filled my mind.

Emma gasped, her hands flying to cover her mouth.

"Do you hear him?" I asked, and she nodded frantically into her gloves. "That is a discovery. He is able to speak to Darcy through my binding, but even Georgiana cannot..." I trailed off.

Yuánchi's attention was fixed on Emma. He had dreamed of *her*.

His voice resumed. *I slept in the deep. The world aged, and I was alone. When the wyfe of healing rose, it was a sun rising. I felt you laugh, and love, and bind. I waited to be called. But you died!*

The last thought was thick with hurt and accusation.

"Yuánchi, you are not making sense," I said. "Emma is standing in front of you."

I felt your death.

"I was in Highbury," Emma said in a confused voice. Her tone firmed. "I have always been in Highbury. I am sorry I did not find you. I was caring for my papa."

"He means Lady Anne Darcy," I realized. "Yuánchi, you are remembering Darcy's mother. She was at Pemberley, near where you slept. She was the wyfe of healing you felt die."

Yuánchi's head stretched closer to Emma, studying her from several yards above the dried rose that topped her bonnet. She stared back, enthralled and guileless as a child, clothed in red from head to hems except for a froth of yellow ringlets shining in the lantern's light.

Yuánchi took a long step back, then laid delicately onto the earth, his neck unspooling until his nose settled by my feet. That pose was new, proprietary and subservient at once, like a hound relaxing by a beloved master. He blew a windy breath, and my skirts fluttered against my knees.

Another wyfe of healing. So soon. The three wyves have come.

"Well, that proves that," I said to Emma. "You are a great wyfe. He would know."

"But what does it *mean*?" Emma said. "To be a wyfe of healing. If I could heal anyone, it would have been Papa—" Her bright tone abruptly caught.

We touch a feather to the scale of life. Those who will die, die. But you are not yet bound. You must bind to find your strength and know your limits.

Emma became intensely still, as motionless as the frozen trees. I watched her breaths plume in the lantern's light. Finally, her chin lifted. "That is like Georgiana. She said her powers would change if she bound." Her lips and brow pursed. "Do you mean I could bind a dragon?"

You cannot bind a dragon, Yuánchi answered.

"I thought not," she said sadly. She seemed both disappointed and unsurprised, as if a shop had refused her order for roses in the midst of a bleak January. Still, her quiet acceptance felt peculiar. This was a woman accustomed to privilege.

"There is only one dragon," I pointed out. But Yuánchi gave an anxious, chesty groan, and his head dragged back across the ground until it was a reddish shadow at the fringe of the lantern's light. I eyed him suspiciously. "*Are there more dragons?*"

You cannot bind a dragon because your dragon—the dragon who shares your purpose—is already bound.

Emma's eyes went round. Her cheeks paled to snow. "You were to be mine," she whispered.

I tried not to smile. "That is *not* what he means." Another groan heaved from Yuánchi's chest, and a gleaming shiver whispered over his scales. An unpleasant, unwelcome realization crawled into my belly. "That cannot be."

Yuánchi turned his gleaming gaze to me. *When the wyfe of healing died, I despaired. I had waited an age of your world. Her death was the start of another thousand-year night. Then, you swept your fingers through my lake, and I felt your passion. I reveled in your love. When you called, it was the most powerful call of any wyfe...*

"What are you saying?" My hand was in the air between us, pushing back against absurdity. "You bound the *wrong wyfe*? It was... what? A mistake? An infatuation?"

A binding is no mistake. It is inviolate. It is for life.

"You mean it is irrevocable. Inescapable. Like a despised marriage in some pathetic comedy!"

"Lizzy," Emma said. "That is not what he said."

"Do not speak for him!" I cried. "You have no right."

Elizabeth Darcy Bennet. Yuánchi's voice flooded me like a torrent, my maiden name ringing—draca prized female ancestry. *You and I are bound. It is for life. Nothing else matters.*

A spark of distrust survived that onslaught and kindled to fury. "Nothing else? Then let her touch you. Show me that nothing else matters."

Yuánchi drew back a step, his body bunched and anxious.

Emma said hesitantly, "Lizzy, let us go inside. We are both very surprised. I have seen a dragon, after all."

She gave a shaky laugh, but what I heard was artifice, cleverly disarming and overly harmless. No, that was ridiculous. She did nothing to cause this. Other than not visiting Pemberley before me.

"You go," I said, and the words tasted bitter. "I wish a moment with Yuánchi." I held the lantern out for her. "Take it. It is a short walk. I can find my way without it."

"Are you certain? I can send a servant. Or are they not allowed to see…"

"Mrs. Reynolds will tell you. Ask her who knows, and who does not. I do not need the lantern. Emma, please go."

She took the lantern. "He is wonderful, Lizzy. You are blessed." I nodded, not trusting my tongue, and she followed the path back to the house, stopping once to look back.

The door closed behind her. Yuánchi became a shadow barely revealed by the glow of the house windows.

I breathed the icy air, trying to calm a storm of emotions. Finally, one held long enough to understand. "You said my call was 'the most powerful call of any wyfe.' Is that because I am the wyfe of war?" The winter cold chilled my words.

The wyves of war have the strongest call. Among those wyves, you are the most powerful I have known.

"So this is a dalliance? To escape boredom, you bound a novelty wyfe? Is this a habit?"

No dragon before has bound outside their purpose. Yuánchi's muzzle emerged from the night. *Elizabeth Darcy Bennet. Child of the Lake. You burn with anger. You reek of shame. None of these are just feelings.*

"They feel just to me!" I cried. "You have peered inside my head and given an excellent summary."

Nothing has changed. You are a great wyfe and bound to a dragon. The love of your marriage is strong.

"That is what this means to you. A way to spy on my human passions!" An icy tear scraped down my cheek.

Stabbing with words will not infuriate me, or shame me, or drive me away. Draca minds are not like yours. We see what is, not what we wish. I have no curtains you can tear away to reveal painful truths.

I blew a wordless syllable, half gasp, half unarticulated curse. "That makes you most unsatisfying for arguing."

I have been told that. His head tilted, eyes shining. *Do you recall these words: 'No archaic verse rules me. My destiny is my own.'*

"I said that to you. When we bound, and you asked if I was the wyfe of war."

The Child of the Lake is old and wise. Your destiny is your own. But you choose for more than yourself. Your choices bind me.

The wild swings of my feelings diminished like an exhausted pendulum. Finally, I hmphed. "I am irritated that I am no longer angry." I rethought that. "*Less* angry." Yuánchi huffed his laughter. "What does this mean for Emma?"

She will marry, and bind, and become whole, and be the wyfe of healing. More than that, no one can know.

"She does not need to bind with you to be a great wyfe?"

All great wyves bind. Few bind dragons.

"So, there *are* more dragons?"

Would it not be stranger if there were only one?

HANDSOME, CLEVER, AND RICH

EMMA

The door closed, sealing me in the walls of Chathford, but my soul stayed in the night, a giddy leaf riding a mighty scarlet ocean. Every step I had taken toward the creature thrilled me. That siren still called, vital and intoxicating, but forbidden. Lost.

Lizzy's young maid, Lucy, curtsied. "Ma'am. May I help with your coat?"

Only long practice hid my turmoil. "I do not wish to take you from your mistress's tasks."

"It's no bother, ma'am. Mrs. Darcy is no work at all!"

"How nice." The scarlet surged, flooded my lungs, ebbed. Lucy raised an impatient eyebrow.

I said, "Can you keep a secret?"

Lucy's face flushed with excitement. "She showed you! Oh, I knew she would. You are so pretty, he must like you. He's the most amazing thing alive!"

"He is very wonderful. But this is another secret." Lucy grew a proud inch, and I smiled at her. "I play a silly game. I do not like to see my winter clothes while they come off. Will you help me?"

She gave a dubious nod, and I closed my eyes. Quick fingers replaced my leather gloves with cotton, then undid clasps and silk ties on my front. My heavy pelisse slipped away. Layers of scarlet seemed to sheet away with it.

The touches stopped. "My bonnet," I said through tight teeth.

"Sorry, ma'am." The bow under my chin was undone. The cotton lining lifted from my hair.

"Are they put away?" I asked.

"Yes, ma'am."

I opened my eyes and beamed at her. "There! Was that not fun?"

"That was *strange*, ma'am." She winced. "Mrs. Darcy says I am to say what I think."

"How nice," I said again. The scarlet flood had receded, but I was still immersed in Darcys. "Where is Harriet?"

Lucy led me to the drawing room. I waited at the threshold, and Harriet came over, her forehead creasing. "Miss Woodhouse, you are so pale!" Every eye in the room turned, curious and overly aware.

"Let us visit our room," I said. Harriet took a candle, and we climbed a daze of stairs and halls before I sat on my bed.

Harriet lit candles and sat beside me. "What is wrong?"

Papa's death. The most fabulous creature in the world, lost. "We must leave. Return to Highbury and the lives we know."

"Oh," she said, diminished.

I had expected that. "Do not fret. Country gentlemen are superior to city gentlemen in any case. I shall simply insist that you are able to bind. But London has been all horrors."

Harriet's chin set with unexpected determination. "I have been scared sometimes, but it is not *all* horrors. There are good things, too. We have friends that help us."

"You cannot mean that you wish to *stay?*"

"Oh... We should do whatever you choose, Miss Woodhouse. You know best..." She trailed off, but her lips shaped soundless thoughts.

I patted her hand. "Harriet, always speak your mind. I would welcome advice from someone who is *not* a Darcy or a Bennet. They are too full of secrets and legends."

Harriet bit her lip, her eyes pure black in the sparse light. "If I *should* speak... I know you are not well, Miss. Not since old Mr. Woodhouse passed."

Startled, my gaze fled her eyes, hunting the room before settling on a candle flame. "What have you imagined! I am perfectly well."

"You are not yourself, Miss." She took my hand. "You hardly leave Hartfield house. You speak of Mr. Woodhouse always. It is as if you are still caring for him, day and night, like at the end. It was a hard end, Miss Woodhouse. You were a brave daughter. But do you not see that, for you, the memories in Hartfield are horrible too? Do you not see how much better you have been in London?"

"*Better?*" The word was shocked from my throat.

"Yes, better! Like you were before. We ride in coaches, and when they let the step down, you do not stare for minutes before you enter. We meet people, and you speak and smile, instead of falling silent to fix your clothes, over and over."

"I cannot do those things! I am too—" I bit away the foolish denial—too *careful*—and used my ultimate proof. "I know how they talk about me. Emma Woodhouse is handsome, clever, and rich. Everyone says so!"

Harriet whispered, "Not everyone. Not anymore." Unexpectedly, she squeezed me in an embrace, her cheek on my shoulder. "But I know you are still Emma Woodhouse. Who has been so kind to me. That is why I came with you to London. To *help* you."

My breath squeezed past a jagged shape in my throat. Help *me?* Help the mistress of Hartfield?

"It seems I have been mistaken," I managed. "I thought I was a good friend."

"You are a good friend," she said. "You have made my life wonderful. Cannot I help yours?"

I laughed, and it was as coarse as a beggar. All this time, I had been secretly mocked. Pitied by a girl in a boarding school.

Despair made the truth easier. "Then help me! I must leave London. The Darcys say I am some healer from legend, as if that is good, and I should be proud or happy. They do not understand it is dreadful. Each time they speak, they announce my sin. Harriet, if I had married and bound, I might have saved Papa!"

Harriet uttered a long "Oh..." Then, puzzled, she added, "Married *whom?*"

That question was so practical—so *futile*—that it calmed my racing pulse. "I do not know."

Harriet crossed her arms, musing. "Only a very fine gentleman could have married you." She became still. Cautiously, she said, "Mr. Elton?"

"No!" Anger drew me rigid—at myself for letting him hurt Harriet, and at him for hurting me. "Mr. Elton is vile. We shall both despise him forever." I shook my head to drive him from my thoughts and felt curls rustle. "Marriage does not interest me. But if I married, it would be someone far better mannered. And richer. *And* more handsome."

Harriet giggled. "Like Mr. Darcy! But you are tired of Darcys."

A memory rushed to mind—Mr. Knightley defending me from the violence by the river. But that hardly seemed well mannered.

I filled my lungs and sighed it all back out again. "It is Bennets who are wearing me down. Perhaps I can find a lost Darcy cousin. Then at dinner, Lizzy will call out 'Darcy!' and the whole table will turn." Harriet gave an impertinent laugh, which cheered me up. Enough talk of marriage. "The Darcys have bound a dragon."

Harriet leaned from her perch on the bed to see me better. "Truly?" I nodded. Her face lit. "Oh, it is like Princess Una and her Redcrosse dragon!"

"I do not think Lizzy battled the Errour crawler. But, yes. It is secret, of course. Like everything here."

The last of the churning scarlet had drained while we talked. My shame had drained with it. All that was left was Emma Woodhouse, sitting on a bed. The space inside my ribs and limbs felt hollowed, but not empty. I was lighter, like a bird.

"Did you *see* the dragon?" Harriet pressed. "Is it as big as a horse, like Princess Una's?"

I raised my eyebrows dramatically. "Bigger!"

"I should love to see it!"

"It is a 'him.' Lizzy's maid has visited, so I am sure Lizzy will take you. I will not go, though."

"Is he too frightening?"

Each time Yuánchi's gem eyes had met mine, they had pulled at my soul. "He is too wonderful."

"Oh. May we stay in London, then? With our friends?"

While I had stood, enthralled that this hallowed creature sought me, Lizzy's face had been wretched. "We are too dependent on our friends. I will ask Lizzy to recommend lodgings in London, and we will move there."

Firmly, Harriet said, "I wish to visit Mrs. Darcy's school."

"We have already agreed to that." I touched Harriet's hand. "We will visit the Darcys. But we had a purpose in visiting London. I must establish your right to bind."

"Why do you think I *can* bind?"

"It only matters that society thinks you can bind. Then you can marry a gentleman."

"What if I do not *wish* to marry a gentleman?" Harriet said stubbornly.

She had dared formidable London and survived terrors. Naturally, she would have new ideas. But obligation burned in my breast. I had failed Papa. I would not fail her.

"I shall not give you any advice," I said slowly. "Only remember that a woman is never secure without a proper marriage. Even my own situation is precarious." Harriet frowned. I interlaced my fingers, pressed my gloves snug until my knuckles ached, and chose to reveal more. "Papa became fond of you in his last year. He felt as I do. He wished you would marry a gentleman."

Harriet cocked her head. "That is considerate. I do miss him. He was a nice old man." She sighed good-naturedly. "Shall we ask Mary for help, then?"

"That is my *last* resort. Mary Bennet dislikes me." Harriet's surprise was so innocent that I laughed. "I am quite convincing on my own. I will write a letter tonight and post it before breakfast. Let us see what I stir up."

12

THE MARTIN SCHOOL

EMMA

efore breakfast, I found Lizzy writing a letter in a well-lit nook, her hair loosely gathered.

No, not a letter. There were columns of numbers in a thick volume. She saw my glance and said, "Monthly accounts for the school. I have the habit from when I helped Papa at Longbourn. I suppose that sounds odd."

"A lady must understand money." She looked pleased, and I continued, "In that spirit, would you suggest an inn where Harriet and I could stay in London?"

"What? You are very welcome here. We certainly have room."

"I do not wish to impose."

"That is nonsense, and you know it." She wiped her pen and stood, skeptical and concerned. "Is something wrong?"

We were alone, and Lizzy's simple question deserved truth. "I am uncomfortable this close to Yuánchi." Her eyebrows rose. I added, "Do *you* not want me away from him?"

Dryly, she said, "Because you are his soulmate, or whatever? He and I have discussed that. We are bound. It is as simple as that."

If I concentrated, I could sense all three of them: Yuánchi blazing behind the house, Lizzy heated with the same fire, and, faintly, Mr. Darcy a few rooms away. "It is not so simple for me."

"Oh, Emma." She reached for my hand, and I stepped back. She smiled ruefully, a few steps between us. "Pardon me. I forgot. When I brought you to Yuánchi, the last thing I wished was to make you uncomfortable."

"I know that. I am sure we will visit endlessly. At the school this afternoon, to start." That was enough to launch Lizzy into enthusiastic plans.

At noon, Harriet and I stood with Lizzy on a London corner. The fabled Martin School was across the street, visible in glimpses between passing carts and strolling dock workers.

I had sent my own letter this morning, and my reticule held an encouraging reply, so this was only Harriet's and my first stop of the day.

The school's classrooms and boarding were in a two-story white wooden building, the same one we gathered in after yesterday's frightening events. It had broad, shop-like windows on the bottom floor, but otherwise it could have been a plain, oversized country home. Two other buildings housed what Lizzy called "practical education." They were red brick and tall as barns, with arched entrances wide enough to admit coaches. Their steeply peaked slate roofs had multiple chimneys and an industrial style.

The three buildings surrounded a grassy yard teeming with children from six to ten, both boys and girls. The youngest squealed and ran in games. The oldest lounged with studied calm.

"The younger classes are on break now," Lizzy said, on her toes to see better. She pointed to one of the red brick buildings. "That is the smithy. The other, we call the factory. It has machines and tools away from the smoke and fumes."

"They are so large!" exclaimed Harriet. Mrs. Goddard's boarding school would have fit in half of any of them.

"How many students are there?" I asked.

"Six and forty," Lizzy answered. "Some pay tuition and return to their homes after school, but most are charity, and most of them board at the school. Although I dislike the connotation of 'charity.' I may rename their status to sponsored or scholarship. What do you think?"

"Charity is a virtue," I said.

Lizzy's curly chignon flung as she shook her head. "You should be right, but society abhors those who require assistance. Providing charity is a virtue. Receiving it is a sin. Even among the students, there were conflicts. The working class sneers at the poor, and the gentry sneer at those who work, but it is accidents of birth or health that dictate who has wealth, and who struggles—" She broke off with a wry smile. "At this rate, I shall be wearing black and marching with Mary. Oh, we have been seen!" Lizzy waved at a lady in her mid-twenties who had raised her hand in greeting from the doorway of the white building. Lizzy crossed the street at her preferred, skirt-thrashing pace. Harriet and I followed more sedately, dodging traffic.

Introductions at the white building were brief due to a class in progress. We looked inside the smithy, where a man in a leather apron was pounding noisily on red-hot metal before a semicircle of boys, then entered the factory building. A gaggle of girls gathered around Lizzy with a mix of curtsies and excited, childish "Good morning, Mrs. Darcys."

Lizzy walked to a mechanism of iron and wood the size of a pony. It was spinning a metal wheel at a leisurely pace while blowing modest puffs of steam. The precise motion and shimmering heat made me think of draca. Lizzy tapped it affectionately. "A Watt steam engine. The Luddites smash them, but I am certain they are wrong. They should protest for more production and higher wages, not break tools that reduce labor." She raised her voice to be heard over the clanks. "Girls, who will show our guests how to thread a bolt?" Excited hands shot up. Lizzy chose a quiet, thin girl around twelve. "Martha, would you please?"

Martha nodded, bobbing fuzzy black braids, and took a metal rod a few inches long from a bucket. "The boys smith these round tenons. They are supposed to be three-eighths of one inch, but we check because boys are not careful." The other girls giggled while she soberly slipped the metal through a plate with several sized holes. "Then we cut the thread with a die." She fastened the metal rod into a clamp.

"How will this bolt be cut?" Lizzy asked in an enraptured tone.

"A three-eighths-inch Martin bolt has sixteen threads each inch," the girl answered. The tip of her tongue poked out while she dabbed a single drop of liquid on the metal—"Linseed oil"—then she gave a sparkling smile and cried, "Watch this!" The pony-sized mechanism began to shriek and rattle, spinning wheels every which way while steam whistled. The metal rod vanished into a whirling silver plate, then popped back out. The girl presented it to Lizzy with a curtsy.

"Is it not beautiful!" Lizzy exclaimed, holding it out for us.

Harriet and I put our heads together. The rod had one square end, and fine lines on the round part.

"What is it?" I said finally.

Harriet was squinting. "They hold coaches together." That insight caused ecstasies of delight from Lizzy, and Harriet cast me a private, astonished glance. Another student brought a small piece of square metal. The two were twisted together, the class applauded, and Martha smiled shyly.

"And what is the impediment to efficient use of bolts in manufacturing?" Lizzy asked in a sing-song tone.

"Non-standardized threads!" the girls chanted back.

Lizzy threw her hands up in delight as if her girls had performed a three-part Bach chorale. To us, she said, "The industry is frightfully disorganized. I am certain it is due to masculine pride. Every blacksmith makes bolts with whatever whim of thread and diameter he imagines while spreading butter on his crumpet. Then they all refuse to cede authority to one another. But we make only four sizes, all with exact threads, and with the steam engine, even a child can cut dozens in an hour!"

"What do you do with them all?" I asked.

"The girls sell them, and we share the funds for cake. There is a carriage maker not ten minutes' walk from here." Softly, she added, "That is to teach them that their work has value. None of these children have families that can provide a livelihood. I hope to start them in their own businesses so they do not die in the mines or sew twelve hours a day for pennies."

While Lizzy thanked the students, Harriet whispered to me, "This is a peculiar school." I nodded, pleased by Harriet's unconvinced tone.

We returned to the white building and visited the classrooms, which we had seen briefly yesterday, then went upstairs to the boarding rooms. There were eight rooms with two beds per room, each bed shared by two children. It was as pleasant and spacious as most family homes, although simply furnished. Lizzy explained, "I would rather teach more children than hang paintings. This enterprise has taken six months, and it is a token against the teeming children in London with no chance of education." She sighed. "It is overwhelming if I think of the numbers. But when I think of the children we do help, I am encouraged. It is so much more than sponsoring a favored child in the country, which is the fashion for wealthy London couples."

The last door of the hallway was closed. Lizzy stopped with her hand on the knob, unusually hesitant, and her deep brown eyes met mine. "One of our young ones, Nessy, is in here with a cough. When I come to the school, I visit to cheer her up. Emma, I wonder if you would see her?"

I heard the question in her tone. Could I enter a sickroom without collapsing? And, hidden but more desperate, the thin thread of hope.

I rested my lace-enclosed fingertips on the doorjamb. "I would like to visit, if I may prepare first. But Lizzy... I have been in sickrooms. Do not imagine I am your husband's legend. I am the same as I have ever been. It will not help." Lizzy nodded tightly, her eyes overly bright, and I knew this child had no passing cough.

I began the ritual I used with Papa. My dress was hidden under my long coat, but I aligned the coat clasps, then perfected each seam on each gloved finger. But something was different. Already, the threat of illness felt distant. An echo of the scarlet that filled me yesterday remained, smoothing my mind.

Was I the same as I had ever been?

I nodded to Lizzy. She opened the door, and we filed in. The air was sharply cold, the window propped wide to the winter day. This treatment was described in the newspapers, and my heart sank. I knew what sickened the girl.

One bed was made and untouched. The other held a solitary small figure curled beneath stacked quilts and wool blankets.

I sat in the chair beside the bed. "Good morning, Nessy. I am Emma."

The girl turned her face from the pillow. Her childish plumpness had melted to hollow adult beauty, her eyes sunken, huge, and brilliant, her cheeks porcelain white with bright roses—the false bloom of consumption that was perversely celebrated by fashionable cosmetics.

"How do you do, miss," the girl whispered. The handkerchief in her hand was stained dry brown and damp crimson.

"I have been touring the school," I said. "But they tell me I am too old to attend!" I pouted, and she gave a weak smile.

"Nessy has been a student for four months," Lizzy said behind me. "She sold me a daisy in St. James's Park, and she had no home, so I asked if she would like to learn to read. We are only waiting for her cough to improve so she may begin her classes." Lizzy's voice was brittle with cheer.

I picked up a book beside the bed. "Shall I read to you?" The girl nodded. I opened it at the marked page and resumed a story about a plucky young rabbit. By the time the rabbit had escaped a fox, the girl's eyes were closed. I fell silent and watched her thin chest rise and fall.

What did it mean to be a great wyfe of healing?

I closed my eyes, then loosened each finger of my lace gloves. Swiftly, I tugged the gloves away and dropped them behind me. The lingering hint of scarlet within me stirred, cooling a rush of fear.

I opened my eyes to the girl's resting countenance. Behind me, Lizzy and Harriet were so still, they might have been holding their breath.

I placed my bare palm on Nessy's forehead, then had no idea what to do next. Outside the window, a sparrow chirped the finish of its song and fluttered away.

I began to feel something. To become aware, like the moment on the river when I sensed the wyfe's terrible injuries. Knowledge of the girl's illness grew in my mind. The unthinkable vileness. The evil rotting her lungs.

Go away, I thought ferociously. I pressed with my palm and said aloud, "Heal!" Nothing changed, and I felt foolish.

Curls of colorless miasma were seeping between the floorboards. They searched hungrily, climbing the girl's bed. I took my hand back and hid my palms in my coat, and they faded.

Nessy's eyes fluttered blearily open. "Are you the angel come for me?"

"No, dear. I am just a friend who likes to read to you." My voice sounded perfectly natural, the sole skill I had mastered while caring for Papa.

"WE HAVE HAD PHYSICIANS VISIT," Lizzy said when we were in a small office downstairs. "The last one said I should not have taken her in. He had the temerity to scold me! 'Do not make yourself anxious over sick orphans. Hundreds die every day.'" She blew out a furious breath. "I should ask Dr. Davenport to come. Mary is a good judge of people." She gave me a tiny smile. "It was good of you to try. Did you... learn anything?"

I had felt the girl's lungs rotting to mush within her. Anger filled me—at the cruelness of illness, and at grandiose legends. "I felt enough to know I did nothing. This talk of healing is a bad joke."

Lizzy nodded, her thin smile lost. There was no hint of accusation, but I remembered Yuánchi's words: *You must bind to find your strength and know your limits.*

To Harriet, Lizzy said, "That is the hardest part of caring for these children. But for every sorrow there are a dozen joys. A dozen children embarking on wonderful paths through life. If I have not frightened you away, may I show you something more pleasant?"

"I am not frightened," Harriet said, who had not spoken since we left the girl.

We joined a classroom of rambunctious younger girls. A harassed older gentleman with gray hair sticking in every direction was helping them fit leather straps around a life-sized straw model of a horse's chest, shoulders, withers, and neck. This was Lizzy's harness making project.

Lizzy sent a girl with a message, and she returned with Lucy, the lady's maid from Chathford. She must be a student, or perhaps an assistant. Harriet and she greeted each other, then crowded around a table with three of the younger girls. I watched Harriet beam at Lucy and a tableful of penniless urchins, and I frowned. Harriet Smith was not a Darcy who could condescend in gracious charity. The more precarious one's status was, the more caution was needed. The more perfect one must be.

Lizzy nodded toward seats beneath a slate illustrating knots and buckles, and we moved there.

"Perhaps Darcy's legends are wrong," Lizzy said dejectedly. "The wyfe of healing may be a story, or a wish. The great wyves celebrated in song may be inventions to justify a handful of women with power."

"I have no power," I said. "But I believe what Yuánchi said."

"I trust him, too. But everything sounds profound when it is delivered in booming thoughts. His explanations are frustratingly incomplete. I do not know if he relates grand truths or tells draca folktales." She sighed. "It is nice to be able to discuss this with a wyfe."

I snugged my gloves more firmly. Despite disliking Harriet's interest in the school, I could not help liking Lizzy. She was enthusiastic and caring. But I did not enjoy admiring the wonders of Mrs. Darcy's fabulous binding.

Martha, the girl who threaded the bolt, approached Harriet and whispered in her ear. Harriet smiled and dipped her head so the girl could stroke Harriet's hair, elegantly styled but as black and curly as the girl's own. Together, they positioned a metal punch on a piece of leather. Martha struck it with a hammer, admired the neat hole, and ran to fit it around the straw model.

Lizzy's thoughts seemed distant. She mused, "I really should ride more."

THE BRITISH MUSEUM

LIZZY

When we left the school, Emma walked swiftly ahead. Harriet, though, all but danced around me, tromping on my toes while she enthused about the young students.

"I think I must love schools!" she announced, face tilted to the sky. "Do you know that Mrs. Goddard scolded me on my first day? I was six, and I did not know the rules, and she was so strict that I cried! But I still loved school. Reading stories, and learning to compose letters, and forming lines two-by-two for our outings. And your girls love *this* school, and I loved helping them!" She ended by flinging her hands exuberantly toward the school, launching her excitement like a dove.

That seemed a good finish, so I sent Harriet on her way. Emma, fur-trimmed and lace-gloved, had observed us silently, but when Harriet linked arms with her, she gave her a fond smile, and they boarded discussing whether to shop for boots or gowns. The coach departed, and I found myself even more perplexed by their friendship. The surface was all asymmetry: of class, of influence—that was what disturbed Mary—but beneath the surface, there were roots deeply intertwined from both sides.

A four-horse town coach waited for me, the latest expansion of our London household by the formidably organized Mrs. Reynolds. It was a lumbering, oaken beast equipped with a driver and a pair of footmen. Even a single footman was ostentatious for Darcy, who preferred anonymity, but their purpose was evident from their military posture and the narrow wooden gun cases they had stowed behind the coach. Mary's and my unaccompanied stroll the day before had been noted.

While a milk cart clopped down the street, I watched the footmen—guards, really—and thought about soldiers. England had been at war since I was eleven. In quiet Meryton, the main effect was that I often dined and danced with officers. Yet, not once had we discussed guards or sentries. That seemed an oversight, as their methods were interesting. One guard remained in the elevated seat beside the driver, watching the street, while the other stayed two paces from me, examining each passerby.

Still, two men could be overrun in seconds. It was like... what? I lost the thought, then was disturbed by a lingering interest in martial topics.

Interesting or not, the guards and their wooden cases were a token against the weapon I had brought. I closed my eyes, and my mind filled with the elevated perspective of the Duchess of Wessex's firedrake. Her Grace was a notorious bore, and her firedrake, a clever creature, was every bit as bored by ducal life as the aristocrats trapped in the Duchess's luncheons. He had cheerfully accepted my invitation to our outing, and was perched across the street, his stippled bronze-copper scales largely hidden behind a chimney. His eyes saw the street in colors that were distorted to human senses, but anything alive—people, horses, even the mouse creeping toward a dropped crust of roll—shone warm against the cold paving stones. Motions were slowed, and the detail was terrific. I could see the mouse's trembling whiskers.

I pictured myself riding in the coach and felt a mental *chirp* of acknowledgement. To the driver, I called, "Montagu House on Great Russell Street," and we set out, hopefully to resolve mysteries rather than add to them.

MARY WAS STANDING in the park that fronted the British Museum and studiously ignoring nods from passing gentlemen. She was striking in a sweeping gown of heavy black cloth that exposed her collarbones and a fringe of crimson petticoat. Her ink-dark bonnet was decorated with black lace, and her gold musical note, a gift from Georgiana, sparkled on her chest.

"You are very stylish today," I said in greeting.

"This is not in *style*," she said with such disdain that, had her salon been within earshot, there would have been orders for crimson petticoats at every dressmaker. Her scornful expression became uncertain. "Do you like it?"

I could not remember the last time Mary had asked my opinion of her clothes. "Well... it is dramatic. Such dark black..." I hesitated, sensing that this answer was important.

Mary grew visibly tense. "It must be black. I am mourning the unjust death—"

"—of our fellow sentient animals," I finished with her, having heard this before. "I understand. However, it is very *unremittingly* black. The red is becoming. You could have more color without undermining your message." Mary bit her lip, and I resolved to be less obtuse than our last heartfelt conversation. "It is not my opinion that matters. Why do you not ask the person you care for?"

Her bit lip whitened. She nodded, touched my arm, then walked briskly toward the museum entrance. I hurried to catch up.

Outside the doors, an officious, round-headed gentleman stepped into our path. "Ladies. May I be of assistance?"

"We wish to visit the museum," I said.

His lips puckered, then his forehead. When he did not move, I tried sidling to one side. He stepped in front of me and said, "Then your husbands are bringing the tickets?" dragging out the final S.

Tickets. I glanced at Mary, saw her preparing to erupt, and hastily said, "I understood the museum is public."

"It is public for those with *tickets*," he enunciated through bared teeth. "The collections are for serious visitors. Ladies' tickets are requested by those with"—his gaze strayed down our skirts—"proper credentials."

"Are proper credentials a physical appendage?" Mary snapped.

"Madam?" he said, gathering his lips into an offended rose.

I was reading an elaborately engraved brass panel on the wall. I sighed theatrically. "My aunt will be *so* displeased. She had specifically requested our report."

He curled his lip. "How sad."

"I have witnessed Lady Catherine's displeasure," I said cheerfully, which was perfectly true as I had been the cause of it. "Displeased is severe enough, but I fear she will be *seriously* displeased, and that is frightening to behold." My hint did not seem to be penetrating, so I added, "When we last dined at Rosings, I fondly remember Lady Catherine *de Bourgh* reminiscing about her patronage of the museum. You must give me your name so I may compliment your service to her."

The man's eyes grew round as his head. Doubtless, her ladyship had visited to ensure her funds were properly spent. She invariably left an impression.

"Your tickets were likely held in reserve," he stammered. "Do you recall your guide's name?" I stared blankly, so he prompted, "A museum curator? Or the area of interest..."

"Dragons," I said as Mary replied, "Tudor royalty." The man smiled as if that were perfectly sensible and dispatched a young boy.

The boy returned with a scarecrow of a young gentleman. His coat dangled from shoulders sharp as folded paper, but his smile was full and welcoming, and he said, "Tudors, is it?" and led us to the entrance.

The museum entryway was grand, with twenty-foot ceilings, endless pillars, and elaborate wrought iron banisters. Mary mentioned the Pendant of Fiery Justice, and our guide studied his shoes, muttered "east wing," and wandered off. Mary and I exchanged a glance and followed.

The east wing was secured by a locked door that swung open with a hoary groan. The airy spaces vanished as we wandered through a cluttered mess of dusty display cabinets, crates that were closed and obscurely labeled, crates that were open and empty, and peculiar items of art and nature in baffling locations.

As I passed an enormous stuffed owl head-down in a basin, our guide stopped in front of a rack of ancient cabinets. "The first Queen Mary," he announced. "Not her remains, but rather the museum's stored artifacts from her reign. The pendant..." He opened a drawer and began piling the contents on top of the cabinet.

"I doubt the pendant is here," I said. "We saw it elsewhere."

"Oh, no," he said reassuringly. "I remember it. It cannot have been more than four years ago." He extracted a snuffbox, gave a delighted cry, and peered at the underside.

"The *pendant* is not in your collection," Mary said sharply. "We hoped you would know who possessed it."

"The Pendant of Fiery Justice," he said. "Beautiful piece. I saw it, no more than four years..." He bent double to peer deep in the drawer. Mary sighed very audibly, and he shook a finger in the air without interrupting his examination. "Do not be impatient. I understand you perfectly. The pendant was in the museum collection, and it was here. Nobody could move it without my knowledge." He straightened and frowned. "Yet it appears to be gone."

Despite Mary's hope that this would provide a clue, I was not surprised. Anyone who secured both a royal artifact and deadly crawler venom was clever and resourceful. "Can you tell us about it?"

He ticked off facts with his fingers. "Crafted in gold by the royal jeweler. Four oval sapphires, each three carats. Twelve minor stones. Despite the incorrect hue, the blue gems represent dragon breath. Originally it was worn with a leather strap, then fitted—"

"What?" I said. "You know that dragon breath is not blue?"

He blinked as if I were an errant entry on his list. "Yes. Dragon breath is not blue. At least, not the dragons I know of."

The blue flame of regular draca was a terrible weapon, hotter than any forge, but Yuánchi's breath was something else. I was not even sure it was fire. He had used it twice in my presence, and it was too blinding to view and too thunderous to hear. It was like a fragment of blazing sun torn away and smashed to earth.

"Do you know of many dragons?" Mary asked, which was good because I was too surprised to speak.

"The historical record describes several dragons," he said. "The accounts are consistent, even across cultures. I prefer the Chinese records, which are less fanciful. The red dragon is prominent and symbolizes vitality and life. They describe its breath as molten light."

"And the other dragons?" I asked, my tongue finally working again.

"Their records are murkier, but there are distinct creatures. One is obscured by poetic description—tiresome rhapsodies on heavenly hues and such. But the shadow or black dragon is straightforward, even though the references are second hand. They inevitably follow disasters—razed cities, lost civilizations, that sort of thing. Some argue the black dragon is a metaphor for plague or drought."

Mary made interested, academic noises, then asked, "How is a scholar of Tudor royalty so knowledgeable of dragons?"

He smiled modestly. "One cannot study one without the other. Draca and dragons are intimately connected to the Tudors. Mary Tudor bound a golden wyvern on her wedding night, and she had tremendous empathy with the creature. It followed her commands, even the most brutal. She claimed they conversed, and from their conversation, she learned of dragons. Then she sent her knights searching for relics that would raise a dragon."

"A dagger?" I suggested.

His eyebrows shot up. "An excellent guess! I have only recently researched the dagger. It is a difficult subject as Queen Elizabeth purged it from the royal archives when she ascended the throne. Doubtless, she wished to protect the Tudor name. But I hope to document the provenance so we may add the dagger to our exhibit."

My heart jumped. "You *have* the dagger?"

He turned and opened a wide, shallow drawer.

The dagger lay alone, nestled in green velvet. The same dagger I had seen in the painting of Queen Mary at Chathford House. The hilt was wrapped in plaited brown leather and had a small, gold medallion. The blade was long and slightly curved, black as night, and lustrous as obsidian. The outside of the curve was smooth and thick as my finger. The inside gleamed with wicked serrations.

"Gramr," Mary said. She was reading a card beside the hilt. "That is from legend. The dagger that Sigurd used to kill the dragon Fafnir."

"Whether this is the legendary dagger, I cannot say," our guide answered. "But this dagger has carried the name 'Gramr' for centuries. Queen Mary acquired it when her knights"—he hesitated, choosing his next word—"*liberated* it from a noble house in Denmark. That family had documented the dagger's history to ancient Germania."

I could restrain myself no longer. "It is a dragon's tooth."

He made *hmm*-ing noises. "The blade resembles the draca teeth in our collection. But even if one accepts that ancient dragons were the size of a horse, this length is preposterous. My article will state that it is sculpted ceramic."

"May I touch it?" I asked. He smiled and nodded. I ran a finger along the leather-wrapped hilt, then touched the golden medallion. It was engraved: 愤怒. "What are these symbols?"

"They are Chinese characters," Mary said. Her black bonnet dipped to read the paper in the drawer. "It has been transliterated as '*Fennew.*' Chinese sounds are not fully described by our alphabet, so that is likely inaccurate." Our guide gave an offended sniff.

I stretched my hand beside the blade. Yuánchi's longest teeth were five inches. This was twice that. Bigger. Much bigger.

I touched my fingertip to the flat of the blade. Cold rushed into my body, climbed my spine, and overcame my senses.

MY HAIR, loose and black, whipped behind me. The wind dashed tears from my eyes. I shielded my face, leaning and squinting to look down. Below, our huge, winged shadow rushed over the forest at incredible speed.

Far ahead, I saw the soldiers marching in their rhinoceros hide armor. The same soldiers who burned our peasant village and killed our parents. Behind them followed the wagons of tribute, heaped with rice and silk, and the palanquin that jailed my sister.

I leaned farther, keeping my seat by pressing my body into the rushing air. The woven hemp of my jacket buzzed in the wind. Our speed was reckless. Exhilarating.

"Keep her safe!" I cried. "Show the rest my fury!" But I closed my eyes, afraid, until the storm was done.

We landed, and I skidded from my perch, tearing my clothes on the scales. Around us, every green leaf and brown clod of earth sparkled with crystalline ice. Cold mist flowed around my ankles like water.

The palanquin, abandoned, lay fallen on its side.

Frightened, I drew aside the curtain. My younger sister, dressed as if she were an Emperor's daughter, not a poor peasant, stared back in shock.

I smiled in relief and held out my hand. "The Dragon Queen came."

"LIZZY!" Mary cried. Her face was in front of mine and so close that her height advantage was very apparent. One of her hands gripped my left shoulder. Her other held my right wrist like a vice while I twisted to break free. She had pushed me away from the open drawer. Out of reach.

I stopped fighting her grip. "I am b-better." My teeth were chattering.

"What happened?" she said. "You shouted a strange language..."

Cold lingered in my jaw. My teeth ached. "C-can you touch the blade? I need you to touch it."

"Lizzy, it hurt you. I had to pull you away from it!"

"Please. I must know what happens."

Mary bit her lip, then nodded. Gently, she backed me another step away from the blade, leaving me beside the open-mouthed museum guide, then returned to the drawer. She did not hesitate, just tapped the blade with her finger, then rested her finger on it. "It feels cool, like iron or silver, but more so.

Heavy and dense." Cautiously, she drew her fingertip across the serrated edge. "It is extraordinarily sharp."

"Thank you," I said. "You have answered my question." Whatever reaction I had, it was not shared by Mary. That meant it was exclusive to great wyves. Or to me.

"That was strange," our guide offered.

I managed a smile. "I was overcome by the thought of touching an item held by Queen Mary."

He nodded enthusiastically. "It *is* remarkable. This dagger altered history. When the queen acquired it, she claimed a divine revelation: Three winged seraphim had been cast out to become dragons, and the greatest of them hid in England. She believed this dagger would raise that dragon, restore God's favor, and reconcile England's Church with the Church of Rome. But her quest for the dragon became brutal. And, obviously, it was fruitless. All she gained was her bloody title."

Mary and I thanked our guide, and he escorted us to the museum garden.

When we were alone, Mary hissed, "Tell me what happened!"

"I had a vision," I said. "I was flying. And I had perfectly *black* hair. That was peculiar. I think it was a memory of some other wyfe. I did not understand much. There was... a black storm..."

"Flying? Like a bird?"

I did not feel ready to answer that. "Did the museum list the meaning of the dragon's name?"

Mary straightened. "*Dragon's* name?"

"The Chinese word on the dagger is a dragon. Fènnù." The name felt natural on my lips, but it had a different lilt than when Mary had pronounced it.

Mary drew her shawl around her neck. The air had become bitterly cold while we were inside.

"The card listed several translations," she said at last. "They all mean the same. Wrath. Fury."

14

THE HONORABLE MR. TINSDALE

EMMA

"Here we are, at last!" I said to Harriet while the coach bounced. "Two ladies exploring London on their own. And this evening, staying in a hotel!"

Harriet did not turn from the window. "I am happy you are well enough."

That soured my mood. I was tired of concerned companions. Today, I was Emma Woodhouse, mistress of Hartfield.

"We are meeting a prominent gentleman," I said.

Harriet abandoned the window. "I thought we were shopping for boots!"

"We will shop. But first things first." I checked the directions in the letter I had received—a reply delivered by private courier. "There!" I pointed ahead.

The road ended at the river. Coaches were stopped every which way. Festively garbed people thronged the cobblestones, the shore, and even the ice. Colorful flags rippled in the breeze, and bright tents and booths had been erected on the frozen white.

"What are they doing?" Harriet cried.

"It is a Frost Fair, the first in twenty-four years. The Thames did not freeze once in our lifetimes! We are clever to be in London now."

We disembarked and joined the crowd rushing to the river. The ice was several feet lower than the seawall, so wide planks had been laid like angled bridges. Harriet and I descended, our arms playfully stretched for balance, and a sturdy lad of sixteen took our hand for the last steps. I gave him a penny, and he winked. "I'd help two lovelies anytime." Harriet giggled, and I laughed outright, feeling more festive than I had in a long time.

Harriet caught my arm. "Who is the prominent gentleman? Is it Mr. Knightley?"

That was unexpected, and for a moment the thought of him drove the correct name from my mind. "We are meeting Mr. Tinsdale."

Harriet's brow furrowed. "The man with the big eyebrows?"

"You must not think of him like that! He is a member of Parliament, and very distinguished." Harriet looked let down, so I said, "He is an important man, and this is an important meeting. He has influence. You must present yourself perfectly."

"Yes, Miss Woodhouse," she murmured.

The Frost Fair was a gigantic, jumbled event. More booths and tents were sprouting even while we strolled. At least half were stocked with casks and packed with rollicking drinkers—gentlemen, tradesmen, workers, even women, all mingling in joyful familiarity. Mules pulled carts filled with meat pies, kegs, rolled-up canvas, and clucking chickens. The walkways were sprinkled with straw and fronted with shops for all manner of goods. One even sold shoes. Harriet browsed but did not buy. They seemed more expensive than their land-based brethren.

When my watch showed quarter of one, I began searching for our meeting. Requests for directions received happy, useless shrugs, but I finally spotted what the letter described—tiered benches and a podium. We rushed through the crowd, arms linked so we would not be separated, and I spotted Mr. Tinsdale's imposing frame with two other well-dressed gentlemen, all in black silk toppers and belted black coats.

I pulled Harriet to a stop before we were seen. "You must wait by that coffee booth. I will speak with Mr. Tinsdale first. Then I will pretend to see you and call you over for a grand entrance!"

"A grand entrance?" Harriet said, her eyebrows squishing.

"You were not introduced in our first encounter, so it will naturally be grand." Harriet looked even more concerned. I patted her arm. "Fold your coat on your arm, be your lovely self, and all will be splendid." I gave her a little push, and she headed to the coffee booth.

I approached Mr. Tinsdale and raised a lace-covered hand. He immediately excused himself from his friends.

"Miss Woodhouse," he said, his smile pink-cheeked in the cold. "This is a delight. I was charmed to receive your unexpected letter."

"You are very kind," I said. "I was not sure you would remember. We could hardly meet properly under such terrible circumstances. I feared you would think me forward."

"Not at all," he said jovially. "I was intrigued by your mention of draca."

"I could not help but notice that you were aware of the Darcys'... *exceptional* affinity to draca. I hoped I could approach you about my own unusual situation."

Under his eyebrows—which now I could not help but think of as "big"—his eyes became shrewd. "I gather you are in the Darcys' close confidence?"

"Naturally," I said with a confident smile. "Seeing the government's interest, I thought you should know that Mrs. Darcy is not the only lady with exceptional affinity."

Mr. Tinsdale's mustache wiggled. "I see this is more than a delightful social meeting. The government values wyves with such ability." A man shouted from the podium behind him, and Mr. Tinsdale frowned. "I am afraid I am the first speaker. Perhaps we could continue after?" He looked me over with an appraising eye. "Have you come alone?"

I blushed at the notion. "My friend is with me, which is why I wished to meet. Her affinity is remarkable, but unfairly hampered by the silliest oversight in records. Of course, that could be easily corrected by a gentleman of your influence."

"Your *friend*? I thought—"

"I seem to have lost her..." I shielded my eyes, looked high and low, then waved at the coffee booth. "There she is!" Harriet noticed my wave with an artful start, then promenaded toward us. As she arrived, I said proudly, "Mr. Tinsdale has requested an introduction. May I present Miss Harriet Smith."

"Sir," she said with a perfect curtsy. I had selected her clothes for today, a rich green velvet gown and bonnet, my gifts for her last birthday, and a cheerful red shawl for warmth. They deepened the rich hue of her complexion.

Mr. Tinsdale's reaction exceeded my hopes. He seemed dumbstruck. He finally muttered "Miss Smith" but so late that Harriet was already rising. That meant he could not take her hand, but I was satisfied.

"I have been researching the matter," I said. "It seems only a question of having her rights documented—"

"You must pardon me," Mr. Tinsdale said. "I am overdue for my speech." He bowed stiffly, then strode off.

"Is that all?" Harriet asked as his broad back vanished into the growing crowd.

"For now," I said cheerfully, although I was disappointed. "His speech cannot be long. Let us wait."

A substantial crowd had gathered. The tiered benches were packed, and the overflow strained behind flimsy rope barriers. Mr. Tinsdale mounted the podium, which I realized was a wooden crate draped with a blanket. That was disappointingly makeshift.

Then he began speaking, and my disappointment vanished. His voice was confident, his charisma magnetic. This was a new aspect to the man—and a taste of the excitement of London politics, which never reached our tiny town in Surrey.

To a man, the crowd had cropped hair and belted coats that matched the speakers'. The darkness made their upturned, milk-pale faces shine. Mr. Tinsdale's voice projected effortlessly. "I come to you with a new and revolutionary conception of politics, and of life itself..."

"He is an orator," I whispered to Harriet.

"Miss Woodhouse, I do not like this," she whispered back. "There are no ladies here. Must we stay?"

"It is naturally men," I said to reassure her. "Women cannot vote."

Mr. Tinsdale's voice rolled, and the crowd amplified each cadence with shouts and surging motion like a restive herd of animals. They spanned society, from well-dressed gentlemen nodding sagely to rough-and-tumble workers punching their fists into the sky.

Mr. Tinsdale's voice cut through the crowd's cries: "...this ceaseless warring against the French, our natural allies in the struggle against inferiors, is bought with your blood..."

A man's violent salute jostled my shoulder. "I beg your pardon," I said. He glanced at me, then stared at Harriet.

"...Britain Awake!" cried Mr. Tinsdale, and an answering cheer rang out. In our pocket of the crowd, faces turned inward. Mouths shrieked "Britain Awake!" like taunting schoolchildren.

Harriet was tugging my arm. "We must go! We are in danger."

"Perhaps you are right—" I said just as a strong arm circled my waist, spinning me irresistibly and pulling me through the crowd.

"What are you doing here?" Mr. Knightley hissed in my ear. My entire side was pressed against his, and my stomach gave a surprised flip. He had an arm around each of us and was half-guiding, half-pulling us away from the ruckus.

Answering was impossible in that chaos, so I concentrated on keeping my feet under me. Frightening memories of yesterday's violence by the river flickered, but the crowd and noise diminished swiftly. In twenty paces we had reached a straw-scattered walkway. People were tossing pennies into bowls to win a prize. A gaily dressed gentleman and lady passed us arm-in-arm. Only the distant racket proved the frenzy had been real.

Mr. Knightley faced me, his hands clasping my forearms. "Are you mad to stand in that? To bring *her* here?"

"Do you mean Harriet?" I said, although he could not mean anyone else. I realized Harriet was gasping in panic. I tried to reach for her, but Mr. Knightley had my arms locked in place. I raised my eyebrows, and he freed me with a start.

I took Harriet's hand. "Are you well?"

"That was terrible," she said shakily.

"We are safe. Mr. Knightley is taking care of us." I smiled at him. "Will you, sir?"

He blew out a hard sigh as if that were an astounding statement. "Let us move farther. Those scoundrels will be spoiling for trouble when they finish." He tugged his tailcoat straight, which was snuggly fitted and very stylish, then offered us each an arm.

"Why do these London crowds become so agitated?" I asked as we set out at a more traditional stroll.

"This mob's anger was cultivated," Mr. Knightley said. "Fliers have been posted with lies of conscription to the navy, and the dock workers seek a scapegoat for lost jobs and poor wages. Then rabble rousers play on their fears to inflame bigotry and violence."

"Rabble rousers?" I asked.

"Rosdan Tinsdale, for one." Mr. Knightley said his name with profound distaste.

I frowned. That was an unwelcome complication.

"His speech was horrid!" Harriet exclaimed. "All that 'Britain Awake' and 'defend our mighty past.' How do you defend the past?"

I had not listened that carefully. In fact, I was feeling unpleasantly unsure of my plan for Mr. Tinsdale. But a good remedy for uncertainty is to reverse the discussion. "Why were *you* there, Mr. Knightley?"

"My work with the Freedom Society requires that I monitor dangerous politics."

"Is that where we are going?" I asked. We were walking farther onto the river.

"To the Freedom Society? No. I am meeting friends. We plan music if our frozen fingers permit." He looked over his shoulder. "I was thoughtless. May I assist you to shore?"

Harriet shuddered. "I do not want to walk near those horrid men."

I was not eager, myself. Brightly, I said, "A musical gathering sounds lovely."

15

A SHIP IN FROST

EMMA

Halfway across the Thames, the tents and booths were left behind. Frozen stillness stretched. I felt like a sailor becalmed on a whitened sea. Ahead, the silhouette of a lone ship grew, low-slung and long with a single bare mast.

The ice was stupendously cold and solid. We walked briskly along a trail of straw trod into the ice. Mules or small horses had made this trek before us; their sharp-shod hooves had cut toothed crescents in both directions. Patches of yellowish mist brought a tinny bitterness to my nose while the sky churned toward the burnished copper of yesterday's strange weather. The light diminished, brightening three twinkling lanterns on the ship. Tones flitted through the air, then connected into a tune. A man's trained voice sang. A pennywhistle played a measure of a jig.

"Knightley!" hailed a voice from aboard the ship. It was fifty feet long, one of the broad, squat freighters that glide the wide rivers. A frosted hawser angled from the bow and vanished into the rigid ice.

Harriet hurried up the steep gangplank and cried, "Permission to come aboard!" Mr. Knightley chuckled behind me, and I recognized the words from a pirate novel she and I read last summer. I was on the ice and too low to see the deck, but I heard jovial greetings. A man's head and nautical hat came into view over the railing, then Harriet vanished.

I made my way up, bracing my boots on nailed cross strips. The gunwale rose eight feet above the ice, and the gangplank was a mere eighteen inches wide. While I inched up, I puzzled over the height of exposed hull. It seemed excessive.

I reached the top and stepped onto a large, upright barrel placed as a receiving platform. The ship had a flat deck and a twenty-foot mast with furled sails. A dozen two-foot-square bales of cloth were pushed haphazardly against the sides. Three gentlemen in evening dress stood with Harriet, already in conversation, while two sailors grinned up at me. One was the sailor with the naval hat, his merry chestnut eyes sparkling in a weather-carved face. The other was a lad too young to shave.

"Why is it so high?" I asked.

"We were hoisted by the freeze," the older man said, his voice Irish atop an American twang. His uniform was cut like a navy officer but sewn of workaday browns and tans. "Good thing, too, for that was the fastest freeze I've ever seen. I'd rather have my ship spat out like a cherry pit than crushed like a walnut." He doffed his hat skyward; I still stood on the barrel. "Captain Olaudah Freeman, at your service. Welcome aboard the *Hearty Meal*."

I laughed. "Is that the name of your ship?"

"And why not? What's better than a hearty meal, save a pint of grog, and my crew does not need reminders in that regard. May I help you down, ma'am?"

"I will assist her," Mr. Knightley said behind me on the ramp. Deftly, he jumped to the deck and offered his hand, bare despite the cold.

I handed down my fur muff, then eyed the three-foot drop to the deck and the heavy coat around my ankles. "I think a hand will not suffice." Mr. Knightley raised a second hand, but he seemed uncertain where to put it. We looked at each other, at an impasse.

Captain Freeman snorted and gave Mr. Knightley a jovial shove. "Grab her, ya fool." I tipped forward, Mr. Knightley's hands caught my waist, and I arrived safely on the deck.

"That worked nicely," I said cheerfully, looking up at Mr. Knightley's long-lashed eyes. He nodded and gestured to precede him. We joined the small party of Harriet and the three gentlemen, who I learned were musicians.

"This is Knightley's lark," one explained. "He is always inventing strange concerts."

"I call it the Frost Fete," Mr. Knightley said. "It is friendly music in a rare setting, not a concert."

"Are more people coming?" Harriet asked.

"A few musicians," Mr. Knightley answered. "Not many. Captain Freeman welcomed company while standing watch, but we must not impose. Musicians are a rowdy lot, far worse than sailors." There was laughter at that, and good-natured barbs between the professions.

The young sailor lit a brazier, more for heating tea and wine than warmth. The air was milder onboard, as if the chill clung to the river's surface. I learned that the *Hearty Meal* had a crew of four, but the others had gone to enjoy the Frost Fair, and that the deck was usually piled high with bales of wool and linen, but most had been carted away to improve the balance when the ice thawed.

Another musician clambered up the gangplank, then a married couple, the woman a singer and the man hauling two instruments. Mr. Knightley claimed his cherrywood violin case with effusive thanks. Harriet and the other lady began chatting, and our gathering was abruptly festive, like the parties we used to have on the grassy hilltops of Highbury. My memory of friends in the sun, and how long ago that had been, summoned a happiness that was uncomfortably keen, like beautiful music that brings a tear to the eye.

I drifted apart from the others, trailing laced fingers over cold bales of wool until I stood alone in the bow. The frozen river spread around me, unmoving and antiseptic, the white turning silver in the fading light. The air was fiercely clean. Here, the idea of illness—of the miasma hurting those I loved—seemed a child's fancy. Perhaps I should become a sailor or an arctic explorer.

A forested point drew my eye, the land wilder than the rest of the London shore. Chathford House. I whispered, "Can you hear me?" but I did not have Lizzy's tie to the dragon. The answer was breeze and the happy chatter behind me.

Still, I could sense scarlet in that distance, like how I sensed a binding. The feeling stirred the strength trapped within me—the strength I had borrowed. Or stolen. Was that why I was so calm? So... healed?

"Do I disturb you?" came Mr. Knightley's voice.

"No," I said, without turning.

He leaned on the rail beside me, ungloved and unhatted, clad in a charcoal tailcoat, his shoulders square to the distant lights of the Frost Fair. "What were you thinking of?"

"Mr. Darcy," I answered. In a way, it was true, and it was a nicely confounding response.

Sure enough, there was a long silence before Mr. Knightley spoke again. "Has Mary seen your coat?"

Now I was confounded. I turned to him. "Mary *Bennet*?"

He nodded. His hand left the rail, and I felt his finger graze my collar. "She disapproves of fur."

"I expect this rabbit was eaten, so the poor creature had no use for its fur."

He chuckled. "That argument will not convince Mary."

"You know her well," I said and found I was not eager to hear further intimacies of Miss Bennet.

"She is a good friend," he said. "I admire her. She is a genius."

"I have never met a person proclaimed a *genius*." That emerged too pointedly, so I said more gently, "Not sincerely, at least."

"I knew another genius, so I know something of genius and the world. I insist on proclaiming her. She composes music before its time, but she is ignored outside of ladies' salons. I fear her work will be forgotten, as brilliance from unexpected sources often is."

"That is sad," I said, and meant it. I forced a playful tone. "I am glad she has an admirer."

"It is not a romantic admiration. Her heart is elsewhere."

Discussing romance felt like flirtation, and it left me off balance, as if our frozen ship had swayed. Perhaps I was starved for the little rituals that pass between men and women. Or out of practice. I hugged my padded arms and turned back to Chathford House, but it had vanished in the spreading night. "What a strange conversation we are having."

"Have I made you uncomfortable?"

"Not at all. I say whatever is on my mind. You may, as well. Now I am wondering why Mary Bennet dislikes me. I do not recall her seeing my furry coat."

"She is jealous. Georgiana is intrigued by you."

I chuckled. "I do not believe *that*. Georgiana must have scores of friends. I think you are protecting Miss Bennet. I know she disapproves of my assistance for Harriet." Mr. Knightley stirred, but he remained silent. "Do *you* disapprove?"

"May I ask what you intend for Miss Smith?"

His tone was neutral, but a protective heat rose in my chest. "Harriet must marry a gentleman. She is a lady. Her status must be secured and irreproachable."

"What if she chooses an easier path to happiness? With her status unclear, she risks humiliation—"

"You speak of *my* dear friend, sir," I said coldly.

"Your pardon." He bowed. "I will leave you."

"No," I said quickly. "That is, not on my account. May we speak of something else?"

He nodded, but no other topics came to mind, and he was silent. I watched the night. Finally, I said, "You know the Darcys well."

"I met the Darcys when I returned from my studies in Germany. I was to perform Herr Beethoven's ninth sonata at a musical soiree, but the pianist refused to accompany me."

"Refused?"

Mr. Knightley extended his arm into the deepening night, fingers flared. His dark skin was vivid against the white river ice. "He had not known I was the 'mulatto violinist' and refused to participate in a coarse stunt."

I spun to him so fast that my hem swatted the gunwale. "That is unutterably rude! Did you call him out?"

"If I called out every man who insulted my skin, I would be dead or hanged."

"Well, I am very angry with that man!" Mr. Knightley bowed in acknowledgement. Less heatedly, I asked, "How were the Darcys involved?"

"Miss Darcy offered to accompany me. She was a slip of a girl, not yet fifteen. I thought it a joke at first, or the naivete of a child, but the excitement of the guests was so obvious that I realized she must be a prodigy. I brashly declared we would perform. That *was* a stunt, but I wanted to prove myself. The sonata is fiendishly difficult for both the violin and pianoforte, so performing it without joint rehearsal was absurd. The audience knew that."

"I hope the story ends happily, and the performance was a great triumph, and that rude man was shamed!"

"It was all that, and more. My understanding of the piece was enlightened with no more communication than the intimacy of performance. Afterward, I met Georgiana's brother, who towered over me and scowled, which Georgiana explained was Darcy exhibiting delight. Then she apologized for her performance, as she had missed notes at a page turn because she was unfamiliar with the composition. She had played the score sight unseen—" Mr. Knightley interrupted his story with an amazed laugh, shaking his head.

"I must hear her play," I said. "And you, too. Perhaps you will play together?"

"I would be honored."

I realized his answer was not a polite nicety. He could arrive at breakfast with his instrument. "We are both intertwined with Darcys."

"It seems so," he said. "I have wondered at your connection. I know you carry a burden." I did not answer, and he added, "You and I meet in strange ways. I carry you up flights of stairs. We flee angry crowds. That is unusual for a lady of Surrey visiting London."

"I am as surprised as you."

"The Darcys are unusual, themselves."

"They are," I said, wondering how to interpret that. "Do they share their secrets with you?"

He answered seriously, "I cannot be specific outside their presence."

"Of course."

"What of you, Miss Woodhouse, who has been surprised in London? Do you know Darcy secrets?"

I crossed my arms, thinking. He stood leaning his elbow on the railing, in profile to the lamps. His hair was tight ringlets tied back in an old-fashioned style, and the coils gleamed.

"They have shared secrets," I answered.

"And do you tell the Darcys your secrets?"

"Not all of them," I whispered, and my heart shivered. "Will you excuse me?"

I crossed the lamplit deck to where Harriet was laughing with the others. She looked beautiful and happy, and my determination to protect her warmed me.

"Miss Woodhouse," she cried out. "Are you not cold? We have wine mulled with cinnamon." She hiccupped.

"I see that," I said. The heated wine was in coffee cups much larger than any wine cup Harriet had encountered. "Perhaps you have had enough?" She blinked at me unevenly, so I took her cup and said, "Yes, you have had enough." She gave a whimsical shrug, and we settled beside each other on the fabric bales.

The music began. After talk of genius, it was simple tunes—folk songs of the Irish, Celts, or farther places, all tending to melancholy and reminiscence. Each was introduced by a single musician who explained where he or she had heard it, the mode or key, and musical details beyond my knowledge. That person would begin, singing or playing a violin or a flute, then after a few bars, others would join. The ensemble was perfect. They were clearly skilled beyond our Highbury performers. Mr. Knightley did not unpack his violin, which was a disappointment, but he sang, harmonizing in his tenor.

After a half-dozen songs, true night had fallen, and the light was all from our lanterns. I checked my watch.

"It is after five," I said to Harriet. "We should depart. We are moving from Chathford this evening." She pouted but nodded, so we rose, shook out our skirts, and asked how, in fact, we *could* depart.

Captain Freeman immediately protested. "That's what comes of dreary music! The ladies leave. Why not play a happy tune to finish?"

"A reel!" Harriet cried with a clap of her hands. "You did say you could play a reel, Mr. Knightley."

"I did," he agreed, smiling. He took out his violin and began tuning the strings, clucking in dismay at the effect of the cold. I watched Harriet's face fall as she realized this meant he would not dance, but she cheered up and accepted Captain Freeman's offer. The married couple joined them in a square, and I sat down to show I was content to watch.

Mr. Knightley and the other violinist started a wildly spirited tune. It was immediately apparent that Captain Freeman's concept of a reel was different from a reel in Surrey—he seemed to be dancing a jig despite the conflicting time signature—but it all blended into laughter, the clop of heels on the hollow deck, and flamboyantly waved hands. I applauded loudly at the end.

Amid the congratulations and jokes, Mr. Knightley approached and offered his hand. I pulled with unladylike enthusiasm to rise from my bale of wool.

"Thank you, sir," I said.

"Will you not have a dance before you go?" he said.

"I have not danced for some time. I have forgotten my steps." I had not dared a ballroom since Papa became ill.

Mr. Knightley had a considering smile. "There is a dance with simple steps."

I eyed him skeptically. "That does not sound like a proper dance."

"Society would disagree. It is the highest fashion of the season." He raised his voice to his friends. "Gentlemen! What dance is the highest fashion in London?"

"The German waltz," they replied as one, with eye rolls and groans as if they were very tired of it.

"The German waltz," Mr. Knightley repeated. "May I have the honor?"

He presented his hand. We were in a pool of lamplight, every face watching. His posture was formal, and it suddenly seemed a ball, where courtesy required that an offer to dance was accepted.

"Thank you, sir," I said. The words sent a reckless joy through my body. "But I cannot dance in this coat."

My pelisse fastened simply in front, but my fingers stalled as they touched the top clasp. The pause stretched to become uncomfortable, as frozen as the river.

Mr. Knightley said, "If you prefer to depart, we shall set out. It is becoming cold—"

"No," I said. "Would you assist me?" I turned my back to him, drew a breath and closed my eyes. My fingers fumbled the top clasp apart, then the lower one, and the coat fell loose. I jammed my arms stiffly by my sides, knowing I must look bizarre, but I kept my eyes squeezed tight...

A touch drew the cloth from my neck. The shoulders eased free, then the furred collar slipped down the back of my dress. It was an extraordinarily gentle sensation, like a caress over my shoulder blades, or how I would imagine a caress. Then there was an awkward tug at my wrists. I forced my arms a little looser, and the cuffs fell away.

"Put it away!" I gasped, unable to invent a reason.

"That is done," he answered after a few seconds, sounding tense himself.

I opened my eyes, braced for fetid disease, but there was only Harriet, who had come close with a worried expression. She looked perfectly healthy. She relaxed when I opened my eyes, then became a little wistful, perhaps thinking she should have offered Mr. Knightley her shawl.

But she smiled and mouthed, *Go dance.*

I swirled, swishing cloth around my ankles, and felt utterly triumphant. "What is the German waltz?"

Mr. Knightley did not answer. Finally, he said, "I did not expect... your gown is very striking."

"Oh." I looked down at my dress, which was ivory and quite simple. I rarely wore it now—there were no fringes or ribbons to ward off disaster—but today it had seemed comfortable. It gleamed in the lamplight, but any satin would do that. "I imagine that is the night, with the dark wood, and all our dark winter clothes." When he continued to just stand there, I added, "It is not a very *warm* gown, you know."

In answer, he offered his left hand, palm up. "May I have your right hand,

Miss Woodhouse?" I took his hand. Our skin touched through the open lace. "Your left will rest on my shoulder."

"Your *shoulder*?" I confirmed. He nodded.

I placed each fingertip gingerly, having to step forward. We were now as close as I had ever stood in a dance.

"A little nearer," he said. I took a miniscule step, and he raised his other hand. "I guide you from here..." He placed his hand on my waist. In the icy air, the heat of his fingers passed through my thin satin and silk in a heartbeat.

I rose on my tiptoes to peer over his shoulder at his friends. "Is this *really* a dance?"

"It is, Miss Woodhouse," one of them replied. "The Prince Regent has danced it."

I frowned up at Mr. Knightley. "*That* does not mean much." The prince was a notorious rake.

"It is danced by the court as well," Mr. Knightley replied. "Step back with your right foot." He stepped with me, and the musicians played a single, opening note. We took halting steps, and the musicians followed, which was a peculiar experience. We began turning, and the music steadied.

As the lamps circled us, he said, "In German, it is *walzen*, to roll."

"Is this all there is?" Most dances were far more complex. It took a week to master the crossings and steps for a cotillion.

In answer, he gave my waist a hard push and whirled away, raising our joined hands over our heads. The lights swirled, my skirt flared, then I was caught against his chest.

"Oh," I said.

The married couple joined, dancing expertly. The music sped up. We twirled faster, and he turned me inward and outward, then showed me how to release hands. Finally, he tried to walk us backward side-by-side, and I said, "What *are* you doing?" then tripped over someone's foot. He caught me, and we clung while the music continued.

"Are you hurt?" he said.

His hands encircled my waist. My white-laced hands had grabbed his upper arms. I had held Papa's thinned arms to help him stand, but Mr. Knightley, his muscles tensed to support me, was a far more formidable handful.

I found my footing, and we straightened. I felt safe. Carefree. Healed.

"I am happy," I said.

Far away, from the dark of Chathford estate, scarlet glory erupted into the sky.

"He flies," I said, my heart thrilling.

"I beg your pardon?" Mr. Knightley said.

A rumble grew. The lanterns flickered, then fluttered. Captain Freeman shouted an order but stopped mid-word, remembering his ship was not afloat.

The air pressed down, thick as an ocean and snapping our scarfs and hems stiff as flags. It lifted into a floating, eerie stillness. My head turned to track an invisible arc, then the wind returned in thumping, gusting gales—the beats of monstrous, unseen wings. They drove to the root of my lungs. They shook my heart.

The night quieted, leaving exclamations and wondering murmurs. The hidden scarlet soared away to the north.

16

AWAY FROM MAYFAIR

EMMA

Harriet and I packed our things with help from several servants. Then, lit by lamps, we met Lizzy on Chathford's circular white gravel drive.

"You might try Mivart's Hotel," Lizzy suggested. "It is very respectable. But are you sure you will not stay? Yuánchi will be away for at least two days."

Yuánchi had flown north so the Darcys could repair the boathouse. That much was planned, but Lizzy had been surprised by his abrupt departure. I did not mention his approach to the ship. I would not know what to say if I did.

"Thank you, but we shall enjoy the shopping districts," I answered. "There are so many affairs to attend in London."

The Darcys had lent their huge coach for our move. I watched the footmen pile luggage and realized that was lucky. Four chests of clothes had been delightful when they arrived from Hartfield, but the rear rack was nearly full with two strapped in place.

"Do you know how much luggage a hotel expects?" I whispered to Harriet as the footmen hoisted the third with theatric grunts.

"*I* never left Surrey before," Harriet said sullenly. She had been moody since I insisted we leave. But she thawed enough to add, "Do you not know?"

"I have never stayed at an inn," I admitted. "But people do. I shall ask Isabella." My sister and her husband, John, lived in London. The only London "affair" I had planned was a visit to their home on our way to the hotel.

"Could we stay with them?" Harriet asked hopefully. Staying with family was always safer for traveling ladies.

I adjusted the corner of my shawl and said simply, "No."

A footman raised a lamp while two others levered the last chest onto a pair of seats inside the coach. It thumped into place, and the carriage rocked.

THE COACH PULLED up outside my sister's house. The coachman aimed one of the driving lamps to illuminate the walk, then unlatched the door and let down the step.

I stayed in my seat, fingers laced, practicing arguments. And summoning courage.

"Are you sure you do not wish me to come?" Harriet asked. She had abandoned her resentment while watching me stew during our ride.

"You are kind, but this is a private matter. I shall be swift."

Her concern bolstered my resolve, so I stepped down from the coach, climbed the three steps to the house door, and rang the bell. A maid exclaimed "Miss Woodhouse!" and escorted me to the parlor.

Isabella arrived in a flutter. "Emma! How are you in London?"

We each took a stuttering step, then it became a tight embrace. Isabella smelled of my childhood, that lilac soap she had always loved, and of her London life, coal smoke and bustle and children. She had five already.

"It has been so long!" she whispered into my ear.

"Since Papa's funeral," I said. I meant no ill will, but she stiffened and stepped back, her face averted and her eyelids fluttering.

Her husband arrived in an unbuttoned day coat, a pipe drooping from the corner of his mouth. "Emma," he pronounced. The pipe bobbed.

"Good evening, John," I said.

"How are you in London?"

I laughed despite myself. "The same question, twice. How does anyone come to London?"

He sucked air through his pipe, which was evidently empty. His tone became gruff. "You have quit Hartfield, then?"

"John..." Isabella warbled, her fluttering eyes skittering between the two of us.

"I have not," I answered. "Hartfield is my home."

"*That* is false," John snapped.

"Papa made me promise to stay!" I had not wanted to start like this, but those words—the truth—burst out.

John plucked the empty pipe from his lips and jabbed the wet end at me. "How convenient. Your secret conversation at Mr. Woodhouse's death bed."

"It is not my fault you were not there. I wrote to you." I bent to intersect Isabella's fluttering, lowered gaze. "*Both* of you."

Isabella clutched her skirt. "I... I could not bear it. Being among all that sickness, and Papa so wretched. And what of the children? I could not forgive myself if it spread to them."

"Papa's malady was old age," I said. "Children are not at risk."

"You do not know that! Well... of course *age* does not infect them, but what if he spread some horrible ague?"

My over-protective sister hoarded her precious children. I lived in terror of imagined disease. The irony was as subtle as a thrown stone. Still, there was a difference. I had not fled.

John adopted a lecturey, pompous tone. "The legal record of Mr. Woodhouse's wishes is his will. I am the sole male relation, so Hartfield is my property. I would say you are living there on my good graces, but it is far past the required date of your departure, so in fact you are *occupying* it like"—his lips worked wetly as if collecting spittle—"like some loathsome debtor!"

"I have been mistress of Hartfield since I was twelve," I said and was ashamed that my voice shook. I sucked in a breath and tried to recall my carefully scripted arguments.

He shook his head. "Emma." He reached for my shoulder but missed when I stepped back. That drew a scowl. "You have a fortune. Thirty thousand pounds! Find yourself a new accommodation."

"And what shall I do with *my* fortune? Beg you to buy me a cottage in Highbury, then use the shillings you dole out to attend tea with Mrs. Bates?"

He snorted. "Buy a *husband*. That is what other women do. You are two and twenty. You are lucky this happened while you are young. Imagine if your father had lived a few more years. At least you still have..." The stem of his pipe sketched circles at my body. "You might even bargain to keep five thousand for yourself."

Being assigned the shelf life of a preserved peach was so infuriating that my purpose snapped clear. "I have not come to debate Hartfield. I have business."

"Business, is it?" John thrust his chin out, then flicked his fingers at Isabella. Head hanging, she scurried from the room. John gave a false smile. "What is it, then?"

"First, I require funds. London is expensive."

"Until you surrender Hartfield, I will *not* supply spending money. I already pay the servants. If you love the house so much, run back. They will feed you, at least."

"Our family has appearances to maintain. *You* have a reputation to maintain. In London."

He grunted and tapped the pipe stem against a stained tooth. "How much?"

"Funds for two weeks. Twenty pounds."

"Ten," he snapped. "Or nothing."

"Very well." I held out my hand. He frowned, so I added, "It will not protect your reputation while sitting in your pocket."

He stalked to his desk, looked over his shoulder to ensure he had blocked my view, then hunched. Paper and coins rustled. He returned and dropped two five-pound notes into my gloved palm.

A success. My breath eased, and suddenly the rest seemed easy. "Second, I wish to alter the terms of my inheritance."

He burst into laughter. "Do you never stop? I have just said no."

"This is not for my benefit."

"No? For whom? Some tiresome charity?"

"I wish to establish a dowry for Harriet Smith."

He gaped like a fish. "That colored woman? You cannot be serious."

"I am quite serious. As the money does not come to me, it will not impede your effort to drive me out."

"What would people say? We would be laughingstocks!"

"John, please. It is my money. Papa willed it to me. I should be able to do with it as I wish."

He smiled broadly. "Fortunately, I administer the funds. For *your* benefit. As this demonstrates, women are incapable of financial judgment."

"Why do you argue? If I have fewer resources, it will only aid your ability to seize Hartfield."

That made him squint. He plodded through the implications. "I have an obligation to protect your interests. If you become destitute, Isabella will insist you live with us."

I gave a dry laugh. "Is that my interest you protect, or yours?"

"It happens that they align," he said snidely.

My smile was sweet. "I have a legal right to make requests of my guardian. If you find the prospect of assisting Harriet so offensive, then I am sure you do not wish this to be a public petition before a judge."

His eyes widened. "Are you threatening me?"

"I am *asking*. Please."

He wiggled the pipe stem. "I will consider it. A hundred pounds would make the girl prize stock for some pig farmer."

I gritted my teeth until I could speak. "Her dowry shall be fifteen thousand pounds."

"What?" he shrieked. "Are you insane? That is half your fortune! You would ruin our family. That is madness. Get out."

I swallowed. "That is the amount I wish."

"Has she cast African witchcraft on you? Or... you are scheming together! She will marry a Caribbean slave and slip you the money."

"There is nothing false about my request. You may make it as legally exact as you wish."

"You are under a *spell*." He reached for the five-pound notes in my hand. I pulled my hand away, and he scowled. "Give those to me."

"No," I said.

He grabbed my wrist and turned, shoving his back into my face and trapping my elbow between his arm and his side. My nose ground against his smoky coat. Bones grated in my forearm. I felt him pry at my clenched fingers, then a yank and tearing paper.

Release was so sudden that I stumbled, my chest heaving and my heart pounding. My elbow hurt like fire. My wrist and hand crawled where his fingers had clutched like I was coated with fetid slime.

He buttoned his coat, sniffing in irritation. "I am protecting you from yourself. Good day."

THE DRIVER HAD the coach door opened and the step lowered before my second boot left my sister's threshold. I slowed as I approached him, then stopped. "I have decided on an adventure."

"Ma'am?" he said politely.

"Mrs. Darcy's suggestion seems conventional. Where would a daring tourist stay in London?"

He frowned. "Not Mivart's, then?"

I shook my head. "I should like something truer to the London experience." He looked baffled, so I tried, "Away from Mayfair. Away from all those... shops."

"Something less dear, then?" he said slowly.

I gave a little laugh. "I suppose that would be a benefit."

"Can't be a coach inn, ma'am, or a tavern. You wouldn't be safe."

"How interesting. What would be safe?"

His cousin lived on a street I had never heard named. The explanation rolled on, alien and unintelligible, thick with his London accent. I crushed the worthless, torn corners of two five-pound bills in my palm.

When he finished, I said, "That sounds charming!"

THE COUNCIL, DENIED

LIZZY

It was three days after our first, contentious meeting with the Council
of War.

The oaken town coach delivered Darcy and me to the street outside
Westminster Palace, then rattled off. I stood unmoving, my gaze tracing the
jagged stone walls and rough-topped towers. The rock and mortar were
ponderous with history.

After a minute, Darcy said dryly, "Has it done anything yet?"

"I know the theme of our ball," I announced.

He looked at me in surprise. "I was unaware we were having a ball."

"You agreed," I pointed out. "Or were about to, at least. To collect politicians, or important personages, or whatever it was."

"That sounds more vague than my usual agreements." His eyes were stern,
which I thought handsome, but a corner of his mouth twitched, quite ruining
the effect.

"We will host the ball at the British Museum," I explained. "That requires
we invite Lady Catherine, which requires the affair be extravagant or she will
decline. Do you mind if I invite Mamma, Kitty, and the Bingleys? That will
level the playing field."

He abandoned sternness and snorted. "I cannot imagine why you require
permission for them when you are inviting my scurrilous aunt."

"The theme," I continued firmly, "will be a new exhibit: the legendary dagger Gramr. Somebody killed a dragon with it, then it was stolen by Queen Mary to..." I toyed with phrasings. "How does this sound: to raise the Dragon Queen of Seraphim! Is that too much? It should be impressive." I looked up for his reaction.

His dark eyes were thoughtful. "You believe that whoever stole the Pendant of Fiery Justice sought to raise a dragon."

"You *are* quick," I said, impressed.

"And with the pendant destroyed, they will attend your ball, attempt to steal the dagger, and be captured."

"Exactly!" I felt a rush of happiness. These effortless agreements were a true joy of my marriage.

"That is a contrived and foolish plan," Darcy said dismissively. "Now, may we tell the War Secretary that he will not have his dragon?"

"*What?* It is not foolish!"

He drew a long breath. "Why would the thief steal the dagger at a ball when they could choose a dull day at the museum and avoid witnesses?"

I tapped my toe. "The dagger will be restored to the royal vault after the event. It is far too potent to leave in a dusty drawer."

"Why not an exhibit *without* a ball?"

"Because *you* need influence to fend off the powerful gentlemen you are about to infuriate. And because a ball will publicize itself. We will not have to wander London shouting about magic daggers and hoping to be overheard." In the spirit of spousal honesty, I admitted, "And I would enjoy a ball. We have been married six months without hosting more than dinner."

Darcy scowled, having to think this time. "What if your culprit is unable to secure an invitation?"

"The culprit is an aristocrat." Darcy arched an eyebrow. Stubbornly, I said, "I am certain. This person seeks power, not wealth. They have allies and resources. They are cruel."

"A cutthroat in an alley is cruel."

"Not like this. This is the cruelty of entitlement."

Darcy's brow furrowed. If he were a Watt engine, he would be puffing steam. "The culprit is Bonaparte."

I sighed. "Not that again."

"Elizabeth, it is evident and obvious. There is a scheme to raise a dragon, a scheme to attack the English navy, and a scheme to kill the sole English wyfe bound to a dragon. Our enemy even used crawler venom, which was the tool of Bonaparte's last agent, *Wickham*."

Even now, with Wickham horribly killed, Darcy spoke his name like a curse.

Well, another joy of marriage was knowing one's spouse. "Will you agree to the ball if I admit you are right?" Darcy's eyebrows soared, and I pressed my advantage. "Napoleon will not attend, but his agent will. Then, one way or another, we will know." On the last word, I hooked my arm through his and set off toward the iron gate.

I HAD EXPECTED to return to the War Secretary's office, but a page escorted us on a trek through endless anterooms and halls. We passed lawyers garbed in formal robes and wigs. They cast interested glances at Darcy and narrow stares at me.

"Where are we going?" I whispered to Darcy. He shook his head, unsure.

We entered a large, empty room—a courtroom. The judge's bench was empty, the rows of seats abandoned, and the staring galleries vacant. The War Secretary, Lord Wellington, and Mr. Tinsdale were seated around a table near the front.

The page left us at the door with a bow.

"I do not like this," I whispered. "They seek to intimidate."

"Remember that I must deny them, not you," Darcy said. This was our strategy, and a sound one, at least for Darcy's goals of law and honor. For myself, I would have been content to inquire politely how the government intended to conscript an unwilling creature who flew.

We walked forward, our steps echoey, and the gentlemen greeted us. The War Secretary was smilingly eager. Lord Wellington was watchful. Mr. Tinsdale was notably friendly, and I returned his smile.

"Well, Mr. Darcy," the War Secretary said at last, rubbing his hands as we arranged ourselves in chairs. "Let us get to it! How will this proceed?"

Darcy bowed slightly from his seat, acknowledging the transition to business. "First, I thank you, the Council, and the King's government for the confidence you have shown in our advice. I have reviewed relevant precedents of law..."

While he spoke, I watched their reactions. Any attentive person would already discern that Darcy's answer was no. Lord Wellington, Darcy's close friend, clearly had. He slouched back in his chair, eyes hooded like a chess player pondering a difficult position. Mr. Tinsdale also knew. A smile played on his lips. This was the outcome he wished.

The War Secretary was beaming and enthused. He was an experienced politician, so that could only mean he had not imagined the possibility of rejection.

Darcy concluded, "...we must, respectfully, decline to offer our support."

"Decline!" the War Secretary repeated, his graying eyebrows compressing in shock. "You cannot decline!"

"I am certain this is the correct path for England," Darcy said. He added pointedly, "Irrespective of that, even if Yuánchi were our property—which he is not, being a creature with his own will—it is our *right* to decline."

"You shirk your duty to England," the War Secretary said.

Darcy's cheeks hollowed. He said nothing, but I was angry on his behalf. Privately—so privately that he had not voiced it even to me—the claim of duty gnawed at him. One evening when Lord Wellington was visiting Pemberley, Darcy had shared his guilt over not volunteering as an officer. Lord Wellington dismissed that as idiocy given the other roles Darcy played, but Darcy's heart could not banish the fear that he had unjustly avoided personal sacrifice.

Mr. Tinsdale spoke next. "I support Mr. Darcy. The firedrake that attacked the *Dapper* is lost. Would you have us burn French troops like straw rather than engage in civilized conflict? History would judge us, and England, unkindly."

The War Secretary pushed to his feet, his lip curling. He seemed more angry with Mr. Tinsdale than he had been with Darcy. "*You* are the last person who should judge England."

Mr. Tinsdale stood, chest thrust out with affront. "I claimed no such authority."

The War Secretary scoffed and turned, fists on hips, to scowl down at Darcy. Darcy rose in silent response, his motion measured.

I was beginning to feel very short. I stole a glance at the slouched Lord Wellington and found him watching me. He raised an eyebrow.

"Your legal niceties are well studied," the War Secretary said to Darcy. "But they mean nothing if the Crown orders it."

I bristled at that, and Darcy whitened, but the tension along his jaw was anger, not fear. His answer was exact. "The law is no nicety, nor does the Prince have carte blanche. Even in war, ethics and morality—"

"Spare me your lily-livered morals," the War Secretary said scathingly.

I shot to my feet. "That is enough! You have repeatedly insulted my husband. In the face of disreputable behavior, he shows gentlemanly restraint and honors the institution you represent. Where is your respect for the rights and honor of a loyal Englishman?"

The table became still. The War Secretary glared at me, chewing his bottom lip in furious silence.

Lord Wellington rose and wrapped my forearm in his. "Mrs. Darcy, let us step aside." I spun to him, furious at dismissal, but he whispered, "Your point is scored. Come with me." Unruffled, and with my arm firmly clamped, he led us across the room and murmured, "The Secretary has overstepped, and you have called him out. Darcy will prevail. It would be wise not to focus more of the Secretary's attention on yourself."

At an infuriatingly relaxed stroll, we reached a distant bench of the gallery. Lord Wellington released my arm and bent to examine some words scraped into a wooden armrest. He shook his head. "How crude."

Seething, I watched the three gentlemen converse, their tones now muted and polite. My whole being was alight with fury. With shaking fingers, I stripped off my overheated spencer and threw it past Lord Wellington's nose onto the bench. He straightened reproachfully.

"You support us, then," I said tightly.

"Do not call it support, exactly," he said. "I am tempted by a weapon that would end the war in days and save English lives. If England's sovereignty were at stake, I would wield it in an instant. But the Secretary has never seen a ship burn, nor a cannon cut down a row of friends enfilade, nor a dragon pour flame like the Almighty's wrath. If France no longer has a firedrake, I cannot unleash unmitigated destruction. England would emerge a victorious pariah."

"Darcy could have used your support."

"Darcy had you." He said that with such simple regard that a flicker of gratitude cooled my anger. Of course, that was likely his intent. I eyed him, then turned back to the conference, lifting the back of my hair to cool a sheen of sweat on the nape of my neck.

Darcy listened gravely to Mr. Tinsdale, then answered deliberately. Everyone was stiffly proper, and Darcy was calm and confident. He was satisfied.

The courthouse windows were a long row of shining rectangles high on our left. A shift of cloud brightened them, then the space filled with reverberating silver so intense that it needled my eyes and raised a spasm in my throat. Surreal gleams raced across the lacquered rails and molding, each shimmer haloed with brilliant colors as if the room had filled with rainbows.

The effect faded. I rubbed my clammy temples, feeling the bite of a headache. Strange colors still flickered in the corners. I muttered, "The sun is too bright," and Lord Wellington gave me a mystified look.

18

VANISHED WYVES

LIZZY

With Yuánchi flown north, it was time to replace the boathouse gate. The battered remnants of the last one were precariously propped in place, splintered edges and all.

The school carpenter came to assist our yardmaster. He kicked at a three-foot-long gash in the hard-frozen clay and cast me a questioning glance.

"We have ferocious moles," I explained, amusing myself but wondering how long even more serious attempts at deception could succeed. At remote Pemberley, secrecy had felt foolish, but in the bustle of London, it grated at me—a disavowal of something worthy.

Indoors, a letter waited, addressed in Jane's rounded hand:

"My dearest Lizzy,

I am most excited by the news of your ball! Charles and I would not miss it, even if they must roll me into the carriage, for I am swelling with baby like a rising loaf. Mr. Jones assures us it is safe to travel, and I know it is true as I feel wonderful, but Charles frets as men do. Whatever shall I wear, though?..."

A long discussion of dress styles followed, then an inventory of every wardrobe at Netherfield to ensure there was room for another garment. I read it smiling but bemused as Jane was usually levelheaded about such things.

Mary entered the morning room and sat at the tea table, thumping down a massive embossed-leather volume fringed with the scraps of ribbon she used to mark pages.

"Jane has written," I said, passing the letter to her. "She declares pregnancy to be frolicking puppies and blooming daffodils. In other words, she is Jane."

Mary smiled wryly while she read. "She is in her sixth month. All mothers are in ecstasies then. Ask her in eight weeks."

I curled in my chair to see her better. "Do you know about it?"

"Dr. Davenport originally sought a female assistant for a midwife's experience at deliveries. I convinced him that training a female physician was more valuable. But we agreed I should learn from a midwife."

"Then you have attended births!" I said, surprised.

"Of course," she said mildly.

I looked at her fastidious outfit, which was very unlike the practical clothing of our Meryton midwife. "I thought you... read books for him, or something."

Mary gave me a level glance over the gold rims of her spectacles. "Books aid diagnosis, but they do not turn a foot-first baby."

"Well!" I exclaimed. Mary resumed reading. Apparently, astonishment did not merit a reply.

I watched her turn a ponderous page and considered mentioning my queasy stomach. But for all that I respected Mary's knowledge, Jane and I had always been first to share intimacies, usually whispered under our quilt at Longbourn. That ritual of sisterhood was lost to marriage, but I would see Jane soon, and the thought of telling her made me glow.

Mary slammed her book, scowling. "I cannot read today."

"Perhaps a thicker book?" I suggested.

Mary peered at the massive spine, then shot me a sharp glance as she recognized the joke. "The binding is not the issue. I am worried. A woman has been missing for a week. Wait, let me show you something."

She left and returned with a handful of the advertising fliers that endlessly cluttered London. "This is her." She smoothed a sheet on the table: "Miss Joane Rees. MISSING. CASH REWARD."

The drawing was a girl around twenty with a heart-shaped face and a slightly bony nose. She was smiling and very fashionable. And missing. "How sad."

Mary lined up four more fliers on the table. The size and printing differed. One was crumpled, another rain stained. Each showed a different young lady.

"It is more than sad," she said. "It is peculiar. These are four months' worth. The others are strangers, so I did not notice the pattern until Joane vanished. Joane is one of..." Mary plucked irritably at her black dress. One of the Marys, the ladies who marched at Mary's protests and, to her frustration, obsessively copied her fashion.

"Have you asked the constables?" I suggested.

"Her family has. The constables searched. It is *the* Rees family."

I looked again and saw the resemblance to her mother. Mrs. Rees was a society gadfly, pleasant if a little trivial. She had bound a lindworm which afforded modest prestige.

"All the missing women are gentry," Mary continued. "All unmarried. Every family has a history of strong binding. It makes me think of the wyfe who died on the river."

"She was married and bound," I pointed out. Mary shook her head, dissatisfied, and I added, "It may be less sinister than that. Girls of good family regularly elope from London."

Mary smoothed the drawing of Miss Rees. "There was no hint of a romance. She was always wanting to talk to me. Chirping trivial gossip. On a good day, I would mutter a syllable back. But she still attended every march, rain or muck." Mary fiddled with her gold rims. "I was annoyed because she enjoyed the protests. She had money. It was like her hobby."

"We have money, now. Even if you never spend it."

Mary sighed. "I know." She tugged the sleeve of her dress. "What color should I wear to the ball?"

I eyed her layers of black fabric. "Is that a trick question?"

"I do not want to vanish into the shadows. People vanish too easily."

19

BENEATH THE ICE

LIZZY

The boathouse repairs finished the next day. That night, I lay awake listening to Darcy's deep breaths and feeling Yuánchi sweep toward the city. When he was near, I stole out alone under a sky of black clouds, the silver-edged rifts agleam with stars.

Yuánchi settled on the icy shore and slipped neatly into the boathouse. I closed the river gate behind us, then walked past his curled tail, crouched flank, and folded wing, resisting the urge to run my fingers along his side. The scales cut if you rubbed against the grain. He had arrived lazy and garrulous, his belly filled, and he told me a bloodthirsty story of crashing through winter-bare oaks to catch the deer hiding beneath. The lamplight reflected from his flexing scales and cast chevrons on the walls that jumped like fleeing whitetails.

Late the next afternoon, after a bleary morning at the school due to lack of sleep, I went with Lucy to the sitting room to meet Mr. Needham, the school's instructor for harness making. He had brought two hand-picked students, older girls of fifteen or sixteen.

Mr. Needham was slightly wary amid Chathford's gilt and polish, but the girls' eyes were wide as saucers. Even though we met daily, they curtsied to me far too deeply, then to Lucy as well, which made her eyebrows shoot up.

Fortunately, tea calmed things. The girls asked shy questions about the house while Mr. Needham listened and stroked his chin. He was in his sixties, retired from serving in both the cavalry and the engineers, and originally answered our advertisement for "liberal teachers" with an account of training his sole child, a daughter, in tack and harness. His blunt outlook reminded me of Mr. Rabb, a dear lost friend who taught me of draca and life in equal parts.

"I have a project," I announced when the teacups emptied. The room became quiet. "If you agree to help, you must be perfectly discreet. That is for the privacy of our household and to protect the security of England."

The girls' eyes were wide again. Mr. Needham rubbed his jaw. "Would this be harnessing steam to carts?"

"I have not heard of that," I said. "To pull the carts, you mean?"

"Yes, ma'am. Coal carts, on rails. They're working on it in Newcastle, and it's secret, but I heard about it in the pub."

"That is intriguing, but it is not that." I hesitated, disturbed by how easily secrets spread.

Mr. Needham's lips twitched. "I don't gab in pubs, ma'am."

That made me smile. I asked the girls, "Can you keep this secret? Even from your friends at school?"

They answered promptly, "Yes, ma'am" and "Yes, Mrs. Darcy." The pair were fierce friends who had survived as young orphans in London, something perhaps one in ten children managed. They were deeply suspicious of strangers and had attended the school's classes—and meals—for two months before abandoning whatever filthy nook they shared to board at the school. Then their sharp loyalty embraced the school, where they flourished in practical studies but were shy about their childish reading and writing.

I led everyone outside, explaining, "I wish a secure seat on an unusual steed. I know it has been done before, but no example survives. You shall have to invent."

"Is it a cow?" asked one of the girls.

I smiled and swung open the boathouse door.

THIRTY MINUTES LATER, the boathouse was festooned with chalked strips of leather. The girls were draping pieces around Yuánchi's neck while debating buckles. Yuánchi observed with interest, doubling his neck up like a swan to compare perspectives.

Mr. Needham suggested reversing a buckle, then came to stand with me, thrusting his hands deep in his pockets. He grumbled, "Were you not worried the girls would be frightened by this beast?"

"Thus far, every girl who has met Yuánchi has been in raptures. I was more worried about you." It helped that Lucy was comfortable with Yuánchi. The girls had not wanted to appear timid.

Mr. Needham gave a short laugh. "I admit I was taken aback. He's a wonder for the ages." He sucked at his teeth. "He's well made for a rider. The base of the neck is the girth of a horse, and the shoulders make it a saddle. Easy to sit astride." He eyed me. "That is, *I'd* sit astride. Were you wanting to fly sidesaddle?"

"I think astride. Balance will be that much more important in the air." I frowned, realizing a complication. "I suppose that means trousers."

Mr. Needham's eyebrows soared. "*Trousers?*"

"Perhaps not. Was there a horsewoman who altered her dresses to ride astride?"

"Rings a bell. Pleats, or some such. I'm no dressmaker."

"Of course not. I shall inquire." Mary must know an adventurous seamstress.

"You're sure no reins?" Mr. Needham continued.

"Definitely not. We will agree on our destination through polite discourse."

"The harness needs a rear anchor. Could we wrap straps around the wing joints?"

"Let me ask..." To Yuánchi, I thought, *The harness maker suggests tying straps around your wing joints.*

Yuánchi swung his neck around to examine his own back, then shrugged his wings until they brushed the walls. Huge flight muscles flexed in his breast, and the room filled with glinting scarlet. The girls squealed excitedly.

Yuánchi swung his head back to look down at them. *They are friendly*, he thought affectionately.

Straps? I reminded him.

It was not done before. My wings flex when I fly. A strap would break. I remember rope lashed to my back ridge.

The back of Yuánchi's neck had a series of rounded, bright-red knobby protrusions. They conveniently ended above the natural saddle Mr. Needham had noted, then resumed as larger ridges along his back. They were pretty, smooth as painted porcelain, and very solid.

I conveyed that to Mr. Needham, who nodded and rubbed his chin. Perhaps he used to have a beard.

Lucy had gone to fetch snacks, and she returned with a chunk of cheddar, a basket of rolls, some pickles, and Georgiana and Mary.

"Oh, this is fabulous!" Georgiana exclaimed, throwing her hands roofward when she saw Yuánchi draped in leather straps.

"This is *insane*," Mary said, but her pressed lips curved in grudging admiration.

"Miss Darcy caught me with the tray," Lucy said to me.

"I suppose that was inevitable," I said. I raised my voice to address everyone. "But this is secret!"

Mary surveyed the crowded boathouse. "Secret from *whom*?"

"Mr. Darcy," Lucy replied, accurately but more bluntly than I would have chosen.

"That is even better!" Georgiana said. "You can surprise him at his fencing club. They have a huge courtyard."

AFTER ANOTHER HOUR, I accompanied the girls and Mr. Needham to the coach while he mused about lap belts and weight tests. The short-lived winter sun had already set. By the time I caught up on the household and returned to the boathouse, I carried a lantern.

Yuánchi was sprawled on his side, throat and muzzle flopped comfortably on the ground. I pulled a square of scrap leather beside his nose and sat.

"Any thoughts on our project?" I asked cheerfully.

It was long ago. I will remember more when we fly together.

"That seems rather late."

He snorted in amusement. Yuánchi was utterly confident that flying together was safe. I hoped he remembered I did not have wings.

I added, "When I touched the dagger, my vision of flying showed a wyfe with long, black hair and copper skin."

The wyfe who flew with me had sunset hair and snow skin.

"Red hair? Where was that?"

Yuánchi gusted air from his nostrils and did not answer. I never knew if these silences were forgetfulness, or reticence, or an inability to express human concepts like geography.

"If you did not fly a wyfe with black hair," I pointed out, "then my vision is of another dragon." His muzzle slid close to my hem, gem eyes gazing without response. I decided to be more direct. "What other dragons are there?"

We do not speak the names of those who sleep or are lost.

"Why not?"

Those who are lost take their names with them. Those who sleep rise to new lives, and their names change. I would not know how to name them while they sleep.

"You mean when you sleep for ages, under the water?"

Yes. Even the youngest of draca rise to new lives and names after the water.

This was a flood of information. I considered what to ask next. "Did your name change? Were you not Yuánchi before?"

I was Yuánchi before. But Yuánchi is my human name, not my true name.

"What is your true name?"

His head rose from the ground, eyes coming level with mine. *A true name is a song. But I will not sing it to you.*

"Why not?"

You would not understand any draca song. But my song is unfinished. He huffed and added, *Do not ask 'Why?' No dragon song has been finished for an age.*

I opened my mouth to ask "Why *not?*" and got a hot snort blown in my eyes, so I folded my arms instead.

My vision of flying on a dragon occurred when I touched the blade at the museum. But my other vision had been here. When I touched the water.

I picked up the lantern and threaded the dragon-wall gap to the river gate. The lip of water beneath was frozen. I knelt, rubbed the ice with a finger, then rapped it with my knuckles.

"I wish to test something," I said. "We must be outside. Would you like to try opening your gate?" The carpenters had fixed a wide board that would undo the latch from inside. Hopefully that would reduce repairs.

Yuánchi looked over his shoulder, and the tip of his tail curled upward to press gingerly against the board. The latch clicked, and the gate swung open. I shuttered the lantern to hide us as the cold night air rushed in.

Leave first, then I will follow.

I went out, fastening my coat and testing each step in the dark. When I was beside the building, Yuánchi's mass poured out in a rush. He stretched his wings into a vast tent of whispered wind and vanished stars, then folded them away.

"May I share your vision?" I asked. "It is too dark for me."

I reached out with my mind, and my vision shifted to Yuánchi's eyes. The black blur of trees became sharper than day, each wrinkle of bark and edge of dried leaf perfectly rendered in shades of violet. I was centered in his view, my face bright warmth against my cool hair, my clothed torso and limbs dimmer but also shining. The golden aura of a great wyfe surrounded me.

Curious, I raised my hand. The motion appeared reversed. Or unreversed. Which was correct, this or a looking glass?

"Would you show me to the river?"

Yuánchi turned his head, and the view swung. I picked my way to the frozen riverbank, struggling to navigate through someone else's eyes and leaving footprints that glowed with borrowed warmth. I felt sticky and hot in my coat, but the frigid air bit my eyes and nostrils. I sensed Yuánchi's perception inventorying nearby creatures. The closest humans with line of sight were specks across the river.

There were gouges in the river's surface where Yuánchi's claws had scraped, but no cracks. The ice must be thick. "Are you able to break a hole?"

His wings spread again. Through our link, I felt the balance they provided. He stretched a clenched foot over the river, then deftly extended a single scaly toe as thick as a man's leg. The tip of his claw touched the ice and sank in. The motion was as smooth as pushing a finger into warm butter, but the river ice chattered and shook. His toe hooked, the ice groaned, and with a heavy crack, he levered up an irregular chunk several feet around and eight inches thick. He caught it like a cat flipping a mouse in its claws, then placed it aside.

I walked carefully onto the ice, then abandoned pride and crawled to the edge of the hole. Falling in would be terrifically unpleasant. Yuánchi stretched his neck above me, and I looked over my own shoulder into lapping black cold.

What are you doing? he asked, sounding extremely curious.

I drew my vision back to my own eyes and looked up at red glimmers in the night.

"Have you not guessed?" I said. "Do you not sense the presence?"

Yuánchi's wings tensed and spread. He backed onto the shore, claws grinding the frozen earth. Each step vibrated the ice under my knees, and through our binding, I felt heat gather in his chest like the stoking of a god's forge.

When his thoughts came, they were stripped of his usual comforting, human-like cadence. They chimed pure and alien.

A great wyfe's senses are unknown to us.

"Well, this great wyfe is about to either feel very foolish and very cold, or to make a discovery." I lowered my fingers into the water.

DAWN REVEALED THE FLOODING RIVER, *swollen and silty. My god-falcon swooped to my feet, folding her limber wings. Her silver-bronze scales gleamed red in the early light.*

The royal physician pointed his hand at the god-falcon. "Queen, abandon this ritual. Your husband is entombed, but your god-falcon remains bound. Only the greatest queens have this blessing. Your divinity is proven."

I shook my head. "A god-falcon will not defeat Rome's armies. A god-falcon will not save Egypt, nor protect me from being led through Rome, a spectacle for Octavian's triumph." I turned to Imhotep, my high priest. "You swear you can raise Ra?"

Imhotep was a lesser man than his famous father, but he too spoke with the authority of magic. "I have read secret histories. In the great river, the scarlet sun god sleeps. This is Ra's winged form. I know the sacred song to call him." He licked khol-blackened lips. "To bind him, you must journey to the hall of Ma'at. You must die and return." He raised a stone cup half-filled with a foul-smelling tar. "I bring the venom of one hundred vile scorpions. We must add the god-falcon's blood, freely given."

I drew my god-falcon to my lap, her folded claws hard and warm on my thighs. To her black eyes, I whispered, "Aid your queen," and she did not flinch when I pressed a bone needle into the soft flesh between her toes.

Imhotep held the cup, catching drops as golden and clear as sun. Exalted sky mixed with crawling foulness, a blasphemy that hissed and spat. Imhotep cackled, added a handful of withered leaves, then a dank powder. A vile scent spread, and my god-falcon fell from my lap, thrashing on the ground.

"It is not enough that I drink the poison," I said. "Octavian will discover soon that I have fled. Death must be quick."

I held my hand to Charmion, my most loyal advisor. Unwillingly, she passed the dried jaw of an asp, fangs proud. I coated the fangs in the bubbling black of the cup, then punctured my arm. The poison burned up my veins, through my shoulder, and into my heart.

I fell to my knees, stunned.

Through blurring eyes, I saw Imhotep splash poison from the cup onto the god-falcon. Charmion shouted, "Betrayal!" as the god-falcon writhed and stilled, then was lifted high by Imhotep.

Imhotep sang strange words, and my spirit journeyed from my body. Betrayed or not, the underworld summoned me.

I threw my spirit deep into the river and found a magnificent presence. A goddess.

"I am dying," I whispered. "Honor my command. Fight my war."

The earth shook. The river parted, and a goddess rose, but not the scarlet glory of Ra. Her wings, broader than ships, were black as night.

In triumph, Imhotep shouted, "Apep!" the name of Ra's terrible serpent enemy. He stabbed a bronze knife at the god-falcon's breast until the scales parted. Clumpy, yellow bile spilled—the corrupted blood of an unwilling sacrifice. He scraped it into the stone cup. Globs of smoking brown-black spat from the rim.

The monstrous flint-fanged head approached us, her spread jaws dripping river water and cold mist. Her goddess voice filled me: I seek the passion of your vengeance. But the wars of your kind are without purpose. They flicker, endless as the seasons—

Imhotep threw the cup of poison into the goddess's throat, then the twitching carcass of the god-falcon. The goddess reared and roared.

Imhotep cried, "Rise, Apep! Bring your darkness! If Egypt falls, the world falls with it!"

The silver thread of binding pierced my stopped heart, weighing it for worthiness, and our minds became one. As the poison smothered my dying thoughts, I felt Imhotep's potion break the mind of the winged goddess. Her judgment turned hard and brittle, then fractured into fury and madness.

I CAME BACK TO MYSELF. Frantic, I yanked my dripping hand from the water and clutched at the suffocating compression in my chest. My fingers were so chilled they were senseless, but I felt my lungs inflate. My heart beat. The jeweled, olive-skinned hands I had seen were not mine.

I pushed my hand inside my coat, shivering and shocked. The familiar cold rattled my bones. Mist roiled on the ice around me. The air tasted metallic and tinny.

The open patch of water skinned with silver, crackled, then froze with snaps and pops, shuddering upward into a block inches thick. Like the Thames had frozen when I stepped from the pier onto the ice.

Yuánchi was a motionless shadow on the riverbank. The binding between us was vivid. He had shared my vision.

"What horror was that?" I whispered.

The fracture. His voice brimmed with loss. *The breaking of dragon names.*

"That is why no dragon song is finished? That... ritual? Why did you not answer when I asked before?"

I did not know. The fracture was a mystery. You saw a lost memory.

"Not lost. It is the memory of another dragon." Yuánchi furled his wings but did not answer, so I voiced what I knew to be true. "That is the dragon I touch through this water. The dragon that sleeps in the Thames."

CALL ME EMMA

EMMA

Harriet lifted her spoon of porridge and slowly upended it. Misshapen lumps plopped into her bowl. "I never thought I would miss Mrs. Goddard's oatmeal."

I smiled until I could pry my glued teeth apart to answer. "It is very wholesome." Harriet's answering sigh was so tremendous that I added, "We could have our luncheon at the school."

"Will you stay that long?"

Harriet planned to spend today at the Martin school, assisting with something or other. That made me uneasy, but it was convenient as well. I had returned to the school with her yesterday, and I felt a desperate need to go again.

"I thought I would read to Nessy," I said. "We are at an exciting point in her book."

Mrs. Hickinbottom, the widow who rented the spare room where we boarded, scurried into the parlor, her fluttering cotton bonnet framing a hopeful smile. "Is breakfast to your taste, ma'am?"

"It is nice, thank you," I said. Harriet coughed dramatically, and I continued more loudly, "Is there tea?"

"Oh!" Mrs. Hickinbottom ran out, ran back with a teapot, and poured two cups of a liquid dark as dirt. I thanked her as the bitter scent of over-steeped leaves spread, and she scurried out again.

Harriet sniffed her cup warily. "Must we drink this?"

"She is trying her best. A lady is always polite."

Harriet muttered, "Yes, Miss Woodhouse."

My brother-in-law's casual contempt of Harriet rose in my memory, and I said, "Emma."

Harriet was poking her spoon in and out of her porridge. She looked up, puzzled.

"You should address me as Emma," I repeated.

"I could not!"

"We are two ladies traveling together. It is proper."

After a dumbstruck silence, she said, "Yes, Miss—" then winced and stammered out "Emma" with a flustered blink. We both laughed, and I felt a surge of affection.

Harriet jiggled her teacup handle, the inky surface wobbling. "Why do you wish me to marry a gentleman?"

"You are a lady."

"But I met my father last year. He is a tradesman."

Postponing my answer, I picked up my gloves from the table edge and closed my eyes to put them on.

Yesterday, I had dressed with my eyes open. I even enjoyed the amateur assistance of our host's young daughter. But today had been a tense terror. Harriet rescued me when the girl could not fasten my dress quickly enough. The reservoir of strength I had gained at Chathford House was draining.

Eyes still closed, I fastened the pearl button at each wrist and said, "What was it like? To be told who your father was when you were seventeen?"

Harriet's voice was soft. "When I was little, I dreamed my father would ride to Mrs. Goddard's on a huge horse and give me presents wrapped in pink paper. Then he did come, and he did give me a present but not in pink paper, and we stared at each other in the school parlor, and he had saggy whiskers and a bent hat, and he seemed frightened of me. That was after you helped me survive my foolish infatuation for Mr. Elton, and I thought... I have been on my own all this time. What good is a father now? And he never visited again. So not good for anything at all."

Tears stung the inside of my closed lids. Firmly, I said, "Put him out of your mind."

"I am not a lady, Miss Woodhouse."

I opened my eyes and gave a smile. "Miss Bennet would say you have a right to bind, and she is quite correct. Read this." I passed Harriet the letter that had been folded under my gloves. The thick paper had been addressed to Chathford House in a weighty, masculine hand, and one of the Darcys' footmen had delivered it this morning.

Harriet read aloud:

"Dear Miss Woodhouse,

I have thought upon our discussion of your friend's plight. I plan to lunch with Mr. John Debrett next week. I am sure you understand the significant opportunity this presents. If this interests you, speak with me at the Darcys' upcoming ball.

Yours, &c.
Mr. Rosdan Tinsdale, MP."

Harriet's features crumpled in dismay. "Mr. Tinsdale? That horrid man!"

"His politics are unpleasant, but politics are irrelevant in polite society. What matters is that he is willing to help."

Harriet shook her head desperately. "Did you see his face when he met me?"

"Whatever you imagined, put it aside. This is an introduction to Mr. Debrett! *Debrett's Dracal Lineage* includes all of England's prestigious wyves. When you are listed, no gentleman will doubt your ability to bind."

Mrs. Hickinbottom returned with a nervous curtsy. "Pardon me, ma'am, but a gentleman is at the door for you. Your brother, he says."

"John is here?" I exclaimed. Harriet had met my sister and brother-in-law in Highbury, and she smiled in happy surprise. That faded when I said, "Excuse me, Harriet. I will speak with him and return." I sounded nervous even to my own ears.

I followed Mrs. Hickinbottom from the parlor, but she slowed in the corridor, then stopped well short of the closed front door.

"Is there something else?" I asked.

"If the gentleman is your brother... ma'am, it is just the matter of the bill. I mentioned that we settle each morning. It is three days now."

I bit my lip. My funds had shrunk to a handful of crowns and shillings. But success was so close. I would find the money. Emma Woodhouse was rich, handsome, and clever.

"It slipped my mind." I smiled. "I do not have my purse. May I pay you this afternoon?"

"Of course, ma'am." She dipped nervously, then opened the front door and hurried toward the kitchen.

John was pacing outside, pompous and frowning. "Emma."

"John. May I ask how you knew I was here?"

"I listened to you fraternize with your driver as you left. Although it was a chore to find which of these *homes* you were in." He swung an accusing finger toward the row of modest houses, then peered past me into the hallway. "Can we speak?"

"The parlor is occupied. I prefer to converse in public." I stepped past him onto the small landing so we were in plain view to passersby. My elbow still ached from the wrench he had given me.

His jaw worked, then he held up a folded piece of paper. "This is a doctor's bill. A copy was delivered to me as a 'courtesy' because the amount is past due." He unfolded it and read mockingly, "'A consultation for vapors and illusions of the mind.'"

The terror of discovery jammed my thumping heart into my throat. I swallowed twice. Treat this as business, nothing more. "I will pay that."

He squinted at the paper and pursed his lips in an airy whistle. "Nine pounds, seven shillings. Such an expensive doctor."

"I said I will pay it." I had saved half the sum last month—ransacking old purses and collecting the change from butcher orders—but all that had gone toward this trip.

John smiled. "The money is no concern. Not between *family*." His smile became a vicious sneer. "My concern is your *safety*. A woman who is so unwell cannot be unsupervised. She cannot live alone in a monstrous house like Hartfield."

Wild thoughts for how to raise the money vanished. I was lost. My attempt to be healed had ruined me.

"Miss Woodhouse is perfectly well," Harriet announced, stepping out onto the landing between us.

John backed a step. "Miss Smith. You are interrupting a private conversation."

"But I cannot let you worry!" Harriet exclaimed, her eyes wide with sincerity. "Miss Woodhouse and I went with my friend to the doctor, then Miss Woodhouse offered to pay for the visit. She was wonderfully generous. My friend was worried that some horrid person would"—Harriet leaned conspiratorially close and finished ferociously—"*pry.*"

"I do not believe you," John said bluntly.

Harriet elevated her nose. One would never know she had delivered a massive fabrication. "Ask the doctor, then."

John folded his arms, eyes flicking between us. He crumpled the paper into his pocket. "Very well. I will pay this. From *your* accounts." He waved disparagingly at the door behind us. "But do not imagine I will fund your gallivanting about London!"

He stomped to a waiting coach. The driver craned around in his seat, waiting as traffic passed, then snapped the reins and rolled off. Still I stood, paralyzed by the specter of disaster. If I had said one more word—if I had asked for help or begged for sympathy—he would have had his proof. He could have destroyed me. Ejected me from Hartfield. Placed me in an asylum.

"Miss Woodhouse," Harriet said gently. "Will you come inside? We must get ready. I do not want to be late to help with the class."

"Call me Emma," I whispered.

21

THE PHYSIC GARDEN

EMMA

In Nessy's winter-cold room at the school, with the fur-trimmed collar of my pelisse pulled to my chin, I read aloud how a little rabbit nibbled a carrot held by a farmer's young daughter.

Nessy's eyes had closed a page before. Her thin breath was slow and easy, settled at last after the coughing fit tearing her when I arrived.

I whispered, "Nessy?" Her thin eyelids fluttered but stayed closed. I marked the page and set it aside.

Try again.

I counted the stitches around the fingers of my right glove, a long seam so Nessy would be sound asleep—she rarely rested this comfortably—and because I needed all my calm.

The last stitch was four hundred, two and twenty. The room had balanced and stilled. I closed my eyes, pulled off my glove, and ran my fingertips over the cold pillow. They found the softness of a child's fine hair, then touched Nessy's temple.

As if sensing my own body, I became aware of hers. Her lungs were fouled with hard nodules—the tubercles of consumption. They were bad but no worse than the day before. Could they be slightly better? She had held her ground against the disease, at least.

"Heal," I whispered. Nothing happened.

Yuánchi said, *You must bind to find your strength*. For all his wisdom, Yuánchi did not know how useless his words were. I would never be able to bind.

Outside the closed door, I heard a distant man's voice. Firm steps climbed the stairs and approached. I drew on my glove and placed a warning finger on my lips as the door opened.

Mr. Knightley, dressed in a sweeping dark gray redingote and white wool scarf, saw me. He released the door latch carefully and gave a short bow in silence.

I was speechless, and not only because Nessy was resting. His hair, curlier than mine, was pulled back and tied in the same old-fashioned style he wore when we danced on the frozen ship. That memory flooded me, as fresh as if he had just released my hand, as immaculate as a treasured childhood recollection.

We stepped into the corridor and closed the door. After greeting each other, I asked, "Why are you here?"

"To plan music lessons for the students. Then I saw Miss Smith and learned you visited as well. She told me you were up here..." He frowned as he finished. "Is someone hurt?"

I had brought the bloodied cloth I held for Nessy while she coughed.

"It is from this poor girl," I said. "I do not like her to see it when she wakes. Her name is Nessy."

"That does not disturb you? I thought illness triggered your... affliction."

"Not if I am helping." I struggled to express the rules that dominated my life. "It is inaction that distresses me."

I put the cloth with another in a bowl and covered them. There was a pause while Mr. Knightley and I watched each other. It should have felt awkward, but we seemed at ease. Thoughtful.

In fact, a thought occurred to me. "When we danced, I felt you were very fit."

Mr. Knightley's ease vanished. He plucked at a sleeve and muttered something unintelligible.

I was not put off that easily. "I was plotting to steal a footman from the Darcys, but perhaps you would help me? I wish to take Nessy on an outing, but I need a pair of strong arms. She is too ill to walk far."

He stopped shuffling his feet. "I would be honored."

"The school has a chair with wheels for when she visits the schoolyard, but our destination is a garden, so there is getting the chair into a coach, then I am

149

told there are steps and a rough path..." I was delighted with my plan. "I know you will manage!"

I DID NOT WISH to wake Nessy yet, so we strolled downstairs to the student's yard. The air stung my cheeks and chilled my front teeth. I had an uncontrollable happy grin. This had worked out so neatly.

I tapped a child's red ball aside with my toe. "Will you attend the Darcys' ball?"

"They have been kind enough to invite me."

"That is a very proper answer," I teased. "I thought you were a madcap musician who played the violin on frozen ships."

He chuckled. "The Darcys' ball is the talk of London. A musician would be a fool not to brush shoulders with wealthy patrons. There! I have revealed myself to be selfish and mundane."

Mr. Knightley was always fashionably dressed and, apparently, at leisure. One would think him an idle gentleman, not someone who sought money. Then again, I was strolling in an extravagant pelisse and layered silks while counting shillings.

He asked, "Will you attend the ball?"

"I had not expected to remain in London that long, but it appears I shall. So, yes." I had avoided balls since Papa became ill. But I had danced, and the sky did not fall. There was only wind from a dragon.

However, a ball required funds. I was clever at shopping without spending —Harriet always exclaimed that she bought more than me—but we would need dancing slippers and shoe roses at least. On top of our expenses until we met Mr. Debrett.

I stroked the fur cuff of my red pelisse. It was embroidered and silk-lined, and had cost tens of pounds. It was a favorite, but I had other coats at Hartfield. They said one could buy or sell anything in London. The answer might be draped around my shoulders.

Mr. Knightley stopped, and our linked arms drew us together as I turned inquisitively.

His full lips had an earnest smile. "May I have the first dance at the ball?"

I smiled back. "Of course."

His smile faded. "I meant it seriously."

"I am answering seriously."

"You would dance with me before all the elite of London?"

"You did not say the elite will attend. I shall have to consider, now." I felt his arm tense. "That is a joke. Did you wish me to hem and haw, and say I must consult my dance card? I know nobody in London."

"So your choices are few," he said stiffly.

I stepped back to scowl at him properly. "Why are you cross? Did you think I would refuse because you are a musician seeking patrons? It is a dance, not a marriage."

Unexpectedly, that made him bark out a laugh that crinkled his eyes. "Is that my flaw? A lack of wealth that renders me unsuitable for marriage?"

"Well, I did not mean to make it a flaw. That would be horribly coarse. In any case, I have no intention of marrying. If that relieves you so much that you laugh, very well. But it means I may dance as I wish." He continued to chuckle, and I added softly, "That night, on the ship, it was not easy for me to dance. So I know I am able to, with you."

His expression became somber. He offered his arm, and we resumed our circuit of the yard.

Nessy's thinned face beamed when I announced an outing. I stepped into the schoolroom to tell Harriet I would meet her later—she had promised to help the students all day—then Mr. Knightley and I wrapped Nessy in blankets and flagged down a hefty carriage. Nessy and I settled in seats first, then we pointed out obstructions and called encouragement while Mr. Knightley and the driver hoisted the wheeled chair and fought it through the door.

"'IN THIS YEAR of our Lord, 1673, by the Worshipful Societie of Apothecaries,'" I read, then I had to squint. The words were carved in a stone block atop a plinth, and the letters were stained, mossy, and crumbling. "'Here, Invoke Healing through the Wondrous'—I think it says plants?—'of the Physic Garden. Delight, for these are found Nowhere Else on these Great Isles. Within are Remedies and Medicines of...' I cannot read the rest."

We had passed a large riverside gate to enter. It had a peculiar emblem, a golden man astride a wyvern-sized draca.

"Are we here to give me medicine?" Nessy said with profound distaste.

"These are herbs, so they make tea. You must like tea."

"If it has..." Her breath hitched, and she tried again. "If it has honey—"

Her cough struck—wet, convulsing hacks that rose from far too deep for such a little girl. I embraced her in her chair, whispering, "It will pass."

At last, her fit eased, and she clung in my arms, exhausted. I wiped her lips and smoothed dampened hair from her eyes. "Save your breath. We will explore the garden, and you must listen. They say the herbs speak. It is a game."

I stood. Mr. Knightley's face was gray with shock. He had never seen one of Nessy's coughing fits. I aimed a bright smile at him until he mastered himself, then we began wheeling the chair along a walk beneath three towering cedars.

"What do you mean, the herbs speak?" he said finally.

"Georgiana's mother, Lady Anne Darcy, was a healer. She said the herbs spoke to her. This garden is so old and full of herbs, I thought it would be fun to visit."

Mr. Knightley absorbed that with skepticism. It did sound like a thin excuse, but if there was a scrap of truth in these stories of a great wyfe of healing, Nessy deserved that I find it.

The groomed walk became wandering, wild paths, each as likely to peter out as to open onto obscure bird baths or benches. The physic garden nestled beside the Thames and was lush even in the dead of winter. Some plants had been wrapped in muslin or canvas to protect against the cold, but there was no sign of caretakers and only an occasional glimpse of another walker.

We reached a fork in the path. "Which way?" I asked Nessy. She pulled her thin arm free of the blankets and waved it playfully, then pointed to the broader path, well-trod and gravel lined. I watched her happy smile and thought of Papa's frustration when he could no longer walk unaided. When had she last chosen a left or right turn for herself?

The gravel resisted the chair's wooden wheels, so Mr. Knightley took over pushing. Greenery enveloped us. Nothing appeared exotic, but it was diverse and wild with overgrown bushes that reached above our heads.

"When I attend balls, my status is defined by my appearance, not my fortune," Mr. Knightley said.

We had returned to the choice of dance partners. He meant his skin, obviously.

"When we came to London," I said, "I did not believe how widespread that prejudice was. It is not like that in Highbury." Mr. Knightley raised a doubtful eyebrow, so I said, "Truly, it shocked me. Although I think I did not always notice the subtle intolerances of country society. Harriet has told me disturbing stories since we came to London."

"England's tolerance for blatant prejudice is growing. Ambitious men encourage hate that supports their beliefs, or they exploit it for cynical gain. But British soil is free. America has the grotesquery of slavery in the south, and the cowardice of appeasement in the north. I watch their politicians debate the Missouri Territory, and I know commerce will triumph over humanity again. And the American slave states are strengthened by this new alliance with Bonaparte."

"At least that alliance carries no weight in England."

"I fear you are mistaken. English extremists admire Bonaparte. Mr. Tinsdale and his like aspire to unchallenged power, so they worship dictators."

I preferred to avoid the topic of Mr. Tinsdale. "You are very informed about America."

"My father was born there, a slave. When the colonies rebelled, King George announced freedom for any slave who joined the loyalist army. My father escaped that evening. He walked a night and a day to find a regiment camp." Mr. Knightley chuckled wryly. "My father named me George to honor the King, but he always said I was named for another George as well: George Washington, the slave owner who so frightened the King that he welcomed Black men to Britain."

Mr. Knightley and I were walking side-by-side while he pushed Nessy's chair. His coat was of the best woolen weave, his buttons polished silver, his enunciation refined and educated. This history only made him more of a puzzle.

I decided to pry. "And his son is a gentleman musician? That must be a remarkable story."

Mr. Knightley smiled oddly, but he did not answer. Hmph. Perhaps I could ask Georgiana.

Our trio stopped at another fork. This had a half-scale statue of a wyfe, her features weathered and blurred. She cradled a winged draca in her arms—a fire-drake—as if it were a complacent goose. That was nonsense. Only tykes were safe to handle, and then only by their bound wyfe. Although there were fables of wyves who could charm any draca. Perhaps Lizzy could hold a drake.

I asked Nessy, "Do you think this lady has a name?"

"Miss Bunny," she whispered.

I hid a smile. "I recall that the Bunny family boasted many great wyves."

That accidental phrase, *great wyves*, felt potent here. The overgrown greenery embedded us in a natural shrine. Nine rays of carved stone radiated from the statue's head and shoulders like an overlarge halo, although the church did not permit draca in religious scenes.

Nessy squirmed around in her nest of blankets. This time she asked, "Which way?"

The wide gravel path curved benignly to the right. To the left was little more than a trail, overgrown with frost-nipped clover and drooping branches. The foliage gleamed jade and turquoise, the twigs swollen and streaked with purple as if poised to burst forth in spring, not frozen by frigid winter. Their hues gleamed over-colored like the false luster I saw when the miasma struck, but this felt living, not filled with sickness and threat.

"Left," I said. "Those plants look talkative."

It was narrow, so I led, lifting the occasional branch or weedy stalk which Nessy then raised over her head to be caught by Mr. Knightley. Grass and leaves brushed the sides of Nessy's chair and crushed beneath the wheels. Heady aromas freshened the air, crisp and springlike or musty like rich loam. The path thinned, wound, then widened.

"I did not think the garden was so large—" Mr. Knightley began.

I raised my hand. "Listen." Leaves were rustling. Ahead, a patch of hedge swayed, then thrashed. It looked distressed, not threatening, so I stepped closer.

A silvery shape the size of a modest dog was hidden in the overgrown stems and lush, rough-edged leaves. I crouched, and a chisel-shaped draca head lifted on a swanlike neck.

"A firedrake," I exclaimed. I saw her wings now, one furled, the other awkwardly half-extended among the weeds. Nessy squealed excitedly and Mr. Knightley said something cautioning, but I was too amazed to listen. The drake's scales were a color I had never seen, a silver warmer than polished sterling, as if rubbed with copper. Her shining black eyes stared into mine, mesmerizing in their depth.

One did not simply find firedrakes in public gardens. Was she bound? Bound firedrakes were extraordinarily rare, but I had never even heard of a feral drake.

The drake's shining head dipped into the green. A stalk shook, then her head rose to resume observing me, now with a rough-edged leaf sticking out of her mouth at a comical angle. She chopped at it ineffectively with obsidian teeth better suited for flesh, then a startling black tongue snagged the scraps, and the leaf vanished with a gulp.

"I want to see!" Nessy begged. After reassuring Mr. Knightley, who seemed convinced we faced a mortal threat, the three of us formed a tiny arc around the drake.

"She is hurt!" I realized.

The drake's wings were longer than a swan's and jointed differently, but the half-spread wing was clearly crooked and slack. I pushed weeds aside to see. The last rib of the wing hung at an angle. Broken.

"Miss Woodhouse, I must insist you are careful," Mr. Knightley said. "A wounded animal is dangerous."

"She is more than an animal," I said. Those black eyes sparked with intelligence.

"She likes you," Nessy whispered.

I offered my gloved hand, palm up as one greets a strange dog. She ignored my fingers, so I leaned closer. Her eyes, polished as dark mirrors, stayed fixed on mine. The silhouette of my face and bonnet reflected in the opal surfaces like a pair of distorted miniatures. They rippled gold. My hair, I suppose.

The silver head darted forward, quick as a striking snake, and touched my cheek. I said "Oh!" and sat back, but she had only brushed me.

The touch tingled. When I touched wyves, I sensed their bindings. This draca was not bound, but a similar brilliance was curled up within her.

The colors around me grew vivid with hidden hues—striations of rust and violet on leaves, jade in the feathery spines on the green stalks, and a pattern on each draca scale like copper filigree embedded in silver pearl. I became aware of the sharp heat of injury in her wing. An image of violent struggle filled my mind, a fight beneath towering forest trees against a writhing, armored, worm-like creature a yard long. Then a flailing, pained flight by night to reach this spot.

"She fought a foul crawler," I said. "A huge one. Several feet long. That is how her wing was injured."

My gloves dangled in my left hand. I looked at them, not remembering removing them. I tucked them in my reticule and studied the broken wing again. The drake's swan-like gaze finally left me and swung to study it as well. She gave a concerned chirp.

"It must not heal crooked," I said. That much was obvious. I touched my fingertip to the drake's sprawled wing. She jerked, rather like my father had done when I bandaged the sores on his feet. I clucked disapprovingly. "That makes it no easier." I reached out again, and this time the drake stayed still. My fingers traced the front of her wing, crossed the joint, and neared the break. Awareness of crushed hollow bone and torn muscle filled me.

Quickly, I closed my fingers around the ribbed front, then grabbed below the break with my other hand and pulled the wing straight. Mr. Knightley exclaimed "Good gracious!" and a strident *squawk* rang in my left ear—I had leaned past the drake's head to see properly—but I held the wing firm.

I sensed the drake's heart pounding. Golden ichor swirled through her veins. The crushed ends of bone seized each other and mended impossibly fast, like sealing wax pressed by a cool signet. The heat of injury faded.

I let go and sat back on my heels. The drake scrambled to her feet, sinewy and birdlike, then spread her wings. They spanned six feet, the bones armored by silver scales, the flight membranes thin and translucent as sheer muslin. She flapped experimentally—I blinked in the gust—then she launched and was gone.

Nessy laughed and clapped her hands. Mr. Knightley said, "That was extraordinary."

I plucked a leaf from the plant the drake had eaten. It was green, an inch long, and had serrated edges. I crushed it in my fingers. A minty scent filled the air.

"The herbs do not *speak*, exactly," I said, "but I think we should try this one."

22

THE BALL

LIZZY

Darcy and I stood arm-in-arm under a night sky and a soaring full moon—the ball had fallen on the first clear night in weeks. We were in the museum courtyard, fifty yards from the main building where we could admire its breadth. Each towering eight-pane-high window framed lamps decorated with blue glass shades to mimic draca fire. The museum's two smaller wings had the same decor, so the courtyard surrounded us with a hundred glimmering blue flames.

We had arrived early, but carriages were already queued, their coach lights casting yellow ovals gridded with thin shadows from the paving stones. Under the silvery moonlight, it looked like a stupendous, cross-hatched drawing splashed with blue watercolor.

"Shall we?" Darcy said, snugging my arm tight.

"You sound peculiar," I said in a worried tone. "It cannot be... do I detect enthusiasm for a *ball*?"

I expected a dry response. Instead, he drew me to face him. "Every ball I have attended with you has thrilled me."

I cocked an eyebrow. "I rather thought I irritated you the first time."

"You transfixed me, and I am sincere. My life is transformed in the year we have known each other." He recited, "My love is a smoke kindled in your eyes."

I stifled an amused snort, which rather ruined the moment. "Shakespeare would turn in his grave if he heard how you butcher his prose."

Darcy was unfazed. "It is verse, not prose. I have tailored it to your beauty."

A blush climbed my cheekbones. "If we are being *that* romantic, I wish to be Juliet, not Rosaline." He laughed with easy affection, and we set out across the stone-paved yard.

The entrance had a row of flaming torches. The glare made the back of my eyes ache. I shaded my gaze until we had passed, then I heard a familiar man's voice outside the open doors.

"I am sure it is expected. Mrs. Darcy's note clearly said—"

"Charles!" I called, skipping up the remaining steps and into a flurry of Bingley greetings. Jane and I hugged joyously, then I pushed her to arm's length to see what on earth I had thumped. Even in her winter coat, her belly was prominent. "Goodness! You grew that much more in a single month? Is it twins?"

"Mr. Johnson says no," Jane said. Her happy smile warmed me to my toes. "But I did not know one baby could be so heavy!"

"Mary knows all about these things. She says you will be a grump in a few more weeks."

"Oh," Jane said, her face falling. "Must I?"

Caroline Bingley was eyeing me from beneath an elaborate poof of yellow curls. Although nothing could have stopped me from embracing Jane first, it was also perfectly proper. Caroline's unmarried status rendered her inferior to married Jane. That thought brought a sincere smile to my lips as Caroline and I curtsied to each other.

"Mrs. Darcy," she said.

"Miss Bingley," I answered. "But I must be Lizzy to you. We are sisters."

"Eliza, then," she said with a blazingly false smile, and I wondered if mine was equally transparent.

Charles was next, his hair as tousled as ever, and after greetings he began a flustered explanation. "This gentleman at the door is concerned, but I assured him it would be fine. Have we done this right?"

I looked at the gentleman in question and recognized a particular round-headed museum employee. "Is there a problem?"

"They have brought a *monster*," he said, pointing a trembling finger at Jane's glorious golden wyvern, who was sitting patiently a little aside.

"There will be draca in attendance," I said. "It is in the invitation." I had borrowed the wording Mary used in her salon announcements.

"That is not a *draca*," he spluttered. "That is a... a *dragon*."

Jane and I exchanged amused glances. Wyverns were powerful and rare draca, heavier than lindworms and with wings that spanned ten feet. Not to mention four-inch razor claws. Still, even the Bingleys' wyvern, which was unusually solid and muscled, weighed less than a hundred pounds, so she was an unconvincing dragon regardless of which mythologized account you preferred.

"I assure you she is not a dragon," I said. "All draca may enter. I suspect Lady Catherine will bring her wyvern as well. Do say hello for me." I began to turn away, then turned back. "I mean, say hello to her ladyship, not to her wyvern. Unless you wish to greet both?" The man shook his round head desperately, looking like a befuddled globe.

The Bingleys proceeded in. As Darcy and I followed, he whispered, "Bringing small draca I understand. But why did Jane bring her wyvern?"

"I asked Jane to bring her. Just in case."

We passed the doors, and he caught my elbow and drew me away from the crowd. "In case of *what*?"

"Well, you know. Trouble. Yuánchi cannot fit through the doors."

"Is that a joke?"

"Of course," I said, grinning, although really it was just a practical observation.

"You cannot unleash a wyvern in the British Museum!"

"Love, do not worry so. Lord Wellington is overseeing security for the dagger. He and I agreed—"

"He *and* you! Are you involved with the security?"

"I cannot imagine what 'involved' means," I said, a shade guiltily as Lord Wellington and I had walked a full circuit of Westminster Palace while scheming. "I am the hostess. Naturally I care about all aspects of the evening. Now, come. We are ignoring our duties. *You* are supposed to be acquiring influence in government."

I spied Emma and Harriet at the door. Emma was dressed in the same striking golden silk gown she wore to Mary's salon but with only a wool shawl for warmth. She looked positively frosted. I fussed over her and asked, "Where is your beautiful red pelisse?"

"I am tired of fur. It makes me sneeze!" She declared this with wide eyes and a crinkled nose, and Harriet giggled.

Darcy and I quickly passed our coats, mittens, and boots to the coat clerk so we could move to the foyer, where it was warmer, if only marginally. I had enlisted Mrs. Reynolds and Lucy to organize the decorators, and their two personalities were apparent. Formal jade scarves draped the banisters, while lively sprays of green holly and hothouse crocuses were tucked in nooks and vases.

There was a surge of arrivals, and Darcy and I were engulfed in London acquaintances, some good friends to me if new, others remote enough that I had to nudge Darcy for hints. He never seemed to forget a face. Then I spotted Mamma and Kitty in the crowd and shamelessly abandoned him to run to them. They wore traditional white muslin over layered petticoats for warmth. Kitty was on the arm of an unfamiliar gentleman in naval dress uniform, while a second uniformed gentleman walked a step behind. A spare, perhaps.

"Dear Lizzy," Mamma said with a firm embrace. "Oh, and Mr. Darcy!" She curtsied as he joined us, and he bowed gravely, which never failed to leave my mother clucking with delight. She peered around the museum's massive entry hall. "Is this your London house?"

"This is the *museum*, Mamma," Kitty chortled, "You know that! How are you, Lizzy?"

She hugged me, and I was in ecstasies to have all my family together, then shot through with loss because Papa would not insert a dry remark, nor Lydia her laugh—the Lydia I cherished in my memories, younger and more innocent than what she became.

Kitty introduced the companion on her arm, a clean-shaven young gentleman in a naval officer's uniform of dark blue tailcoat with gold buttons, white waistcoat, and white breeches. He had a reckless grin, and Kitty whispered proudly—and far too loudly—"He is a *purser!*"

"To think I used to like a red coat," Mamma exclaimed. "Blue is much more handsome."

That comment came while the officer bowed to me. He rose with a good-natured chuckle and confided, "My mother has been saying the same thing ever since I received my Navy coat." I decided I liked him.

Both officers met Darcy and Charles, and then I drew Emma and Harriet into the muddle, as they had been watching with polite smiles at a distance. The entire group—even Kitty—became reserved while greeting Emma. I had seen this effect before, but this time I tried to put my finger on why. Emma was a beautiful woman in a beautiful gown, but the room had more spectacular gowns and more daringly dressed ladies. It was something particular to her, an eerie perfection of presentation. Her smiles and greetings were pleasant, but her person seemed untouchable. Ethereal.

Out of curiosity, I closed my eyes and sought the perspective of a ferret-worm perched on the second-floor banister. The flood of detail from ladies' lace and gentlemen's cravats was astonishing, but once I dragged my attention past that, Emma and I were obvious in the crowd, shining with the aura of great wyves.

Opening my eyes, I found Harriet and Kitty heads-together in intimate discussion.

"I read the most wonderful novel about a dusky heroine!" Kitty said. "I sat in the sun for days, but it was hopeless! I hardly tanned at all. That was silly of me, but I do so envy you. You must have all the gentlemen in pursuit."

"That has not happened yet," Harriet said, thankfully looking flattered rather than offended. "There are few single gentlemen in Highbury. And they shoot all day."

"All gentlemen shoot," Kitty commiserated. "I do not understand why. They cannot do it with ladies. Do you have officers in Highbury?"

"Not one," said Harriet.

"You poor thing!" She called to the second officer, "Henry, would you not like to accompany Miss Smith?"

My eyebrows rose at Kitty tossing gentlemen's Christian names about—perhaps she was under the influence of the navy's famously rough language—but the fellow stepped forward smartly. "It would be my honor, Miss Smith." Judging from his uniform, he was another warrant officer, although I did not know navy ranks as well as army. Exact rank aside, he cut an impressive figure in his coat and snug breeches, and he offered his arm handsomely. Harriet smiled shyly, and the four of them vanished toward a table with punch bowls.

"That was quick," I observed, as it turned out, only to Emma. Everyone else had been claimed by surrounding conversations.

Emma did not answer. She was staring at the room and still as a statue.

Softly, I said, "Are you well?"

"Of course," she answered immediately with a charming smile, but I was unconvinced.

There was a flurry at the entrance, and an aged, stentorian lady's voice sliced through the babble. "What can you possibly intend by speaking '*Hello*' to me?"

"Ah," I said. "She has arrived."

The crowd parted, and Lady Catherine sailed forth, an eighteen-inch ostrich plume cutting the air above her hair. She spotted me and changed course with resolute disdain.

"Aunt." I greeted her with a curtsy.

"Hmm," she said, ignoring me and studying Emma. "Who is this?"

"Lady Catherine," I said, "may I present Miss Woodhouse of Surrey."

"You are smartly put together," Lady Catherine declared. "And Surrey is tolerable."

"Your ladyship," Emma said, rising from her curtsy. "I am fond of Surrey myself." She looked both unintimidated and friendly. In my experience, that was an unprecedented combination when encountering Lady Catherine.

"Indeed." Her ladyship scowled at me. "And have you filled the museum with bolts? Recall that I do not share your fascination."

"There are none, madam. Our featured exhibit is a dagger."

"Weapons? That is more practical." There was a shocked cry behind her, and people scrambled apart. Her ladyship smiled in triumph. "I am attended by my wyvern. London has been too long without the presence of a truly magnificent draca."

"You are generous," I said, and to be generous myself, I headed off a faux pas by adding, "Jane has brought hers also, so London is doubly blessed." Lady Catherine exhaled in sharp annoyance.

Lady Catherine's wyvern, shining beautiful bronze amid the hundreds of candles, approached us, drawing gasps and murmurs. Wyverns have the same general form as other winged draca, two-winged and two-legged, but they are shorter necked, solid, and heavily muscled, quite different from the lithe elegance of the smaller firedrakes or huge Yuánchi.

Lady Catherine loftily addressed the room. "Do not approach her. She is exceedingly dangerous." Lady Catherine appended a quelling glance at me with a clear message: *hands off*. I had demonstrated my ease with her wyvern when she last visited Longbourn, but I had no desire to embarrass her, so I simply smiled.

Her wyvern, however, had spotted me and was trotting forward with her usual enthusiasm. I sent a silent thought, *Please wait. I shall give you a scratch later*. Like dragons, wyverns communicate with articulate thoughts—or at least, thoughts I could comprehend as articulate. With other draca, I communicated through images and feelings.

Disappointed, the wyvern stopped beside Lady Catherine and sat on her haunches, wings snugly furled and the tip of her tail flicking. Then her gaze swung to Emma and fixed there.

Another great wyfe. An unfamiliar one. While planning the ball, I had worried about the mysterious dagger, Gramr, but I had forgotten this would be the first meeting of other potent forces.

Emma sank down until her eyes were level with the wyvern's, her posture perfect as a ballerina. As she dropped, her gloved fingers skimmed her spreading skirt so it fell symmetrically on the gray granite, her hands finishing behind her so the hem formed a golden oval. The bronze wyvern approached until their noses were a foot apart, and the room silenced.

The great secret of this meeting was that this wyvern was unbound. Decades ago, Lady Anne Darcy, a powerful great wyfe, had summoned a wyvern to conceal an embarrassing truth: her sister, Lady Catherine, failed to bind when she wed. Ever since, Lady Catherine had flaunted her prestigious draca, unaware that the wyvern accompanied her solely to honor her dead sister.

Like dragons, wyverns have faceted eyes that shimmer in a rainbow of reflected colors. Those prismatic glimmers now stared unblinkingly into Emma's hazel eyes.

23

THE PRINCE REGENT

EMMA

The wyvern's eyes shimmered, and the chaos around me faded.

The day before the ball, my compulsions began a wicked spiral. By the time Harriet and I entered the museum doors, the crowd was blurring—a wet oil painting smeared by an unseen palm, first one way, then the other. Isolated details stuck in the air. An unbuttoned cuff. A gold cross hanging crooked below a necklace. Miasma trickled thirty feet from the ceiling, pooling wetly on the floor, splashing hems and slippers with colorless pestilence while hunting a victim I would mourn.

Now, the wyvern's eyes shone, steady as summer sun. A single word chimed in my mind like a crystal bell:

healer

"I hear you," I whispered—not even whispered, just shaped words on my lips. I knew she heard.

The wyvern's thought, *healer*, did not thump my skull like Yuánchi's mind, but it sang of inhuman wisdom. Then my disbelief bristled. I had served Nessy tea brewed from the green leaves from the physic garden. It tasted pleasant enough—I had tried it, as well—but there was no miracle. This talk of healing was a fool's dream.

it is long since great wyves gathered. together, you are strong

"I do not feel strong."

you must bind for strength

That again. Aware of the watching eyes, I did not even mouth my next words. I only thought, *I would fail if I tried to bind.*

The wyvern's head cocked, avian in her curiosity. *the dragon songs broke. together, the wyves are strong. healer, can you heal a song?*

"I do not even know what that means." Frustration swamped the last of my awe. "Stop saying I can heal! My papa died in my arms."

I remembered the firedrake healing in the physic garden. But that was like a country doctor straightening a bone. Everyone knew draca healed quickly all on their own.

the great wyves gather. the great ones stir. a messenger awaits to the north

The facets of her eyes glimmered with the gold of my gown and the yellow pinpricks of distant candles. Then she simply trotted off, her tail lifting in a curl and her claws rasping the stone. The flex of her muscles hinted at untapped, explosive speed.

The world flooded back as I rose. I half expected a miracle of my own—the miasma banished—but the room resumed its skittering and shifting.

The wyvern reached the isolated corner where Jane's gold wyvern had settled. The two touched noses, and the crowd's silence burst with amazed exclamations and admiring claps. As a rule, draca ignored each other.

"What triviality," Lady Catherine said. "Why has my nephew not presented himself?"

"He is engaged with other guests," Lizzy said. "Shall we rescue him?" They excused themselves, Lady Catherine parading first through a thickening rain of miasma.

"Emma," said Georgiana's voice.

"Yes?" I said, forcing the expected smile, my gaze on a lady's bare forearm swelling into huge, red pustules.

Georgiana's voice came again, urgently. "Listen to me." Melody flitted through my mind, then I heard it in my ears, a barely hummed tune beneath the bustle of the crowd. Layers of crumpled fear folded into tolerable apprehension. The trickling miasma thinned to flickering illusion, a conjurer's trick that could be ignored.

"Is that better?" Georgiana asked. "The world was all dissonance about you."

"Much better, thank you," I said, although fear still scrabbled at the underside of my mind. Had I been this bad at Hartfield? No wonder Harriet had guessed the truth.

I realized Mary Bennet stood at Georgiana's shoulder. "Good evening, Mary." At first, I thought the daring color she wore was a trick of my mind, but the hues shifted too subtly with the light and shadow. "What a beautiful gown."

Mary wrapped her arms around herself and muttered, "I regret it already." Her dress was night-black satin and vivid crimson, with more crimson than black. The dark, slim sleeves and dagged cuffs exposed red lining and black lace.

"It is beautiful," Georgiana told her. "I am so happy you wore it." Her middle finger grazed the side of Mary's wrist, the touch gone almost before I saw. Their gazes locked, and their posture became so still they could have been caught in unseen chains.

Feeling extraneous, an intruder who had stumbled onto a private intimacy, I looked away, hunting unsuccessfully for Harriet. Imperfect clothes snagged my gaze, but at least the crowd was no longer putrid madness.

Instead of Harriet, Mr. Tinsdale emerged from the throng. He bowed. "Miss Woodhouse. You look bright as a summer day."

Unease tensed my cheeks, but I forced an untroubled expression. This was his proposed meeting—the chance to secure Harriet's status through a listing in *Debrett's*. "You are kind, sir."

"I see you are acquainted with Miss Darcy." He bowed to Georgiana, who returned a polite greeting. His gaze shifted to Mary's dramatic form. An impressed smile stretched his mustache.

"I know who you are," Mary said with scathing distaste. "An introduction will not serve us well."

Georgiana blanched. Mr. Tinsdale frowned. "We have never met. Miss?"

Mary uttered a scoffing laugh, apparently at his foolishness for ignoring her advice. "Bennet. Mary Bennet."

Mr. Tinsdale's barrel chest puffed. His face reddened. "Not *that* Mary Bennet. The one who writes offensive letters to newspapers and parades her black-clad Marys?"

Mary smiled fiercely. "Not *that* Rosdan Tinsdale, the Jacobin turned royalist who parades his Blackcoat bigots?"

"Excuse us," Georgiana said with a brilliant smile and whirled Mary into the crowd. I caught Mary's indignant "*And* he is a Tory!" before they were out of earshot.

"How exciting," I said with a hostess's smile.

"Quite. You met her through Miss Darcy, I suppose."

"Yes." I felt an unprecedented urge to defend Mary, but I did not dare. Once Harriet was secure, I could purge this unpleasant man from our lives.

"Miss Darcy, at least, is a valuable acquaintance. I was intrigued to learn you are a guest at Chathford House. When we last met, I had no idea you were so close to the Darcys." He paused meaningfully. "That you had such *privileged* access."

He did not know I had left Chathford House. But it was not the house that interested him. It was the Darcys.

"The Darcys are good friends," I confirmed, then added firmly, "both to myself and to Harriet. *I* was intrigued to learn you would be meeting Mr. Debrett. Perhaps he could correct a tiresome oversight. Harriet's remarkable affinity for draca should be publicly recorded."

It had not occurred to me to call her "remarkable" before, but it sounded wonderfully important.

"That... disadvantaged woman has the ability to bind?" Mr. Tinsdale frowned and crossed his thick arms.

Despite his offensive tone, I settled for a nod.

His jaw worked as if chewing a tough piece of mutton "I will speak frankly. You know the Darcys are caretakers of an extraordinary creature. The government is eager to protect the beast, so much that they would transgress on the Darcys' rights. I, however, wish to protect the Darcys. Shield them from embarrassing inquiries."

I had no idea what that meant. "What inquiries?"

He lowered his voice to a whisper. "We cannot locate the dragon. The Pemberley staff display such perfect ignorance that the lair must be elsewhere. If I were privately advised of the creature's location, I could reassure the War Secretary. The Darcys would be undisturbed, and their creature guarded." He smiled shrewdly. "His Majesty's government would be indebted for that information. A debt worthy of an introduction to Mr. Debrett."

It was so simple. I could tell him Yuánchi's location with my next breath. But would he deliver his promise? His claim of helping the Darcys was transparent manipulation. Still, Lizzy spoke of him as an ally.

His eyes narrowed. "You *do* know something. Miss Woodhouse, I meet Mr. Debrett tomorrow. This offer ends tonight. Help your friend while you still can."

Mr. Tinsdale's pressure was eroding my precarious calm. The flickering trickles of miasma thickened. I searched the room for a reprieve, spotted a friendly profile, and stared hopefully. I was rewarded when Mr. Knightley turned and caught my gaze. He smiled and began walking over.

Relieved, I returned my attention to Mr. Tinsdale, then realized my blunder just as Mr. Knightley arrived.

"Miss Woodhouse," he said, bowing, then he froze when he saw Mr. Tinsdale, whose eyes had hardened.

"Uh... are you acquainted?" I said desperately. "One discovers the most unexpected connections at a ball."

The two men glared at each other in deadly silence.

I seized the explanation that saved me with Mary. "I believe Mr. Knightley is an acquaintance of Miss Darcy." The silence thickened, and I babbled on, frightened that I had ruined Harriet's chance. "A musician, is it? Have you come to entertain us?"

Mr. Knightley turned to me, his posture impeccable, his neckcloth a cascade of silk between velvet lapels. "Your pardon. I mistook you for a friend." He inclined his head and strode away.

"Callow and rude," Mr. Tinsdale declared very loudly. "Proof that dressing in fine clothes cannot make an Englishman of... that."

"Excuse me. I am unwell." I staggered aside, then dove between strangers, my vision blurring with shame for how I had treated my friend. Whatever hope Mr. Tinsdale offered for Harriet, I could not proceed like this. Tears heated my throat and spilled on my cheeks. With shaking fingers, I groped at the drawstrings of my reticule. If I soiled my gloves, the evening was lost.

A gentleman's hand appeared before me, presenting a handkerchief with a discreet D embroidered on the corner. Mr. Darcy said, "May I assist you, Miss Woodhouse?"

Unable to speak, I took his handkerchief and wiped my eyes. The miasma raged like a sea, churning higher and higher from my emotions. Then the storm vanished behind Mr. Darcy's perfect ivory waistcoat, each decorated button aligned, and a starched neckcloth with fifteen symmetric lobes.

I forced my gaze up to his eyes. He was standing overly close to block my view of the room. Relief shattered my last pretense of strength, and I whispered, "I must touch you."

His brow furrowed. "I do not see how that can be accomplished."

Despite my turmoil, his propriety made me laugh. I shut my eyes, pulled off my gloves, and fumbled them onto the floor. By the time I opened my eyes, Mr. Darcy had retrieved them. I accepted them in my left hand, said "Thank you," and offered my bare right hand.

No gentleman took a lady's ungloved hand without removing his own glove. That reflex of etiquette bared his skin, then our fingers met.

Scarlet roared up my arm. The thickening miasma vanished like a popping soap bubble. My senses exploded—the vital warmth of guests around us, the staircase glows of candelabra, the feathery swansdown on my cuffs.

This health and clarity of perception was astonishing. My pathetic rituals of distraction were a toy by comparison.

I realized our fingers still touched. I opened my hand. "Thank you for my gloves, sir." I drew them on, watching how the yellow cloth filled unevenly and wondering at my lack of distress.

"Miss Woodhouse," he said. I looked up into wondering eyes. "We must decide how to manage this."

"Has no lady fooled you into a touch before?" That sounded silly, but I was giddy with relief. Then I remembered Mr. Knightley striding away, and my relief became shame. "I do not mean to joke. You have saved me this evening. I am grateful."

He bowed with utmost formality and said, "You are welcome. I beg your pardon. I must speak with Elizabeth." He vanished into the crowd.

Was he affronted? Furious? I swallowed through a tight throat. I had offended two upstanding men in as many minutes. And I had not even left the foyer.

I moved to the next room, hoping to spy Mr. Knightley, or Harriet, or anyone I knew. Not Mr. Tinsdale, though. Not yet.

This was an exhibit hall, with suits of armor and weapons around the perimeter, each collecting chattering admirers. Near the back was a roped off six-by-six square with a small pedestal. A black, curved dagger rested in purple velvet. Gramr.

An elegantly dressed lady in her early twenties stopped beside me. She wore white silk, an extravagant jeweled gold necklace, and ostentatiously styled yellow curls. She inspected me heels to hair, then wrinkled her nose in grudging approval. "How delightful to have an addition to our winter society. May I assist you with an introduction?"

The simplicity of social ritual made me smile in gratitude. "I am Miss

Emma Woodhouse. You are quite right. This is my first ball in London. I reside in Surrey."

"I am Miss Caroline Bingley."

We exchanged curtsies. Hers was carefully measured to be shallower than mine.

Miss Bingley nodded to Lizzy and Mr. Darcy on the far side of the room. "Our hosts. The tall one is Mr. Darcy. I fancy that I played some part in their marriage." She laughed lightly. "They are married six months now. You cannot imagine what a relief that is."

That was a peculiar comment. My enthusiasm for my new friend diminished.

When I did not reply, she resumed, "Mr. Darcy was *so* tiresome before." She arched an eyebrow outlined with pencil. "Infatuated, you know."

It seemed I had to speak. "That is charming in a new marriage."

Miss Bingley tittered. "Oh no! Before *that*. He was infatuated with me! It was perfectly shocking. The man followed me like a lost puppy. Finally, I was able to cast him toward Eliza."

"How incredible," I said tightly.

Miss Bingley lifted her face, an actress on stage. "He even danced with me. You cannot imagine how remarkable that is. Mr. Darcy *never* dances. That is the one thing I miss. For all that he was scandalously attentive, he is a handsome figure on the dance floor."

"Miss Bingley," I began, "I am acquainted with—"

She shushed me loudly. Mr. Darcy was threading the assembly toward us. I exhaled the rest of my sentence as a sigh and waited to see what would happen.

Mr. Darcy arrived and bowed. Was that his sixth bow to me this evening? "Miss W—" he began exactly as Miss Bingley laughingly enthused, "Mr. Darcy!"

Mr. Darcy swiveled his bow to her. "Miss Bingley. I trust you are well?"

His adjustment was subtle, but Miss Bingley's eyes darted between him and me. Her smile thinned. "You know each other."

"Miss Woodhouse was our guest at Chathford House." To me, he said, "Are you enjoying your new accommodation?"

I smiled brightly. "It cannot match the elegance of Chathford, but it is convenient."

Mr. Darcy's gaze remained intent on mine. The moment lengthened. He was here for some purpose.

Finally, he said, "Will you dance this evening?"

"I may," I said. It would have been impossible before I brimmed with Yuánchi's strength.

"It would be my honor to accompany you," he said with yet another bow. I nodded, and he departed.

Miss Bingley was rigidly silent. I debated describing the splendors of Chathford House to cheer her up.

Georgiana and Mary arrived smiling with an older, pleasant woman, and I was introduced to Mary's mother, Mrs. Bennet. That caused Miss Bingley to vanish in a jangle of irritated jewelry, after which Mary and Mrs. Bennet exchanged a satisfied glance while Georgiana looked disappointed. At this rate, I would need a list of who disliked whom.

"There are a good number of draca present," Mary said with satisfaction.

"Does that help your project?" I said.

"Society restricts the display of draca to diminish the power of wyves. The patriarchy abhors any sign of female achievement, so they distort binding, a feminine strength, into a moral bludgeon of virginity and virtue. The Britons at Pemberley bind draca without any of that masculine probity, and their wyves have superior relationships with draca."

That was a more interesting answer than I expected. ' How do the Britons bind?"

At that, the crowd fell suddenly silent, and our conversation ended. Every head turned to the entrance as a voice rang out. "His Royal Highness, the Prince Regent."

A buzz rose. People backed to the walls, clearing a large receiving oval for the prince—England's reigning monarch, as King George had been declared mad years ago, causing the establishment of the regency.

"Was he expected?" I whispered to no one in particular.

Georgiana answered, "No. But he is always invited to London events." Mary was backing into the crowd. Georgiana caught her hand and pulled her forward. "You stay right here!"

I could see the prince's black, double-breasted evening coat, a military style though not a true uniform. He was with a half-dozen attendants and members of court. After hearing shocking stories of his infidelities, he looked far more mundane than I imagined. Rather old and stout.

The royal party met Mr. Darcy and Lizzy, then began circuiting the arrayed guests, occasionally exchanging a few words.

"Will he speak to us?" I asked.

Georgiana *hmmed* a knowing smile. Mary, evidently alarmed, began shuffling backward again. Georgiana hauled her forward and whispered, "He is quite harmless. That is Lady Hertford beside him. She keeps him in check."

"Have you met him?" I asked.

"I have played for him. He is a patron of many arts."

The royal party neared us. They seemed to be greeting the titled aristocrats, so I relaxed. Then the prince's gaze found Georgiana, and he stepped to us with a pleased smile.

An attendant rattled off our names. "Mrs. Bennet of Hertfordshire. Miss Darcy. Miss Bennet." A man behind him whispered, and he finished, "Miss Woodhouse of Surrey." I had no idea how they knew.

We dropped in deep curtsies saying, "Your Royal Highness."

"Miss Darcy," the prince said as we rose. "Beautiful as ever. The last pianoforte I heard was played by a boor of a man. You must give us a proper recital."

"I would be honored, sir," she said.

He looked us over, nodding politely to Mrs. Bennet who was audibly gulping, then settled his gaze on Mary. "Very striking. I think you have the gown of the evening."

The crowd *oohed* and clapped admiringly. Mary stammered, "Thank you, sir," then drew a breath and continued more firmly, "The crimson mourns the bloody death of our fellow sentient animals."

The prince's attendants thrust out their lips and sucked in dismayed air, but the prince chuckled. "You must be another performer."

"Miss Bennet is a composer," Georgiana answered for her.

"The Darcys always discover superior talent. We shall have to hear your work." The crowd hummed.

The royal party moved on. Georgiana hugged Mary, who hissed, "I shall burn this dress!"

Across the room, Harriet, attended by her officer, caught my eye with a raised hand. Kitty was beside her, waving madly and mouthing *Mary!* while clutching her laughing purser with her other arm.

I nudged Mary and inclined my head to the display. Mary closed her eyes in sisterly dismay, so I switched my attention to Georgiana, who was ecstatic, and said, "That was remarkable."

"It is wonderful for Mary. He will stay for a dance, you know. It is a great privilege to dance in his presence."

That gave me a thought. The receiving oval was dissolving as people mingled. I excused myself and circled the narrowing space until I spotted Mr. Knightley.

My arrival was met with stiff silence.

"I am ashamed of my behavior," I said. "I wish to apologize." He did not answer, so I forged on. "I am embarrassed that I appeared to deny our... our friendship."

"I am accustomed to being disowned," he said. "It is a recurrent event."

"I do not wish to disown you! It was terrible, desperate behavior that I deeply regret."

"I meet many privileged gentlemen and ladies. They smile at me, then stare past me when society observes them. Actions speak truth, not words."

"You cannot imagine how deeply I regret my actions. I would list my excuses, but none matter, except one: I desperately require Mr. Tinsdale's help for Harriet."

His lip twisted in revulsion. "Do you understand what that man is? You cannot seriously think he will assist Miss Smith."

"I have something he wants." When Mr. Knightley frowned, I added, "Do not worry. I will not give it to him."

Emotions chased across Mr. Knightley's stern demeanor. Finally, he softened. "You must not trust him. Tinsdale is evil. If you need proof that England is not the tolerant society it claims, watch the hypocrites in Parliament as they dance for him. The lords give grand speeches trumpeting English freedom, then they secretly beg for his favor. Tinsdale toys with them and betrays them, and then they start all over again."

"I can use Mr. Tinsdale," I said stubbornly, and realized I had a plan to do just that. "It is only for a few days. Then Harriet's future will be secure."

"You are a fool. Does Miss Smith even desire this future you press on her?"

"She does not know the world well enough to judge."

"And *you* do?" His long-fingered hand swept past my dress. "Wealthy Miss Woodhouse, who resides in country splendor?"

I straightened my shoulders. "I do not pretend to understand your challenges, Mr. Knightley. Do not pretend to understand those of a woman alone, who is a tenant in my own home, and who must beg for my own funds."

He was silent, then said softly, "Is your situation so dire?"

I waved a hand in frustration. "That is not what I wish to discuss."

"What, then?"

"I..." My attempt at apology now felt foolish and self-aggrandizing, but at least it was action, not words. "The first dance will be a royal dance, observed by His Royal Highness. It is the pinnacle of social visibility."

"And whom will you dance with?" he responded shortly.

I gathered my courage. "With you, if you will ask me."

There was a surprised silence. "Have you not been reserved by a parade of stuffy lords?"

"Only by Mr. Darcy, and he wishes to scheme, not dance. He will have his opportunity." Censure and humor warred on Mr. Knightley's features. That was hard to interpret, so I presented a lively smile and said, "Mr. Knightley, would you honor me with the next dance?"

He broke into a laugh. "If you are asking gentlemen to dance, you have spent too much time with Mary. Are you completely corrupted?"

"Not completely," I said with a smile.

24

WYVERNS

LIZZY

L ondon's social set swarmed us after Darcy and I greeted the prince. When that became overwhelming, we ducked and hid behind a battered suit of armor.

"I never expected the Prince would attend," I said, feeling overheated. The crush had been intense.

"Hopefully he merely wished to fill a dull evening," Darcy said.

"What else could it be?"

Darcy's lips pursed uncertainly, the closest to a shrug he allowed himself in public. Then he turned to me. "Would you remove your gloves?"

"What?"

Darcy waited, earnest and intent, so I did. In one swift motion, he removed his right glove and took my hand, then stared at our folded fingers.

"What on earth are you doing?" I said.

"I am recalling the times when ladies tricked me into touching them."

"Goodness. Does that happen often?"

"More than I knew." He bent, and his kiss brushed my skin. He restored his glove.

While I tugged my own gloves on, I noticed something familiar in the next room's collection. I made my way there, trailed by Darcy.

This room held Egyptian artifacts. The Rosetta stone was prominent, four feet tall and covered with engraved symbols. Some claimed it would decipher the mystery of hieroglyphics. But that was not what caught my eye.

I stopped in front of a multistranded, turquoise necklace. A *menit*. "This is like my vision in the boathouse. I was a bound wyfe. A queen."

Darcy frowned. "I do not question what you saw. But there is no record of Egyptians binding draca."

"We cannot read their hieroglyphics."

"True. But the Romans wrote histories of Egypt."

"Mary regularly points out that rulers erase the achievements of those they rule." I was reading an explanatory panel titled *Egyptian Death and Afterlife*. "This describes what I believed. What I *felt*."

A modern painting hung with the exhibit: a beautiful young woman slumped in a chair surrounded by a half-dozen grieving maids. Inexplicably, they had chosen to grieve while mostly undressed. A small snake curled around the dead woman's arm.

The painting was labeled *The Death of Cleopatra*, Guido Cagnacci, 1658. There was an explanation of her despair over the loss of Mark Antony.

For a few seconds, I was fooled by the milky skin and light hair. Then I saw the truth. "What were the names of Cleopatra's advisors? The ones who died with her." Darcy would know. Shakespeare had written a play.

"Charmion and Iras," he said.

The image of loyal Charmion, ebony haired and dark skinned, leaped into my mind. "I journeyed. I found the god. I had the strength to defeat Rome!" I reached out and pried at the sign below the painting. The thin wood splintered, and it broke from the wall. I waved it at Darcy like a blade. "This is *lies*. I drove poison into my arm with a dead asp's fangs. I dared the underworld for vengeance. But Imhotep drove the god mad. If he had not, I would have crushed Rome." I thought of Yuánchi. "I still can!"

"Rome fell a thousand years ago," Darcy said quietly but firmly. "This is England, and you are Elizabeth."

I blinked up at him, untangling memory from reality. My anger faded. "Yes. That... I am sorry. The vision was intense. Dying is intense." I took a settling breath and looked again at that ridiculous painting of pink-cheeked maids. "Cleopatra was a bound queen who summoned a dragon. Imhotep promised she would return from the underworld. He lied."

I dropped the broken sign on the table and turned away. That denigration of history revolted me.

Beyond the strolling crowd, I glimpsed Lord Wellington speaking urgently to a guard. Darcy had begun an involved observation about Cleopatra, so I plucked his sleeve to get his attention, and we hurried over.

Lord Wellington saw me and skipped niceties. "We baited our trap with the dagger, but I did not intend the Prince to be present as well. What do you see?"

I closed my eyes. The perspectives of draca throughout the building filled me—all of them at once. That was unexpected, a peculiar synthesis less direct than sight, more like the unconscious awareness of a familiar room where sounds and shadows can reveal even a person out of view. There were colors, though, spanning the vibrant spectrum of draca vision, and hyper-detailed textures. The guests' strolling steps and motioning hands appeared slowed and clumsy.

"It is more crowded. More excited. People are heated with emotion. There is passion." I saw the gold aura of great wyves among the surge of people, but.... My eyes snapped open in shock. "There are *four* great wyves."

Lord Wellington's urgency sharpened to a steel edge. "Who?"

"I... do not know. Individuals are difficult to recognize through draca eyes. And I was aware of *everything*. They were scattered through the rooms."

"Impossible," Darcy said. "There are only three great wyves."

"Three?" Lord Wellington exclaimed. "I understood there were *two*." He did not know about Emma. His eyes swung between Darcy and me, and his jaw corded. "You have withheld information."

"I will address that later," Darcy said. "Elizabeth, there cannot be a fourth wyfe."

"I know what I saw."

Lord Wellington made his decisions. "I will move the Prince to safety. *You*"—his gaze pinned me—"guard the dagger." He vanished into the crowd.

"I can find her," I said to Darcy as we returned to the room with the dagger exhibit. "If we go room by room."

"You are supposed to guard the dagger."

"With what, my wit? This is why I brought draca."

I had already called for help, and the result was apparent as the crowd made way. Jane's golden wyvern stalked from a widening corridor of amazed faces on our right, and a lindworm and tykeworm from the left.

The tyke scrambled excitedly to nuzzle my hems. I knelt, closed my eyes, and flicked into his perspective. I saw myself, stooped and shining golden bright, but the rest was a forest of trousers and skirts. I scooped him into my arms and stood—a marginal improvement—then placed my hands under his chest, hoisted him over my head, and turned a circle to scan the room. No shining auras.

I placed him back on the floor and opened my eyes to see a thin-shouldered, academic man bouncing toward me waving a handful of handwritten papers— the museum researcher who first showed us the dagger. "Mrs. Darcy!"

"I am rather busy." I tugged Darcy's wrist and headed to the Egypt room.

The museum researcher caught up on my other side, his stack of papers held in front of us like a fluttering figurehead. "When shall I give my lecture on the dagger?"

"We had planned that before the dancing—" I began, then I noticed the thickness of his sheaf of paper. Social self-preservation stopped me in my tracks. "Is *that* your lecture?"

He smiled modestly. "I am afraid that the last pages are mere bibliography. For those who wish additional study? But the lecture should fill an hour."

"An hour!" The room would be glazed stares in minutes. For one irrational moment, this seemed more important than chasing great wyves.

Then a chill like filthy, dripping slush ran down my back. The skin on my arms pebbled. I knew this sensation—from the wyfe on the frozen pier, and from fighting Lydia. I grabbed Darcy's arm and whispered, "There is danger," then closed my eyes.

This time, I held my awareness within, resisting the beacons of nearby draca minds. To my senses, the draca were scattered shining presences throughout the building, but a room away, oily darkness was seething. Blind to my surroundings, I turned in that direction, then opened my eyes. I was facing the wall separating us from the dagger's exhibit room.

Darcy had managed to send the museum researcher away. To find Mary, apparently. She would probably advise adding a chapter. As Darcy turned back, I said, "A wyfe has been dosed with crawler venom. Tell Lord Wellington."

"I must remain with you—" he protested.

"No! Lord Wellington and I have planned for this. He must be told. Go!"

Without waiting, I bumped and squeezed back the way we came. Every fine coat seemed to block me. Every smiling face smirked at my delay. I fought to the middle of the exhibit room, the rough location I had sensed, then slowly spun. I saw polite conversation. Lace and tailored coats. Cups of punch and brandy balanced in poised fingers. Frustrated, I closed my eyes, opened my mind, and turned toward a towering fountain of black filth. Unwelcome memories of my final battle with Lydia stirred, dragging up shreds of buried guilt.

Aligned, I opened my eyes and faced the back of a well-dressed lady five paces away. She was approaching the ropes surrounding the dagger. I rushed after her and shouted, "Stop!"

She turned. This was not a filthy face like at the river, just a modestly pretty young woman with nicely styled light brunette hair and classic white muslin ball attire. Only her eyes showed the effect of the venom, her pupils stretched into huge, coal-black pools.

A man's voice shouted commands in the foyer. Heavy doors slammed—the museum's entrances. Lord Wellington had received my message. Every exit was being locked and guarded.

The woman's heart-shaped face and bony nose were familiar... a sketch... the pamphlets Mary had shown me. Although the face had changed. Her happy plumpness was thinned and gaunt.

"You are Miss Rees," I said. Her eyes pinched oddly.

I closed the distance between us. She waited passively. Cautiously, I took her hand. Her arm lifted bonelessly.

"You have been missing for weeks," I said. "Were you abducted?" An empty stare. "I am Mrs. Darcy."

A spasm climbed her spine, jarring her head and clicking her teeth. Her fingers clenched mine with manic strength, grinding my knuckles.

Her blank stare became a mindless grin. "I have you."

Black, foul strength flooded past me, crossing the room as swift as dark lightning. There was a scramble on a packed stairway. A body fell. A scream.

I cursed myself for being off guard. Then my urgency, my frustration, and the grating pain in my hand were all washed away by delighted fury.

Battle. At last.

The locations of draca aligned in my thoughts. Two behind me and one on the stairway were caught in this wyfe's oily, black tentacles of command. One by one, I crushed the tentacles with my mind. Through our gripped hands, I felt Miss Rees quiver as each snapped.

"You have me," I whispered. "And I have *you*." My strength was swelling fantastically, unlike anything I had experienced. I swept up the black potency around her and crushed it back into her. She was making sounds now. Gasps and whimpers.

Alarm was spreading through the assembly, but not panic. People helped a grimacing young man to his feet on the stairway. No one understood what had happened. The draca who clawed him, a lindworm, had retreated to sit on his haunches. Waiting.

The eerie blue of draca flame flashed from another room. Even that indirect reflection threw heat on my cheek. I released Miss Rees's hand—her grip had weakened to water—and she collapsed to her knees as I turned to the new threat.

Shouts erupted in the other room, and pounding, running feet. The orange flicker of mundane fire grew, and the entrances to the room jammed with panicked guests. Bodies collided, sending men and women reeling.

I reached my awareness through the wall and sensed another wyfe boiling with black strength. *Two* opponents. I bared my teeth, ecstatic, excited by the chaos of running people and spreading smoke, then shredded her oily trails of command. One trail I ignored. She had attempted to seize control of Jane's wyvern, and my mind sensed a glowing silver orb surrounding the wyvern, sizzling the attempt into nothing. Wyverns had their own defense, much like our Longbourn firedrake had used against Lydia, but even more potent.

"Elizabeth!" A broad hand took my arm. I looked up at Darcy, his jaw set, a smudge of soot on his temple. He looked very severe and grave.

"Do not fret," I told him cheerfully. "I did not expect two, but I have them controlled." Voices in the other room were calling for calm. "Where is Lord Wellington?" Had he caught anyone at the doors? The wyves dosed with venom were unimportant. We needed to catch their abductor.

Yuánchi's voice filled my mind. *Are you safe?*

Stay away! In the delight of battle, I threw the thought as a command. It bounced off his distant strength like scrunched-up notepaper bouncing off a stone rampart, but I felt his astonished surprise.

"We restrained a crazed wyfe in the Egypt room," Darcy said. "A draca burned some drapes. Is there another affected wyfe?" He squinted at me. "Are you *enjoying* this?"

"Two wyves were dosed with venom," I said gleefully. "This one is strong-est..." I turned, but the wyfe who hurt my hand was gone. "Miss Rees escaped! Oh, there." I pointed to her, behind the downed ropes around the pedestal for Gramr.

"She has the dagger," Darcy said.

Miss Rees had lifted the ten-inch curved blade vertically between her eyes. She turned it slowly as if admiring the dark gleam. She would have made a convincingly mad Lady Macbeth. People backed swiftly, leaving Darcy and me nearest.

She saw us and moved her left wrist near the blade. A threat.

"I thought you had her controlled," Darcy hissed.

"I meant I isolated her from draca."

But I could do more. I called the wyverns. My excitement had cooled enough that I made it a request, not a command, but of course they came. As the crowd pressed to the walls, the wyverns emerged, flanking Miss Rees and settling in taut crouches, each seven or eight yards away. Close enough.

The exhibit room stilled to frightened whispers. Traces of smoke drifted, laced with the stink of burned wool.

Lord Wellington stepped smartly to my other side.

"This is Miss Rees," I said to him, loud enough to include her. "She was abducted. She has been mistreated."

Lord Wellington bowed, his gaze never leaving her. "Miss Rees. No one has been seriously injured. We are here to help. Would you assist us by placing that dagger on the floor?"

She tilted the dagger. Reflections rippled along the serrations. Precisely, she touched the blade to the fleshy base of her left thumb. Her motion was so measured that the well of blood seemed unconnected—a gory coincidence.

Mutters and gasps rose from the onlookers. Darcy and Lord Wellington shifted their stances, trading glances as they prepared to rush forward.

"It does not hurt," Miss Rees said with the simple relief of a child. "See?" She held out her cut hand. Drops ran into her palm, trickles of dark red that pooled in her bone-white skin. She closed her fingers, wetting the tips, then rubbed them along the flat of the blade, smearing a crimson streak.

From a dozen points, the flat of the blade began to smoke. Miss Rees waved it as if frustrated, trailing thin, parallel streaks in the air, then held the flat horizontally in front of her face, eyes narrowed to see through the smoke.

In a well-trained, musical voice, she sang words of strange syllables in a peculiar melody.

My gut smashed into a knot like an icy hand had grasped my insides. The room vanished. My vision turned black, but I was not unseeing—I was in another perspective, dark and ferociously cold.

"Darcy..." I said uncertainly. Blindly.

Swirling chill sucked the heat from my arms. My legs. Then Yuánchi's presence erupted around me like a yellow sun. His voice bellowed *No!* like thunder.

Again, my vision changed, but this was a relief. I had fallen into Yuánchi's cradling presence. I shared his inhumanly exact vision. He had launched from the ground and was climbing past the treetops, branches tossing with each beat of his wings. An expanse of the Thames came into view. The frozen surface shone like mercury in the moonlight but was spotted with hot torches and celebrating people.

The cold and dark perspective returned, dragging at me, but was forced away by Yuánchi's commanding thought—*Stay with me.*

London rooftops began to pass. Uneven wood shingles. Rough slate. Heated plumes from chimneys. The view swerved to follow a street. Stunned faces turned up as we passed.

They see you, I thought.

It does not matter.

"Elizabeth!" Darcy's voice shouted. My human ears had been hearing crashing stone, yelling, and thumps.

"I cannot see," I answered, trying to hold my voice steady.

"Jane needs you!"

Do not go! Stay with—

Violently, I slammed my self closed and forced Yuánchi's thoughts away. Human vision returned.

Miss Rees stood a dozen paces away, Gramr smoking in her hand. A blur of writhing bronze and gold tumbled between us. The wyverns were fighting. Chunks of stone sprayed as they strained for purchase, their claws gouging the floor.

I opened my mind, and the invisible conflict was revealed. The venom-fueled potency I had pushed back into Miss Rees had broken free, vastly strengthened. A writhing black leash had captured the mind of Lady Catherine's wyvern and commanded her to attack. If Jane's wyvern had not blocked her, we would be dead.

Jane, big belly and all, was beside me, her hand stretched toward her wyvern, her face straining. "Help me!" she cried. "I am losing her."

A second black leash was attacking the mind of Jane's wyvern, held back—barely—by a shaking silver orb that surrounded the wyvern. Jane was supporting her wyvern's defense, pouring strength through the silver thread of their binding, but the silver orb was failing.

This, at least, was a situation I had faced before when Lydia tried to take Mamma's drake. I grabbed Jane's hand, found the gleam of their binding, and added my strength to hers.

The golden wyvern's defense flared blinding bright. Every trace of the vile black filling the room burned away like mist in a blazing noon.

The slashing frenzy of the wyverns ceased. They separated, feinting and wary, hissing through bared teeth. Ripped strips of wing hung. Gashes in their scales dripped golden blood.

Miss Rees collapsed to her knees, her white gown puddling around her. Her sobs filled the deathly still room. The dagger slipped from her fingers and rang on the floor.

"Thank you," Jane said softly to me. "I did not know what I was doing."

"You were doing very well," I said.

Mary emerged from the crowd. She took a cautious step toward Miss Rees. "Joane?" Miss Rees turned her tear-streaked face to Mary, eyes wide with recognition.

The crystal chandeliers tinkled. The floor vibrated under my toes. Yuánchi had arrived.

I reached for his mind, expecting to see the museum courtyard, but his perspective was high in the sky. An astonishing panorama of moonlit London narrowed as he plunged toward the silver, frozen Thames.

Eyes closed, I felt the floor shake under my feet. Tipped objects clunked and smashed. I struggled for balance, hands outstretched, but I stayed in Yuánchi's view while the stone floor jerked and shouts rose.

Yuánchi was diving, his wings tucked, air thrumming. The scene on the ice became distinct, late-night celebrators fleeing, lamps and torches falling, people sprawling. Then the ice buckled. A black crevasse split, unlit, cold, and deep. Huge, wet wings splayed over the ice, then a lithe, black neck emerged.

Yuánchi's thoughts filled with awe. *She wakes.* Then, with an urgency I had never heard, *Elizabeth Darcy Bennet. Hold fast to me.*

The black head rose. A colossal body clambered free. Each clawed step smashed thick ice. The faceted eyes turned toward Yuánchi—and looked through his eyes into mine.

Violence, ruthless as bitter winter, filled me. A dragon's voice, feminine and ecstatic, caressed my soul. *My wyfe of war.*

A cyclone of black strength filled my veins. Fear melted away. I laughed and shifted back to my own vision.

Mary was kneeling beside Miss Rees and holding her hand. Miss Rees's other arm was extended, propping up her swaying torso, her palm flat on the floor.

Her fingers were inches from the hilt of Gramr. The hilt she had dared to hold.

"Thief," I whispered. "The dagger is mine."

Issuing judgment was a long-lost delight. The sentence of punishment was effortless, a command I sent that crushed the defenses of Jane's gold wyvern and seized her mind—a command that made the wyvern dig her claws into the stone floor and hurl herself forward.

A wyvern's attack is not the floating leap of a wolf or a bear. It is the streak of a loosed crossbow bolt. The gold wyvern struck Miss Rees faster than a human eye could follow, but I felt the scythe claws cut and the blood and flesh spray.

Yuánchi's mind fell on me like an ax, shearing away the mad, dark presence that had filled me. His embrace trapped me in featureless quiet. The chill of black strength drained.

Only my weak, human eyes remained to view the carnage.

25

FURY

EMMA

Harriet and I stumbled across the museum courtyard. Around us, gentlemen and ladies trotted awkwardly in their formal attire, or called out names, or stood dazed.

"We are safe here," Mr. Knightley said, and our group stopped beside a pair of decorative torches, panting in the chill air.

Kitty was clinging to the arm of her officer. She did not cry, but her eyes were wide. The other officer supported Mrs. Bennet, who was shaky and frightened.

Kitty's officer nodded to Mr. Knightley. "Thank you, sir. That was well done."

We had been trapped between the surging crowd and the locked doors, a pressing mass that suffocated our breath until Mr. Knightley kicked loose a metal latch and the remaining lock broke under the mob's weight.

"What happened in there?" Harriet asked. No one answered. None of us knew. When the shouts began, we fled. Then came metallic brays and bangs like knights battling in armor, and screams, and panic.

Through the crowd, I saw a distinctive black-and-crimson gown descend the museum steps. I called, "Mary! We are here," and she turned. By moonlight, half her face was white as death, the other half stained inky black.

She walked to us with quick steps. When the torchlight lit her, Kitty gasped, "Heavens, Mary."

The light had reddened the stain on Mary's face to blood. Her loose hair hung wetly. Sodden locks stuck to her forehead, temple, and neck.

Mary said in a grating tone, "Joane Rees is dead." She gathered a thick handful of her skirt in one hand and wiped her other bloody palm, then scrubbed violently at each finger. Both her hands were drenched.

"I do not..." Kitty began, then tried again. "I am sorry. Who is that?" When Mary only shook her head, Kitty said, "How did it happen?"

"Fast," Mary breathed. "Jane's wyvern killed her." Her head lifted to search the courtyard. "Where is Jane? I was looking for her. She is distraught."

"Is Lizzy safe?" I asked.

"Yes," Mary said flatly.

Mr. Knightley offered his handkerchief. "Your face, Mary." She blinked at the white square, then took it and wiped her forehead. The cloth came away red-soaked. She stared as if amazed, then her shoulders hitched in a stifled sob.

"Look!" Harriet pointed at the sky.

"Where?" Kitty asked, then a huge wing eclipsed the moon.

"Yuánchi," Mary said sharply.

"No," I said. There was none of Yuánchi's scarlet pull.

"Where did it go?" someone said. Heads turned, then the stars and moon blotted out. I shielded my eyes as freezing gusts slammed us. The torches extinguished and rolled away.

The earth shook as giant feet struck the ground. With a clamor like grating chains, the blotted dark folded away. Moonlight reached the gleaming, jet-black scales of a hulking dragon, her wings tucked close, her sinuous tail lifted taut and twitching. She was tremendous. Bigger than Yuánchi. Her huge head and long neck swung to survey the museum buildings. I could sense her presence like the impressions I felt from draca, but armored, icy, and vast.

At least a hundred people were throughout the courtyard. The guests began fleeing while gawking late-night Londoners swarmed in. The two waves collided in a crest of humanity.

The dragon's head abandoned the building and turned to us—out of all those people, our tiny group. In four thudding steps, she crossed thirty yards, and her dark muzzle stopped ten feet up and a dozen feet away. Her faceted eyes shone with images of the silver moon, the blue lamps in the museum windows, and the yellow of fleeing lanterns.

"Do not run," Mary advised tensely.

The jewel eyes rested on Mary for one heart-stopping eternity. Then they settled on me. The sense of presence deepened as I stared into her eyes, but it was jittering, flailing fragments.

Words came, halting and imperious as a mad queen: *My wyfe of war is claimed by another. She is hidden. Drowned in your song.*

Crazed images fluttered—women's features blending one to another, a stutter of complexions, ochre and cream and ebony, then sweeping sheets of beaten gold and briny blue and swirling, inky clouds.

"Her mind is a ruin," I said. "Mad."

The air was still, but a gale-like shriek was climbing. A scarlet presence filled my mind, and I shouted, "Get down!" as a huge shape flashed out of the dark and slammed into the black dragon with a thundering thump. The black dragon tumbled, her tail striking a carriage and spinning it crazily, the horses screaming in their traces while the wheels chattered over the stones.

Fast as a cat, the black dragon was crouched and hissing. Her wings opened and drove wind that forced me to my knees, then rolled me across the ground.

The rushing air settled. I pushed to my feet, a banged knee smarting. The others staggered up. Swaths of the crowd had been flattened like wheat in a storm. They clambered up, exclaiming and sobbing.

The dragons were gone.

TEN MINUTES LATER, we waited for Mr. Knightley and Mary to return from the museum building. Harriet and I sat on a stone bench with Mrs. Bennet and Kitty, attended by the two naval officers. A dozen constables were circulating through the clustered onlookers, taking statements and directing coaches. Everywhere I heard the wondering, frightened word "dragon."

Mr. Knightley emerged from the crowd. "The rest of our party is safe. The Darcys will depart soon, but Mary wishes to stay. She is helping another wyfe who was poisoned with crawler venom. We agreed that this group should proceed to Chathford." His sweeping hand included Harriet and me. "The sooner the crowd is cleared, the better."

The officers offered to assist us in finding a carriage. That prompted the rituals that conclude an evening, comforting and ridiculous in the chaotic scene. Once Mrs. Bennet, Kitty, and Harriet finished thanking the officers, the conversation turned to Chathford House, and Harriet found herself an unexpected authority.

While she described the house in lively detail, Mr. Knightley squatted by me, his forearms on his knees. His neckcloth was missing, and his collar hung open. I stared at my dirtied gloves, not sure which was the greater risk to my sanity and wondering at my calm.

Softly, he said, "Mr. Darcy strongly suggests you stay at Chathford tonight. That creature was interested in you, and Chathford is more secure. Also, the wyverns are injured. Georgiana has soothed them, but I thought you could help." I shot him a look, and he winced. "I felt I must tell Mr. Darcy what happened at the physic garden."

That gave Mr. Darcy more reasons to imagine I was his mythic healer. I sighed but nodded. "If we are admitting things, do you know what the Darcys bound?"

"I do," he said simply.

"Is Yuánchi at Chathford?"

"Mrs. Darcy says no. That is the sole word she spoke in my presence. The crowd's gossip is of a mad woman stealing the dagger and of rogue draca, but it was the Bingleys' wyvern that killed that woman. Both the Bingleys and the Darcys are shaken to the quick. There is more to the story, but I could not ask."

That and the cold air drove a shiver through my body. A moment later, Mr. Knightley wrapped his still-warm coat around my shoulders. I gave him a grateful smile. "We missed our dance."

He made a dismissive noise, then said earnestly, "You must abandon the inn and stay at Chathford. This is not a time for pride. I will settle the bill in the morning and have your things sent."

"Pride is not what keeps me from Chathford. But for tonight, I will go."

"If you will not stay at Chathford, let me arrange other accommodation for you."

I smiled ruefully. "Would other accommodation be safer?"

"It would not cost you funds you do not have." Mortified and a little frightened, I stared at the paving stones while he continued, "A musician walks all tiers of life. I notice when Miss Woodhouse forgets her beautiful pelisse on a frosty night." When I said nothing, he added, "There is neither merit in wealth nor shame in want."

"I do not require your support," I said. Emma Woodhouse is rich.

"I know you do not. But you are welcome to my friendship. Now, let us try to find a coach."

RAVING

LIZZY

For an hour, I waited. When Darcy took my elbow, I followed him, docile, until I could wait again.

Where were the pointing fingers? The accusations?

Finally, Darcy assisted Lady Catherine, Georgiana, and me up the stair of our coach, and my daze began to break.

Despite it being the middle of the night, Darcy had found a wagon for hire, and it followed us carrying the wyverns, too hurt to fly. Jane refused to be separated from her golden wyvern, so she and Charles rode with them.

As we clattered through the streets, Lady Catherine was ashen, her jowls sagging as if she had aged a dozen years. Somehow, her ostrich feather still floated above her head. I watched it sway with our motion. It was better than meeting anyone's eyes.

"The wyverns will recover," Georgiana said. "I saw worse injuries when the army tried to apply draca in war. Draca are immensely tough."

Lady Catherine cleared her throat with a rattle. "What *are* you people?" She turned to Georgiana. "My niece sings, and wounded, crazed draca lie down like sheep. And *you*!" Her pale blue eyes pinned me. "You challenge a madwoman like some sorceress—"

"For once, hold your tongue!" Darcy snapped. "You criticized my mother through her entire life. Do not criticize my sister or my wyfe. You have no idea of what you speak."

A rough laugh split my lips. "Criticize me? Better to condemn me outright. I deserve it."

Georgiana squeezed my hand. "That is not true! It was frantic. You cannot manage every draca."

"I *killed* that woman. I condemned her because she touched the dagger." My memory of those moments was unforgivingly clear, but my reasoning was lost. Incomprehensible. Why command Jane's wyvern to attack?

"Mr. Knightley saw another dragon," Georgiana said to Darcy. "A black dragon. Is that what the dagger summoned? When that woman sang, it was like the bedrock of London awoke. Something sang an answer."

"She raised Fury," I muttered. "The dragon's name is Fènnù. It means *Fury*."

"The dagger is gone," Darcy said.

That penetrated my murk of self-despair. "What? Gone where?"

"Missing. Wellington's guards searched the area, then the buildings. Even amongst Miss Rees's... remains. Someone took it."

I closed my eyes and again tried to reach out with my mind. *Yuánchi. Where are you?* But my awareness was crammed within my own head—locked in by Yuánchi's strength, like a lunatic locked in an attic. Presumably so I would not murder more innocents. All I could sense was that he was far away.

"I assure you that I shall *not* offer my museum for future balls," Lady Catherine announced.

The horses reined in. We were at Chathford. Lady Catherine disembarked and spied our servants with a hair-thin smile, finally having someone to order about. I trusted Mrs. Reynolds would keep her in check and walked to meet the wagon. It was little more than a wheeled box of planks pulled by a single horse, the sort that delivered cheap goods to back doors throughout London.

Two pairs of scintillating wyvern eyes met mine as I arrived, astonishingly beautiful but as opaque to my mind as real gems. What had Yuánchi done to me?

Charles helped Jane down, and she pulled me into an embrace. "Dear Lizzy." I clutched her like a scared toddler and found I was leaking tears onto the shoulder of her gown.

I swallowed my sobs. "How is your wyvern?"

"They have both stopped bleeding. I do not have your gift to hear her thoughts, but"—she gazed at her crouched, tense wyvern—"she is not yet herself. She is withdrawn. Or... frightened."

"What have I done?" I whispered.

"Oh, Lizzy." She pulled me tight again. "You are my beloved sister. I wish you did not face such trials."

Here I was, unharmed, being comforted by Jane, who had almost died twice in the last year. "You are too good. But I seized your wyvern's mind savagely. You cannot imagine the power I had. I was euphoric. Intoxicated." Two disparate facts linked in my mind. "I have felt that before. It is what I sense in wyves who are dosed with crawler venom. But it flowed from the black dragon. From... Fury." I whispered her name, afraid that the sound would summon her. Or change me.

Emma and Georgiana ran up, breathing hard. Georgiana must have searched the house to find her.

"Oh." Emma's gloved fingers caught at her lips, her eyes wide at the wyverns' gashes and scrapes glistening with golden ichor.

"Help me," Georgiana said.

Emma shook her head. "I cannot."

"You can." Fearlessly, Georgiana cradled the bronze wyvern's jaw in one hand, then she took Emma's hand with her other, fingers meshing tight, and began to sing. Her voice was beautiful, the tones strange and foreign, but that was all. I did not sense the power she unleashed.

"Is something happening?" I asked uncertainly.

"Can you not feel it?" Jane asked breathlessly. Rapturously.

I turned away, digging my teeth into my lip until I tasted blood. The front door stood wide open. I went through. Lady Catherine's strident tones echoed from one direction. I turned the other way.

After two rooms, I found Darcy in quiet conversation with Charles. I did not even wait for privacy. "I killed that woman."

Darcy caught my arms, his grip firm. "That is unjust. Remember my self-recrimination after the death of Lydia. You helped me then, so apply your own counsel. You had an instant to choose—"

I shook my head. "No. Whatever madness drove Miss Rees had ended. She was harmless. I *knew* she was harmless. And Mary was holding her hand! She will never forgive me." I leaned into his body. "Miss Rees had claimed that dragon, but I... coveted him. And the black dragon seeks me. She called me her wyfe of war. Do not let me become that! Stop it!"

I stuck on that, crying *Stop it* over and over until his hands stroked my face. Darcy was always warm, but his fingers felt cold as freezing spring water. Simple surprise silenced me.

"You are burning up," he exclaimed. His icy palm pressed my forehead.

"I do not feel well." My gorge fluttered. My knees wobbled. Unconnected thoughts blurred together. I had planned to tell Jane my secret tonight—that I was with child. Had I told her? Not yet. The clash between happy anticipation and violent reality made my head spin.

The candle flames sprouted strange, round glows. The room rocked.

"I think I am tired." My knees gave way.

I WOKE IN BED. The window showed day. Blue sky, even.

There was a note in Darcy's fine hand on his pillow:

"Dear Elizabeth,

I am meeting the Council to discuss urgent events. Do not worry. Rest.

Yours in love, Fitzwilliam."

I sat up in bed. My body felt vastly better. My mind... the terror and guilt sprang to life, savage and accusing, but an obstinate, rational part woke as well, buzzing like an irritating fly and trying to impose order. To set priorities and fix problems. But a killed woman could not be fixed. I shoved my fingers into my tangled hair and pulled until my scalp ached.

What happened to me last night? A black dragon burst from the frozen Thames, and I lost my mind.

There was a soft knock, then the door opened, and Lucy stuck her head through. "I thought I heard you. Mr. Darcy asked me to check on you, but I would have, anyhow. You were raving last night! Also, he says you are to have Miss Bennet examine you."

"I see." Raving was not an encouraging report.

She helped me put on a morning dress and tidied my hair, then I went downstairs, not sure what I would find. The answer was breakfast, attended with ferocious normalcy by almost everyone—Charles and Jane, Lady Catherine, Georgiana, Emma and Harriet, Mr. Knightley, Mamma and Kitty. Only Darcy and Mary were missing.

The gentlemen rose when I entered. I greeted them and Lady Catherine, from whom I received a scowl, and then Emma and Harriet.

"Where is Mary?" I asked. I had no intention of being examined by anyone, but I was desperate to speak with her. To... apologize? Atone? I had no idea.

Kitty shrugged to my question, but Georgiana said, "Mary is not back yet. She sent a note. She is helping an injured wyfe."

"Will you find me when she comes in, please?" Georgiana nodded, her blue eyes dark and serious. Had she seen the wyvern's attack? I could not remember.

"The wyverns are much better today," Jane said to me. I nodded, feeling relief, then guilt for the pleasure of relief.

A maid entered. "Pardon me, ma'am. Lord Wellington is here." Mamma clucked and turned to fuss at Kitty's lopsided hair bun.

"Were we expecting him?" I asked the room. Heads shook, so I went with the maid.

He was waiting at the doorstep and greeted me with a nod. "Mrs. Darcy." He still wore his gray evening wear from the ball. It was wrinkled and soiled, and his eyes were bloodshot.

"Have you slept?" I asked. He shook his head. "Please come in. Breakfast is set, if you have not eaten."

"I cannot. I am to escort you to the Council."

"Did Darcy send for me?"

"Is he with the Council?" When I nodded, Lord Wellington's tired eyes narrowed. "I was with the naval command. Then I received this." He lifted an opened, official envelope. "It says I am to escort you to the Council."

"So you said." The government coach behind him had two armed soldiers perched on the back. "Am I being invited, or arrested?" The latter had a black appeal.

"We are both summoned. I choose to treat it as an invitation." For the first time, his wry smile twisted his mouth. "Perhaps my judgment should not be trusted. But I have grim news and wished to speak with you. We can talk while we ride."

WHEN THE COACH DOOR LATCHED, I decided to preempt his news. "I know the dagger is missing. That was my error. I have been a total fool."

"You and I planned the security together. Blame is useless in war. Save it until the need for action has passed." His fingers meshed restlessly. "Guilt, on the other hand, I indulge in the dead of night. A bedroom ceiling is an excellent stage for reviewing my failures."

He said that with moving honesty. What was my trial against the deaths that weighed on the commander of England's armies? "I am sorry. You have faced far more serious circumstances."

He rubbed his eyes. "I hope you are correct, but I fear otherwise. My news is worse than a missing dagger. The naval command received a communication at daybreak by messenger bird. In short, England's navy is defeated and in retreat."

"What?" I must have misheard.

"The bird was from a flotilla patrolling the Dover Narrows. There were twelve ships, including four ships of the line. The entire flotilla is sunk. Fishermen are pulling wreckage from the water. Bodies. We have no survivor account as yet."

The implication was obvious. I wet my lips, afraid of the answer. "Were they burned?"

"It seems not."

I breathed again. "That is a relief. I feared you meant the black dragon."

"I do mean the black dragon. The message was four scrawled words: 'Black wings. Black breath.' Do you understand that last part?" I shook my head. "Those few words alone would mean little. But when I add the witnesses on the Thames where the dragon rose, and those outside the museum..." His eyes met mine. "Why did the black dragon come to the museum?"

"She was summoned by the wyfe." Give her the courtesy of her name. "By Miss Rees. She summoned her with the dagger."

"Summoned *her*?"

"The dragon is female. She is called Fènnù. It is Chinese for Fury. That is all I know."

His fingers drummed the armrest. "That woman died. We captured another mad wyfe at the museum. Does she control the black dragon?"

"That wyfe was also dosed with crawler venom. She is a victim, not mad."

"Your sister Mary has been loudly insisting the same thing. She is with her. However, my question was whether that wyfe controls the dragon."

"No. She never touched the dagger. Is she recovered?"

"Slightly. Miss Bennet reports old wounds from brutal mistreatment." His tone pressed harder. "Our naval losses are not an animal lashing out. Those were military targets. Who controls the black dragon?"

My heart was thumping. "I have no idea. It may be whoever has the dagger." Sounding more defensive than I liked, I added, "It is not *me*!"

"I know that much. More's the pity." He blew an angry sigh. "A second message arrived a half hour ago, this from the French coast. It, too, is sparse, but English ships are sunk, while French ships are untouched. Not even a dragon can survey an ocean in a night, so our enemy had foreknowledge and intelligence of our positions. The third and last message was from Brighton. American warships and slave cutters are standing four miles off England's south coast, unchallenged." He gave a humorless laugh. "The English navy is dropping like mayflies. The admiral has dispatched a general order to scatter and hide. But that leaves our shores unprotected, and without naval support, our armies in Spain—*my* armies—will exhaust their supplies in weeks." He slammed his fist into the side of the carriage, rattling the glass panes. I had never seen him display physical anger, not even when he shot a man in the hills of Pemberley. "In one night, the war has turned. If we do not turn it back, England's strength will be cast down. We will be invaded."

"That cannot be possible."

"We have done it to others often enough. I assure you, they are eager to return the favor." He wedged a smile onto his lips. "You see why we are summoned. England must fight fire—or whatever 'black breath' means—with fire. The Council will ask for Yuánchi. How will you answer?"

The coach wheels chattered. The springs creaked.

"My answer will disappoint you, but hear me out." I swallowed and tried to sound sane. "There is something wrong with me. The black dragon influences me. Attracts me to... to violence. I lose myself. I dare not be involved in battle. And I am certain Yuánchi will not participate without me." Lord Wellington drew a breath, but I held up my hand. "There is more. Yuánchi has isolated me. Shielded me from my own ability. It is like being wrapped in cotton. I cannot even sense where he is. I am useless."

"If not you, the Council will try another great wyfe. They know of Miss Darcy."

I shook my head. "She cannot even speak to Yuánchi."

"Who are the others? You said there were four great wyves at the ball."

I had forgotten that. "The fourth may have been Miss Rees." But I had viewed her through draca eyes. She had no aura. And the other dosed wyfe was weaker.

"Perhaps the *third* great wyfe, then?" he said dryly.

The third was Emma.

After all I had been through with Lord Wellington, I refused to pretend ignorance, but neither would I cast her into this madness. "I have no permission to reveal her identity."

He considered me with narrow eyes. "Mrs. Darcy, I count you as a friend. I do not know the Council's plans, but do not delude yourself. England's survival is at stake. They will insist you deliver Yuánchi. Your husband may support them."

What if Darcy asked me to fight? Could I deny everyone?

I closed my eyes and reached out. London, usually a constellation of glowing draca minds, was a woolly void. Was I shielded? Or had I been permanently neutered, my skills burned away forever?

No, I still sensed one thing. My binding to Yuánchi, silver and shining.

Even if I could speak to Yuánchi—convince him or command him to fight —the thought of unleashing destruction on the French army was like sinking my fingers into a rotten carcass, abhorrent and revolting. And frightening. It would corrupt me. I would become worse than the monster we already faced.

"There must be another way," I whispered.

27

THE KING'S BENCH

LIZZY

L ord Wellington said a few words to a guard, and the iron gates of Westminster Palace yard swung wide. Cobblestones rattled the wheels as we passed through a dark, arched tunnel into a courtyard. Soldiers rushed to open the carriage and let down the step.

Lord Wellington descended first. He offered me his hand while asking an aide, "Will we meet in the Secretary's office?"

"The summons is to the King's Bench, my lord," the aide answered. Lord Wellington's grip on my fingers stiffened.

"What is the King's Bench?" I asked.

"The high court of England and her monarch. Currently, the Prince Regent, although he rarely attends. This way." He set off, fortunately at a fast pace so I could burn off nervous energy.

Like my last visit, we passed through antechambers and halls, but instead of gowned, frowning lawyers, we saw hurrying officers with grave faces. I was accompanied by the commander of England's armies, so every man bowed, sometimes with a hand at their brow in the formal military salute.

We reached an oversized pair of doors. Two guards in braid-trimmed uniforms swung them wide to reveal an even more imposing courtroom.

The War Secretary sat at the elevated judges' bench. He was dressed in his usual conservative day attire, but he was flanked by two judges in robes and wigs. Twenty other gentlemen, sporting a selection of graying whiskers and straining waistcoats, were scattered in the area for counsel and court staff, some standing, some sitting.

Loud, bickering voices halted when the doors swung open. Heads turned to us.

Lord Wellington did not move. He remained two paces from the threshold, studying the assembly. My heart beat a half-dozen times before he said softly, "Remember that I am with you."

"Is that intended to reassure me?" I whispered back.

He walked in without answering. I followed, lagging while I searched the room for Darcy. I looked twice. He was not here.

The gentlemen scurried aside as if we were contagious, but Lord Wellington took no notice. He stopped in the center of the court and addressed the War Secretary. "You requested our presence."

The War Secretary nodded. "Lord Wellington. The full War Council is assembling, and His Royal Highness will grace us as well. Please take a seat. Our interest is in your companion." He looked at me and sprouted an immense smile. "Mrs. Darcy. We appreciate you attending."

"I was summoned," I said. For the first time since I woke, my sea of bleak guilt mixed with hotter emotions. Distrust. Suspicion. "I expected my husband to be present. Where is Mr. Darcy?"

The War Secretary gave a magisterial chuckle. "Ah. We get right to it, then. That is for the best."

The crowd of gentlemen settled into chairs with creaks from aged wood and arthritic knees. Lord Wellington stayed standing beside me, but I could read nothing in his posture.

"Where is Mr. Darcy?" I asked again.

"Your husband is nearby," the War Secretary replied. "But the news I must reveal is shocking." His over-broad smile folded into stern concern. "Please sit, Mrs. Darcy. Fainting or hysterics would be natural."

The next time Mary stomped into Chathford House muttering about the male establishment, I would sympathize more. But for now, my distrust sharpened. "Say your news. If you are overcome by hysterics, I shall sit while you recover."

Disapproving whispers skated across the audience. The War Secretary scowled and adopted a solemn and official tone. "As His Royal Highness's agent, I speak for the Court of the King's Bench. Mrs. Darcy, you are present as an innocent, and you are charged with no crime. But you have been manipulated and made a pawn. Fortunately, the harm can be repaired with swift action." When I said nothing, he resumed, "Your husband, Mr. Fitzwilliam Darcy, has betrayed England. He is charged with treason."

Despite Lord Wellington's warning, that word, *treason*, was a shock. Then common sense returned. "My husband would never commit treason."

"He was arrested this morning for refusing to surrender the King's property to the Crown in time of war."

A part of my tension drained. At least I was not opposing Darcy. "Is that the purpose of this theater of intimidation? To claim Yuánchi?"

The War Secretary unfolded a paper and squinted at it. "That is the name of the creature. But the court sympathizes with the predicament of a young wyfe, freshly married and eager to serve her husband. You, Mrs. Darcy, are held harmless for your husband's transgression. In fact, the law *protects* you. Your husband's commands were unlawful, so you may do your duty. Your service can both aid your country and save your husband."

I was angry now, but was this sensible anger or the onset of madness? I chanced a look at Lord Wellington. He had been watching me, and our gazes barely grazed before he turned to the War Secretary. "Lord Castlehurst, may we speak privately? This is poorly done. And *unwise*."

The War Secretary ignored him and pronounced, "Mrs. Darcy. As a bound wyfe, you have influence over the creature known as Yuánchi. If you are able to summon it to His Majesty's service, the scales will tip toward leniency. In time, you may enjoy a happy reunion with—"

Clearly, being angry was perfectly sane. "Deliver Yuánchi for *leniency*? Sir, your words corrupt decency and common sense. There is no man more honorable or loyal than my husband. You presume in announcing his guilt. And when you claim a dragon as if he were *any* person's property, you reveal profound ignorance."

Lord Wellington broke in even more urgently. "Henry! This is madness, and it is *dangerous*. Darcy is no traitor—" Another gentleman protested, the War Secretary thumped his fist, and an argument erupted.

For a moment, I stood ignored in the ultimate court of England—even though I was guilty of killing a defenseless woman. But I was not the accused. Instead, this farce threatened an innocent man to force my compliance.

If my guilt drew judgment, so be it. But until then, guilt would not hobble me.

I closed my eyes, sinking into an awareness of draca that was shrouded in woolly silence. I concentrated, drawing my senses fully within. The bellow of men's voices faded. The world turned eerily blank.

I prodded the barrier surrounding me. Pressure turned the wool into unyielding iron, but I recognized the sensation. When I had first reached into the depths of Pemberley lake, Yuánchi had walled his self away for his centuries-long sleep. Then, it had not been force that penetrated his resistance. The strength of a human, even a great wyfe, was nothing to a dragon, but they cherished passion.

I stopped pressing and opened my heart. My love for Darcy—my fear for his safety—suffused a simple thought: *Yuánchi, I need you.*

Like a shutter cracking on a sunny day, a ray of his awareness streamed into my mind.

Child of the Lake. Why do you fear?

"They have taken my husband."

The barrier fell away. Released, my mind fell with it, then was caught and drawn into a tremendous awareness. My senses exploded. My innermost self altered.

I was soaring over blue-and-pearl ocean, rising without effort as flight muscles, bruised but healing, rode a current-warmed thermal. I banked with the lighter, wetter air, tracking the sun-violet compass through thin clouds until I faced west, and the multitude called London, and the tug of silver binding.

There was a pungent, fishy aftertaste in my mouth.

Enthralled by a hundred novel sensations, I thought, *This is more than shared vision.*

Yuánchi's answer was realization, not speech. *I have drawn our minds close so I will know if she reaches for you.*

"If Fènnù tries to take me," I whispered. Fear tinged my thoughts, then eased. I trusted Yuánchi.

My wings stroked. Descent quickened like a sled speeding down an endless hill. Air sang around my body in wind-cheating paths guided by the tensing of ridged scales.

I am coming, Yuánchi thought. *Tell these men who have taken your husband. Tell them that you are a great wyfe.*

I opened my eyes. A full dozen red-faced men were now shouting like children. Around me was wind. Below me were waves.

"Yuánchi is coming," I announced firmly and rather louder than I had intended. Surprised silence fell.

The War Secretary turned gloatingly to Lord Wellington. "There! Mrs. Darcy is quite reasonable when isolated from selfish interests." He turned to me, cloying as honey. "When Mr. Darcy is told of your service, he will thank—"

"Do not speak for my husband," I said. "He and I will do our duty to England. But duty does not answer to a court that levies false charges as extortion. When Mr. Darcy is released, then I will speak with"—I turned pointedly to Lord Wellington—"honorable members of the Council to provide what aid we may." The Thames rushed beneath my wings. "But first, release Mr. Darcy. I suggest you hurry."

The War Secretary's brow furrowed. He said to Lord Wellington. "Have you put her up to this?"

Lord Wellington threw up his hands in disbelief. "Castlehurst, have you not heard a word I said? You sought a dragon that could lay waste to an army. That dragon is *coming here*."

I spotted a door below the windows. "Does that go to the yard?" I walked toward it.

"You do not have permission to leave!" the Secretary shouted.

A portly, gray-haired gentleman harrumphed and stepped into my path. He grasped my wrists, and I stopped, astonished that a gentleman would physically accost me. I tried to pull free, and the gentleman pulled back—a stalemated tugging match.

But our contest summoned a memory. My father's battle-hardened hands once held me this same way. But not to restrain me.

It had been a lesson:

"Do not fight a man," my father—but not my father—announced in the commanding tones he used to address his army. "A man is too heavy and too strong. But his size breeds arrogance. He will grasp you like a child." He seized my scrawny forearms, so hard that it hurt. "Do not fight a man. Defeat him! Strike once. Strike hard."

The motions of our drill returned, rehearsed as a dance. I reversed my futile tugging and stepped forward, aided by the pull on my arms, and planted my heel behind the gentleman's shoe. Overbalanced, he began tipping backward. His arms lifted, and I twisted my palms hard toward my face, wrenching his wrists and breaking his grip.

His desperate, balancing backstep smacked my planted heel, and he began to fall. He had sparse, gray eyebrows and a lumpy, red-veined nose. Too much brandy, too much snuff—an old man who heaved himself into a coach to travel a hundred yards. A weak man. A harmless man.

Barely in time, I checked my blow. He teetered, arms windmilling, then crashed clumsily to the floor.

My skirt was stretched taut between my firmly placed forward foot and my half-turned rear foot. My right fist trembled by my shoulder where I had frozen my strike. Already, soft, little-used muscles in my arm were protesting.

I had never struck anyone. I had never made a fist. Not even as a child. It was unthinkable. And Papa did not have gold-hued skin, and he certainly did not teach me to fight. What had I remembered?

The gentleman was grumbling and groaning at my feet. Shock and shame roiled my mind. The room stayed silent until Lord Wellington spoke warily behind me. "Mrs. Darcy?"

Move.

I hurried to the door, banged it open, and emerged onto a stone balcony. No steps down. No other exit. Wonderful.

Yuánchi was close. West. I squinted at the sky and thought, *Did you see the memory I had? That was not my father. That was not me.*

A past life, he replied. *Each life is a part of the self. Their layers build the next mind.*

"That is how draca minds grow," I said aloud. "Not human minds."

The lives of wyves are shared with their bound draca. Their draca remember.

"That memory was from you?"

Stillness stretched. *No. From her.*

From Fènnù.

Men's voices whispered behind me. I looked back and saw faces peering out the door. Blustering, frightened faces. Pathetic. These men led England in war?

Wind rose. Yuánchi swept low into the garden, a hunter's stealthy approach that was hidden by the building. He settled with fast, short flaps that rippled the grass, tucking his wingtips to avoid walls and trees.

There were shouts and scuffling behind me, then Lord Wellington strolled up to lean on the balcony. He took a long look at Yuánchi, then a longer look at me. "May I ask what you intend?"

"I intend to retrieve Mr. Darcy," I said. "Our binding passes through me to him. Yuánchi can follow that to find him." I looked at Yuánchi and asked belatedly, *Can you?*

Yuánchi's head swiveled. *He is not far. But I will not leave you with enemies. Come down.* He took two thumping steps and crouched to lean his shoulder against the balcony.

That was unexpected. I licked my lips in the chill air. I had not intended to attempt my first mount of a dragon in front of members of Parliament. Not to mention the armed guards running into the garden, pointing at Yuánchi, then at Lord Wellington.

Lord Wellington acknowledged the guards with a relaxed wave that commanded calm, but when he spoke to me, he was soft and serious. "In the coach, you said you feared an attraction to violence. You must not commit violence to free Darcy."

"I intend to ask nicely," I said, then wondered how true that was. I had almost punched a man. But Yuánchi's awareness flowed with me, ancient and dispassionate. "Would you help me, please?" I nodded to where Yuánchi's shoulder pressed against the balcony.

Lord Wellington smiled an unreadable smile, then offered his hand. I hoisted myself to sit on the rail, held his hand while swinging my legs over, then very inexpertly slid onto Yuánchi's scales. I grabbed a knobby neck ridge for balance.

My feet now dangled fifteen feet above the courtyard. Nervously, I thought, *Could you let me down, please?* but Yuánchi sank to the ground so smoothly that I hopped off as easily as dismounting a carriage.

That worked out quite well. I waved up at Lord Wellington as a gaggle of gentlemen's faces popped over the rail on both sides.

Yuánchi strode off. I hurried to catch up, nodding to the open-mouthed guards. We rounded the building's corner, and Yuánchi set off toward an older, two-story wing. Somewhere, a bell was clanging desperately. Another dozen soldiers charged up, muskets ready and bayonets fixed, but they only stared, disbelieving, as we passed. Without Lord Wellington to reassure them, I resorted to waving and smiling as if this were a summer promenade.

Yuánchi stopped outside the building. He curled his neck to peer through a barred window on the bottom floor, and I distinctly heard Darcy's voice say, "Blazes!" I had never heard him swear before, which made me smile. He must not realize I was in earshot.

"I am here, too," I called. "I will ask for the jail manager—"

Yuánchi lifted a foot, hooked his claws through the window, and pulled.

Iron bars and foot-thick stones tumbled across the ground with a cloud of mortar dust.

"—or not," I finished.

Darcy stepped through the gaping hole. He flicked dust off his coat. "I was expecting a lawyer, not a dragon. Are you aware that the Secretary and I argued?"

"He has charged you with treason."

"A petty bluff," Darcy said dismissively. He toed a chunk of mortar on the ground. "I gather the charge is not yet dropped."

"Not officially," I admitted.

"I think we should not depart until that is resolved. Wellington!" Darcy waved to Lord Wellington, who was striding across the grass with a half-dozen ministers. And the War Secretary.

Another heated argument began, indistinguishable from the last one. I was learning that a group of arguing gentlemen has a specific sound, their voices starting low for weightiness, then popping to stridency as they become frustrated.

In a rush, exhaustion swamped me, followed by a surge of sweaty heat despite the chill morning. I leaned my shoulder on Darcy's arm. He squeezed my forearm, reassuring me, but my weakness was not nerves or relief. What was happening to me?

When Yuánchi arrived, my intense immersion in his senses had ended. I tested now to see if my awareness was restored. His presence blazed beside me, but if I focused, I could sense something beyond. I was no longer locked in.

Abruptly, the argument silenced. Darcy bowed deeply, and in reflex, I curtsied with him even before I recognized the prince a half-dozen yards away, fists on his hips, staring up at Yuánchi.

"So *this* is England's scarlet dragon," he said. "He is certainly tremendous." The prince spotted me in the group and gave a worn but sincere smile. "Wellington rushed me away from your ball. Wisely, it seems. But I did wish to speak more. Wellington praises all you Darcys, but his tales of Mrs. Darcy are especially intriguing."

Unsure how to answer that, I curtsied again. "Your Royal Highness."

The prince's smile became grim. "Entertaining stories must wait. The news is dire. I was entering the King's Bench when I heard this ruckus. But before we return to the court, I must ask..." He eyed the broken stones at our feet. "Why are you tearing apart my jail?"

I looked at Darcy, who looked at Lord Wellington, who cast a stony stare at the War Secretary. The weather seemed to chill as well. A thunderstorm was rolling in the distance.

"A misunderstanding," the War Secretary answered smoothly.

The thunder had not faded. It shook and grew. Through my freed senses, the distant presence became huge, but it was captive, trapped in cruel, oily power. Fènnù, controlled by the dagger.

And despite the rushing threat, I recognized another victim of my failure at the museum. I feared being forced into dark and violence, but I had condemned this creature, a prisoner, to that exact fate. My redemption and hers must be won together.

The sky darkened, and a twenty-foot-thick torrent of stormy black slammed down like a dark thunderbolt, smashing the High Court of the King's Bench like a crystal sculpture beneath a falling column of iron. The balcony where I had stood with Lord Wellington shattered. The walls and roof collapsed.

Yuánchi spread his wings with an unearthly howl and launched into the sky, then black covered us.

28

REVELATION

EMMA

"Here it is," I announced to Harriet. The shop doorway had a small, engraved brass panel: *Debrett & Assoc., Publishers.*

We had come directly from breakfast, earlier than any gentleman would call for business. That was my plan—be gone before Mr. Tinsdale arrived for his meeting.

I had thought less about how to begin, though.

The wool tassels on Harriet's shawl were uneven. I straightened the first, but that made it worse.

As I fixed the fourteenth, Harriet said, "Are you nervous, Miss Woodhouse?"

"No," I said. "You must call me Emma." I began fixing the other side.

Gently, her gloved fingers stilled mine. "You *are* nervous. There is no reason. I know nothing will come of this meeting. I do not know why you try." She looked up at the sky. "Should we even be out today?"

The streets were almost deserted. The few coaches rolled dangerously fast behind skittish teams, and the scarce walkers hurried, hugging building fronts and ducking from awning to awning. When they crossed roads, they cast frightened glances at the sky like mice hearing an owl's hoot.

I forced my hand away from Harriet's shawl. Mr. Darcy's touch from the ball still filled me. The perfection of her clothes was habit, not necessity.

"You are right," I admitted. "I am delaying. That is foolish. We are out today because this meeting must be today." I knocked firmly.

A harried man of thirty opened the door. He straightened oval spectacles with ink-stained fingers, then his expression became resigned. "Good morning, ladies. I am afraid that Mr. Debrett does not hear personal appeals."

"We are here for Mr. Tinsdale's appointment," I said. Harriet drew a surprised breath. I brightened my smile to compensate.

The man frowned. "You are early. That is not for an hour."

That was nearer than I had guessed, but not near enough to be a problem. I invented an explanation. "Mr. Tinsdale asked that we review the materials before he arrived."

"I see. Very well." He waved us in distractedly.

For such a prestigious publication, Debrett & Associates was both untidier and smaller than I expected. It was, however, overflowing with books. The walls were filled with shelves of mismatched, faded volumes, some as thin as a pen, others as fat as a loaf of bread. The countertops and floor were buried in crates spilling identical, thick editions, their titles embossed on the leather binding: *Debrett's Dracal Lineage of England, Scotland, and Ireland, containing all Wyves' Descent*. The odor of fresh ink and old dust tickled my nose.

We picked through the mess and arrived at an open office door. Our guide announced "Mr. Tinsdale's associates" and departed without a backward glance.

Mr. Debrett was white-haired and spindly, with wrinkled skin like parchment, but he maneuvered vigorously around his desk and extended his hand. I shook it and gave my name.

"Would that be the Woodhouses of Surrey?" he asked.

"It would," I said.

"That is very favorable! A rare and potent maternal bloodline. The 1764 wyvern."

He shook hands with Harriet. He could hardly rattle off the history of Smiths, but as we sat, he gave her a lingering glance. "Given the nature of Mr. Tinsdale's request, you are not the associates I would expect."

"Whatever do you mean?" I said. Perhaps he would explain the purpose of Mr. Tinsdale's appointment. That would be convenient as I had not the slightest idea.

"Well... ladies on business is unusual enough, although I am told there is demand. The Prince himself is scouring shops for some new novel 'by a lady.'"

He sniffed. "I do not publish fiction. Although I have considered it. The business of print is an endless struggle... though I suppose... if it were lucrative?" He ended with a tentative smile, as if expecting us to present a manuscript.

"It was not our being ladies that surprised you," Harriet said. I had not expected her to chime in.

"Ah. Well, that brings us to the nature of Mr. Tinsdale's request. It has weighed on me these last few days, so I am afraid I must decline." He gave a sheepish shrug. "There are those who say 'business is business,' you know. But my life's work is documenting English binding. Mr. Tinsdale's terms are generous, but an edition that purged wyves due to ancestry"—politely, his wrinkled fingers acknowledged Harriet—"would be indefensible. There is no deficit of affinity in women of foreign blood. Draca were once bound in the Far East and Africa. The English monopoly on draca is a comparatively recent phenomenon, and due solely to the absence of draca beyond our shores. I call it the 'Anglo-Saxon dracal migration' and it is a puzzle, although a comforting one for an old Englishman like myself. Can you imagine if there were American wyves? Draca in log cabins!" He snorted as if caught off-guard by his own humor.

Flatly, Harriet said, "Mr. Tinsdale requested an edition that lists only white wyves."

"That would be the effect of his criteria," Mr. Debrett said. "He wished to title it, *Strong Blood, Strong Britain*. But you know this already."

No gentleman would marry a lady thought unable to bind. If that edition became accepted, women of color would be purged from the gentry in a generation. It was a duplicitous, hateful scheme, and it would have been frighteningly easy if Mr. Debrett shared that prejudice.

Mr. Knightley had warned that Mr. Tinsdale would never help Harriet. But the very vileness of Mr. Tinsdale's plan could help us now.

"Mr. Debrett," I said. "We are not visiting as Mr. Tinsdale's associates. I find his project quite repugnant."

"Oh." Mr. Debrett relaxed into his chair, relieved.

"I merely require your assistance to document the right to bind of Miss Harriet Smith. Due to an accident of missed records, her history is regretfully lost." I laughed delicately. "You must agree that her status as a lady is evident."

Mr. Debrett's posture stiffened. "I fear there has been a misunderstanding. As I have said, *Debrett's Dracal Lineage* is forged on integrity. This has been a charming visit, but I document verifiable records, not personal appeals. I cannot help you."

Harriet rose, more dignified and ladylike than I had ever seen her. "You are very clear, sir. We are sorry for taking your time."

I held up my hand. "Harriet, wait."

The bluntness of his answer, and Harriet's grace, and that word, *records*, spun in my mind and became resolve. My third secret must be revealed.

I drew a deep breath. "Harriet Smith has the right to bind. I can prove that Miss Smith is gentry."

Mr. Debrett eyed me skeptically. "Prove it?"

I beckoned Harriet. Uncertainly, she sat back down. I turned to her and squeezed her palm between mine. "Dear Harriet, I can think of no other way to say this but the simplest. We are sisters."

She shook her head. "Miss Woodhouse. I am embarrassed. It is time we left."

"I swear it is true. We share a father. You are the natural daughter of my papa, Mr. Woodhouse, a gentleman. He told me with his last breaths."

She became still. "That cannot be," she whispered. "I met my father. A tradesman."

"You met a tradesman who owed my father a great deal of money." I opened my reticule, pulled out a bundle of papers—I had carried them to the ball, unwilling to leave them unprotected in our rented room—and held them for her. She shook her head, tears swelling in her eyes, so I placed them on Mr. Debrett's desk. "He owed one hundred and twenty pounds. Papa canceled the debt after he went to Mrs. Goddard's school and pretended to be your father. A gentleman should have revealed himself to you, but Papa... did not intend to do so. He thought offering a tradesman was a kindness compared to silence." Hot tears of shame ran down my cheeks. Shame, but relief, too. "He regretted it."

Harriet stared, her lips a little apart. "Why did you not *tell* me?"

"I... I do not know. I was stunned when he told me. Ashamed for how he treated you. For how I had treated you."

"How *you* treated me? You are so kind to me. You have been my dearest friend." She drew back. "Is this why?"

"No! We were fast friends before I knew. Our friendship is why Papa confessed to me. Why he changed his mind."

Mr. Debrett was leafing through the pages on his desk. "Mrs. Goddard's was your boarding school?" Harriet nodded without looking away from me, and he continued, "There are receipts for each year's fees, paid through a London lawyer." He chuckled. "You would be astounded by how many natural children I discover. They spring up like daisies. But it is rare they are so well documented."

Harriet's stillness broke. Her hand flew to her mouth. "My mother! Do you know who she is?"

"I know her Christian name. Abigail."

"Is she alive?"

"She survived your birth. Then she moved away. I do not know where." Harriet's hands muffled her shocked cry. I drew a shaky breath and said it more bluntly—harder for me but perhaps easier for Harriet. "She did not abandon you easily. Papa arranged to send her away. I am sorry. That is all I know."

In a surge of skirts and fury, Harriet stood. "It was lies. *You* lied to me. You are ashamed of me."

"No, Harriet! I promise. I had just lost Papa. It was all so strange..."

"Strange!" She gave a crazed laugh.

"I had to think of what to do," I said desperately. "How to protect..."

Protect what? My father's reputation? My fortune? The weeks after Papa's death had been a whirlpool of grief and confusion and then—slowly—wonder and love.

Why had I waited? "I should have told you sooner. But Papa said—" I stopped.

Harriet's voice was soft. "What did he say?"

My hands twisted in my lap. "He was not well. His mind was confused."

"He said not to acknowledge me." Her voice sharpened. "Not even to *tell* me?"

Without warning, she ran from the room. I ran after her, slipping on books, then catching the outside door as it bounced after her exit.

She stood motionless a few steps into the street, her back to me.

I stopped an arm's length behind. "Harriet. Papa is gone. I am struggling to honor his dying wishes. I am failing, over and over. But he told me his wish for you. You are to have the life you deserve. You should marry a gentleman, and bind, and be a lady." My voice broke. "I am trying to achieve that."

Mr. Debrett emerged from the door, my papers in his hand. He saw us, then looked awkwardly aside, *hmming* to himself as if admiring the deserted street.

"Will you ever forgive me?" I said.

Slowly, wordlessly, Harriet extended her hand behind her back. I touched her fingers, and for a moment, she squeezed mine.

A large, private coach, four-horsed and gleaming with black lacquer, was clattering down the street. It rolled to a stop in front of us. The footman glared at us, then opened the door.

Mr. Tinsdale stepped out and said in a puzzled tone, "Miss Woodhouse."

I smiled despite my wet cheeks. "Your pardon, sir, we are departing. You should know that Mr. Debrett has declared Miss Harriet Smith to be a documented wyfe. I am certain she will bind brilliantly. She has extraordinary affinity to draca."

Mr. Debrett passed me my papers. "She is at least properly documented. I look forward to listing her in our next edition." He gave Mr. Tinsdale a cool smile. "I am afraid that Miss Smith and the many wyves like her make your proposal of an expurgated edition impossible."

I waited for Mr. Tinsdale to show embarrassment at his exposure. Or frustration at being denied. But he simply answered, "What of the other project?"

"The... uh... *personal* research?" Mr. Debrett flicked a glance toward Harriet and me.

"Proceed," Mr. Tinsdale said. "There is nothing secret about it. On the contrary."

Mr. Debrett fell into a businesslike tone. "I confirmed your relation to the royal family. You are eighteenth in line to the throne. Although that separation will grow as heirs are born and then the next generation." He laughed politely. "When one is more distantly related, the line of succession changes rapidly."

"It does," Mr. Tinsdale said gravely. There was a silence.

Mr. Debrett resumed, suddenly chattering and nervous. "Historically, the succession is more malleable than the layman presumes. Parliament may even alter the Act of Settlement. The wyves' movement has achieved notable support for abolishing male primogeniture. But you would know more of that than I."

"I would," Mr. Tinsdale said. He looked up at the sky. "I think I shall return home. For safety."

Mr. Debrett followed his upward gaze. "Safety?" he said uncertainly.

Mr. Tinsdale smiled. "Have you not read today's newspaper? I should think it would fascinate a man of your profession." His voice strengthened like an actor's, and he recited, "'Behold a great red dragon, having seven heads and ten horns, and seven crowns upon his heads.'" His voice dropped to a carrying whisper. "'And there was war in heaven.'"

He bowed to Mr. Debrett, then to me, then—with mocking formality—to

Harriet, to whom he added, "Miss Smith." He entered his coach. The driver whipped the horses to a gallop, and they raced down the empty street.

Mr. Debrett turned to Harriet and me. "Was there news today? I slept in the office."

Harriet looked at me, as if I could provide a neat explanation of a pair of dragons at the British Museum.

"There are—" I began, then my voice faltered. Scarlet had tugged my heart. I began walking to the street corner. "A dragon rose from the Thames."

Mr. Debrett hurried beside me. "A draca, you mean? Was it witnessed? There are historical accounts of draca from water. Was it a greater draca? The arrival of a firedrake would be extraordinary."

We reached the corner, and the Thames opened to our left. I pointed. "I meant a dragon. Although that is not the one from the Thames."

Yuánchi was gliding above the ice, his sunlit wings spanning a third of the river. With a flick of his wing tips, he rose over a bridge, then skimmed the ice again. He banked, effortless as a soaring gull, and vanished behind the riverside wall of Westminster Palace.

Mr. Debrett pushed stiff fingers through his gray hair. They stopped halfway, leaving him in a pose of shock.

On my other side, Harriet said, "Why would he fly in broad daylight?"

"He was summoned," I said. I could feel it in the Darcys' binding, a tautness in my borrowed scarlet strength.

We watched for a minute, but Yuánchi did not emerge.

A rolling rumble began. Like thunder, but endless. Like a waterfall, but stupendous. It was behind us.

I turned just as a monstrous black form blew over the rooftops above us. Windowpanes rattled. A wind of biting cold swept the road, tossing leaves and papers.

There was only a hint of shape—a suggestion of head and the leading edges of wings. The rest was billowing black cloud, darker than thunderstorm and blacker than coal. Straight as an arrow, the trail stretched toward the palace, a roiling, soiled path that widened unnaturally fast and blotted the day.

I hugged my arms close, shivering. My exhalation misted, and flecks of frost landed on the fringe of my bonnet and my eyelashes. My drawn breath was a knife of cold in my lungs.

"What is that?" Mr. Debrett gasped through chattering teeth.

The black cloud obscured Westminster Palace. It writhed and rolled, then ripped open in golden radiance, brighter than the sun. We shouted inarticulate, amazed cries, shielding our eyes. The buildings around us glared, too brilliant to be distinguished, then darkened in dazzled gloom. My heart beat once, twice, then the air itself struck us, sharp as being slapped with a thick book. Shopwindows smashed as if kicked.

"Get inside," Mr. Debrett shouted, pulling us toward his shop. "It is a hurricane."

"It is dragons," I said, but he could not hear me.

PART II

PEMBERLEY

MARY BENNET

MARY

Mary Bennet's journal, 1st day of December, 1812:

After eight creeping days, our coaches near Pemberley. The earth, frozen in this darkest season, is further chilled by war, but Georgiana, a being of music, hums and sketches. She sits opposite me, undisturbed by the clunks and slips of our wheels upon rutted snow.

While her sable lashes are lowered, I stare, entranced, and dream. We coast on the sunlit ocean's surface, dare the twin perils of Scylla and Charybdis with hands clasped, conquer dangerous tempests to leave behind this hostile land of Britain and settle mythically, a saved pair of lovers—

"What are you writing?" Emma asked me. She sat beside Georgiana. Harriet was beside me, while Lizzy and Mr. Darcy rode in another carriage with Lord Wellington. We had been stopped on the road for ten minutes.

I lifted my pen, feeling the shape of that last word, *lovers*.

"A draft of a letter," I muttered. "A ruined one." That word must not be set in ink.

My writing desk was balanced in my lap. I used the quill knife to cut the page from my journal, then a few strokes with an over-wet nib soaked the last passage to soggy black. I folded the page and tore it in halves, quarters, eighths.

Emma turned her bold eyes and blonde curls to Georgiana. "What are *you* doing?"

"Drawing," Georgiana answered, melodious even in that single word. Her slim fingers, their oval nails brusquely short for the keyboard, held a pencil. A sheet of artist's paper rested on her drawing board.

"May I see?" Emma asked.

Georgiana held up the paper, angled so Harriet and I could see as well. It was I—no, it was some romanticized alternate of me, blurred and contemplative, stilled and tense. Seduced. Seductive.

Emma looked between the sketch and me, then beamed at Georgiana. "You are accomplished at everything! It is quite unfair."

An angry twinge tightened my scalp. Beautiful, broken, gifted Emma, who dotes on Georgiana, and when she tires of that, fascinates my sister's husband, and when that grows dull, winds my friend Mr. Knightley tighter around her little finger.

"It looks just like Mary!" Harriet cried; then to me: "I mean, it is just how you *seem*, with your hair down that way you like. But it is a strange drawing. Is it modern?"

Harriet had changed. It was subtle yet sure. The balance between her and Emma had leveled.

Georgiana answered, "Fitz studied the Pemberley paintings for days to choose my drawing tutor. He picked Mr. John Martin, who insists I 'free my hand' from classical style, so I suppose it is modern. Mary does the same thing with her music. I think it suits her." Her sapphire gaze studied me. "I am to paint as well as draw. Shall I make this into a painting?"

Georgiana's paintings burst with color and passion. The thought heated my cheeks. "What would you do with a painting of me?" Georgiana's lips crooked, and the heat spread to my shoulders.

Emma wrinkled her nose. "You must have used up your entire pencil to draw all that *black*."

There was not a thread of black on Emma. Today, she wore one of her yellow and gold gowns, although it was hidden by a khaki wool coat—one borrowed from Lizzy. Some unfathomable whim of fashion.

Georgiana resumed humming. F major. Telemann. I flipped through his scores in my mind's eye. Fantasia No. 5.

Outside, men's voices called out. Harriet sat up excitedly. "Are we near Pemberley?"

"Not yet," Georgiana said. She cleared a spot on the steamed window. "There is another hill before the house. A mile to go." Matter-of-factly, she added, "We have been within the estate for some time."

Outside, I spotted a stout, frowning man wrapped in layers of wool. He gestured angrily at the row of stopped coaches. I leaned and saw an officer and Mr. Darcy listening. "The court protocol man wants the coaches to arrive in a different order. Even though we are disguised and indistinguishable."

"I suppose the Prince must be first," Emma said. "Or should it be the King, even though he is mad? Or is it reversed, and the royal family comes at the end?"

"I imagine that is the debate," I said dryly.

Our caravan was ten coaches, twenty soldiers, and three wagons. A blind spy would guess this was the royal family fleeing London. But Yuánchi had overflown Pemberley's woods for months without a rumor. Pemberley had no spies. It was Camelot-like, as if honor were extant, not a fable.

But our flight to Pemberley was driven by fear, not honor. Only Yuánchi could turn Fènnù aside, and Yuánchi was at Pemberley, so to Pemberley we ran. And fear was justified. Brighton Pavilion, the prince's favored home, had been leveled and four royal cousins killed. Half of Westminster Palace was rubble, and thirty members of Parliament dead. Even a wing of Windsor Castle, that edifice of stone, had been razed, mere minutes after Lord Wellington's men hustled the mad king and his keepers to safety.

And though only Yuánchi could turn Fènnù aside, even Yuánchi was overmatched. The dragons' battle over London had been a clash of gods. Whole stands of buildings were crushed, the worst London disaster in a hundred and fifty years. In the end, the black dragon turned to other targets, but Yuánchi had fled, wounded, to shelter at Pemberley. Now the royal court scurried north while the remade French invasion force, *l'armée des côtes de l'océan*, landed with American slavers on the shores of south England.

"Will you draw me?" Emma asked Georgiana.

To avoid hearing her answer, I pushed open the carriage door and stepped onto the road.

The hills spread, sunlit and spottily snowed. I walked a few paces from the coach. The turf gave little squishes and creaks under my boots: thawed. The great freeze had been worse in London than the north, but when Fènnù left the Thames, the cold spell broke. The freeze followed the black dragon, winter made a weapon.

Emma stepped down next. "I will check on Nessy." She headed to Nessy's coach, her steps effortlessly balanced on a grassy fringe to avoid the mud. I scowled at her back. Beautiful, goodhearted Emma, gifted with healing. I had lugged a traveling chest with twenty pounds of medical texts.

After the violence in London, fear gripped the city. Everyone with a country estate or relatives in the north sent their children to safety. Lizzy had shuttered the school, sending the older children to the Lambton school, near Pemberley, and the younger children to the Bingleys' Hertfordshire estates. But Lizzy had been loath to separate from Nessy, nor did I want Jane to care for a consumptive child. Most London physicians ascribed consumption to smoky air, or uncooked milk, or said it was a cancer, a hereditary defect of the lower class, but I supported a neglected theory ninety years old: the cause was a slow and invisible contagion. Purging class bias revealed the truth: the poor died in droves because they were crammed in tiny rooms. So Nessy traveled with us, but I insisted she isolate in a private coach.

Despite my irritation, I called to Emma, "Keep the windows open while you are with her." I sounded petulant even to myself.

Georgiana came down next and took my hand. Softly she said, "Are you jealous?"

"Evidently," I said sourly; then self-mockingly: "Ferociously."

She whispered in my ear, "You are everything to me."

"Be careful."

"I have no cares at Pemberley. This is my home."

Other carriage doors opened. Even royalty grows tired of sitting. The coach before ours disgorged two uniformed attendants, then the prince, fifty years old, swinging his arms beside his overfed stomach. Georgiana and I curtsied; she did not release my hand. When we rose, a smile played on his lips. "Miss Darcy. Miss Bennet." There was a thoughtful pause before he strode toward the courtier of protocol.

"Be *careful*," I repeated.

"Twice!" she teased. "Are you my elder sister?"

I gave a crooked smile. "I have seen more of the world than you."

"I have been to France and Greece. You have not."

"Last year, Curate Mincekeep rallied his mob against witches at the doorstep of Longbourn. Yesterday, I read the newspaper accounts from Brighton. The invaders persecute those with dark skin, and 'unnatural' men and women vanish into their jails as well. There are no champions for the nonconformant, here or there."

Seriously, she whispered, "Pemberley is safe," and squeezed my hand before returning to the coach. I curled my fingers, preserving her warmth.

Iridescent blue flashed as a feathered draca landed in the tree beside me. It appeared very like the one from London. Whimsically, I called up, "Did you follow all this way?" He cocked his head, a spectacular songbird until you noticed the scaled face.

I visualized a page of a different Telemann, Fantasia No. 8, and whistled the first few notes.

He sang those back, then sang the rest of the phrase.

That was unexpected. "Have I played that for you?"

A second blue-feathered draca winged to the branch. I had never seen two together. The scales on their faces differed. The first was unquestionably the draca from London.

They piped the opening four bars of the Fantasia in two-part harmony, every note perfect although raised an octave. Alongside the coaches, wig-adorned heads turned. I stood uneasily, the image of Telemann's score lodged in my mind while the notes danced.

A third blue draca flipped to a neat landing at my feet. They were astonishingly adept fliers, agile as barn swallows and having the same forked tail, but as large as robins.

More heads turned. I muttered, "Shoo," and kicked a clod of dirt. The draca winged away.

Emma was not the only one with someone to care for. I walked to the coach behind ours, tapped on the coach door, and called, "Miss Bathurst?"

There was a rustle, then the door unlatched, and a drawn, freckled woman's face smiled hesitantly. "Miss Bennet. I was asleep."

"You should sleep, then." She was still recovering from ingesting crawler venom at the ball.

"No. I do not want to. Please join me."

I climbed in and closed the door. "Let me check your bandages." Obediently, she turned her back. I had helped her dress in this nightgown, the drawstrings removed to keep it loose. The bandages around her shoulders and upper back looked and smelled clean, but I unwound a strip to check. The scabs were crusted and rising into angry red scars, but dry. "The cuts are no longer weeping. That is good, but they will become very itchy. You must not scratch." The back of her head nodded obediently.

Gently, I felt the ring of bruises around her neck. At the ball, those had been hidden by a velvet choker. I had rather liked chokers, but after her halting reve-lations of captivity, the thought of wrapping a throat for decoration turned my stomach.

I pulled her blanket up to end the examination. "Your back is healing well. I must find you a proper dress at Pemberley. We will be overrun with royals." That emerged with ill-advised distaste, so I forced a light tone. "Perhaps you will be introduced to the Prince." I lifted her chin with a finger, watching her pupils shrink in the brightness. "How are the cravings?"

"Strong," she said simply. "That poison was so foul. It burned my tongue. But if I even think of it..." A pink flush colored her freckled skin. "I do not shake anymore, at least."

"I think it is like laudanum dependency. That requires weeks of recovery." Her face fell, so I added, "You *will* recover. This was done to you, but you can undo it. You have triumphed through the hardest days. Pemberley has refer-ences on draca and crawlers. An index listed crawler venom. When we arrive, I shall read that for advice."

"I am much better. My memories are less clouded. You make me feel brave enough to speak of them." She drew a long breath. "Mary, they have another woman captive."

An unwanted image of a woman, butchered and dying, snapped into my mind, crisp as an anatomist's diagram. I hid it behind an image of the Pemberley library index. "Do you mean Miss Rees? She also attended the ball."

"Not poor Joane. I know she was killed. It was another woman. They brought her only a day before the ball. She was not yet... fully tested."

"Then you must tell Lord Wellington and Mrs. Darcy." They had inter-viewed Miss Bathurst once already, seeking clues about the captive wyves.

"No!" She clutched my sleeve. "Can I not tell you instead? Mrs. Darcy scares me. After I swallowed venom at the ball, I felt her come for me. She was dark and howling. She was like crushing ice..."

That was unnervingly similar to Lizzy's own description, but I said, "That was fantasy from the poison."

Miss Bathurst bit her lip. "Pardon me. Of course. She is your sister."

"Tell me what you remember, and I will tell them."

"When we were first... caught... they tested us with the venom. To see how strong we were. Only those who survived were brought to be imprisoned in the house."

A lump settled in my stomach. "Some did not survive?"

"Most did not," she whispered. "The man who hurt me was so cruel. Worse than an animal, as animals are not mindfully evil. He joked about how only the best-bred English wyves survived, but it was not really a joke. They argued endlessly about how to choose unmarried women with strong draca affinity. Should it be status? The family's history of binding? For the last wyfe, they chose a friend of Joane, although Joane's mind was so lost by then, I do not think she recognized her." She pinched the black fabric of my dress. "She wore the same clothes as you and Joane. I heard her name, but I cannot recall it…"

Joane had only one good friend among the Marys. Frightened, I almost blurted it out, but that would compromise her answer. When interviewing, the patient's lips speak truth, not the doctor's.

Carefully, I prompted, "Miss Bottle? Something like that?"

"Spoon! Miss Spoon."

My heart froze. "I know her." Not only as a marcher for women's rights, but as a composer of beautiful melodies for the clavichord. She was my good friend, one of the founders of our ladies' musical salon, and now a captive to these monsters.

FANG, SCALE, AND CLAW

LIZZY

"Welcome back, Mrs. Darcy." Mrs. Reynolds curtsied, her head bowed and her back pole-straight, her black gown brushing the granite steps of the main entrance to Pemberley House.

She had not batted an eyelash when I arrived alone and on foot. She simply summoned the staff, now arrayed in two angled wings. Their curtsies and bows followed hers in rank order.

Pemberley was without a butler, so Mrs. Reynolds led the household. When Darcy and I married, there were sixteen servants. That was skeletal for a house this size, but Darcy had blocked hiring for three years while he interviewed butlers and found fault with every applicant. That amused me when I heard—we never had a butler at Longbourn, a vastly smaller house, so the idea was a novelty—and it was irrelevant while we spent time in London. Now, though, I regretted it. A royal visit was a tremendous burden for Mrs. Reynolds alone.

Mrs. Reynolds permitted herself a glance down the empty road. "Will the master be joining you?"

"Shortly," I said. "He is enmeshed in a fuss with the coaches a mile back. The delay is deliberate so I may address the staff." I smiled at Lucy, now officially my lady's maid, so she stood at Mrs. Reynolds's right. Lucy gave me a fleeting grin, but the rest of the staff were stiff and uneasy, their gazes fixed on the horizon. Except for one footman studying the clouds. I watched Mrs. Reynolds eye him, her lips compressing. He would hear about that.

"What have they been told?" I said.

"To prepare for a large party of guests, madam. Only that. As you directed."

Was that the cause of their mood? We did not entertain heavily, but guests were hardly unusual. Anonymous guests, though, were strange. Or was it the war? Every newspaper screamed of the invasion of south England.

Or was their discomfort nearer?

I addressed the group. "Good afternoon. I am certain you all long since discovered that Mr. Darcy and I are bound to a dragon. His name, if that information has not yet spread to every ear, is Yuánchi. Mr. Darcy has appreciated your polite silence and discretion on your master's behalf. However, I must now speak openly."

Tense expressions relaxed. Eyes dared curious glances, both at me and the sky. That confirmed my theory for the source of their tension.

Mrs. Reynolds said firmly, "The staff's discretion is on *your* behalf, madam. Pemberley's wyves are her jewels."

There were many nods. Most of this staff had served Lady Anne. Now that I had seen Emma's struggle, they must have kept many secrets. Not to mention concealing Georgiana's abilities.

"Then I thank you, myself," I said. "I know you have also heard of terrible destruction caused by a dragon. That was not Yuánchi. Another dragon is loose in the world, and she fights for England's enemies. The war, distant for so many years, has invaded our shores." The gazes converged on me. I chose my next words carefully. "Pemberley has a service to perform. We will shelter His Royal Highness the Prince Regent, His Majesty the King, members of the royal family, and members of the royal court." I expected exclamations, but there was disciplined silence. "Whatever secrecy you practiced before must be doubled. The enemy seeks to strike the monarchy. If any rumor escapes, the enemy will come here." I paused, then words I had not intended came to my lips. "We are not soldiers. I do not seek war. But if war comes to Pemberley, I will defend it."

I nodded to Mrs. Reynolds, and she dismissed the staff. Lucy waited with her while the rest hurried to work, resolute.

When we were alone, I said, "When did you two arrive?"

"Four days ago," Mrs. Reynolds said, then added dryly, "It seems your troop was slow." We had departed London at the same time.

"You cannot imagine the inanity of the courtiers," I said feelingly. "I would despair for England if not for a few bright minds in the mix. But most of our delay was due to Lord Wellington's stealth. We could hardly stop at town inns. Are the kitchens open? Larder stocked?"

"All as ready as can be. Pemberley will not fail you."

"The Prince has brought a head of household, and an annoying man who obsesses over protocol, and a head of court who noses into everything. You shall have your hands full. Let me know when it becomes impossible, and I will attempt to intervene."

"Certainly, Mrs. Darcy." Mrs. Reynolds's eye had a steely glint. I suspected she would need little help. "Rooms and meals are well enough, but I am concerned for entertainment."

"Entertainment?" I echoed, rather densely.

"Guests of rank expect to be entertained." Primly, she added, "From what I have read, the Prince is easily bored. Bored guests make trouble. Or do foolish things. Ride off and be seen."

"You are very wise. I did not consider it. See what you can invent." She nodded. A shiver climbed my spine. "But nothing frivolous, please. London ended horribly. I could not stand an endless ball."

Lucy had listened. Now she said, "You look tired. Shall I call for tea?"

"Thank you, but no. I must see Yuánchi."

I TRIED to steady my voice. "Can you fly?"

Yuánchi stretched his wings, filling the clearing where Lucy and I stood. There were uneven ridges where tears in his wing membranes had healed. On his breast, a two-foot-long scar was mending to a line of misaligned scales. Ugly as they appeared, the injuries were vastly less frightening than his condition when he fled London.

I flew last night. Launching from flat earth hurt, but in the air, I was only stiff. I will jump from a ridge next time.

"Please be discreet. Lord Wellington has spread false rumors that the scarlet dragon lives in a watery cave in Wales. He even added some story about their flag. But Mr. Tinsdale is a traitor, and he knows you and I are bound. Neither your presence at Pemberley nor mine can be known."

In the past, Yuánchi responded to such cautions with an overconfident snort. Now, he shifted warily, muscles rippling.

"We've been feeding him well," Lucy piped up, so intrigued that her carefully practiced lady's grammar faltered. "Three sheep a day. The gardener brings them up."

"Thank you."

Peevishly, Yuánchi thought, *I do not like sheep in winter.* His recovery had eased my concerns enough that I laughed.

"What is it?" Lucy asked.

"He does not like the fleece in his teeth."

"Oh." She looked up at those black teeth, eight feet above her head. "A cow, then? Snap once for yes."

Yuánchi showily bit the air.

My eyebrows rose, and I thought bemusedly, *Snap once for yes?*

You were not here. This one is helpful. His gaze turned to where the house lay, hidden by forest and a rise of hill. *They come.*

"You can see through that?"

I sense great wyves.

Wyves, plural. Emma. She had insisted on continuing Nessy's care, and returning to her home south of London seemed dangerous, so she had joined us. Certainly, Pemberley had room.

Three great wyves together. It seemed a portent.

To Lucy, I said, "Would you go to the house and tell Mr. Darcy where I am, please?"

She planted her fists on her skinny hips. "I must stay to keep you safe!" I cocked my head toward Yuánchi, and she relaxed sheepishly, then trotted off.

Yuánchi settled to the earth, his motions lithe and powerful. Any stiffness was too subtle for my human eyes. He ended with his belly and chest buried in the scraggly winter grass, but he did not sprawl sideways to relax. One massive foot landed firmly at each side, his posture alert.

Ask your questions.

Each day since the battle over London, I had pressed him for information. Each day, I was rebuffed. Now, facing his bulk and surrounded by towering, ancient trees, I felt suddenly small.

"Is there some rule I break by asking these things? Some law or custom of draca?" He waited. "Very well. Humans call the black dragon Fènnù. It means Fury. Why is she called that?"

That is her human name. A dragon name is a song.

"Then who named her? The word is Chinese. So is your name. Do you know what China is? What a country is?"

A country is a house like your war castles, but the walls are imagined. He huffed dismissively. *Countries change like clouds, and they vanish when I sleep.*

I sighed. "I asked a poor question. I will try to be specific, but you must explain things in human terms. Otherwise, we shall not get anywhere. I wish to understand the black dragon."

Why? Yuánchi's tone was simply curious, even though he had fought the black dragon twelve days ago.

"Lord Wellington would answer that she is a weapon, ravaging England for our enemies, so she must be destroyed. But he is a military man. To me, she is a mystery. When she rose from the Thames, her mind overcame mine until you protected me. The next day, when you battled above London, I felt her reach for me again." I licked dry lips. "It is not only she. I am attracted to her, as well. The visions I had of past wyves show her, never you. Are they her memories?"

They are wyves' memories. Wyves she has bound. Draca bind to learn what we do not know. Love. Passion. She keeps memories of her bound wyves after they are bone and dust. There was stillness, then, *We all keep memories. The memories of a lost wyfe are treasures.*

That was comprehensible, at least. "In the visions, I saw moments of vengeance and violence. I know I am the wyfe of war. You need not prevaricate about that. Fènnù called me that, and so did you when we bound. But I have been interpreting that label through human concepts. What does a *dragon* mean by wyfe of war?"

The passions of wyves burn bright. An ordinary wyfe is a candle. A strong wyfe, a torch. A great wyfe is a sun. All wyves have... colors. Your passion is the color of a wyfe of war.

"Are there human words for the color of a wyfe of war? Is it anger?"

It is steel and courage and sacrifice.

"Not... madness?" My throat was thick. I swallowed, tasting salt. "Or cruelty? I killed a woman, and I felt no regret. Not until after. When I did it, there was..." I could not voice those words. Pleasure. Triumph.

The one you call Fènnù is broken. The fragments of her mind overcome the wyves she binds. Even when she was whole, she chose wyves seeking strength to right wrongs. When she lost her song, only battle remained. Now, the songs of all dragons are unfinished.

"I need a poet to interpret these unsingable songs," I muttered. I rubbed at a growing ache in my temples. "Well, what is the dagger, then?"

Nothing. Daggers are human things.

"This dagger is a dragon's tooth. Fènnù's tooth, unless there is another dragon larger than you."

Scales rattled as Yuánchi stiffened his wings. *You did not say it was a tooth.*

"I was not sure at first. Did I never tell you?"

In answer, Yuánchi's thoughts filled my mind, but they lilted like a woman's voice: *Fang, scale, and claw. Then death, they saw.*

Well, that was different. I heard Yuánchi's thoughts as words, but that was a comfortable illusion. If I concentrated, his words, like those of wyverns, had no sound. No syllables. They were comprehension without hearing. But this had been true mimicry of a spoken voice.

"That *is* poetry," I said. "Do draca write poetry?"

Those are human words. I woke to a call and crossed seas to the wyfe who called me. She spoke those words. Even then, she told a lost story. Three great wyves had gathered three great items—fang, scale, and claw—to heal the broken song. But they failed and died.

"You crossed seas to reach England?" Yuánchi cocked his head uncertainly, and I blew out a frustrated breath. "England is the large island on which we sit. It is not built of imaginary lines. Neither does it vanish while you sleep. Did you cross seas to come to this island? To find *that* wyfe?"

Yes, he thought, sounding mildly chagrined.

"You must have come from the East, as you had a Chinese name." Yuánchi snorted reprovingly, as if logic were distasteful, but I forged on, "The great wyves gathered the dagger and two other items to heal Fènnù. Or they tried. They failed. Then you came here."

I did not say all that. Those wyves are gone. I do not hold their memories.

"What *exactly* are fang, scale, and claw?"

Yuánchi's head swung, examining me from several angles. Finally, in a fussy tone, he thought, *Exactly, they are three human words. You called them poetry.*

"So I did," I sighed. This was giving me a profound headache. "The dagger summoned Fènnù from the ice. But I do not believe the dagger is a weapon. It was in none of my visions, so it came after Fènnù's mind was broken. I think it was made as a cure." Yuánchi was eyeing me as dubiously as faceted jewel eyes could manage. "But weapon or cure, we must recover it. If our enemies have it, England will lose this war."

A SMALL THING

EMMA

Pemberley House was a massive three-story manse of silver granite, stately and unfamiliar, situated on a grassy rise. Behind, the hill climbed to a peak crowned with ancient forest.

Harriet and I stopped in the entry, amazed by the decorations for the royal visit. Narrow, ten-foot-tall tapestries showed winter scenes of frozen lakes, snowy forests, and proud elk, all agleam with silver thread. Green holly with blood-red berries overflowed from vases wrapped in black ribbon. A few laggard courtiers wandered, nodding their approval. It was dramatic but tasteful, suited for a country at war and a royal family mourning a handful of lesser cousins.

A maid led us to our room. I left Harriet exploring the cabinets and wheeled Nessy to her chamber, adjacent to ours and cozy with wool rugs, embroidered pillows, and a goose down quilt. Nessy climbed under the covers, and I cracked the window so chill air flowed in.

"The air is healthful in the north," I said, tucking the quilt to her chin, then wondered why that sounded familiar.

Nessy yawned, her cheeks hollow. "I'm tired."

"Have a rest. We have traveled a long way."

She curled up, and her breath settled into shallow, uneven rasps, as much comfort as she ever had in sleep. I smoothed damp hair from her pale forehead, but I did not remove my glove. I was afraid of what I would sense. Perhaps I could check after her next dose of tea. The tea did help, for a while.

I eased her door closed. Notes drifted down the hallway from a distant violin. I walked that way, past an unused parlor and several guest rooms pleasantly but sparsely furnished, then stopped by the open door of a small sitting room.

Mr. Knightley was playing; through the doorway, I glimpsed the expert motions of his bow arm. He had practiced during our trip, technical studies I heard muffled by closed doors, but this was a virtuoso performance—dazzling runs and thrumming double stops as dark and throaty as a pair of singers in intimate duet.

The phrase halted on a sour note with an exclamation of *bah!* Music sheets shuffled noisily.

I knocked on the door jamb. Mr. Knightley took a step to see me, blinked, then bowed, the curves of his violin complementing his form. "Miss Woodhouse."

"I do not wish to interrupt. But I *was* listening, so I should not pretend otherwise. That is beautiful. I have never heard it."

"It is Bach. The Partita in D minor. A brilliant work, almost lost. But Simrock's edition is half illegible..." He scowled at the score.

I hesitated, my toes on the threshold. We had walked together every day while traveling, but it would be improper to linger alone in an isolated room.

Mr. Knightley apparently had the same realization. He set his instrument aside. "May I show you Pemberley?"

We strolled down the hallway. Mr. Knightley had visited before, and he named paintings and rooms. He rapped his knuckles on a passing mantle with a smile. "As you see, there is no deficit of walnut."

"Like your home?" I asked innocently. This had become a joke—I would pry about his lifestyle, and he would defer. This time his evasion was a flourish of his deft hands, so I pouted. "You are hiding something. I think you are a secret baron!" He laughed, so I asked, "*Have* you a home?" Perhaps a musician slept in tavern lofts and patron guest rooms.

Abruptly, he was solemn. "I live in Chelsea. The city has not yet swallowed all the farms, so I watch the sun set into an orchard. One might think it was the country."

"Oh," I said, disconcerted that our game had ended so suddenly.

"My room is positively foul with music manuscripts," he added. "You could not bear it."

"I like happy clutter. It is clothes that disturb me."

He nodded in silence, then nervously corrected a cuff. The quiet pooled around us like a tide of intimacy.

We were at a stairway with a north view. The stillness broke when he pointed. "The town of Lambton is over those hills."

"And another Darcy school," I sighed. "Harriet chatters about it."

Mr. Knightley tugged harder at his cuff, spoiling the crease. "The Lambton school is seeking an instructor. I have written a recommendation for her."

"A recommendation?" Then I understood. "For *Harriet*?"

"It is a good match," he said, squaring his shoulders. "Harriet Smith has first-rate qualities."

"Precisely! That is why she will marry a gentleman. I did not go to all that trouble to have her listed in *Debrett's* so she may teach!"

Mr. Knightley's eyes narrowed. "Harriet Smith is listed in *Debrett's*?"

"In the... next edition." Harriet and I had not yet announced our sisterhood. To fend off troublesome questions, I hurriedly added, "That is thanks to my clever use of Mr. Tinsdale. Which *you* said would not succeed."

That unsettled Mr. Knightley. He caught my gloved right hand in his bare fingers and spoke. I hardly heard. He had lifted my hand to his heart, and for a moment I thought—I almost thought—he would carry it to his lips. My temples thudded, and a blush heated the nape of my neck.

"He is a dangerous man," Mr. Knightley repeated.

I stammered, "I know he is dangerous. I am not a fool."

"You are not. But you are reckless with your influence. You lead a life gifted with cleverness and beauty and wealth. Do you appreciate the effect you have on others?"

My fingers were still caught in his, my racing pulse barely concealed by silk, but I recovered enough for a bright smile. "That is a very roundabout way of congratulating me on Mr. Tinsdale." Mr. Knightley gave a startled laugh, and I said, "You see? You like that I am clever."

"I would *like* you to face a challenge."

My smile broke. I had thought he understood my life.

Instantly, he was contrite. "That was an idiotic thing to say. I apologize. You fool me with all... this." His free hand sketched the air past the brim of my bonnet, my flushed cheek, the sleeve of my gown. He released my hand from its press against his muslin neckcloth and stepped back, then watched me, the fine lines beside his eyes deepening as if he were deciphering a difficult passage of music.

Like the arrival of a wrathful angel, a memory of Mr. Elton filled my vision —that day in Highbury when, resplendent in his vicar finery and brimming with the holy authority of the Church, he pronounced that I could never bind. Shouted that I could never be a proper wyfe.

I heard my name and hunted blindly to find Mr. Knightley, waiting yards down the hallway. He must think me mad.

"I beg your pardon?" I said.

"I thought this would interest you."

He stood by an arched stone entryway. I steadied myself for a few breaths, then we entered a large hall.

It was a gallery, long and wide with open arches at both sides. Five statues were equally spaced along the center. A few large portraits hung on the stark, white walls. The effect was dramatic and sparse, very unlike my beloved Hartfield, crammed with needleworks and knickknacks and friendly, amateur watercolors.

Mr. Knightley stopped before a life-size statue of a young wyfe in white marble, standing with her arm stretched to grasp something unseen. A wyvern, poised for flight, crouched at her feet. Two feet of red cord hung looped from her other hand.

"Lady Anne Darcy," he said simply.

The healer of Pemberley. When she died, six years ago, I was sixteen. My symptoms, or whatever they were, began that year.

"Thank you. I am interested," I said and circled her slowly. She was carved from marble so pure it was translucent. I stopped when we faced each other. Our gazes—lady, stone lady, and stone wyvern—met there

I realized what had seemed familiar when I settled Nessy in her bed. The wyvern at the ball said *a messenger awaits to the north.*

I peeled off my glove and grasped the statue's outstretched, questing hand. The fingers were unyielding. Lifeless. The hope that had welled within me, a child's imagined fable of healing, slunk away.

Lady Anne shared the high cheekbones of her children. Her expression was focused and driven. But that was a choice of the sculptor.

"Caring for the sick is not like this," I said. "It is not great or noble. Healing is a small thing. Little courtesies. Smiles when life is bitter."

Mr. Knightley, observing from a respectful distance, said, "You never shy from Nessy. When she is wracked with coughing fits, you comfort her, then wipe the gore and smile. It is astonishingly brave."

"I should think she is the brave one." I patted the wyvern's head. The stone scales felt sharp, but they were cold as well. No message here.

"I mean that you do not shy from the challenge. I criticized you unjustly. You help that girl."

I said nothing. His praise was unjust, not his criticism. When I tucked Nessy into bed, I feared to remove my glove.

Mr. Knightley continued, his voice resonant in the empty hall. "You have a life, Emma. If there are lessons to take from Lady Anne, find them. But do not let Darcy enlist you with his ghosts and guilts. You do not need Pemberley."

I veiled my thoughts with lowered lashes. Yuánchi was at Pemberley. I could not explain the relief I gained from his strength—not when that relief depended on touching Mr. Darcy. That secrecy, and Mr. Knightley's undeserved praise for my care of Nessy, heightened the color in my cheeks.

The silence stretched, then Mr. Knightley said, "I must travel to Brighton."

It took a moment to believe my ears. I turned to him. "You cannot! The south coast is occupied."

"Slavers have begun to transact their vile business on English soil. The Freedom Society is building a chain of households to shelter escapees while they flee north. I must go to assist."

"That is madness. You are the last person who should go!"

"Because of my skin?"

"Yes!" I exclaimed. This was no time for false delicacy.

His gaze was level, the line of his chin dark and decided against his starched collar. "I have been privileged with freedom my entire life. Until now, my help for others has been an easy task. A gentleman's pastime. I must do my duty, or I could not live with myself."

Miss Taylor, my governess—practically my mother—had left for her marriage two years ago. Then, I lost Papa. Now, my new sister chafed to leave, and Mr. Knightley aided her while planning to leave as well.

I tugged my glove into place, then held my hands side-by-side to check that the trim was identical. The ribbons were trembling. "Send someone else. Please."

"I cannot. I would not, if I could. We all have duties, Emma. This is mine. I will travel south in a few days. But I will pass through Surrey. I could assist your return."

Mr. Elton's condemnations mocked me. What business had I holding hands with a gentleman? This was inevitable. This was for the best.

"Do your duty," I said and left, my steps dragging as if through icy water.

3 2

THE DAGGER

MARY

Lord Wellington rose from his chair in the south sitting room. "Miss Bennet. I have been meaning to thank you for your care of Miss Bathurst. And to compliment you for your composure on the night of the ball. You were as steadfast as any army surgeon."

That was untrue unless army surgeons wept when someone died in their lap. Perhaps they did. The Greek heroes all wept.

Pemberley, for all its size, was thoroughly familiar after spending July and August with Georgiana, but this room I had entered rarely. Mr. Darcy favored it for private work, and it channeled his masculinity: thick-legged oaken furniture and a shelf of brandies and ports. Lord Wellington had swamped the writing desk in papers and maps. That mess looked more like Georgiana, who existed in a cyclone of manuscripts and disassembled keyboard mechanisms.

I muttered "Lord Wellington" and began: "Miss Bathurst is why I have come. She has remembered information from her captivity."

Lord Wellington frowned and offered a chair before ringing for a servant and asking them to find Lizzy. He strolled to the shelf of liquors, weighed a crystal glass, and raised it questioningly toward me. I shook my head—was that a joke?—and watched him slosh in a half-inch of amber liquid that shot scents of oak and alcohol. It was late morning, not even one o'clock.

He lounged into the desk chair, studying me, then sniffed the tumbler.

"Darcy keeps Scotch whiskey. We use it to toast his Scottish gamekeeper, the poor fellow." He sipped. "I am bracing myself for your news. Miss Bathurst's stories are ghastly. You must agree, given your own work."

I did not understand the purpose of his last sentence. "My work?"

"Condemning the establishment. Your cause is..."—he tapped a finger on his glass while he thought—"the right of all women to bind. I recall a spirited condemnation of England's war effort as well." He pursed his lips for another sip, but the glass stopped an inch short. "You know, they do not come any more establishment than I. Well, His Royal Highness, I suppose."

I thought I understood him now. "Are you interviewing me to determine if I am a spy?"

Finally, he drank. His throat bobbed in a heavy swallow. "If I thought you were a spy, you would not have joined our excursion. This is curiosity. The Bennet sisters are, without exception, remarkable. Mrs. Darcy, obviously. Mrs. Bingley has her wyvern. Your sister Lydia, frankly, was terrifying. What is your distinction?"

"You excluded Kitty," I noted. "If you explain whatever innuendo or intimidation you are attempting, we could be done with it."

He swirled his glass and raised it in a mock toast. "The efficient sister, then." He slung his head back against the chair and rubbed his eyes. They had harsh shadows, dark as bruises. He was exhausted.

Lizzy arrived, changed from traveling clothes to promenade dress. That was gaudy for at home but sensible when a prince or princess might lurk around any corner. I doubted she had clothes for presentation to court, and if she did, Lizzy was too clever to wear them. The formality would scream royalty if a stranger called.

Lizzy had worn this same gown, cheerful sky blue and cloud white, in the summer when we called upon homes in Lambton. It hung too loose, now.

There were niceties and shifts of chairs, then Lord Wellington said, "Miss Bennet has news from Miss Bathurst."

Lizzy looked at me, her eyes wider and her expression sadder. Reminders of the ball stoked her guilt. I wished that trauma would mend, and that I was not one of those reminders.

I fiddled with the binding of my book, organizing thoughts. "Miss Bathurst recalled several details about why and how the captive wyves are taken." I started my mental list: "When these criminals abduct a woman, they dose her with crawler venom. Immediately. It may be in the alley where they took her, or the garden. It is a test of tolerance. The dose is so strong that most do not survive. They leave those behind, to be ignored as victims of London's random violence." I showed them the book I held, a thin, water-stained volume. "Wickham and Lydia stole volumes of draca lore from the Pemberley library. Those are in Napoleon's possession, but hundreds of references remain. This is an old Briton pharmacopeia, and it lists lethalities of crawler venom. One drop will kill a man. A bound wyfe survives four or five drops. An unbound wyfe with strong affinity for draca can tolerate higher doses. That is the purpose of the first venom test. The criminals abduct women of good family because, in England, only those families have public histories of binding. So they select wyves whose mothers or grandmothers bound strongly."

"They are choosing strong wyves to control the black dragon," Lord Wellington said.

"Correct," I said, advancing one topic on my list, but he held out his hand for the book. Irritated by the delay, I passed it to him.

He flipped it open and squinted. "What on earth?"

"It is Scottish Gaelic," I said. He passed it back with an elevated eyebrow, and I resumed, "Before preparing to control the dragon, their captives are tested on an easier task: controlling a common draca. That 'testing' is the brutality Miss Bathurst described to us: feigned rewards, vicious punishments, and drug-enforced stupor. Miss Rees was their strongest captive wyfe, so she was taught to use the dagger to control Fènnù. Miss Bathurst did not receive that training; she was sent to the ball to assault Lizzy and to cause panic. But she heard the instructions. The dagger's blade has an inscription revealed when wetted by a wyfe's blood. A song that establishes a connection to the dragon."

Other than their revolted expressions, Lizzy and Lord Wellington offered no comment. I had a sour taste in my own throat and needed a steadying breath before advancing a topic. "To raise Fènnù, Miss Rees carried a huge dose of venom to swallow once she had the dagger in her possession."

"The venom boosts a wyfe's power," Lizzy said. "That is how Lydia used it. Even with the dagger, I am sure they need it. A dragon's mind is unimaginably strong."

"You would know," I acknowledged. "I deduced it was required because the dose inflicts a severe cost. Miss Bathurst said even the doses necessary to control common draca killed wyves in days. Her memories are clouded, but she believes this occurred twice, forcing the abduction of yet more women. I think that, once a wyfe takes the huge doses required to control Fènrù, she cannot survive long."

"Lydia Bennet took the venom," Lord Wellington said. "She did not die in days."

Lizzy's response was quiet. "Lydia was no ordinary wyfe. I battled both her and the wyves at the ball. Lydia was far stronger."

"Because she was your sister," Lord Wellington said. His gaze found mine. "Miss Bennet, you avoided my earlier question. I must ask directly. What is your strength?"

"Reading Gaelic," I answered. "And irritating lords. It depends upon my mood."

He grunted—perhaps he laughed—then he shrugged. "If wyves do not survive long, that explains the gap in dragon attacks. After Fènnù rose, there were raids on the fleet, then on the royal residences. But in less than a day, the black dragon vanished. The French and American invaders at Brighton fought conventionally. Even with our regular army trapped in Spain, we had mustered the militia and could have cast them back. Then yesterday, the black dragon returned." His jaw corded. "I have an account from a militia lieutenant who survived. His first combat. It reads like the end of the world." He squared the knuckles of his fist against the table, then pressed until his fingers turned white. "Can we rely on that gap each time?"

"It is impossible to predict," I said. "This gap was due to insufficient strong wyves. They lost two at the ball, and their replacement wyfe was not yet... tested. She must have become ready. I do not know if they have others to follow her."

Lord Wellington tapped a small, curled piece of paper, a message that had been carried by bird. "Yesterday, the enemy controlled Brighton, Canterbury, and Portsmouth. They could be halfway to London today. What if they collect wyves from those cities?"

My stomach twisted. "That is a vile thought. You may judge the French army's morals, but the brutality of slavers has no limits. The man who punishes the captive wyves speaks like an American. You have seen the marks of his hand-iwork. It is rank torture."

Lizzy was flushed. "We must get the dagger back. This is evil, and it is my fault. Think of the nightmare for those women."

"For those women and many more," Lord Wellington said. "Without the dagger, England will lose this war, and swiftly. Tinsdale is an open traitor. Bona-

239

parte has declared Tinsdale king of England—a vassal king who swears loyalty to France, and only for those regions he subdues. And even though Tinsdale is odious and dishonored, there are demonstrations supporting him in London. His agents post lies throughout the city: that England's monarchs feed on the blood of infants, and that France's war is a divine crusade to liberate Catholics imprisoned by English devil-worshippers. I do not know who he expects to convince with such falsehoods."

"More will believe than you think," I said. "England's oppression fosters rebellion. Catholics are one of many minorities—"

"Mary, stop," Lizzy muttered. I looked at her, surprised—less for being scolded than for the weakness of her reprimand.

Lord Wellington stomped to his feet and glared southward as if anger could spy an enemy two hundred miles distant. "I will *not* be defeated on English soil. The black dragon must be removed from the field of battle, so we must retrieve the dagger. Darcy and I have almost completed Pemberley's security. When that plan is done, I will depart south to have swifter command." He turned gravely to Lizzy. "Mrs. Darcy, the soldiers I leave here will be straw in a storm if our enemy discovers the royal family. Only your dragon can stop Fènnù. It is no exaggeration that England's fate relies on you. If His Highness is killed, Tinsdale's claim to the throne becomes uncomfortably close to the truth. England's crown has been taken through blood and assassination before."

Lizzy shook her head doubtfully. "Yuánchi cannot overcome Fènnù."

"You drove him away from London."

"Yuánchi was severely injured."

"I saw Yuánchi's breath rip the heavens. The power was unimaginable. Fènnù must have been as injured."

Lizzy did not answer. It was unlike her to abandon a debate; her response should be that Fènnù could not have been injured as the attacks on the royal residences came afterward.

Instead, she said, "We need the dagger but not because it is a weapon. It is a cure."

Lord Wellington arched an eyebrow. "A cure for what?"

"For the damage to Fènnù's mind. Yuánchi calls it 'the fracture.' Thus far I have only hints of how to proceed, but Pemberley has the largest collection of draca lore in England. I hope to learn more."

Lord Wellington clearly held Lizzy in high regard as he did not challenge that exceedingly vague explanation. He said only, "What would be the effect of curing Fènnù?"

"She would no longer fight in this war."

His answer was deliberate. "I do not yet have a battle plan to defeat a dragon. My priority must be retrieving the dagger. But when we regain the dagger, rendering Fènnù unable to fight is ill-advised."

Lizzy sat unmoving and silent—she must have guessed his plan—but I exclaimed, "You cannot mean to *use* the dagger!"

"Our navy is weakened, the remnants scattered," Lord Wellington said. "Our army is stranded across the channel, and our militia is crushed and reeling. France has a ruthless and powerful ally in America's slave states. I need strength to cast the enemy from our shores."

I jumped to my feet, bristling. "That is not the *point*. Who would wield the black dagger? Will you abduct an unmarried wyfe and poison her with venom? Employ a slave master to torture her?"

"I will ask a powerful wyfe to wield it of her own free will. Gentlemen volunteer their lives for England. There are ladies equally brave." His smile was thin. "I should think you would approve of my attitude."

I shook my head. "You are mistaken. Lizzy cannot do this. The black dragon drives her mad."

"I am aware," he said. "I intend to ask Miss Darcy. She is a great wyfe, and she has assisted the army before. Or will you volunteer?" I blinked at him, too stunned to speak. He resumed, gravelly and tired, "I must leave to finish planning Pemberley's security. Darcy is enlisting the Britons in Pemberley's hills. Miss Bennet, thank you for the information." He bowed and left.

"He is mistaken," I said after the door closed. "Georgiana would never *fight*. She has only ever aided injured draca and wyves."

"I am certain you are right," Lizzy said. She did not sound certain.

I was desperate to run to Georgiana, but I could not. We had not finished my list from Miss Bathurst.

"There is a last item," I said. "The identity of their current captive wyfe, who has likely begun using the dagger. It is a... a detail. Unimportant... but she..." My words tangled as the fears I had knotted away came loose. "Miss Rees was strong, so they hunted her friend, Miss Rebecca Spoon. She is a friend of Georgiana and mine. A member of our salon."

Lizzy stood and put her arm around my waist. "Oh. I am sorry, Mary."

I shook my head, striving for control. "Dr. Davenport says a doctor must put aside failure and focus on the next patient. But I cannot stop thinking of Rebecca, trapped with those beasts."

"Then think about this," Lizzy said. "Where is the dagger?"

The specificity of her question caught my attention. "They would not take it to France. They need strong wyves, and French families have no binding history. That is why Napoleon wanted Lydia." I saw why she had asked. "It would be extraordinarily risky to move the dagger to the occupied south. They would have to cross the line of battle. They could be interrogated. Searched as spies."

"Exactly. Did you notice that the demonstrations supporting Mr. Tinsdale are in London? Mr. Tinsdale is a self-important, arrogant man. I cannot imagine him orchestrating such events where he could not steal a glimpse to gloat."

"He is in London!" I exclaimed. "Why did you not tell Lord Wellington?"

"Lord Wellington has had agents searching London since we left. But that is hopeless. London could conceal a thousand traitor kings. But your news gives me a half-hatched idea. The problem is Lord Wellington will never agree. The risk to the royal family is... the risk—"

Lizzy shuddered and collapsed in my arms.

3 3

PROMISE ME

LIZZY

I dragged my eyelids apart and saw Mary's frightened gaze framed by her hanging brown hair. Her arms were straining to hold me upright.

I set my feet and found my balance. "What happened?"

"You fainted," Mary said worriedly. "Briefly."

I rubbed my aching eyes. "I am tired. The maid did not set the fire right in that last inn. I woke soaked with perspiration and freezing as well. I sat on the floor and shivered half the night."

"Lizzy. Let me see your eyes." Mary spoke so intently that I obediently moved my shielding fingers, then squinted when painful light glared off her golden rims. Mary tilted her head left and right. "Your pupils are giant. Have you taken some tincture? Laudanum?"

"What? Of course not. I do not trust it since Mr. Jones tried to give it to Jane." Mary appeared so concerned that I blurted out, "Could it be the child?"

Her eyebrows shot upward. "*Child?*"

"I am with child. Or... well, I thought so—" I was cut off as Mary swept me into an embrace. That was unexpected, but I let out a breath and closed my eyes, enjoying the respite of darkness. "I did not mean to announce it so clumsily..."

My words tailed off. Mary's hands were methodically pressing my body—an examination, not an embrace. Briefly, she cupped my breasts, then pushed me to arms' length. Her brow was furrowed. "You are skin and bones. I have never felt you so thin."

I swallowed. "Why do I feel that you are not about to congratulate me?"

"Why do you think you are with child? Have your menses stopped?"

"They had. But they were only late. Weeks late."

Mary scowled. "And you think you are *pregnant*?"

"I... we are not all doctors, you know. I had gotten used to the idea, and... my brain has been addled for this entire trip. It was the battles at the museum, I think." Mary pulled the window curtain wide, and daylight blazed in. I squeezed my eyes closed. "Please do not. Light hurts. Perhaps I need spectacles? You had headaches before yours were fitted." I heard the curtain thump closed and the room dimmed. Cautiously, I opened my eyes.

Mary's hands were clutched together as if she did not know where to put them. "Light hurts. You have chills and sweats at night. How are your days?"

"Well, I am sometimes boiling. People tell me I am hot. I thought... I know ladies with child are often overheated." Mary was very still, her eyes bright. "Mary, you are frightening me."

"I must examine your neck," she whispered.

The precision of her request filled me with foreboding. I nodded, and she touched both sides of my neck, her fingertips pressing exactly where I had feared. When she drew back, her face had blanched.

I managed a breath. "I noticed that, too, a few days ago. Little bumps, like dried peas. They do not hurt. I suppose I sound even more foolish when I say that I wondered if they were due to pregnancy."

Mary spoke in a rattle of words. "Education of women regarding conception and childbirth is poor. The bias of religious stigma and male medical establishment..." She stopped.

"What is wrong with me?" I said as steadily as I could.

"I am not a doctor."

"But you know. Do not torture me with delay."

In a whisper, she said, "You have consumption."

For an instant, I was shocked, then the rush of relief was overwhelming. My dread fell away, and I laughed. "Do not misunderstand when I say this, but I rejoice that you are not a doctor. I cannot have consumption. I do not even cough!"

Mary said in a desperate, tiny voice, "It is not that kind of consumption."

"Is there more than one kind?" Mary gave an unwilling nod. "What kind is it?"

"Lymph and..." She swallowed, then set her shoulders and stepped closer, studying my eyes. She steadied my forehead with her left palm, placed her right hand behind my neck, then pressed in at the top of my spine. White-hot pain lanced down my neck and up into my skull.

I gritted my teeth. "Ow."

"I am sorry." Those words were polite reflex, but when she stepped back, white as a sheet, the rest came raggedly. "The bumps in your neck are tubercles of consumption. In some cases, they spread to the spine and brain. Meningeal infection, it is called. It is unusual, though not... not truly rare. I have attended cases at Dr. Davenport's public clinic. Your eyes hurt because the optic nerves are infected, locking your pupils wide. You see haloes? Shining auras?"

I nodded mechanically. My relief at Mary's supposed inexperience had vanished. This was the most precise diagnosis I had ever heard.

"Consumption is so slow, though," I said. "People live with it for years and years. I have heard that recovery is a matter of lifestyle. I do not even have the cough yet. That must be good."

Long seconds dragged, then Mary said, "It is good you do not have the cough. The cough is painful."

The truth was in her tone. "The cough is painful and slow. The kind I have hurts less because it is quick."

"Lizzy, do not ask me these things! Let us find the royal physician."

"No." My own voice was thick, but I forced words out. "You must advise me. *How* quick? I do not ask from morbid curiosity, or to... to argue, or to beg. The sole dragon protecting England is bound to me. I must know how long I have."

Mary bit her lip. "Can you detect any change within the last week?"

"It is worse in the last week. *Much* worse. It is noticeably worse every *day*. Mary, how long? When will I become unable to... perform duties?"

"A week," she whispered. "Or days."

Her answer fell through my chest like an anvil. I was twenty years old. I would not live to be one and twenty. I would not finish my first year of marriage.

"First Papa," I said. The words stung. "Then Lydia. Bennets are dropping like flies. Thank goodness Jane is doing her part." Mary made a desperate sound, but I waved her silent. "Miss Bingley will weep copiously at the funeral.

You must judge the sincerity of her tears, then be touched or vexed as appropriate. Either will gratify me."

Mary pulled me into a ferocious embrace—far tighter than her examination. Some perverse anger made me push against her, then I collapsed and clung. She whispered, "Do not practice your wit on me," and my tears burst free. They flowed for a long time.

Finally, though, I was simply leaning my forehead on Mary's soaked shoulder while she sniffled in my ear. I pulled my head up. "I am very thankful that I married. Darcy and I wasted months staring at each other and exchanging trivialities. What fools we were to be bound by society's strictures." I pushed Mary back to see her red-rimmed eyes behind round glass circles. "You told me that you are in love. Do not waste it. Promise me."

Mary choked, swiping at her eyes with both hands, then nodded.

Then, unexpectedly, hope burst into my mind. "Emma is a healer! She is treating Nessy *for consumption*. She has that special tea!"

"I am considering that. But... Lizzy, I recognized the leaves of her tea. I have tasted it. It is common spearmint. Nessy improved for a time, but now she weakens quickly. I say nothing because Emma's care does no harm." Mary must have seen my crushed expression because she became resolute. "I *shall* speak to her. She has a remarkable skill to diagnose."

"I am already diagnosed." I knew Mary was right. Something had been seriously wrong with me for weeks. I had been deluding myself. Hiding from the truth.

"We will pursue every chance," Mary said. "The issue is... the complication is that Emma must touch a patient to see."

I breathed an ironic laugh. The great wyfe of healing's skills required touch, but Emma could not touch me because I had bound her dragon.

Darcy, though, would never accept that Emma could not help. He would not accept that *he* could not help. Every doctor within a hundred miles would be summoned.

Like my despair had been a fogged window to push aside, my choices turned clear. "Do not tell Mr. Darcy. Do not tell anyone."

"This cannot be hid!" Mary exclaimed.

"The slavers use venom to 'test' their victims. I can sense a wyfe affected by venom. With Lydia, I sensed it miles away. I could search London in hours, find the wyves, *and* find the dagger. But if Darcy knows I am ill, he will insist I am stuffed in a bed for a parade of doctors. And Lord Wellington will insist I stay to guard the royal family. Both would be foolish. If Fènnù attacks, Yuánchi cannot stop her. And if I delay for hopeless treatments, I will grow too weak to recover the dagger." I grasped Mary's fingers. "And I must free your friend. To atone for what I did. For the death of Miss Rees. It is all the more urgent to me now."

Mary was staring in disbelief. "It is winter. If there is snow, the trip alone to London could take a week."

"Not if I fly."

Mary's jaw dropped. "Lizzy. You are too ill. You cannot do this."

I squeezed her hands between mine. "You do not know what I can do. I am the wyfe of war."

MYSTERIOUS ERRANDS

EMMA

I entered Pemberley's great dining hall through a stone arch thick as a medieval castle wall, the root of some ancient foundation that supported the modern building.

I arrived alone. I had dressed in the last hour, but Harriet had not come to our room. Her moods flickered, cool then friendly, all without cause. More likely, due to her newfound sisterly independence. Well, if independence meant she would go her own way, so be it. That did not mean I could not assist her success.

I had chosen a ruby silk gown, slimly fitted. Lines of tiny shell buttons decorated the breast while flat bows of red ribbon, all tied identically, adorned the shoulders and sleeves. It was a defensive dress, heavy with aligned detail. Luckily Lucy had looked in. She dismissed the chambermaid, then shaped bows and pinched buttons until the rows matched.

My cotton gloves formed the final defense. Their embroidery drew my gaze from the miasma glistening under chair legs and puddling beneath drapes.

When did I last touch Mr. Darcy? Three days. Too long.

This predinner gathering was social, although any gathering risked becoming another of Lord Wellington's lectures on secrecy. The dining hall held a tremendously long table, twenty-five feet at least, partially set for this evening's dinner. There were white linen runners and fifty unlit, white wax candles high and low in silver holders.

A few members of the court wandered the room already. Freed of the trip's prohibition against extravagance, velvet and fur swished. Beads and ruffles rustled. The layers gave them puffy, irregular silhouettes that marred the symmetries of Pemberley's décor.

A lord whose name I had forgotten greeted me with drawling languor. "Miss Woodhouse. I gather your day has been as boring as mine?"

That was a joke because we had both arrived at the scheduled time. After a week of watching Lord Wellington fume over late courtiers, I knew timeliness was not a royal virtue. "I am simply interested, my lord. And I have no rank that requires formal entrances."

"You understate your prestige," lord whoever said gallantly. He had reddened his lips and darkened his eyebrows with something greasy. "I am sure you will regularly brighten our court when these French interlopers are tossed out."

The white-wigged, frowning chancellor of the Exchequer joined us. "Killed, I should hope," he pronounced. "It is past time to crush Bonaparte. If Wellington had not been so soft on him, he would not have dared send troops to England."

"I recall a dragon..." said lord whoever, one greased eyebrow arched.

"Nothing stout English shooters could not end. Think of Agincourt."

"Agincourt was four hundred years ago. And with bows. Surely, it would be cannon. Like shooting pheasant, but bigger."

I curtsied, left them debating tactics against dragons, and went to a window. Pemberley's front gardens were a grand landscape drawn in winter greens of olive, sage, and moss with damp browns from the bark and earth. The plantings swept down the hill in flowing shapes pierced by a boisterous, rain-swollen stream. Below, Pemberley lake was dark as wet slate.

Mary Bennet entered, surveyed the room, and strode to me. "Emma."

I smiled, surprised she sought me out. "Good afternoon, Mary. Are you happy to be home?"

"Longbourn is my home—" she began curtly, then scowled. "Then again, Longbourn is properly Jane's since she and Bingley bound, and presently overrun with children from the London school. Doubtless Jane is delighted, but I am unsure where home is."

"That is an unpleasant feeling. I worry that my home will be occupied by French soldiers. I am sure they would ruin it."

Tightly, Mary asked, "How is Nessy?"

"Happy to be out of coaches. Mrs. Reynolds found a toy rabbit for her. She was cuddled with it when I left."

"Her medical condition, I meant." Mary's verbal delivery was peculiarly intense, even for her. "Have you seen change? Improvement?" When I hesitated, she tossed her head, her straight hair flying. "You know! You have... your insight. I have seen you do it. You lay a finger on her brow and then you *know*."

"It is hard for me to speak of it." What did she want? An admission of despair? "You see she is not well."

"Why can you not heal her?" Mary whispered tensely. "What is missing?"

"I do not know. I have never healed anyone. I do not think I can. Mary, why are you upset?"

Her lips pressed tight, then she flew in a new direction. "Do you require more energy, or whatever this mystical force is? What if you held Mr. Darcy's hand while trying?"

That would be a shameful display, but I answered simply, "It is not like that. The strength from Yuánchi settles my sensitivities, but it does not grant powers. It does not *change* me." Mary scowled, so I added, "Do you not think I would try if it could help?" She took a breath, then, reluctantly, nodded.

Lizzy and Mr. Darcy had arrived and were circulating through the court crowd. The Darcys' dress suited the measured elegance of Pemberley, but the gathered silks and dangling scarves of the courtiers were unraveling the room's balance. A dragging hem tugged my gaze across the polished wooden floor, miasma burbling in its wake.

I was yanking my gloves brutally snug by the time Lizzy arrived and greeted us. Surprising myself, I asked, "Do you know where Harriet is?" The words emerged wistfully.

"I needed an errand done at the Lambton school," Lizzy said. "She kindly offered."

"*What* errand?" Mary said sharply.

"*An* errand," Lizzy answered equally sharply. They glared at each other, Lizzy squinting oddly. It appeared I was not the only one in a sisterly standoff. Then Lizzy scooped up Mr. Darcy's arm and pulled him toward Lord Wellington, who had just entered.

Mary tapped her toe, then turned to me. "Can you sense Yuánchi at a distance?"

"This is not the place for such questions," I whispered. "Will you tell me what is wrong?"

"Please," she implored. "Determine where he is."

She was so sincere that I glanced around, then pressed my gloves together as if in prayer, filling my eyes with their design, and tried to feel the tug—the enthralling attraction—of Yuánchi.

He was near enough to sense, though not toward the lake or any of the windows. I turned slowly, head bowed, seeking, until the tug was directly forward. I straightened and found Mary had followed my turn to hover in front of me, looking apprehensive.

"He is directly behind you," I said dryly, then added more nicely, "and distant. I cannot say how far, but into the hills. Near as far as I am able to sense him."

Mary spun to look at the wall behind her, then studied each window in turn. "I know where." She gave me an unwilling, "Thank you."

Georgiana arrived next and came smilingly to Mary, speaking of plans for a music performance. Mary interrupted her with "I have an errand" and rushed from the room. Georgiana, disappointed, went to speak with Lizzy.

What were all these errands? Alone again, I stood for a while, then wondered if I should escape to some barren, calming corridor. Pemberley had an endless supply. But before I did, a bustle rose, silence fell, and the royal family entered: the prince's daughter by his old marriage, Princess Caroline, sixteen but womanly in an emerald gown; the Prince Regent himself, slightly graying and unpretentious in gentlemen's evening dress but with a sheaf of medals on his breast; Lady Hertford, affixed to the prince's arm, a scandal that had long since lost its bite; and last, poor King George, his hair a mess, wearing little more than a thick nightgown. He was steered by two stern doctors while his head twisted blindly.

The king's arrival was greeted with murmurs of "Your Majesty." He had been paraded by his doctors before—they were hardly more than jailors—and each time, an irritated spark within me rose hotter. People had ignored Papa this same way at the end of his illness. He would sit stoically as if he did not notice, then fume and moan about it at night.

Whatever a person's illness, this treatment was cruel. A king should either be dressed and greeted as a monarch or granted the dignity of solitude. Instead, his keepers prodded him about with snide contempt as if he were no more aware than a cow or sheep.

The court, as usual, had clustered around the prince like bees to a hive. But my irritation launched my feet, and I found myself walking to the king. One of his doctors, a wiry and grimacing man, waved me away, but I ignored him and curtsied, the court curtsy I had practiced when a dance instructor still called on Hartfield—a full sweep with one pointed toe, then sinking deeply on my back leg to wait with head bowed and gown spread. I said, loudly enough to carry, "Your Majesty."

The room quieted. Every pair of eyes pressed.

I hoped the king would recognize courtesy, but I did not expect him to respond—he had been thoroughly mad for years. Yet, in an old man's hoarse voice, he said, "Rise."

I recovered smoothly from the curtsy, thinking that my dance instructor would have been pleased, and looked into the clouded, hunting eyes of the king. His face roamed up and around the room, then toward me again. Fretfully, he said, "Who are you?" Gasps sounded from the court.

"Miss Woodhouse, sir."

"What is this? Where am I?"

"Pemberley, sir."

"Oh." His lips, unevenly stubbled from a poor shave, thrust out like a petulant two-year-old's. His lined face furrowed and became tragic. "War, is that it?"

I had no idea how to answer, but Princess Caroline rushed past me, her emerald gown flapping. "Grandpapa!"

The tragedy etching his face fell away like a shattered mask, and he beamed. "Darling girl!" She embraced him, and there were delighted whispers and approving taps of over-polished fingernails on palms.

Seeing the king happily engaged with his granddaughter, I backed away, then dodged the courtiers' grasping congratulations until I was behind the mass of the crowd.

Mr. Knightley stood there, hands clasped behind his back. I halted, toes bent mid-step. I had steadfastly avoided him since he announced he would travel to the occupied south, but I found I was smiling happily.

"That was nicely done," he said. "Boldly."

He had come from practicing; I scented the pine rosin he rubbed on his violin bow. My smile wobbled amid rushing, conflicted feelings. I settled for asking, "Are you still leaving?"

"I must." He angled his head toward the troupe of courtiers. "These indulgences rub me wrong. They mock my leisure."

"Can you not invent a few hardships and be content to stay?"

"Most gentlemen would. Do you think that satisfactory?"

"I know you do not." I surprised myself by announcing the brash resolution I had formed. "I am going to help Nessy."

"You have some new insight?"

"I am simply determined."

"Nessy is a sweet girl. Her illness is unfair." He drew a breath. "But a child bedridden with consumption—"

"Do not! Do not say it is impossible." If I was to be alone, could I not have these successes? Aid my sister. Aid Nessy.

He nodded slowly. "I admire your devotion. But there are other hurts in the world. Other callings for your care. I have seen a hundred lives transformed by the Freedom Society."

"I cannot imagine helping a hundred lives. Helping one child is hard enough."

Lizzy and Mr. Darcy had approached to a polite distance. Mr. Knightley nodded to them, and they joined us, complimenting me on my respect to his majesty.

"He reminded me of Papa," I said honestly.

Mr. Darcy exchanged a glance with his wyfe, then said, "Elizabeth and I wish to extend an offer. You recall my mother's condition?"

She had obsessions like mine. I nodded.

He lowered his voice. "After my father's death, her symptoms worsened. She and I worked together to invent methods to manage her... compulsions. I have wondered if these methods could aid you. If you wish, we can discuss them tomorrow after breakfast. Elizabeth will accompany us."

Mr. Knightley said nothing, but he folded his arms as if frustrated. I did not understand why he disapproved.

"Very well," I said after a moment. "I will try."

Lizzy smiled at me. "I hope you find Lady Anne's methods useful. But I forgot that I am engaged after breakfast. Someone can attend in my place. Harriet, perhaps?" Lizzy's attendance was clearly mere propriety, the third party required when an unmarried lady spent extended time with a gentleman.

"Perhaps," I said. It would be a way to engage Harriet at breakfast, at least. "If not her, I am sure Mrs. Reynolds or Lucy can attend."

Covertly, I was watching Mr. Darcy's bare hand below his sleeve. But dinner would be an easier time to manage a touch. I would be ungloved, and if I hesitated near him, he would offer to escort me to my seat.

Lizzy, abruptly pensive, threaded her arm through her husband's and said to him, "Please ensure you meet. I hope that Fènnù can be freed of that cursed dagger and healed. Emma will need strength to try."

Surprised, I said, "I?"

Her smile was tired. "Yuánchi was destined to be your dragon, and Fènnù mine. Instead, we are hopelessly tangled. There must be a purpose to that."

Her cheeks were sunken and her eyes bloodshot behind slit lashes. I wondered if she was ill. But even if I could bear to touch her, I would sense only the blaze of Yuánchi, not the quiet insight, good or bad, I felt with Nessy.

Lizzy turned to where Lord Wellington was calling for order. "Lord Wellington has promised to explain the security he and Darcy have invented. I am very curious about their new patrols."

While the crowd grudgingly quieted, I stole a glance at Mr. Knightley. The black coils of his hair were raked back, accentuating his expression—frustrated but decided, although on what I did not know.

35

FLIGHT

LIZZY

I sat shivering on our bedroom floor, tendrils of hair stuck to my sweating temples, my shoulders nestled in the quilts hanging down the side of our bed. It was a foolish location to wait, but Darcy was snoring, and the mundanity was comforting.

When two pairs of feet passed in the hall outside—a pair of housemaids lighting morning fires—I felt my way to the dressing room, pulled on my stashed traveling dress, heavy robe, and riding boots, then eased through the door into the hallway, candlelit at one end.

At the stables, a lone, scrawny stableboy sat cross legged in a pool of lantern light, blowing into his cupped hands.

"Good morning," I said.

He scrambled to his feet, tugging his forelock. "Mrs. Darcy." He peered at the night sky and waning moon. "Here I thought they'd told me a joke!"

"Not at all. I enjoy night rides." He looked at me as if I had sprouted an extra head, so I added, "That is why I ride so rarely during the day." It would be fairer to say I never ride at all, but this would be a steep climb, and events had left me unwilling to gamble that I could maintain a fast pace on foot.

"Yes, ma'am," he said, accepting his mistress's nighttime madness. He scampered off and was back shortly leading a mare. "A gentle ride, ma'am, as you asked. I woke her a while back and gave her some warmed oats to liven her."

I patted her, then recognized her from a frightening Beltane morning this spring. It seemed a world ago. I smiled. "You carried me when I saved my husband." A good omen.

The stableboy placed a wooden step, and I climbed up astride. The dress and robe were awkward, but that would be solved later.

With a cluck and touch of the reins we set off at a walk. I brought no lamp, relying on the sketchy moon. Darcy, a superb horseman, enjoyed discussing riding with our guests, so I had heard of horses' superior night vision. If that was insufficient, I could summon a draca to navigate. But our route was familiar for any Pemberley steed, and my mount plodded stolidly into the hills with hardly a nudge.

The lights of Pemberley vanished. Shadowy bare branches surrounded us. The unease of a lady alone in the night crept into my mind, then I smiled. What had I to fear? I, who could level armies. That thought rattled in my skull, feeling misplaced.

A chilly two miles later, a pair of lamps became visible through the trees. I passed a few modest, thatched-roof buildings—the homes preferred by the Britons who managed Pemberley's hills—then entered a wide clearing for village gatherings.

As planned, Mr. Needham, the school's harness instructor, was waiting with his two young apprentices. They were dragon harnessers, now.

Not as planned, Mary stood beside the girls, her arms crossed and jaw set.

"You are out early," I said, pleased with my composure. I slid off, caught my robe on the saddle, and came within a tangled moment of landing on my head. I whacked the robe so it hung properly, then added mildly, "You shall not dissuade me."

"That is evident," she said. "And I am not out early. I am out late."

"I understood Miss Bennet came at your request," Mr. Needham said worriedly.

One of the girls snickered. "*I* didn't believe that. But we did it! Took all night." She ran to where the harness waited, slung over a form. A second seat had been added behind mine, securely riveted on the long leather saddle skirt and straps. It even had a second of what Mr. Needham called lap belts.

"No," I pronounced.

"You cannot go alone," Mary said. "If you wish, I will explain the medical reasons. Convincingly, and very explicitly to ensure our audience comprehends. If you wish privacy, accept my opinion."

If intimidation had the slightest effect on Mary, she would not have spent the autumn marching through London and staring down irate constables. But she enjoyed logic. "You cannot go without goggles. The wind will be tremendous. They did not make *those* for you overnight."

"I have tied my spectacles in place. It will suffice. *You* can ride in front." Mary unfolded her arms, then gently took my hand. "You must not attempt this alone. An inexperienced rider may keep their seat with care, but an unconscious rider is a hazard to herself."

While arguments and counterarguments circled in my mind, the lanterns were growing concentric rings of shimmering light. Each flicker warned of the stabbing headache to follow.

"Is a second rider safe?" I asked Mr. Needham.

"Safe as one," he said. "The added weight is nothing. You'd be two fleas for a beast that size."

The stubborn part of me longed to refuse. But success mattered more than stubbornness. I would never have saved Jane last year without Mary's help.

"Very well," I said and looked into Mary's brown eyes. "You know, I was worried that Darcy would try something like this. *He* would never have convinced me."

Mary straightened her spectacles. "That is because *he* would insist on riding in front."

DRESSED WARMLY—IF wildly unconventionally—in trousers and leather coats, Mary and I waited at the edge of the clearing. Hints of day blued the eastern sky. The villagers had gathered to watch and whisper. I thought it better to wake them than shock them out of sleep. It no longer mattered if word got back to Darcy.

An owl floated across the clearing, noiseless, feathers splayed like fingers. Suddenly, it flapped in a frenzy, fleeing for the woods.

Thundering grew, more like pounding water than wind. The western stars vanished, and the sliver of moon was shrouded. I pressed a hand to my leather cap, forgetting it was securely strapped under my chin, and leaned into gusts that rolled pebbles and churned the trees.

Yuánchi settled, his tons of mass looming as dark ruby glints. His faceted eyes gleamed as his gaze met mine, then turned to Mary beside me, almost looping his neck as he examined her from several angles.

Mary. I miss her music. Will she and Georgiana play?

They had played for him in summer, in the hills, a lark when they brought instruments on our picnic. It made a profound impression. Yuánchi rarely bothered to learn human names.

I said to Mary, "He wishes you and Georgiana would play for him again."

"I would enjoy that," she said, addressing Yuánchi. "But we cannot this morning. Soon, I hope."

Our harness makers stepped forward. Yuánchi prostrated himself, and they began fitting straps and buckles.

There had been two test flights from Chathford House, the second with burlap sacks of rice that certainly weighed more than Mary and I combined. All had gone smoothly, and I was impressed with how the straps resisted slippage, but for a little revenge I whispered to Mary, "Do you think the straps can hold two?" That was met with stony silence.

The harness buckles were tugged tight. Even with Yuánchi flush to the ground, the saddle was high. Stirrup-like footholds reached down like a short ladder. I took a breath, grabbed hold, and climbed.

The lap belt took two tries to fasten correctly. It was wide and padded, buckled around my waist, and attached to the harness in front and back. Really, it was clever. Would it work on a horse? Riders claimed it was better to fall clean than to be caught in a stirrup, but falling sounded unpleasant to me. I suppose one did not want to be dragged, smacking into rocks and trees. That would not be an issue in the sky.

Mary heaved up and swung her leg over behind me. Her trousers stopped mid-calf as they were one of several measured for me, but her ankles were hidden by riding boots. She bumped me while puzzling through her lap belt. This was a true two-seat saddle, far more roomy than riding double on a horse which pressed the riders together. We had a foot between us.

Finally, she said, "I am ready."

"This is quite secure," I mused. "I believe I *could* fly unconscious."

"Too late," she said dryly.

"I have just realized we will be arriving in London during daylight."

"Only now you realize this?"

I had spoken lightly, but I was dismayed. My admittedly vague plan had involved sweeping over London by night. It was not a fatal issue; already I could imagine strategies for day. But I did not make this sort of error. I was the organized Bennet. Well, and Mary, of course.

Maybe it was best not to examine my decision-making skills. I pulled the peculiar goggles down over my eyes, their leather seals snug. "Are you ready?"

"I have said I am ready." But her arms tentatively circled my waist, then she pulled close, pressing her shoulders to my back. I grabbed the handholds on the harness with my gloved hands and thought, *Fly!*

Yuánchi's weight shifted. We rose frighteningly high, then I realized that he had simply gotten to his feet. His wings unfolded, and most of the village and forest vanished. On both sides was dark blue sky and an endless expanse of poised scarlet. His head and neck extended, and his body tilted, sinking into his haunches like a horse preparing to leap. I sensed living muscle under my legs drawing tight like a bow.

With spectacularly poor timing, I remembered something. *Did you not say you needed to launch from a ridge—*

I was slammed toward my seat. My chin clunked my breast while I pushed with my arms to avoid smashing face-first into dragon scales. Mary's death-tight grip around my waist helped, bracing us in a triangle. Weight surged weirdly. Rotated. I floated up against the lap belt, weightless, then smacked the seat again. The sky had broken loose of reality, the horizon slipping sideways at an incredible angle. That must be illusion, as I was being jammed ferociously into the saddle.

Yuánchi's wings, more than ever seeming like the complex sails of a huge ship, were flapping, but their joints flexed in complicated cupping and scooping motions, nothing like a simple up and down. The horizon tilted nearer to level, and the thumping on my rear end smoothed into surging, long pushes. I found the rhythm and relaxed. This was far less jarring than a galloping horse.

My goggles worked fantastically well. There was no hint of wind in my eyes despite the banshee-like howl in my ears. Oh. That was Mary shrieking.

I tried to shout reassuringly over my shoulder, but what came out was, "We are flying!" Treetops were rushing and vanishing beneath the—upper arms? fronts?—of Yuánchi's wings. Would a falconer know the proper words?

Yuánchi's voice filled my mind, thunderous with delight. *We fly. Mary, all is well.*

Mary's howling, which thus far had only paused for gasping refills of air, ended so abruptly that I felt the shocked snap of her mouth closing. She had heard him. I filed that away to investigate later.

The trees blurred past faster and faster. Yuánchi's wings were spread taut but no longer flapping—we were falling with the slope of the hill like a runaway cart. From nowhere, the sprawling roofs of Pemberley appeared, then vanished in a heartbeat. Pemberley lake loomed, then we skimmed across, the modest waves of a still dawn streaking so quickly they appeared to sizzle. Yuánchi's wings began working again, and we rose, following the road that led to Lambton.

Coherence penetrated my amazement, and I thought, *Turn away from the village. We must not be seen near Pemberley.*

Wordlessly—soaringly—our path changed, the horizon tilting more than forty-five degrees before leveling again. This time I noted the pressing heaviness while we turned. That was concealing the sensation of being tipped.

The wind had come. The oversized collar of my leather coat buzzed against my cheek as if infested with bees. The air was ferociously chill, but Yuánchi was warm and Mary was insulating my back. We winged along a forested valley, all dark green murk in the early light, flying below the peaks of the hills. That was my request for stealth.

I patted at Mary's hands until she loosened her grip a notch, then twisted to look back. Her eyes were squeezed tight. I shouted, "Can you hear me? Look. It is beautiful." Facing backward made me dizzy, so I turned back without waiting to see if she managed.

Do you always fly this fast? I thought. The wind was scraping my cheekbones.

This is slow. You would be uncomfortable if I flew quickly.

How fast was "slow," then? Yuánchi could fly from Pemberley to London in less than ninety minutes, although how much less was unclear; there had always been reasons to take circuitous routes. As the draca flies, that was one hundred and fifty miles, so he could exceed one hundred miles per hour. Was this half that speed? No, it must be faster. A racehorse sprinted at thirty miles per hour, and I did not believe any horse approached the speed with which landscape was rolling past.

I could compute it exactly by measuring the elapsed time when we arrived at London. But I had not checked the time when we left, and my watch was buried inside my coat. Being men's clothing, it had a preposterous number of pockets. Well, there was always the return trip.

"This is remarkable!" Mary shouted unexpectedly in my ear. She must have opened her eyes.

"Yes," I shouted back. "If we do not grow too tired, I would prefer not to stop before London." I had considered landing in the hills near Watford to plan —they were mostly empty and just short of London—but clambering down and up no longer appealed. My arms still felt the strain of steadying myself during our launch.

I had forgotten to bring a London map. Whimsically, I imagined plopping down on a street corner to ask directions.

The sun cracked the horizon and lit my impending headache on fire.

"LIZZY." Mary's tone was steady but urgent. I had a vague, aural memory of hearing my name more than once.

The wind had lessened, an endless gust instead of a skin-abrading howl. I was lolling in my seat, arms hanging loose, gloved hands fluttering. I caught a handhold. Mary had reached an arm around me to hold the other handhold while gripping me with her free arm. I tapped her fingers, and she let go so I could grab the second handhold.

The sun was higher. The Thames was recognizable, exactly like the maps. I remembered flying a long time, but we hadn't been close to London. I had lost... an hour? Could I have slept like this?

Yuánchi thought worriedly, *I cannot speak to you when your mind is like that.*

When I am asleep? I thought cautiously.

You were not asleep.

His tone was suspicious. Wonderful. But this was not the time to discuss my health.

We will search the city from the air, I thought. *You must fly as low as you can, so people see only a glimpse. And fly slowly until I am sure how far I can sense a wyfe who has taken venom.*

I could have detected dosed Lydia across all of London, but her strength was incredible. Still, the dosed wyves at the ball were hardly subtle. A half-mile should be possible. So, passes a mile apart. How sure was I, though?

We were descending in a broad spiral west of the city proper, wings unmoving except for adjustments at the tips. I turned my head and shouted to Mary, "We will try one pass. An experiment," and projected the same thought to Yuánchi. Mary nodded.

Slow flight felt much faster when the ground was close. In a blink, we were skimming the Thames. In flight, Yuánchi tucked his legs close and stretched his flexible body like a spear, so I found myself staring over his shoulder at chunky, broken ice and dark water roaring past no more than fifteen feet below. I looked ahead and saw a stone bridge approaching. Were we going over? Surely not beneath. The spans would never fit his wings.

You have not opened your mind, Yuánchi thought reprovingly.

I had forgotten the whole point. I closed my eyes, struggling for the required calm but distracted by every jog and tilt. Abruptly, our motion changed—the sound of wind over wing ceased, and we became weightless and fell. A hard shadow flashed over my closed eyelids, then wings caught air with a powerful snap and weight surged back. Beneath the bridge, then.

Trust Yuánchi to fly. My thoughts settled, and my senses expanded.

Yuánchi came first, a shining cloud of brilliance below and around me. Then sparks of bound draca's awareness passed on each side. I could pick them out even at this speed. Lindworm. Ferretworm. I exhaled, falling into the mindset, willing my mind farther, and then there were too many to name, each a beautiful, flickering being. They flowed past like a storm of fireflies. But no oily dark. No corrupted wyfe.

Too soon, the sparks became few. We swerved and soared upward. Mary whooped delightedly, which was far nicer than shrieking. I opened my eyes and saw the sparse settlements of outer London, though I was not sure where.

"This will work!" I shouted. "But I found nothing yet."

"Try the docks," Mary shouted back. "Search near fishers." She must have clues from Miss Bathurst.

We turned a tight, tipped half-circle that drove me into my seat and made the wind over Yuánchi's wings hiss and moan. The jagged skyline of London came into view, palled with coal smoke. I braced my hands on one of the red knobs on Yuánchi's neck and leaned forward, peering to choose a path.

36

THE WINDOW

EMMA

I woke to a soft rattle from our guest room door. It came again, a tiny but insistent bump.

Harriet was sound asleep, but the window showed the night-dark ridges of Pemberley valley against a faint blue glow. Sunrise was near. My slippers lay precisely side-by-side with my dressing gown folded and fanned on the dressing table above them. Lucy had learned my bedtime ritual as well as any maid at Highbury.

Wrapped against the chill, I stood motionless until I was able to accept the scrabble of disarranged hair on my neck and back, then I eased the door ajar. A little tykeworm turned up her nutmeg muzzle and ink-black eyes, then sat on her haunches. Not the tyke bound to Lizzy's aunt. This one had dark brown paws, as if she had scampered through coffee grounds.

I crouched and whispered, "Good morning." Only closely bound wyves dared touch draca, but, feeling bold after the firedrake in the physic garden, I stroked a finger down her back. The tyke arched happily, so I petted her with my whole hand. Her scales were warm as a cat lazing in the sun. Her skin was supple, but each scale was hard. It was like stroking close-set, smooth jewels.

Like the firedrake at the garden, this draca was not bound—the brightness of binding was curled up within her. Bemused, I asked, "How did you get into Pemberley House?"

She grinned inscrutably, revealing impressive fangs for such a small creature, then padded a few yards along the hall before looking back expectantly. I pulled the door closed and padded after her.

We wandered a hallway of polished wood floors. Windowpanes framed squares of magenta twilight. I passed beneath unlit wrought iron chandeliers and down a wide, curving stairway, the tyke's paws silenced by luxurious carpet. The notes of a pianoforte became audible, and the tykeworm bounded ahead.

Candlelight and music poured from open, elaborately carved wooden doors. I entered and was surrounded by a collection of pianofortes in gleaming walnut, red cherry, and black ebony. One was square, a few were stubby triangles, the rest had modern serpentine curves on their treble side. Most were pushed by the walls as if out of favor, but in the middle of the room, the largest two instruments faced each other, their nestled curves very feminine. I had never seen such large instruments, seven feet long at least.

One instrument was closed. At the other, Georgiana, wrapped in a blue velvet robe with her black hair messily pinned, was playing a baroque composition filled with tinkling trills and ornaments. Without interrupting her music, she smiled a greeting at me, then concentrated on her playing. The mysterious tyke sat at her feet for a few bars, then began exploring the other instruments.

Not wanting to distract her, I walked to the far side of the room—a towering wall of glass. I had never seen anything like it, not even in London. Behind pinpoint reflections of candles, vague shadows of mossy oaks slumbered.

The precise meter of Georgiana's playing relaxed. Skipping the traditional baroque close, the music dissolved into melodic, lingering chords. This was not the composer's work, but a wandering improvisation.

"What do you see outside?" she asked. Her music changed, as curious as her words.

"It is too dark to see much," I answered. That was a dull reply for someone serenaded and facing a tower of glass, so I added, "I am sure it is beautiful by daylight."

Georgiana nodded toward the tyke, who had returned to stalk the hem of her robe with stiff-shouldered pounces. "Mary is shut away working all night, so I came to play. Our friend arrived outside to listen. I was not sure he was real, so I opened the door and sang of you, and he ran in."

"He is certainly solid," I said, quite familiar with wondering if things were real. "He thumped my door."

264

The harmonies of Georgiana's improvisation converged, narrowed, then ended on a single hanging note. She whispered, "I sang of you so you could see. Watch the window."

She leaned into a deep, rippling chord—the start of a composition more involved than her improvisation. Slow chords riveted my attention, glimmering on the edge of dissonance, dancing toward unexpected resolutions, then breaking apart and hunting anew. The harmonies were complex, but the melody was songlike, resonating with romance and sadness, then searching and brightening. It was music of emergence. Music of dawn.

Remembering her request, I turned to the window. The trembling high harmonies seemed to have drawn shimmering, reddish beams among the plum-purple shadows behind the glass.

"This was written for me," Georgiana said, then she began to sing. I did not recognize the language—it was not Italian or French or German—but her voice soared in a descant above a rumbling bass melody, each accented note struck so hard the strings pinged percussively.

Her voice woke the music, then the music woke the world. It was like the mountains stirred.

A silent wind plucked my robe. The glass wall and its dozen reflected candles erased as if it had never been. My slippers nestled in the grassy loam of a springtime forest. Vital pollen danced in the air. My startled intake of breath was sweet with sappy sprouts and blooms.

Freckled beams of sunlight dappled a wyvern, a male with deep brown scales that turned ivory on his chest and belly.

His thoughts filled my mind. *after so long, you have come*

Do you know me? I thought.

Lady Anne saw the rising storm. saw it would surpass her strength. she sent me away to wait for you

Why for me?

so the next healer could be stronger. look to the north. i keep her gift for you

The wyvern vanished as instantly and completely as the glass wall. Daylight darkened to stormy gray. The treetops whipped and shook in squally gusts. Spring-green leaves rained down, decaying in mid-air so they turned splotchy brown by the level of my eyes, then slimy black by my feet. They squelched to the earth in a soggy muck.

The stripped treetops revealed churning cloud. It was darkest toward the east, and my gaze followed.

Far away, across an endless expanse of blue water, an oily blackness spread. It writhed, serpent-like. It burrowed and feasted on corruption. My heart cried to flee, but terror rooted my feet in the rotted duff. The unholy malevolence spread, a vileness that thirsted for cities. For continents.

Even as the tree trunks themselves began to fall in fetid spoilage, Georgiana's bright song penetrated the blackening skies. I clung to her voice, and the destruction faded. The ringing chords of her pianoforte emerged, buttressing her melody, and hope returned.

The glass wall reflected the music room, warm and well lit. Beyond, the old forest waited for dawn. Georgiana's song had ended.

"Did you see anything?" she asked, folding her hands in her lap.

My mind was so overwhelmed that my answer was mechanical. "I saw a wyvern. Then blight. An oily blackness in the east." Georgiana nodded, unsurprised, and my amazement broke loose. "What *was* that? A vision? Magic? I pray it was not prophecy."

"I have no name for it. I see it, also. No one else does. Not even Lizzy. Lizzy has rules in her head, and her rules say windows do not vanish." Georgiana played an idle passage with one hand. "The wyvern was Mamma's. I remember him distinctly. I used to pet him. She said I was old enough. Eleven."

I thought of his bronze and ivory vigil. "He said your mother sent him away."

The bench legs rattled as Georgiana shot to her feet. "He *spoke* to you?" Her hand clutched the pianoforte's case. "I only see him. Again and again, and then the world dies."

"I am sorry you did not hear." There was hurt in Georgiana's eyes, so I tried to share what I heard. "He said Lady Anne asked him to wait for me."

Her hurt became shock, then softened to puzzlement. "Of course, I would not hear. I never hear draca's voices. I hear their music, which is better. But... a message from *Mamma*...." She bit her lip, her shoulders rigid, her willowy frame gawky and thin. "This is why I do not sing while I play. Together, they are too much. Things change."

"Do you know what that... oily blight is?" I asked. Unlike the illusions of the miasma, which seemed implausible as dreams when I remembered them later, that vileness still chilled me. It was real.

"I first glimpsed it in my bedroom window after Mamma's death. I asked Fitz for a room with a bigger window—so I could see more—and he made me this." Without irony, her fingers swept the perspective of the windowed wall, thrice my height. "When Fènnù rose, I wondered if she was the darkness, but when we met her at the museum, she was only broken, not evil. So, it is something else. It reminds me of how Lizzy describes a wyfe dosed with crawler venom, but the blight is not a person. It is a... force. It seeks to swallow the world." Swiftly, she crossed from her instrument to the fireplace and rubbed her hands in the warmth. "The east is where Napoleon leads his armies. But this evil is greater than a man. I think Napoleon is its pawn."

Despite the bleak topic, that amused me. "Do not tell Napoleon. He would be insulted."

Georgiana smiled, too. "Lord Wellington would be as well. He steels himself for the ultimate battle with Monsieur Bonaparte. He prefers enemies of flesh and cannons of iron, not ladies' visions." Her cheeks puffed with a youthful sigh. "The war is part of the blight, but the blight is much bigger. Has Lord Wellington asked you about the dagger?"

Her churn of topics was boggling this early in the morning. "I have hardly spoken with his lordship."

"He knows there is another great wyfe. He suspects it is you or Mary. When he knows the truth, he will ask you."

I imagined Lord Wellington accusing me of being a great wyfe. "Ask me what?"

"If you will wield the dagger. He hopes to find it, then have a wyfe command Fènnù to destroy the French army. He asked me yesterday, before he left." She had settled at the keyboard again—she seemed unable to stay away—and she banged a showy minor chord, the sort overused in amateur theater. "His frown was most grave. He warned that the dagger might kill me."

I looked at this slim beauty, who two years younger I would have called a girl. Her eyes were thoughtful but not frightened. "How could you answer such a question?"

"I said I did not yet know." Georgiana rolled her eyes comically. "Fitz and Lizzy and Mary... they are always certain what is right. They would answer 'no' and cite a thousand reasons. But do their reasons mean I must let darkness consume the people I love?"

I remembered gazing into Fènnù's eyes outside the museum. "I do not think Fènnù should be commanded by anyone. Her mind is ill. It is unfair."

Georgiana played a heroic chord. "I like *your* reason." She tucked a black lock of hair behind her ear. "Will you and Fitz meet this morning?"

Yet another topic. "Mr. Darcy wishes to assist me with 'methods' that helped his mother. Your mother, I mean."

Georgiana grinned affectionately. "He asked my opinion before he spoke to you. He was nervous about discussing Mamma." Not for the first time, I wondered what family history had unsettled him, and she added, "When you stand like that, with your feelings hidden, you are so like her. Not how you *look* —your hair is gold, while there seems a rule that Darcys have dark hair. But your feelings are pent up in the lines of your body, like a dancer before the music begins and they are free to leap and swirl. Mamma tried to hide her feelings, too. But feelings always break free."

Georgiana's fingers had wandered into the composition she played before. The one written for her. The intensity and novelty of the harmonies summoned that long-ago night on a frozen ship when Mr. Knightley described a gifted composer. "That is Mary Bennet's music!"

Georgiana nodded, pleased. "I knew you would realize. She wrote this about her and me. You are the first person for whom I have played it, so you are the first person to know that I love her." Her shoulders lifted in a musing shrug. "Well, perhaps not. I think Fitz has guessed. Still, it is different to say it." She played a shimmering chord. "I do not think love is proven until you tell someone. So, now I have."

"Oh," I said, inadequately, wondering what she had just shared. I had scoffed when Mr. Knightley claimed Mary was jealous of my friendship with Georgiana, but since then I had witnessed their charming intimacies. Had they been a man and a woman, I would have long since declared them wildly infatuated.

Still, it was not unusual for two ladies to set up a household of convenience, and some couples were rumored to be more. The Ladies of Llangollen were a famous pair, but they had money, which made all the difference. Money freed a woman's life in a hundred ways; freedom of love was one. But even for a wealthy Darcy, a non-traditional romance was dangerous. The Society for the Suppression of Vice pursued what they called "husband-wives," and the results were violent.

Georgiana's fingers explored melodies. She was five years my junior, but she seemed vastly more confident of love than me.

"You are right," I said, "Telling someone is a test. A proof." I watched her wrists sweep graceful arpeggios the length of the keyboard. "I shall keep it in confidence. But Mr. Knightley has guessed."

Georgiana smiled. "He would. He knows Mary so well."

"I have never been in love," I said softly. I must not be. It would be too cruel.

Georgiana's music halted. When the overtones faded, she spoke, her head lowered as if addressing the keys. "Mr. Knightley is a good friend, and a great romantic. You make me fear he will be hurt."

I had said that I was not in love.

There was only one circumstance where an absence of love caused hurt. But Mr. Knightley could not be in love with me. He *knew* I would not marry. Was this a caution? A rebuke? Had I encouraged him?

Mr. Knightley had seemed safe. A gentleman without a living could not marry. Then again, he could marry for money. But no man would knowingly forgo the prestige of binding.

Encounters played in my mind, teeming with repressed feelings and resentment, or painful explanations and regret. But even that part of love—heartbreak —was lost to me. Mr. Knightley was leaving.

37

THE CELLAR

LIZZY

I had never seen a London intersection deserted in mid-morning. Even the cries of the fleeing Londoners were distant.

Mary dropped stiffly from the saddle ladder to the cobblestones beside me. She worked her neck with a grunt and squinted at the intersection signs. "I thought we would land at Chathford House."

"Then everyone would see Yuánchi arrive at a Darcy residence. This is nearer our goal." My own legs were complaining, but I could hardly stretch on a public street. "The faster we are there, the more advantage of surprise."

On our fifth pass over the city, crossing a disreputable slum of warehouses and tanners, I felt the oily dark corruption of a dosed wyfe. We had landed a quarter mile away.

"Surprise?" Mary said dubiously. "People ran. People see us *now*!" Although the street had emptied while Yuánchi circled to land, heads crowded every window.

"All they see are two bizarrely dressed people," I pointed out. "Help me." I unbuckled the saddlebag, which appeared tiny strapped to Yuánchi but was tremendous by usual standards. I could have packed three spring bonnets and not creased a ribbon, but as we each grabbed a bundle, the cloth and colors were far more prosaic.

I thought to Yuánchi, *Hide outside London. I shall call when we are ready.*

You need my protection.

I need protection that fits through a door. Go. But frighten away these watching people.

His lithe neck bent until his muzzle faced straight upward like a fountain as tall as a building. He spread the nearest joints of his wings from his body, keeping the rest pinched closed to fit between the buildings. The breadth of one wing curved over us like a sheltering roof.

Close your eyes.

"Take off your spectacles," I said to Mary. Once she fiddled them off—she had tied them to a leather lace behind her head—I pulled her surprised face against my shoulder. "Hide your eyes. And cover your ears!" Her palms clamped in place just before I buried my own eyes in her shoulder.

We were near Yuánchi's chest, and through my own pressed palms, I heard a rumble. It was not inhalation—this was nothing so mundane as breath—but a building tension like the thousand miniature hisses and groans of a steam boiler at high pressure. Then the corners of my buried eyelids flared white, heat flashed every exposed inch of skin, and a roar—did something that loud even have a sound?—shook my lungs within my chest. It ended in a moment, even before my skin goosebumped in instinctive animal fright.

By the time we lifted our heads, Yuánchi was trotting down the street, his tail held awkwardly high so he would not accidentally crush us. In a dozen strides he reached the next corner. He peered both ways, doubtless curious but looking remarkably like a cautious walker, then spread his wings and rose in a thunder of wind. In seconds, he was out of sight.

I tugged Mary's hand. "We can be gone while their eyes are dazzled."

"Look at the sky," she cried.

It was a day of high thin cloud and spotty low puffs, but above us, a round of pure blue sky was spreading. In the center, the air glowed in shimmering greens and yellows that folded like giant butterfly wings. As they faded, leaving a roiling fringe of cloud at the circle's edge, I pulled Mary toward the wharves.

We ducked into an alley, stripped off our heavy leather coats and caps, and pulled on our nondescript brown riding hoods. A few inches of Mary's trousers were exposed, but no one would care if we did not enter a respectable establishment. I doubted that was our destination.

"This is madness," Mary muttered, flapping her shapeless garment.

"Says the sister who waited all night to ambush me."

"*You* are mad," she clarified.

271

"That is a symptom of my impending death," I said, peeking around the corner. There was a distant din from some unseen crowd, but in view there was only a pair of men, pointing skyward and conversing rapidly.

I closed my eyes, settled my excitement, and easily located the pocket of vileness. "This way—" I began, then opened my eyes to see Mary's cheeks wet with tears. My own heart seized. "Mary, you must not, or I will dissolve in a puddle beside you, and we will achieve nothing." Her throat lurched through a swallow, then she dashed her tears off and nodded.

We hurried on. The road was still vacant. That was odd. A dragon sighting, however frightening, should draw the indomitable curious of London.

One street short of the wharves, I stopped at the corner of a rundown, nondescript wooden building. It leaked a reek of dead fish far worse than the usual wet odor of the Thames.

"The wyfe is there..." I began, then hesitated. I was long past committed to this plan, but the realization of imminent violence froze me. What if I lost my mind? What if I hurt Mary?

Mary was surveying the exterior with the obsessive focus she applied to books in dead languages. She sniffed the air. "This is very likely where Miss Bathurst was kept. The odor. The district. It is all correct." She faced me, recognized my hesitation, and her expression became determined. "Lizzy, these men are murderers and fiends. English law would hang them many times over."

"I know." At least my hesitation suggested I would not be possessed by the mad, vengeful thrill of battle. "Let us begin."

I closed my eyes and fell into... not calm, but a balanced and honed focus. I drove the boundaries of my mind outward. Not just awareness, but influence. The strength to command, if needed. The distant sounds of the city vanished, and my headache went with them. I had not noticed it lingering.

The blur of the dosed wyfe resolved, but faint. An old dose, faded. She was below the street and near the back of the building. A cellar.

There were draca all about us, a few nearby, many more distant, each an intoxicating spark, tiny and young or aged and wise. I began surveying them for suitability, then discarded delicacy and sent a summons: *Help me!* It rang out in all directions, even sweeping over the Thames and up the far shore.

"Aid is on the way," I said, opening my eyes. "A great deal of aid."

The door was weathered wood planks with a shuttered face-sized peephole. I looked for a doorbell, then felt foolish when Mary pounded on the wood with her fist.

Steps approached, and the peephole shutter opened. Suspicious eyes gleamed. A guttural man's voice said, "Who are you?"

"We have a message from Mr. Tinsdale," I said. I did not know how Mr. Tinsdale was involved with the dagger, but there were so many hints, his name must be known.

The eyes flicked between Mary and me, then the voice said, "Frig off." The peephole slammed.

Behind us, a patter of running paws approached. I touched Mary's shoulder, moving her to one side of the door while I stepped the other way, then I chose one of the heftier draca minds and pictured the door as an obstacle.

A lindworm, thirty pounds of locking scales, dense draca bone, and surging muscle shot between Mary and me, level with my chest from his running leap. He cannoned into the door with the violent clap of a sledgehammer striking a pile of loose wood. The door burst open, shuddering on its hinges and scattering a splintered locking beam across the stone floor.

The man whose suspicious eyes had watched us stood, jaw hanging. He was tall, ill-fed and hunched, and sported a greasy black beard, a grubby shirt that may once have been white, and trousers drooping from a rope belt.

Scaled shapes streamed past Mary's and my feet like a metallic brook—roseworms, tunnelworms, a ferretworm, a tyke. In the room, window glass smashed inward as draca leaped through, snarling in their peculiar, whistling way. The lindworm, recovered from his spectacular entrance, leaped again, butting the man in his chest and flattening him on the ground where he vanished under a wave of draca.

"Stop!" I cried. Gory memories of my aunt's small tyke killing a French spy filled my mind, and I ran into the room, fearing I was too late. But the man was intact, not shredded, although winded and furious. He was surrounded by draca, several perched on his body, all with fangs bared and hissing.

"Stay very still," I advised him. My floppy hood was like looking through a tunnel, so I yanked it down. This single room spanned the entire building. The only concealment was three vertical timbers to support the roof joists, a stove and stone chimney against a wall, and a modest pile of crates that would have barely hidden a child. Scattered trash and two open, shallow crates of rotting fish completed the picture.

"Who else is here?" I said.

"Ain't no one," the man spat, rebellious but nervous.

Mary was dashing around the room, frantic with haste and half-tripping over the milling draca. "She is not here!"

"There is a cellar," I said and pointed to the crates.

Mary pushed the piled crates aside. They were empty and fell easily, revealing a wooden hatch with a rusted iron handle. Before I could stop her—anything might be down there—she hauled the handle with two hands and threw the hatch aside to clatter on the floor.

The hatch left a square of shadow in the stone floor. Mary knelt at the edge, then recoiled with a grimace. Slitting her eyes and nostrils in distaste, she leaned in again. "I need light. I cannot go down in the dark."

I grabbed a stick of kindling from a pile by the stove and took it to her. "Light it." The stench from the hole hit my face, vile with ammonia that made my eyes stream and my stomach flip. I knew Mary was desperate to find her friend, and abruptly I feared the worst. "Mary, do not go down until we know more."

"That odor is excrement and filth, not rot," she said, speaking in the lightning syllables she used when excited. She headed to the stove. "We have not opened a crypt."

I retreated a few steps into the lesser stench of rotted fish, drained my lungs, lidded my eyes, and was surrounded by a whirlpool of swarming draca minds. Dozens had arrived, and more were coming, dashing through the ruined door and leaping through the broken windows. A roseworm was at my feet. I stroked her awareness, found her willing, and sank into her vision.

I saw myself, shapeless in my robe but massively haloed with brilliant gold, a great wyfe with her influence cast wide. The cracking plaster and old timbers snapped into ridiculous detail. Scent, thankfully, faded. Now that I thought of it, I could not recall ever noticing scent through draca senses. Perhaps draca noses were less sensitive, a tradeoff for their incredible vision. Here, that was convenient.

I shared my curiosity about the open hatch, and the view bounced forward and peered down. A ladder descended to a dirt floor that was a neutral cool spotted with the magenta of soil chilled by damp. Two wooden buckets stood to one side, filled with unpleasantly lumpy liquid. As curious as me, the roseworm's perspective shifted as she trotted around the perimeter.

A person's warm figure, lying flat, came into view, then another beside. The view lowered—I felt the roseworm's jaw rest on the edge of the hole—and I saw farther.

"Oh, no," I said.

"What?" Mary cried into my ear, breaking my concentration. I shook free of the roseworm's view and found Mary distraught, a few pieces of kindling flaming in her white-knuckled hand like a torch.

"There are more than I expected," I said.

"Guard the man!" Mary said. She hitched up her riding robe, got her boots on the ladder, and descended into the black with her wavering flame.

Wondering when Mary ended up in charge, I turned to the man. His rebelliousness had drained. He stared at me in open terror. "You's one of them witches!"

It seemed counter-productive to argue semantics, so I said, "I am," and produced what I hoped was a menacing smile. He quailed nicely.

Faces were gathering outside the gaping door. I put my shoulder to the wood and ground it across the floor pavers, one broken hinge flapping, until the view was mostly blocked. I returned to stand over the man. "Who comes here?" He jutted out his chin, so I waved my hand showily and sent a silent request. The roseworm jumped onto the man's chest, little razor fangs bared. "Tell me, or I shall transform you into a newt and have her eat you."

"That whisperer. The American," he grudged. "But he haven't been here for days. He took one of them girls."

"And Mr. Tinsdale?"

He gave a surprised shake of his head. "Just the beggar lady who feeds 'em."

I reviewed our plan and remembered an important goal. "Where is the dagger?"

"I got a pistol," he said, scowling as if this was some trick. "Broke it lightin' the stove. Got no flint. It been freezin'."

"What do you do here?"

"Add fish every day. Keep people out. Don't see nothing." His list was rote, a child repeating a lesson.

Mary clambered up the ladder and clumsily rolled onto the floor. She stood and shook out her hair, a cleansing fueled by disgust or anger. "Rebecca is here. She is alive but unresponsive. They are dehydrated. We need help. Let nobody in." She ran to the crooked door and squeezed through the gap. Through a broken window, I glimpsed her gray robe flapping as she ran down the street.

"Who's she?" the man asked.

"Witch number two," I said absently while trying to convey the concept of *Keep People Away* as images for the hoard of draca outside. Then I began an

275

organized search, lifting refuse and tossing crates, although I knew it was pointless. The dagger was priceless. It would not be left in filth guarded by a fool.

Finally, I turned up a tiny lamp like the one I had used to write or read in the night when I shared a room with Jane. An ounce of oil sloshed in the base. I lit a splinter at the stove, lit the lamp, faced the dark hole, and found my feet balked at that chamber of horrors.

Mary was unquestionably brave. I could more easily walk to my death than descend into that stinking filth and pain. But that was cowardly and selfish. I had killed one of her friends. Another was down there, with other innocents.

"Do not attempt to flee," I called to the man. "The draca will rip you limb from limb if you rise." Actually, they would simply alert me, but the threat was gratifying.

Step by step, I descended the ladder into dark. The stench crawled up my nostrils. Each breath was clinging filth in my throat. At the bottom, I raised the lamp and counted. Nine women, all in the filthy remnants of dresses that had once been good, now terribly soiled because they could not rise to relieve themselves. There were no beds, only strips of blankets and straw thrown on the floor. The women were packed close as cargo, their feet trapped in horrible, heavy iron shackles. The nearest set lay open, that strip of dirt empty.

A few faces turned vaguely toward me, or to the light more likely, blinking owlishly and unknowingly. No one answered when I spoke. They were drugged to insensibility, but it was something other than crawler venom or I would have sensed them all.

There was a squat table with stubs of candles, metal dishes, and glass jars with tied leather lids. One metal dish held a few ounces of sticky, brown paste. I had to bring it close to my nose before the medicinal fishy odor penetrated the general stench. Laudanum, but stronger. Raw opium.

My eyes had adapted so swiftly to the dark that the lamp flame was a knife. I shuttered it and set it on the table, relying on the dim light through the cellar opening. The darkness was soothing, but peculiar reds and yellows surged and faded at the sides of my vision. That did not seem healthy.

I knelt to examine the shackles on the ankles of the woman nearest me. They were thick iron bolted with a hammered rivet, not a lock. A wyvern's claws would tear it easily, but the nearest I remembered was at an estate twenty miles from London, too far to reach without being bound to the creature.

Work with what you have. I called the lindworm, and he jumped down with ease. I slipped my delicate lady's fingers between the iron, pulled futilely, then pictured him trying. He scratched at the metal, his claw ringing like a hardened file, then began working at it like a dog with a bone, paws pinning the metal while he chomped at different angles. When the rivet caught between his back teeth, he clamped down with a satisfied purr. With a screech, the rivet head popped off and bounced off the ceiling, and the shackles fell loose.

I bent to give him the effusive praise a dog would adore, but the lindworm stepped impatiently around my outstretched hand, found the next set of shackles, and began gnawing.

Just as I noticed a shadowy shape beneath the low table, several pairs of footsteps entered noisily above my head. Mary's voice shouted, "Lizzy!"

"Down here."

Mary clambered down holding her own, larger lamp. I shielded my eyes and said, "We will have the shackles off soon," as another rivet pinged free in the shadows.

Carefully, Mary removed the iron bars from the first wyfe's ankles. The skin was scabbed and bloody, and I looked away while Mary gently examined and prodded. "No bones are broken. She can be moved." Mary called instructions up the ladder, and a man's voice answered.

"The dagger is not here," I said, squatting to look beneath the table. Mary's lips thinned in dismay, but I held up what I found in a box. "Books." That lit her interest.

We climbed up, and I met two black-clad, straight-haired Marys and a burly, mustached constable. The constable was tying the captive man's hands and ankles with a thick length of hemp.

Mary sent the constable into the cellar. He swore a streak at the reek by the ladder, then swore again, softer but more shockingly, when he saw the women below.

With him out of sight, I raised an eyebrow at Mary. The last person I expected her to summon was a constable, and she looked embarrassed, muttering, "He is one of the good ones," before beginning instructions to one of the Marys: "These women need specific care. Provide this note to Dr. Davenport. They must be concealed. The men who took them may seek to recover them. Reopen the old shelter house." She was scribbling on a square of notepaper while she talked. Leave it to Mary to bring pencil and paper.

The Mary she had addressed, an auburn-haired woman around Mary's nineteen years, said worriedly, "*You* must hide. Men came to my house. They frightened my Mamma terribly, but they were seeking you. They asked if you were in Derbyshire. They claimed to be constables, but I did not believe them. Mary, London is descending to madness. Already, there are districts where gangs of men roam shouting that Britain Awakes in the south—"

A strange sensation prickled my mind. I stopped listening and turned slowly, trying to locate it. It was very far. So far, I was amazed I sensed it. But it was coming nearer. Quickly.

"Mary!" I said, interrupting another tranche of rapid-fire instructions. "We must go."

She blinked behind her spectacles. "I cannot. Rebecca did not even recognize me. I must—"

While she spoke, I had grasped the silver thread of my binding to Yuánchi and sent, *Find us. Hurry.*

Aloud I said, "We are out of time. Fènnù is coming."

THE LESSON

EMMA

M r. Darcy's notepaper was thick and rich as cream, with lines of ruler-straight script:

"Miss Woodhouse,

If your schedule permits, I shall meet with you at ten o'clock in the ivory alcove of the north garden. Any member of the staff will be pleased to offer direction. I have invited Miss Harriet Smith to attend with us.

Yours respectfully,
Fitzwilliam Darcy."

The ivory alcove was almost hidden by dwarf holly and juniper. Sculpted angels half-concealed in greenery watched serenely from four compass points. In the center, a garden table and benches of carved ivory stone were swept freshly clean.

I took a seat, bundled, gloved, and scarved in white. Although the savage cold gripping England had broken, Pemberley was high in the Peaks, and the leaves sparkled with morning frost.

Harriet came, stomping the gravel, her arms folded tight against the chill, or more likely against me. She thudded into the farthest seat and glared a hole through the table.

"Are you still vexed?" I said.

She burst out, "How could you say 'Teaching is unsuitable for a lady' in front of everyone!"

I had mentioned that, gently, at yesterday's dinner. I straightened the seam on a gloved finger. "I did not wish you to embarrass yourself. It is proper to guard my sister's prospects."

I was determined to protect Harriet. After reflection, I was skeptical of Georgiana's hint that Mr. Knightley had formed an attachment to me. But it was a timely warning. Even the most well-meaning lady could blunder.

Harriet locked her black eyes to me, and they were blazing. "You cannot resist meddling. I have my own prospects, and I wish to do good." Bitingly, she added, "Mr. *Knightley* admired my plan."

Hearing his name woke a flutter in my belly, but I disliked having him invoked against me. "What does a London musician know of prospects and doing good?"

"What do you know, hiding in your rooms at Hartfield?"

That was hurtful, so I took a turn glaring holes in the table. In the corner of my eye, I saw Harriet shift uneasily. Well, if she was preparing an apology, she should hurry. It was not warm.

However, neither of us spoke until Mr. Darcy arrived. That was short-lived relief as Mr. Knightley followed a pace behind. The flutter in my belly became a flop, and a flush drove the chill from my cheeks.

The gentlemen bowed their greetings, and Mr. Darcy began, "Thank you for meeting outside. I am besieged by requests from our guests and did not wish to be interrupted. Privacy seemed wise."

"Why has Mr. Knightley joined us?" I said, sounding perfectly uncaring.

Mr. Darcy pursed his lips as if that were a deeply insightful question. He turned to Mr. Knightley, raised one eyebrow, and waited.

"I do not approve of Darcy meddling with your mind," Mr. Knightley announced. Harriet *hmphed* approvingly, apparently in support of anti-meddlers even though Mr. Knightley was meddling right in front of her nose.

Mr. Darcy said to me, "As I have assured Knightley, I will do nothing to your mind. The methods I speak of are simple aids. They are neither mesmerism nor manipulation."

That did not satisfy Mr. Knightley. "Miss Woodhouse is an independent woman. She should not be reliant on your arcane projects. Nor should her care for Nessy."

"That is very kind of you, Mr. Knightley," I said. "Would an independent woman choose for herself?"

"I... yes, certainly." Mr. Knightley drummed his fingers in an involved pattern, then blurted, "Just consider your options."

I had no idea how to interpret that.

"These methods are to help Miss Woodhouse's personal wellbeing," Mr. Darcy said. "They are not arcane, and they have no relation to her healing ability as a great wyfe."

"They will not help with Nessy?" I said.

"No." Reluctantly, he added, "My mother treated several consumptives. She was unsuccessful."

That settled like a stone in my belly, but I nodded.

Mr. Darcy began rather formally. "You will recall that my mother struggled with a compulsion for order and symmetry. It was worsened by any perception of illness. She was aware of her condition and discussed it frankly with me, and we experimented with mental techniques to manage the debilitating effects. We were successful, in part."

Mr. Darcy's gloved hand was clenched on the stone table. Georgiana had said he was uncomfortable discussing his mother.

"What does 'in part' mean?" I asked.

"While she remained bound, her episodes became rare and manageable. But after my father died, her binding broke, and her wyvern left. Then..." His throat worked. "Our techniques were then insufficient."

Already, there was convergence with the vision Georgiana summoned through those huge windows. "Lady Anne's wyvern did not leave. Lady Anne sent him away."

Mr. Darcy's clenched hand twitched. He lifted it to knead the back of his neck. "Elizabeth told you this?"

"No. Georgiana showed me a vision this morning. I saw Lady Anne's wyvern, and he spoke to me."

"There are *visions* now?" Mr. Knightley exclaimed. "Are you certain this is the right path?"

I frowned. "I do what I like. Why are you so disagreeable?"

"I dislike being avoided," he said pointedly. "I sought you all last evening."

Why did everyone accuse me of hiding? "You announced you were traveling to your death. I assumed you were packing."

That silenced Mr. Knightley, but Mr. Darcy had his own pent-up exclamation. "My mother's wyvern left years ago. He *spoke* to you?"

"Of course," I said crossly. "He is waiting for me with memories of Lady Anne. I imagine it is a message. At the ball, Lady Catherine's wyvern spoke of a messenger to the north. But wyverns are terribly vague."

Now the whole table was silenced. Their stupefied expressions were much better than being scolded for hiding and meddling. I crossed my wrists on the table edge and added, "So? What is this technique?"

Seconds passed before Mr. Darcy spoke. "I have never known what to make of Georgiana's vision. Your insight is crucial. Elizabeth should hear also, but she is visiting Mr. Digweed and the Pemberley Britons. She should have returned by now..." He trailed off uneasily.

"Then we may as well discuss your technique," I pointed out. All this delay was making me curious.

"True." He set his shoulders. "Let us compare your symptoms to my mother's. The core of Lady Anne's illness was attacks of crippling fear. She became certain that severe illness was about to strike. She believed she could prevent that only through perfection in the clothing and appearance of herself and those around her. Quickly, those compulsions grew and became an illness in themselves."

I had blanched at the exactness of his description. Harriet reached across the table to take my hand, and I gave her a squeeze, remorseful for being cross before.

"That is what I feel," I answered, trying to match his factual manner.

"Yet the threat of illness is always to others, not yourself."

"Yes!" But he had not mentioned one thing. "Did she see the miasma? *See* the false illness strike those around her? Like a dream that is impossible but cannot be disbelieved?"

He answered slowly, "Much later, when she was no longer bound, my mother's fears manifested as visible illusions."

"I am unbound. If this method fails when one is not bound, what good is it?"

"It did help her, even then. It was simply... insufficient."

Harriet asked suspiciously, "What happened to Lady Anne?"

Instead of answering, Mr. Darcy resumed his teaching tone. "My mother experienced her first attacks in her eighteenth year, before she married. She tried to battle them with logic. She told herself that the illnesses she feared would not occur, so her fear was irrational."

"I do the same," I said, remembering the mental battles I hid in my room. "But my papa feared illness all his life, then his health failed. I had reassured him, and I was wrong. My *denials* were wrong." That realization had been harrowing.

"Denial failed my mother, also. But we discovered what helped. She had to accept that illness and injury may occur. Accept that illness is a matter of fate and out of her hands. Then her compulsion to ward off illness through rituals became irrelevant. Instead of denial, we practiced reaction. If the worst occurred, she would be prepared. She would act to help." His eyes considered me. "This may seem a trivial distinction."

"It... I am not sure." I was reliving my struggles. My endless fight to protect those around me. To build a fortress of perfection. "It is very different from what I have tried."

While I thought, my gaze drifted to the north point of our alcove. That statue was the hardest to make out, shadowed by a tough old yew, thick with greenery even in midwinter.

"My mother and I developed exercises to practice the distinction," Mr. Darcy continued. "I believe this difference, though subtle, is fundamental to breaking the grip of compulsion. If you wish, we can attempt these exercises together. Not this morning, though. They may be intense, and I am... Elizabeth should have returned by now." The last was a rush.

Mr. Knightley had watched with narrowed eyes. "You avoided Miss Woodhouse's question. I will ask it plainly. Is marriage required to restore her health?"

"I have only my mother's example," Mr. Darcy replied. "But her symptoms eased when she bound, then worsened when her wyvern..." His gaze hunted the garden while he sought words. "When she was no longer bound."

"Then Miss Woodhouse *must* marry," Mr. Knightley pressed.

"She must marry and *bind*," Mr. Darcy corrected. "Not all who marry succeed in binding."

This had taken an alarming turn. "You both sound like meddlesome grandmothers. I will not marry. And I am perfectly well today."

Hurried steps thudded, foliage flew aside, and a gray-haired gentleman in his sixties burst into our clearing, panting.

Mr. Darcy jumped to his feet. "Digweed! Have you seen Elizabeth?" Mr.

Digweed pulled him aside—I heard *London*—then Mr. Darcy returned looking dazed. "My wyfe has embarked on an unexpected trip. I must... I should..." He bowed and vanished at a run with the other gentleman.

"Good gracious!" Harriet exclaimed.

"Why will you not marry?" Mr. Knightley said as if that drama had not even occurred.

"I cannot imagine *whom* I would marry," I said scathingly.

Harriet had swiveled to watch that. When a deafening silence ensued, she ventured, "How did Georgiana show you a vision?"

"With music," I said. Harriet's eyes sparkled like we were reading a wonderful novel together, and I warmed to the topic. "It was like magic. Beautiful, then frightening. The wyvern said, 'look to the north'..."

My eyes returned to the north point of our alcove. I had thought all the statues were angels, but the north one cradled something winged and scaled, and had nine rays from her head. She was a twin to the statue in the physic garden, but here the alabaster stone was pure, not stained and eroded by the fumes of London.

Beyond her, a trail wound northward into the old woods of Pemberley. It vanished into gloom behind massive, mossy trees thick as carriages.

"It is too cold here!" Harriet said. "Tell me inside." She took my arm, and I went with her into the house. Mr. Knightley followed, wordless, his hands jammed in his pockets.

PURSUIT

MARY

With the captives protected, Lizzy and I hurried into the street. I checked both directions, wondering where a dragon would fit. "Which way?"

"Yuánchi will find us," Lizzy said, but her voice was more detached than confident. Disassociated.

"Let me see you." I steadied her chin to examine her eyes. We had discarded the riding hoods and pulled on our heavy fishermen's leathers and caps. Lizzy's curly dark hair was tucked away except for stray floating locks. The hairs looked black as coal against her drained complexion.

Pallor. Pupils blown to full dilation in daylight. I rested two fingers at her carotid artery. Pulse racing but weak beneath clammy skin. Illness, not fear.

This had worsened far too quickly. "Had you symptoms last night? Sweats?"

"Mary, I know I am worse. Do not bother." Her face tilted to the sky. "They both come. It is a close race." She stared upward, entranced by senses I did not share.

"By the river," I decided and pulled her along. We cut through a shipping yard, drawing stares for our garb from a set of boys braiding hawsers, then heard their youthful shouts when a dozen small draca scampered behind us. We scrambled over a collapsing chunk of seawall and onto the stony shore. Here there was room. A stiff, cold breeze snapped, little impeded by the broken ice. Even so, I was hot in the heavy leather.

Draca leaped from the seawall and gathered around our feet. "Lizzy, can you stop this... summons?"

"I called too loudly. They know me, now. That is how Fènnù found us. I called too loudly..."

Close to shore, the river was a slurry of hand-sized ice chunks, flotsam, and brackish water. Unexpectedly, the water glugged and surged, then a translucent, writhing shape, finned and fishlike and at least fifty pounds, drove itself onto the stony shore at Lizzy's feet. A shadowy shape squirmed inside. Lizzy had described this, the amphibian or chrysalis-like aquatic form draca took after their bindings broke, the form in which they transformed to their next breed. A razor claw split the side releasing a greasy torrent of gelatinous liquid, and a good-sized bronze lindworm crawled free, mewling at Lizzy.

"You! Stop!" A trio of men were running toward us on the street, their stride occasionally interrupted to look over the seawall, searching for a path down. They had the cropped hair and wide belts of Blackcoats.

"There," Lizzy said, pointing high. Scarlet Yuánchi, wings tucked to stoop like a hawk, was diving toward us. I steadied Lizzy as his wings snapped vast, hiding half the sky. The blast of wind launched spray and ice, and the draca around us hunkered low, claws clutching the ground. He hit with an earth-shaking splash, near foot ashore, far foot in the water, the ladder-like steps of the harness facing us.

Lizzy climbed while I stuffed the books from the cellar into the saddlebag, then I followed, strapping my lap belt and tugging hers to be sure she had not forgotten. I slapped Lizzy's shoulder and shouted, "Go!" and the wings drove us into the air. It was as tempestuous as the first launch. I caught a glimpse of the three men who had chased us pointing pistols, but they were too distant to be a danger. Then the sky rocked madly, and I held tight.

We settled into a rhythm, climbing fast. Like the first flight, pain built in my ears, then released with a pop. Pressure, like the effect reported by divers. A page of Valsalva's treatise on the Eustachian tube opened in my mind's eye, the Italian I had comprehended appearing in neat lettering, the parts I had not understood a mushy blur.

Lizzy twisted in her seat and looked left. Above the hills west of London, a black winged form flapped. Even miles distant, Fènnù's black silhouette was clear.

Yuánchi's voice filled my mind, a silent yet roaring basso profundo. *Hold fast for speed.* The force of his message rocked my mind. How did Lizzy manage this every day?

The rhythm of wings sped. The wind of flight, already intense, rose to a gale, then a tempest. Lizzy hunched forward and lay flat. I did the same, spectacles jammed against her leather coat. Still the wind grew, battering my shoulders and arms while an endless, merciless thunderclap howled.

With no warning, our path jagged up and to one side, slamming us into our seats. A monstrous black shadow flashed past. Twenty seconds later, we jagged again, sudden as a carriage striking a curb. My head was knocked up enough that my spectacles caught the wind. The leather cord snapped with an ephemeral tug, and they were gone. Squinting, face averted from the blast, the horizon softened to a familiar blur, rocked crazily, then leveled. Fènnù's black bulk flashed overhead again.

The wind had eased tremendously. We glided in a downward curve toward a hilltop. Lizzy pushed upright in her seat and shouted back, "We cannot outfly her. I told Yuánchi to land." Already, his wings were flared and cupping, and we settled in uncanny grace, his sides heaving like a ship-sized bellows.

Lizzy unstrapped her belt and climbed down. I hurried after, stripping off my gloves as my fingers were numb from effort. By the time my feet struck earth, Lizzy had dropped her cap and goggles in the rough grass. She turned to watch Fènnù's approach. Her expression was manic.

"What are we doing here?" I shouted.

"I have told Yuánchi not to interfere. I must help Fènnù. She is not under the dagger's influence, so our enemies are unaware. She comes only for me."

"That is what I am afraid of!"

A new round of gusts battered us. I shielded my eyes from dirt as Fènnù came down crouched, her chest thirty yards distant. This was my first view of her in daylight. She was longer in body and neck than Yuánchi, and even more broad-chested and muscled, easily twice his weight. The two dragons' necks wove, testing wary perspectives like a pair of belligerent barn cats. But not violent. Not yet.

Lizzy took an uncertain step forward, then another.

I said, "What are you doing?"

"She is mine. I am hers."

I caught Lizzy's wrist. She turned to me, her eyes wide as if amazed I were present, her pupils empty pools.

"You already have a dragon," I said. Her answer was a glassy stare and an impatient tug. Yuánchi towered above us, so I shouted up, "Stop her!"

She is a great wyfe. The will of a great wyfe has power.

"She would never choose this if her mind were clear!" There was no reply, so I took Lizzy's shoulders in my hands. "Lizzy. You are ill. It is time"—my throat balked at the gentle phrase I used at the clinic but had spoken only to strangers —"It is time to be with your family. It is time to go home."

"She calls me," she whispered. "I am not strong enough to deny her." She did not fight my grip, but her head craned, staring at the black dragon.

Fènnù's neck descended until her scintillating eyes were level with ours. The underside of her jaw brushed the grass; her head was as tall as me. This close, my blurred vision was clear. The black scales on her skin did not mesh with the smoothness of other draca; they were disfigured or diseased. Rough sores fringed her lower jaw. Farther away and slightly blurred, the sores continued along the leading edge of her shoulders. They dripped blackish ichor onto the grass, issuing an astringent and biting scent as the grass wilted. Oily, pitch-dark vapors rose, coiling like ink in water rather than gas.

A hot snort, cloyingly humid, blew around us. Lizzy moaned like a sleeper trapped in a nightmare.

I let her go and stepped between the dragon and her. Fènnù's nostrils and the sharp ridge atop her snout aligned at my breastbone. The faceted eyes fixed on mine. The tip of her snout drew closer. A yard. A foot. The rumbling rush of a breath flattened my leather jerkin, then the inhalation lifted it.

"You cannot take her," I said to those inhuman eyes. "She is unwell. If you desire her—if you *care* for her—find the sense to understand me."

The jaws cracked six inches, enough for the gleam of obsidian-black teeth and a rush of bitter air that sank in a chilled, veiling mist, but the gesture seemed puzzled, not a threat. What use had this creature for threats? No force could oppose her.

As another breath began, I laid the flat of my bare palm against her nose. It fit easily between her nostrils; I could have placed both hands side-by-side. The heat under my skin was fevered. The scales were sharp as roughly stacked blades.

I pressed hard, like I would prod a reluctant cow. There was no give, not the suppleness of mammalian skin, not yielding muscle, certainly not retreat. An animalistic fear unnerved the muscles in my arm. This was an adamantine colossus, as old and massive as the pyramids, a creature whispered of in myths of fallen cities.

Her eyes flickered, turbid with spectral hints, each a roiling jewel. But changing. Brightening with beautiful gossamer hints of gold.

"You are aware," I whispered. "The injured mind thirsts even more to comprehend. My sister has seen your past. She told me you rise in vengeance against wrongs. Remember what you were. It is the corrupt and powerful who covet and steal. If you overcome her—if you overwhelm her—you pollute yourself. The memories you treasure would diminish to *ignes fatui*. All you value would become mockery."

So abruptly that I staggered, the muzzle withdrew a yard, then farther. There was a gargantuan wheeling of gleaming black and the metallic grind of rubbing scales, then a blasting wash of fetid, acrid odor, and she was gone.

My outstretched arm hung, shaking. My ankles and feet were freezing. I clenched my fingers, feeling as if my heart had stopped and restarted, then turned.

Lizzy stood, eyes closed and face uplifted, her attention distant—her pose when sharing a draca's vision. Yuánchi's vision. His head was a few yards above hers, his gaze on me.

Yuánchi's thought came. *The will of a great wyfe has power.*

Lizzy whispered, "You are shining, Mary."

"What?" I said. How like my sister that sounded.

"It was you at the ball. The fourth great wyfe. But your aura is different. It stretches like a rainbow to the north. Toward Pemberley."

Fragments of facts fluttered past my mind's eye, like when weeks of research first hint at connected meaning.

"Lizzy," I said, "at the performance tonight. At the musical event for the royal court. I had planned... I hoped to show you a truth about me."

Her eyelids opened, and she smiled through pale lips. "Show me then. Nothing will keep me from your performance. I have another day, at least." She picked up her leather cap with its funny, round goggles and began hauling herself up the harness ladder.

A tiny movement caught my eye. A few feet from my frosted boot, the thick hilltop grass had eroded where the black ichor dripped. A small, segmented worm emerged from the ebon-stained, freshly barren earth. It was the length of my little finger, with dozens of pairs of legs, and pincer stings at the rear. A foul crawler: mundane, small, and deadly. That tiny sting would kill me as surely as the titan I had touched.

All the strangeness affecting our family began when Jane rode to Netherfield to visit our handsome new neighbor, Mr. Bingley, and was stung by a foul crawler. Like the crawlers that answered to Lydia when she drank their venom.

Again, fragmented facts teased my mind. A flickering page from our family journal. The history of the Bennets reached far back. Even the name of our family estate, Longbourn, was a corruption of old lore: *loch bairn*, Child of the Lake.

But no image assembled in my mind's eye. Like the composition of a painting, an image requires clarity of comprehension. Pieces of the puzzle fit, but I did not comprehend the whole.

4 0

TOGETHER

LIZZY

M y feet sank into the damp winter soil of the Briton village clearing. I rested my gloved palms on Yuánchi's side, feeling wobbly after two hours in the air, and thought, *Thank you.* Then I took a bracing breath and turned.

Darcy stood a dozen yards away, one hand firm on the neck of his wild-eyed gray stallion, frightened by proximity to a dragon. Behind him, Mr. Needham and the girl harnessers huddled, apparently attempting to sink into the earth.

From the air, I had seen Darcy wheel his mount when we glided overhead, then gallop like a madman to where we would land. Now, he was rigid and unmoving.

I wet my lips. "Love, I had to. They had captives. Mary's friend was taken. After what I did, I could not go on—"

He rushed forward and trapped me in his arms, then whispered, "You are an insane fool. You are a miracle." That was encouraging, and relief flooded me. I let myself be held, cheek resting on his chest and his heart thumping hard in my ear. He added more sternly, "Never leave me again."

After hours of frankness with Mary, it was a shock to remember I had not told him of my illness. Guilt for my silence and anger at fate's injustice filled me, but there was less fear this time. The rescue of those women had softened it.

Perhaps this was how soldiers survived the specter of death. Count those that you save.

Still, I swallowed, and guilt turned my voice foolishly bright. "About that..."

"*What* about that?" he said suspiciously, but then Mary clambered to earth, puffing in frank relief. He stiffened in my arms and said to her angrily, "You terrified Georgiana!"

"No more than myself," Mary muttered.

His chest filled hugely, but all that came out was, "Did you retrieve the dagger?"

"No," she said simply, "but we saved lives and slowed our enemies. And I have information about... whatever all this means. What happened to Fènnù. I must go to the library." She began taking books from the saddlebag, then squinted at the clearing. Looking very windswept and, missing her spectacles, strangely young, she frowned at Darcy. "You rode all this way and did not think to bring a carriage?"

WE RODE BACK, although once Darcy got a good look at me, he declared me exhausted and insisted I ride with him. So again, I rode tandem, pressed against my husband with his arm around my waist while Mary rode after us on the gentle mount I had brought—a good choice as Mary's spare spectacles were at the house, where the horse was eager to return. We trotted down the narrow trail, and it felt more dangerously steep and bumpy than flying with Yuánchi.

Darcy was working up to something. Finally, he burst out, "What was it like to *fly*?"

I smiled at that. "It was glorious. And interesting. The control is all subtle changes to the angles of the wings. I cannot believe I did not notice before, but flapping is less to rise, and more to maintain speed, like paddling a boat. I am certain a winged device could fly..."

I drifted with the sway of the horse, thinking about it. Yuánchi was certainly heavy, so it was not about weight. But he was immensely powerful. Could a horse fly if its feet were harnessed to power the wings? Equine reluctance aside, I doubted it. Was a steam engine more powerful per pound than a horse? I had never compared them.

"You are plotting," Darcy said. He sounded unaccountably cheery.

"I am considering how to weigh the school's steam engine."

He chuckled, then became serious. "What happened in London?"

The thought of the cruel shackles and vile stench prickled the hair on my scalp. "The men who have allied with the French are consummate evil. Why is it that collaborators are worse than the enemy with whom we war? It was the same with Lydia and Wickham. The French officer had more honor."

"A soldier of any flag may have honor. A traitor has none." We were emerging from the trees, and Pemberley House became visible. The horse picked up to a canter, jingling the harness. "You did not say what happened."

The open sky had driven a pair of needles into the backs of my eyes. Phantasmic reds and yellows covered my vision, then drained away like an emptying hourglass. I tried closing my eyes, and the pain crawled into my skull.

"I am more tired than I thought," I said. "Would you mind asking Mary? She was astonishingly brave." Let her decide whether to speak of her aura as a great wyfe. "She is doing something special at the performance this evening. Promise me that we will attend."

"Of course." I had expected him to question that, but he sounded earnest and unsurprised.

With that secure, I put my hand on his and guided the reins, taking us from the main path toward a secluded garden. I waved Mary on toward the house, but she reined in where we had left the path, watching until we were out of sight.

When we were surrounded by the stark and spare beauty of winter, I said, "Let us rest here. I have something to tell you."

BOX HALL

EMMA

Lucy had delivered these invitations after breakfast:

A Musical Entertainment
Mr. and Mrs. Darcy invite you to an afternoon of music and improvised amusement.

The Box Hall, top floor North, at 3 o'clock.

Pemberley's staff were efficient, so I expected a housemaid that afternoon, but at two o'clock, it was Lucy who appeared at my door asking if I wished help dressing.

"Do you not need to assist Mrs. Darcy?" I said.

"She is off with Mr. Darcy," Lucy said, swinging her hands dramatically. "She and Miss Bennet did something brave this morning, but nobody knows what! Then Mr. Darcy scooped her onto his horse without even stopping his gallop, and they rode into the hills! That's all I have heard." Her excited face swung, then became curious. "Is Miss Smith not with you?"

"She will meet me at the afternoon entertainment." Lizzy was not the only one on mysterious errands. After my morning meeting with Mr. Darcy—and the peculiarly ubiquitous Mr. Knightley—Harriet had taken Pemberley's daily coach to Lambton. I was certain it had to do with the school, but she offered only a tight-lipped smile when I asked.

"I hope she dresses warmly. Miss Darcy is sure the guests will leave all the terrace doors open, and the tunings will be ruined by the cold." Earnestly, Lucy added, "Miss Darcy will play! You must hear her. She is so much more exciting than those kings."

"They are a king and a prince," I corrected while eyeing my sparse wardrobe of formal gowns. When I wrote to my maid at Hartfield, I had not expected to meet royalty. "Let us try the ivory. With warm petticoats for the terrace."

IN MOST ESTATE HOMES, the top floor was attic, short and stuffy, fit for aging aunts and overstayed guests. Here, it was as lofty as the lower floors, with a row of towering arched windows on the house's southern front.

Box Hall was square with a sprung floor of long planks, more an intimate ballroom than a hall. The room was on the manor's north side, sun-brightened by dormer windows, and the windows overlooked the hills and a ragged ravine. A pair of glass doors opened to a long, shallow terrace. Half the floor had small tables and upholstered seating like a salon, suited for the two dozen guests who would attend. The rest was sparsely filled. A grand pianoforte stood imposingly, and I recognized the cherrywood case of Mr. Knightley's violin on a table.

The chairs had been subtly spaced to indicate the royal seats. Eight or nine members of the court entourage were milling. They had indeed opened the terrace doors, and the room was cool.

"Miss Woodhouse," called one of them, Mr. Howell, who seemed to manage royal gatherings and entertainments. His bony face was perched above a ruffled sky-blue silk coat. He swirled his long-nailed fingers, beckoning me to their group.

I was not fond of the royal entourage. The prince, and even the young princess, had gravitas and thoughtfulness, even if they were sometimes lost in decorum or boredom, but the courtiers were downright dull, saying nothing worth hearing and admiring without intelligence. They were all jewels and cosmetics and rude rumors, the staples of London society.

But declining Mr. Howell's invitation would be rude as well, so I joined them, flanked on the other side by a remote royal cousin, one of the few bound wyves at court. She wore a pleated apple-green bodice trimmed with gauze. The members of court had brought maids and dressers, which had a selfish benefit for me: there was not one loose thread, stray hair, or crooked tie.

Conversation pattered among fortunes and rumored courtships and smug allusions to gambling debts. The sole mention of the war was shushed. A white-powdered, bewigged baronet announced he would perform a pantomime for the entertainment, then asked suggestions for his theme. I was invited to join him and smilingly declined while wondering what time it was. Afternoon entertainments usually started promptly.

At last, Mr. Knightley and Miss Darcy arrived, and expectations rose as A's were struck and strings tuned. Satisfied, Mr. Knightley set his violin aside and joined our group. His greetings with the court were casual; we had all mingled during the trip from London. Mr. Knightley's deepest bow was for me, and I curtsied carefully. Perhaps this was his apology for misbehaving at Mr. Darcy's lesson.

I had dwelled on my behavior as well, and decided it was not my best. He had been trying to help.

The next influx of guests provided everyone except Mr. and Mrs. Darcy and the royal family. Harriet arrived radiant and slightly rumpled from her tour to Lambton, wearing the green velvet gown she had worn at our frightening visit to Mr. Tinsdale's rally on the Thames. She greeted everyone very properly, but the responses disturbed me. The courtiers flicked too many glances and lifted too many eyebrows.

Harriet, though, was so happy that she held every eye. Amid that attention, she said, "I have had the most wonderful day."

"Indeed?" inquired Mr. Howell, with a bony half-smile.

"Oh yes! The Lambton school is so charming and modern. The headmistress complimented my explanation of a story. She will recommend me for the Martin School. Is that not wonderful?"

Together, the courtiers' noses lifted an inch. Rouged lips twitched in amusement. One said, "Quite."

I felt myself heat with embarrassment. I had warned her about discussing the school. Clearly, she had forgotten.

Harriet continued with supreme confidence, "Teaching is not a position in His Majesty's court, but it is important. If I improve the understanding of a single child, I should feel tremendous accomplishment."

"Well, modest expectations are best," the courtier said with a rude wink to the circle.

"I assure you, sir, my expectations are not modest," Harriet replied. "You will see what I accomplish."

Some of the courtiers were openly chuckling. It was time for a rescue, and the bolder, the better.

"Harriet is such a dear," I said. "I have explained that professional teaching is common, but she cannot master her impulse to be charitable."

The courtiers hummed and nodded. To my right, Mr. Knightley's head snapped around to stare at me. And at last, Harriet's confident smile thinned. Perhaps she realized these horrid people were mocking her.

Still, the reaction of the court proved my point. Vindicated, I continued, "Charity is wonderful, but a setting like a school suggests a person is comfortable there. When a path to genteel society has been offered, one is obligated—"

Mr. Knightley's foot landed on my toe so hard that I winced. I gave him a hurt look.

"There!" the baronet told Harriet. "You must accept the advice of your better."

"I have heard her advice before," Harriet pronounced carefully, but to me, not to him. Her chin was set. She was angry.

Mr. Howell gave a fleeting laugh. "With a sponsor such as Miss Woodhouse, I am certain doors to suitable society can be opened." He gave me a courtly bow, fluttering his hand.

Harriet's eyes narrowed dangerously. Mr. Howell's words had kindled an uncertain sensation in my breast. I tried to remember what exactly I had said...

Loudly, Harriet said, "Miss Woodhouse is not my *sponsor*."

"Oh." Mr. Howell turned to me, screwing up his outlined eyes in curiosity. Every gaze followed. "What, then?"

She is my sister. The words hung, shy of my lips.

Ever since our meeting with Mr. Debrett, I had been pondering when to announce our relationship. There was no rush, as his next publication was months away. And Harriet had not pressed me to hurry. Not once.

"She is..." I began. "We are good friends, as you see..."

"That is very admirable," the baronet enthused, tapping two fingertips on one palm in tiny applause.

"Is my attendance here obligated?" Harriet asked me with such resounding presence that silence fell and the smirks vanished. "If not, I prefer the afternoon entertainment in Lambton."

"You do not need my permission—" I started, but she turned on her heel and marched from the room. Behind her back, the courtiers traded ostentatiously shocked looks.

The uncertainty in my chest had exploded to burning guilt. That had not turned out as I intended.

"Miss Woodhouse," Mr. Knightley said. "May I show you the view from the terrace?" I followed him, very relieved.

The terrace was high and breezy, stripping the residual warmth of the room. I gave Mr. Knightley a thankful smile. "That was well timed."

He did not return my smile. "How could you be so unfeeling to Miss Smith?"

A startled, hot blush rose in my cheeks, but I laughed his words off. "I was only trying to help."

"She did not ask for your help. She did not require it."

The guilt in my heart surged, but I said, "There is nothing wrong with help."

"Your help demeaned her. Emma, all the time I have known you, you have pressed her to pursue a life she does not want—a life she can achieve only by being dependent on your goodwill. Now, you degrade her accomplishments because they do not align with your goal."

"I only wish to protect her," I protested. "To help her accomplish more."

"Why more? Is it more, or simply different? She is your friend. I know you care for her, and she cares for you. When you are absent, you have no surer defender than Miss Smith. But her entire life has been one of indebtedness. Her boarding school—the nearest she had to a family—was hired by the cast-off coin of a father who rejected her. Then you, her wealthy friend, coddled her. Always, the message has been: My trifling effort has caused your success. But Harriet Smith stands on her own. Have you even watched her in a classroom? The independence you crave for yourself is within her grasp. Yet you celebrate her achievement by belittling it."

I folded my arms to conceal my trembling shoulders. She had asked me to come see her teach. All I had felt was irritation.

"I care greatly for her," I said. "You are breaking my heart by speaking this way."

"I am your friend. It is my privilege to speak plainly, even if that plainness must be endured rather than welcomed. I cannot bear to see you hurt a woman whom I know you care for." I must have looked distraught, because he finished more gently, "I see how much you regret it."

I turned to the rolling hills as they blurred with tears. Harriet had left, betrayed by me. And still, I had not admitted the truth.

"You do not know half the wrong I committed," I whispered. "Harriet Smith is more than a friend. That cast-off coin was paid by my own papa. When he died, I learned that we are sisters. I tried to stand with her in front of those fools, and I blundered terribly. What can she possibly think other than I am ashamed of her?"

The wind shifted and turned before Mr. Knightley spoke, his tone serious. "*Are* you ashamed of her?"

The wretchedness of that scene repeated in my mind, as abhorrent as it would appear to Harriet, a woman who treasured her school memories as a child, a student, and a teacher. I was ashamed of myself. But of Harriet?

"I am frightened of what people will think of Papa," I said. "I am a little frightened of what they will think of me. But I could never be ashamed of her. There is not a better creature in the world. She is a better person than I."

"She is certainly less vexing," Mr. Knightley agreed, rather promptly. But it was true. I gave a big sniff and nodded, and he said, "Thank you for confiding in me. I understand your anger when a sister faces prejudice of class and race. But you cannot save her from those unfair trials. Let her choose her path and her battles. If she needs to unburden her heart, she will find you. Offer respect, not rescue, and she will triumph."

Keeping my gaze on the distant hills, I drew off my gloves and folded them, then felt in my reticule for a handkerchief to dab my eyes. "I am afraid I will lose her if she becomes a teacher. It would be so much nicer if she were a lady with a country house I could visit."

"Nicer for you," Mr. Knightley said. He made it a simple statement, not a rebuke, which was considerate.

"That is not just my selfishness," I said, feeling encouraged. "She has never been alone. Is a marriage not a wonderful thing to wish for? To have a companion for life, full of friendship and love, who helps one, or even"—I gave him a watery smile—"corrects one from time to time?"

"Emma, you cannot presume what is best for her. What Miss Smith desires in life is not what Miss Woodhouse would choose."

He held out his hand, palm up and ungloved. Before, when he lifted my gloved hand to his heart, I had been surprised. Now, a little awkwardly, I reached out and rested my bare fingers on his. Mine were chilled by the winter air, and they looked drained as snow, the nails blue as river ice. His fingers were warm and long and strong, with firm calluses at the fingertips, and skin the color of spring earth ready to burst with life.

"What do you see when our hands meet?" he said.

No image of Mr. Elton arose, shouting accusations. No panic flooded my heart.

If he had the privilege to speak plainly, then so did I. "That you have handsome fingers." That sounded a little silly, but it was honest.

He made an exasperated sound. "But is it the hand of an equal?"

I had gathered my courage for... I was not sure what, but not for *that*. In fact, his tone was very over-satisfied. I looked up at his dark-lashed eyes and found he was scowling, and my courage, which had leaped toward mortification, landed somewhere hotter.

"It is the hand of a musician," I said. "I certainly do not care that it is black, if that is your point. Do you wish to pretend that England treats everyone equally regardless of wealth? That is not my experience. I also see the hand of a man. Shall we pretend that a woman, forbidden from conducting business or holding property, is *your* equal? That would be a tremendous relief. That is, until my jailor brother-in-law starves me so I must marry some gentleman and surrender my wealth, my home, and my body."

He did not take back his hand, but his posture withdrew. "I am sorry my profession offends you. Aside from that, you have misunderstood my point."

"I certainly understand that I hurt Harriet, and I regret it with all my heart. But I have heard enough *points* for one day. Are you not supposed to be rushing to your death? Perhaps you should write your points down so I may study."

There was a stir of activity in the hall. Mr. Darcy and Lizzy had arrived. Lizzy was smiling, flushed and dark-eyed. Mr. Darcy, though, was more severe than I had ever seen him, taut and tall at her side, staring over his guests as if the room were a wasteland.

His eyes met mine, and in an instant, he left Lizzy to stride toward us. He fairly burst onto the terrace and bowed deeply. "Miss Woodhouse."

"Mr. Darcy," I replied hesitantly. His mood was peculiar and intense.

Mr. Knightley murmured a greeting. Mr. Darcy gave him a fleeting glance, then returned his attention to me. "I wish greatly to speak with you."

Suddenly, I did not wish my conversation with Mr. Knightley to end. "We had not yet—"

"I have said too much already," Mr. Knightley interposed roughly. He bowed and pulled the terrace doors closed as he left, leaving me with Mr. Darcy.

The instant the doors shut, Mr. Darcy said, "My wyfe is dying. You must heal her."

He spoke with profound clarity, but it took me seconds to cast off my last conversation and understand. Even then, his meaning was impossible. "She is walking in the hall behind you!"

"She has a most rapid and deadly form of consumption. You are her sole hope. And mine." His eyes were brimming, his brow furrowed, his hands clenched. That, and his absolute integrity, drove the truth of his words, and my heart broke. Lizzy was so vibrant with life.

"That is horrible. I cannot say how sorry I am." His eyes beseeched me, and I stammered, "You cannot expect me to *help*? You know I cannot heal anyone. All this time, I have tried with Nessy, and she..." I could not finish that sentence.

He grabbed my hands in his, so violently that I shied back but was prevented by his grip. "You must embrace your destiny. You are a great wyfe. If you bind, you can heal her!"

Through his grasp, the power of Yuánchi's binding climbed my arms. The touch from yesterday's dinner had barely faded, and the added potency was distressing.

But this was madness. "You said even your mother could not cure consumption."

"You will exceed her!" he cried. I had never seen him so impassioned. His face was lit. The rushing scarlet binding made my heart stutter. In the hall, a head turned to peer through the glass.

"I cannot bind," I gasped. The admission was like a snare tightening around me, squeezing the air from my lungs. I had thought I was done with secrets.

"You will bind if there is passion and love. Why do you wait when you can save Elizabeth, and Nessy too?" He pulled me closer, fervid. "A life without love is a husk. Throw aside the foolish procrastination of courtship. Are you blind to the worthiness of your admirer?"

Confused feelings rushed in from my conversation with Mr. Knightley, but sense, cold and cruel, triumphed. "I would fail to bind. I shall never marry." I tugged futilely at my trapped hands. "You have no right to speak of this. You are hurting me."

His intensity jammed to an appalled stop. He flung my hands away. "Forgive me. To advise you on this personal matter was reprehensible." He gave a rigid half bow. "I must return to my wyfe." He swung the door wide and strode into the hall's crowd.

I stood impaled by my own words. It was one thing to accept that marriage was closed to me, but it was unbearable that my loneliness harmed others.

I fumbled my gloves from my reticule. They were Chantilly lace sewn so each hand mirrored the other's pattern of openwork. I drew them on and spread my fingers flat on the terrace railing, tugging and tightening until the shapes matched perfectly.

The north gardens of Pemberley were spread below me. The ivory alcove was farthest, the old yew at its northern point a tousled torrent of dark green. Beneath that, hidden, was the twin to the statue at the physic garden. Beyond that, a path led north. *To the north...*

I turned to the hall and stopped short, almost colliding with Mr. Knightley at the terrace door. He had waited.

He backed a step, his hand half-extended in entreaty.

I said, "The north path—" but bit away the rest and dashed around him, hurrying toward the sweeping stairs.

ARIA

LIZZY

I n the last year, my young and complacent life was transformed by moments of lucid decision. When my father died, I chose to save Long-bourn. When Jane was ill, I chose to cure her. When Lydia seized my husband, I chose to fight. Each time, my world shattered, and I answered: *No*.

Learning of my own illness was different. Even in little Meryton, lives regularly ended without rhyme or purpose. A fever spiked. A childbirth was hard. A scratch blackened and swelled. Why should I be immune to the scythe? If there were purpose to death, I was a sensible choice—either judged for the violence I had unleashed, or simply a fool, a country girl who traipsed through London's slums as if fresh wealth and good intentions were proof against pestilence.

But when I cradled Darcy in the privacy of our gardens—when I listened to him moan and shout—I realized I must choose again. Not for myself. After all, I would be gone. But other lives continue. So, I decided: I would be strong for my husband.

"Wait here," Darcy whispered to me when we entered Box Hall, then he rushed to Emma on the terrace. I knew he would seek her out—to ask her to cure me, or to demand it—but I did not expect him to return so... eviscerated. Riven to his core. Darcy believed in Emma. He was her prophet and her champion. His surrender extinguished a secret glimmer of hope I held as well, but it strengthened my choice.

I pulled him to the corner, away from the chattering bodies. "I am glad that is done. Now you will not be distracted while Mary performs." When he did not answer, I said firmly, "This is important. You promised we would attend. That means in spirit, not staring through the walls like a blind wraith."

He breathed deeply several times. "Yes."

While he collected himself, I surveyed the room and considered the mysteries of illness. I felt quite good now, other than a buzzing glare around each window. This followed a pattern that had built in the last few days: a few hours of normalcy, then a surge of symptoms. Each surge was harder, but the timing worked well for this.

Georgiana joined us, happy, excited, and wearing her Chinese gown of red silk and golden, web-footed dragons.

"I have not seen that dress since Jane's wedding," I said.

"Mary has been composing like a madwoman. She was gone before I woke, and has hidden in the library all day. I am sure this will be special, so I have dressed to celebrate."

Mary entered the hall while she spoke, and Georgiana summoned her with a wave. As she arrived, Georgiana announced, "Mary is adapting the third act of Purcell's *Dido and Aeneas*."

"Not that!" Darcy burst out, so loudly that nearby conversations stopped.

Georgiana made a scolding noise at him, then gave Mary an apologetic smile. "Fitz is worried because the aria is *so* sad. He is all stony nods in life, but he cries if there is the least drama on stage."

Mary said seriously to Darcy, "Do not be apprehensive. I have altered the ending." She was dressed in fastidious black, the most dour of her Mary-ish outfits, although the most dramatic as well. Across her shoulders, a roll of cloth was bunched and tied.

"Is that a costume?" I asked. Mary played the pianoforte endlessly while composing, but I had expected her to remain behind the scenes. She was not a confident performer like Georgiana.

"Belinda," Mary answered, which meant nothing to me. She passed several pages of handwritten music to Georgiana. "Your part."

Georgiana took it eagerly, then quieted as she scanned it. "I thought the courtiers would sing. You know I do not perform vocal work. Things... happen when I sing."

"England is invaded," Mary answered softly. "Every life is unsure. I wish to sing with you. This once, while we are all together." Mary's gaze touched Darcy and me as well. When Georgiana hesitantly nodded, Mary said to me, "After the performance, we must speak with Emma also. I have had only an hour to read since London. But those books reveal a greater danger than we knew."

I was battling a swell of emotion from Mary's brief speech, but Georgiana removed any need to reply by saying sharply, "*London*?"

"Later," Mary repeated. "Where is Emma? We will need her, too."

"She left," Darcy said.

The royal family entered, and formal greetings rippled outward. The old king, pouting and mumbling, settled in a chair between his doctors, but the prince came to us. "Mr. and Mrs. Darcy. Thank you again for your accommodation. Lord Wellington did tell me this extreme secrecy will be brief. I hope we will not long require Pemberley's unique defenses." His smile at me was polite, but curious also.

Lord Wellington doubtless uttered whatever words soothed restless monarchs. But what would happen once I was gone? Draca bound through their wyfe, so when a wyfe died, the binding ended, and the draca left. Everything I knew suggested that Yuánchi would leave after my death. Pemberley would be a poor fortress without its dragon.

Lady Hertford, the prince's acknowledged mistress, patted the prince's arm. "Prinny, let them prepare. Miss Darcy must herd all these squawking geese into place."

"I am sure Miss Bennet will assist," the prince said. To Mary, he said, "Will I hear your music today?"

"In the last piece, sir." Her tone was tight, which surprised me. Mary was no royalist, but she had been precise in observing court etiquette. Perhaps she was nervous about performing.

The prince watched her thoughtfully. He seemed intent to make some point. "I look forward to it. I have been curious since the ball. Wondering what woman could so captivate Miss Darcy." Mary's tension was now visible in her clutched fingers. Darcy, too, stiffened. More softly, the prince added, "Do not be concerned. A royal life fosters sympathies for impossible situations." He took Lady Hertford's arm, and they proceeded to chairs beside the king.

Everyone exchanged meaningful looks. Everyone, that is, except me, who was baffled. "What was that?"

"Unexpected," Mary said, releasing a breath. She squeezed my hand. "I must herd geese." She vanished into the crowd, saying, "Where is Mr. Knightley?"

We took our seats, and after the confusion necessary for all improvised affairs, the entertainment began with a skit that featured, unexpectedly, the master of protocol. I had thought him an utterly humorless man, but he portrayed himself perfectly, remaining in character through a farce of tripping court buffoons. At the end, the court laughed uproariously, and he bowed stiffly. Perhaps he thought it was real.

A song followed, then a pantomime, pleasant in the way amateur performances are, but I did not know the players, so my mind wandered.

Yuánchì, I thought.

I am here. Our binding brightened, west and slightly upward. He was atop one of Pemberley's hills.

It felt like cowardice to tell him this way, but more delay was cowardly as well. *I am sick.*

I know.

Somehow, I expected that. Our last connections had been so intimate, so integrated to his sensations, it stood to reason he felt mine as well. *Will you leave when I am gone?*

I must sleep when a binding ends. I will dream of you.

That was nice, but I was in a practical mood. What that really meant was that we needed to recover the dagger. Or at least free Fènnù from its control. Perhaps Mary had found a clue. Or Lord Wellington might recover it in London. Mary had enclosed a note to him with her letter to Dr. Davenport.

There was another round of applause, then a discreet conference between Mary and Georgiana. I realized that Mr. Knightley's violin sat untouched on a table. Had he missed his performance? Emma and Harriet were absent as well.

Georgiana took a seat at the pianoforte, adjusting her music, and the audience hushed.

Mary faced us, her voice carrying and strong. "For our last work, we adapt the lost myth of Dido, Queen of Britannia. The time is long ago. Britannia is at war with the Gauls, but the war goes poorly. Desperate for allies, Queen Dido has agreed to marry Aeneas, a prince of Troy. But Aeneas was ensorcelled and withdrew his engagement. Dido's heart is broken, and Britannia is doomed."

There were intakes of breath from the audience, either due to Mary's delivery, which was riveting, or because she had dared allude to the war.

"I do not know this myth," I whispered to Darcy.

"That is because it is wildly altered," he whispered back. "For one thing, Troy is inconveniently far from Britain."

Mary finished her introduction with, "I, Belinda, Dido's loyal maid, have come to comfort her." Georgiana played a chord, and Mary began to sing.

The keyboard music was an old style, a spare continuo to lead the voice, nothing like Mary's strikingly modern compositions. I knew Mary's singing, of course. Neither of us were gifted vocalists; Mary was more accurate, while I was more sweet—Papa once called Mary's singing "furry," which had upset her. This music, though, somber and slow, fit her beautifully, and she sang with a confidence I had never heard as Belinda beseeched her mistress to put aside unworthy Aeneas and heal her heart.

While she sang, my binding to Yuánchi, a constant in my mind, brightened like a spiderweb catching sun. The sensation strengthened, and around me, the forces of the draca world began to rotate and fold, like the flow I felt when Georgiana invoked her strength. But these were structured and purposeful, a dressmaker sewing panels into a gown, not a paintbrush blending watercolors. The exactness was quintessentially Mary. Her aura as a great wyfe was real, even though it was strangely dispersed. She had power.

Outside on the terrace, motions caught my eye. Those iridescent small draca had gathered, landing on the rail and tables, heads cocked and listening.

Still playing the keyboard, Georgiana added her voice—the voice of Dido, Queen of Britannia, although oddly costumed in a flame-red Chinese gown. In all this time, I had only ever heard her sing short phrases, the notes she used to invoke her powers as wyfe of song. Now, her voice rose in a bell-clear soprano that blended beautifully with Mary's earthy timbre. The melody grew more complex as well, and the harmonies more daring.

Georgiana sang a dark refrain:

> "Belinda; darkness shades me,
> death is now a welcome guest.
> When I am laid in earth,
> remember me, but ah! forget my fate."

This heart-wrenching melody I recognized—Dido's lament, the devastating death song of the queen—but already the music was forging a new path, and the queen did not complete her death song. Instead, the harmonies, resplendent with the shimmering contrasts of Mary's composition, swelled with hope.

Georgiana sang a wordless counterpoint, her eyes closed as her hands swept the keyboard in a ringing challenge that shivered my skin.

Mary sang again, and the crowd muttered in surprise. Purcell's sad ending had been discarded. These words were solely Mary's:

> *"Beloved Dido, descend not to death.*
> *Forget your faithless prince of Troy.*
> *Behold: Faithful Belinda has a secret."*

She pulled a bow at her shoulder, and the cloth unrolled, a cape decorated with strips of purple and violet silk. The room had become brilliant with sunlight, and the colors shone like fine vestments.

Georgiana played a celebratory resolution. There was no more music. The last page of Mary's handwritten score was on her music stand. Uncertainly, she looked up at Mary. The story was clearly unfinished.

Mary lifted Georgiana's hand from the keyboard. "Rise, Queen Dido." Georgiana stood, her eyes very wide, and Mary took both her hands and sang:

> *"The Fairy Queen commands me.*
> *Thy engagement must be honored.*
> *I, secret princess of Troy, and a sprite, replace him at the*
> *   altar,*
> *so Troy's ships and men shall defend Britannia."*

She fell silent. Their cheeks were flushed, their gazes transfixed. A hundred past hints rushed into my mind—they would have been declarations for a more sensible onlooker—and, finally, I understood Mary's brave love.

Shocked whispers spread among the courtiers. They quieted as Mary recited, no longer singing:

> *"Let us not to the marriage of true minds*
> *Admit impediments.*
> *Queen, will you take a princess as your bride?"*

Georgiana took a shaky breath, but her answer was steady. "Love looks on tempests and is never shaken. I am yours."

Mary finished in a whisper that filled the silent room:

> *"What may express my love or my dear merit?*

Nothing, sweet girl; yet music as prayers divine.

Thrill my heart that throbs with unwonted fervor,
Chasten mouth and throat with immortal kisses,
Till I yield on maddening heights the very
Breath of my body."

She kissed Georgiana, a gentle brush of the lips which drew loud gasps from the audience.

Those folded forces of the draca world erupted in an invisible structure mitered of form and melody—twin aspects of these wyves of song. It grew high as the hills and hung, trembling, then careened upon itself and vanished.

On the terrace, the iridescent small draca burst into harmonious song.

As if that were her release, Mary turned to the audience, presented a dazzling actress's smile, and bowed elaborately, pulling an exceedingly distracted-looking Georgiana into the bow beside her. That pretense of performance was necessary. Their entire lives would be performance, an endless fiction. How unfair, and yet how inspiring that love triumphed regardless.

Their bow was met with silence. The courtiers' heads swiveled, seeking guidance. Then from the corner, the mad King's voice croaked querulously, "Britannia is saved, then? That is good."

The Prince Regent rose from his seat. "Well said, father. A brilliant debut." He began clapping, and the courtiers burst into applause.

Darcy and I stood as one, but he had my hand tight in his, so we could only add our voices to the approval. With his other hand, he dug a handkerchief from his pocket and wiped his eyes.

Georgiana knew her brother well.

THE NORTH PATH

EMMA

I slammed the guest room door behind me and thumped my back against it, digging the points of my shoulder blades into the wood to bar entry, bracing my toes. Harriet might come, or Mr. Darcy, or Mr. Knightley. One I had betrayed, the next abandoned, the last angered.

"Selfish girl!" I cried out. "You are hiding while Lizzy is ill." With her, I had been my best. And with Nessy, too. I had only failed them by not achieving a miracle.

To the north, to the north, the wyvern said. I gathered the cloth bag with the last teaspoon of herbs for Nessy's tea, dried now but a lively green, and an ivory coat and bonnet that matched my gown. Ivory seemed lucky for an ivory alcove. I hurried down more stairs and rushed through the gardens, the twin skirts of my gown and coat flashing. I patted the radiant statue at the north point as I passed.

The north path was natural, widened by deer, an easy walk, although damp and weedy where the earth dipped. Soon, I was climbing the hill, scattered sunbeams at my back.

The human noises of Pemberley House vanished. The mild afternoon had brought animals out to forage. Birds sang and squirrels chittered. Other than the tremendous, mossy girth of the bare-branched oaks, it could have been a forested walk near home.

The ground roughened with knotted roots and rotting mast, and the path steepened. Rowan and holly joined oak. Finally, puffing, I stopped to catch my breath. The path behind me stretched back—it had not magically vanished as happens in fables—but the hilltops I glimpsed through the trees were unfamiliar. How far had I come?

"A half mile," I announced, to hear a voice, and to say something unfrightening. "Not far." The day seemed darker, but that was the canopy of unthinned forest. I had left the house before three, so there would be hours of light. Well, two hours. Perhaps.

Lucy had matched my short boots of supple ivory kid to my gown. They looked dismayingly dirty already, caked with black mud and dead leaves. My calves ached. Sighing, I resumed the climb.

It grew harder, as happens in fables. The path stayed clear, but downed branches and trunks crossed it. I removed my Chantilly gloves, aligned the lace holes between the left and right, and folded them into my reticule. With my reticule fastened to my waist, I could now pull on branches to step over rocks and rotting logs. But the low branches had loose, dead bark, the wood brittle from summer shadow. Some snapped without warning, even sticks an inch thick.

I stopped again, panting. My thighs burned. I was hungry, my stomach growling, my throat dry. The left seam on one boot had popped several threads. The sky was unquestionably darker.

"Three quarters of a mile. That is far enough." The woods listened. "Should you not come out?" The woods did not answer, but distantly, I heard an echo as if a tenor voice had shouted. I called louder, "Mister Wyvern?" but that felt foolish.

In the fading light, my palms had red scratches and smears of sap and mold. I rubbed them, the skin stinging and the sap sticky. Better to harm my skin than my gloves. The hems of my skirts were soiled, so I should preserve what defenses I had.

But these trees had deep, vertical crevasses in their bark. In each, cunningly hidden, miasma glimmered, a subtle trickle to soak the earth. I was alone, but how far could it seep? Where would it rise in a malignant spring? Harriet had stormed off, furious with me. She must be safe in Pemberley. Or did she look for me in the gardens? She might be wandering and lost.

I caught myself opening the drawstrings on my reticule. I tugged them tight again. Lace gloves would be ruined by dirty fingers.

What had Mr. Darcy said? I forced my memory past the wretched terrace to the lesson in the ivory alcove. Denying the possibility of illness would fail. That was true. I knew that spiral of what-ifs and the hopeless chase for perfection. Accept that you cannot protect people from being hurt. Instead, help them if they are.

The glisten of miasma had thickened to a flow. I shouted, "I am prepared to help!" but the fear stayed.

I needed a stronger talisman than an unpracticed lesson. I dug into my reticule, avoiding the gloves, and found the little cloth bag of Nessy's tea. I pressed it to my nose, breathing flowery mint, and my mind filled with calm stories and her smile at the foolish rabbit. The fear eased.

Words whispered in my mind: *climb, healer*

"Thank you," I cried. That was just like the fables Papa had read me as a child. "I *knew* this was right!"

Up, then. I climbed, ignoring the cramping hollow in my belly and my loose boot. The twilight made inky pools under raised roots, then around them, then swallowed the ground. I splashed through water, my torn boot waterlogged and my toes numb. The trunks turned to shadows against an iron sky, then black against silvered, slipping clouds. Direction was impossible, but always there was only one path ahead. I tripped, fell, and fell again, batting at unseen bushes and hanging moss, cloth snagging and dragging, bonnet pulled askew and straightened fifty times. But all that damage was swallowed by the dark.

No hilltop of Pemberley was this high. Had I gone up and down and back up again?

I stumbled into a rough meadow, the sky cleared by the fall of an ancient tree. The stump was a softening mound tufted with ivy. Without branches overhead, it was lighter, the sky the purple-blue of elderberries and glowing rose in the west.

No. If I was facing north, that was east. Was I lost, or was that the dawn?

I blinked and was surrounded by mid-morning sunlight on a spring day. Cheerful blooms nodded their heads. Life boiled everywhere: ants searching and birds singing, gnats dancing, rabbits nibbling, their ears alert and listening. I trembled with exhaustion, every muscle aching, but my clothes were as pristine as a final fitting.

Where the mounded stump had been, Lady Anne's wyvern stood. The proud strength I saw in Georgiana's vision was lost. He was wasted and skeletal, his bones propping wrinkled leathery skin, those lustrous brown scales reduced to a few ragged patches. Pity stilled me, and fear that I came too late.

healer. i have waited

"I am here. For my message." That was not nearly urgent enough. "There are people I must heal. A child and a wyfe."

the song is broken. blight spreads in the east

"I do not know how to help songs or blight. I want to help two people. Please."

only two? show me what you carry

I pulled out the little bag of tea leaves, enough for a single cup. When nothing happened, I walked close and sank on my heels.

In the grass around us, fallen scales gleamed. The facets of the wyvern's eyes were pitted and cloudy like poor glass, and his head had an uncertain cant, so I opened the bag and held it close. He leaned to bring one eye near.

you are as she thought you would be. the heiress to her skills, but stronger. already these have power

"Not enough. The child is too ill. Every day I see the disease eating her away."

one child. the world is besieged

"Healing is a small thing," I whispered.

The wyvern's weary head lifted in startled surprise. When at last he resumed, his tone was wondering.

my eyes rot, wyfe, but my vision clears. the wyverns hold the lore. never has one waited so long. never has one's vision seen so far. say for a third time: how many would you save?

"Two. Just two. A child and a wyfe."

The wyvern took a step. His feet had lost their claws, and his gait was unsteady, his toes scabbed and webbed. In the clearing around us, leaves and grass rustled. Small creatures of the forest were gathering—rabbits, crows, squirrels, foxes. Watching.

He pressed his cheek to my hand so the bag and tea were beneath his eye. A single golden drop gathered and rolled into the dried, green leaves.

her gift. to cure the child. only the child

That eye clouded until it was the opaque gray of dusty stone. Along his flank, a strip of brown scales shed like dense seeds, each descent sudden and quick.

"What of the wyfe?" I said. "I must save her, too."

He turned his head the other way, and his remaining eye clouded to stone as a golden tear gathered. It rolled down, and I caught it on my palm as it fell from his jaw. It shone in the sunlight, then sank into my skin. A sense of pureness filled me.

"I will give Nessy the tea. But what do I do with this?" He did not answer. "What message did Lady Anne leave for me?"

you already knew her message: 'healing is a small thing, born in love.' stay true to your path, wyfe, and you will save three lives today

Save a third life. That sounded more ominous than good.

The wyvern's head shuddered and clunked down a handbreadth. Gleaming, jet-black shoulder blades split the skin of his back, then he collapsed in a mound of skin, scale, and clean bone.

The gathered creatures swarmed forward. Rabbits and crows caught leathery shreds or tiny phalanges in their mouths and left. Squirrels stuffed their cheeks with scales and climbed trunks. Foxes lifted the heavy bones and padded off, tails waving. All were common creatures, not draca, and they carried their burden with reverence.

The bright sunlight vanished as if it had never been, leaving cold twilight, but brighter than before. Dawn.

The decayed mound of the fallen tree was at my knees. I touched the ivy, felt a hard edge, and tugged free an obsidian jaw bone with a few knife-edged teeth attached. Hard clay and tangled roots clung from years of rest.

In the dawn light, my clothes were completely ruined, my boot seam hanging. My belly had shrunk to a cramped, empty knot. My throat was thick with thirst.

Ahead of me, the path continued through the trees. I looked behind. The path I had walked was still there, not vanished. But retracing all those steps was quite unappealing.

I tucked the jaw bone back into its bed. "You were most loyal and brave. It is strange that the message is one I already knew, but I think 'Stay true to your path' means just what it says."

I pushed to my feet, tucked loose strands of hair into my bonnet, and slogged north.

THE PINNACLE

LIZZY

"A new day," I croaked. The words made the cracks in my lips sting. "I feel much better."

Darcy was seated on the floor behind me, steadying me. I had tried to steal away in the night, but he found me.

He wiped sweat-soaked curls from my temples and felt my forehead, then got to his feet and returned with a dampened towel and a cup of water. I wiped my face and neck, then chanced a few sips.

He said, "When I was a boy, I helped my mother care for her patients. You do not need to hide."

"I am preserving my dignity." I dabbed the soaked neckline of my robe. "What time is it? I should like to visit breakfast, at least. To see Mary and Georgiana." My fever had roared back after the performance. I had only blurry memories of being guided through the crowd, then thrashing in bed.

"Lucy looked in already. I will ring for her."

Lucy returned, and I banished Darcy to go find his valet. Lucy made me presentable, chattering only one notch too cheerfully and never breathing a word about my health, for which I was stupendously grateful. After fastening my dress, she became quiet, then said, "One thing more," and gently dabbed rouge on my lips. I had worn it perhaps twice in my life. Despite her effort, the face in the looking glass looked like death absent the courtesy of even a tepid warming.

There was no routine yet with our guests, but the household breakfast was private. Darcy and I walked down together and found Mary with a dozen books spread over a third of the table. She had her nose inches from the page, which meant she had been at this for hours, but she leaped up when we approached, looking doctorly and concerned.

I ended that by pulling her into a long embrace, then I held her at arm's length to show my smile. "I feel very foolish about misunderstanding you in that London park. I am all joy to know I have a sister in love, and to someone so admirable. You were clever about it, too. Will you have a royal commission?" Mary frowned, so to head off a lecture on the evils of monarchy, I said, "I do have a question about the opera. Why was Belinda a sprite as well?"

Mary smiled then. "When I was four, I wished to be a sprite. So why not?"

I nodded to her array of books. "Is this what you wanted to speak about?"

"We should wait for Georgiana and Emma. I have both questions and answers."

The staff began placing breakfast, and Mary and Darcy greeted them while pouring coffee. I took one look at the silver coffee pot, every gleam a scintillating needle that stabbed my waking headache, then I turned my back to it to sip hot water with a thin splash of tea.

That left me sunk in morbid thought, and it took a minute to notice Darcy had stepped into the hallway. I followed and found him with Mr. Digweed and Mrs. Reynolds, who were so rushed that they were speaking over top of each other. Finally, Mr. Digweed deferred to our housekeeper, and Mrs. Reynolds began.

"Master and madam, I am afraid that Miss Woodhouse, Miss Smith, and Mr. Knightley have not been seen since the Box Hall entertainment."

"Harriet went to the school," I said. For some reason, the courtiers had thought that the hottest of gossip. "Perhaps they all went."

"I thought so too, madam, and the staff assignments were topsy-turvy all evening, so I thought they only missed dinner. But the maids have been in this morning. Their beds were untouched."

"Mr. Knightley was preparing to leave," Darcy said. "Miss Woodhouse may have chosen to depart at the same time."

"Without a goodbye?" I said. "Darcy, that is impossible."

Rigidly, he said, "Miss Woodhouse had cause to leave. I behaved poorly."

There was an awkward pause. Darcy considered it poor behavior if he was not the first to rise when a lady stood, but clearly his conversation on the terrace had been difficult.

Mrs. Reynolds spoke into the silence. "Mr. Knightley's trunks were not yet packed. And nothing was taken from the ladies' room. Not a comb. Not a shoe."

Darcy's comment had left me more curious than concerned, but Mrs. Reynolds's news filled me with alarm—a strangely dispassionate alarm for a discussion of missing friends.

"I must add my news," Mr. Digweed said. "The patrols we set up for Lord Wellington caught a pair of suspicious men in the hills. We are holding them in the east village, and they are angry about it. One is a laborer from Lambton. I do not know the other man, but his accent is Sussex. He is protesting loudly that they are hired to scout for a birding party and lost their way."

My sense of urgency had soared, but Darcy's answer was hesitant. "I am no soldier. What does the captain recommend?" That was the military officer Lord Wellington had left to manage the royal guards.

"He is unsure. Call a constable, perhaps. But they have broken no law." Everyone pursed their lips as if this were cause for consideration.

Why were they so thickheaded? "They are spies," I said. "It is a classic pairing. A local guide, who is bribed, ignorant, and untrusted, and a master, who will survive and report. Did the Lambton man have too much money?"

Mr. Digweed's eyebrows rose. "Three guineas. That is a good guess."

My alarm condensed to certainty. "We should not have brought the royal family here."

"Wellington chose it," Darcy objected. "No other path was safe."

"Lord Wellington commands armies, but he is not a spymaster. Deception is key. When a single path is safe, you choose *any* other." Dusty lessons skittered through my mind. "It is my fault, too. Mary and I took their reserve of captive wyves, but they had moved one wyfe. Their captives do not live long, so they must use her. It no longer matters that Lord Wellington's precautions hid the royal family. Our enemy is forced to attack, so they will gamble."

"Elizabeth," Darcy said intently. "You are not speaking like yourself."

I looked up at him, and the final realization whispered into place. "These are lessons learned by others. But if I can feel these memories..." I closed my eyes and threw my mind wide.

Yuánchi filled me first, a blaze of awareness a mile distant. He sensed me reaching, but I blocked his query, hiding his mind to search elsewhere like a night sentry shielding a torch to see beyond.

There. The oily black of a dosed wyfe, and from that, a tendril reaching south over the hills of Pemberley. And at the end of that tendril, a powerful, broken mind was reaching for me, but restrained by an iron grip.

"They are using the dagger," I said. "Fènnù is coming. They will destroy Pemberley."

I opened my eyes to three disbelieving stares, and the confidence that had carried me—the discipline to forgo emotion—drained like spilled water. My body was wretchedly ill, my head aching. Fear filled my heart. I had no idea what to do.

"We must move the royal family," Darcy said. He watched me, waiting, then said, "Do you agree?" That seemed sensible, so I nodded. He rushed off with Mr. Digweed and Mrs. Reynolds, and they gave orders. Servants ran down hallways with instructions.

From the frenzy, Mary appeared, half dragging Georgiana, whose undressed hair hung loose to her waist.

Mary said, "Lizzy, we are to leave!"

"No!" Georgiana cried. "Pemberley is safe. It is always safe." She had tears in her eyes.

"Not today," Mary said. She took my hand and rushed both of us past the breakfast table and out a side entrance onto a garden path. A handful of the iridescent blue song draca were perched outside the door and window. They burst into the air, swirling over our heads.

The morning light burned. I narrowed my eyes and said, "Please go slow." I had to feel for the path's spaced flagstones through my slippers.

Yuánchi's awareness was pressing at me, so while Mary led me, I reached for him. *Yuánchi.*

People flee your house.

I had forgotten he did not have the senses of a great wyfe. *Fènnù is coming. She is commanded by our enemies. You must flee as well.*

I will fight her.

No. You will lose.

I felt him rise into the air. *I will not let her harm you. I will not let her take you.*

You sound as foolish as a human. I will be dead within a day. That truth had been driven home while I fought through the night. The next surge of this illness would be the last.

There was no response, but that did not matter. I could not command him, but he would accept reality. Draca were not captive to emotion like people.

I thought, *Can you see her?*

In answer, his vision replaced mine. That was an unexpected relief as the aches in my eyes vanished. The sky, variegated in a hundred shades of blue and violet, spun as he searched, ferociously acrobatic. This made the twists when we rode him seem as tame as a child's ride on a pony.

His voice filled me, quieter than usual. *I do not see her. But she will be close before I do.* There were hills and ravines and lumpy, low-hanging clouds. Ample cover for a hunter.

I could guide him to her. I knew her rough direction. But she would kill him. What if I lied, and sent him the wrong way? Morals aside, our mental communication was so intimate that I doubted I could deceive him.

But Fènnù, for all her danger, was not the true enemy. "Mary, stop!" I cried. "I must concentrate." Holding Yuánchi's vision, I spread my other senses as well.

There. That stir of oily black.

Yuánchi, look here. I tried to convey the position and felt him puzzling over my request. The skies flipped fully upside down, inverted trees rushing overhead, then Pemberley House came into view and spun right-side up. His vision fixed on a hillside beyond the lake.

I felt myself uselessly squinting my own eyes. An old memory made me ask, *Can you look farther...*

There was a tightening. The view faded at the edges but sharpened in the center.

There was a dark gash in the hillside. A cave mouth. The Britons called it Pemberley Cavern, although it was small compared to the huge caverns farther north in Derbyshire. Still, one could walk twenty paces into the hill.

If I wished to hide from a dragon, I would hide underground, too.

Yuánchi, I must speak with Mary privately. I will find you again soon.

I drew my senses back within myself, opened my eyes, and found Mary waiting in front of me. The yard was full of rushing servants, the clatters and bangs of carts moving, and urgent voices.

"You are still here," I said, a little surprised.

"You told me to stop. I stopped," she said. Mary, as perfect as always. "Georgiana has gone to fetch Mr. Darcy."

"I know where the dagger is. Where their captive wyfe is wielding it." Watching the disciplined exodus from Pemberley, I knew why. "Our enemies need to be close. Pemberley is not a ship isolated at sea. Forewarned, the royal family could escape. They need a vantage to watch the house. To hunt down every fleeing person."

I thought that a strategic insight, but Mary said impatiently, "*Where* is the dagger?"

"In the cave across the lake. It is a two-mile ride through the hills. Too far to reach in time. But Yuánchi can be there in a minute. Mary... if he throws his breath into the cave, this would end. The cave would collapse to a molten tomb. The dagger would be destroyed. The men who control the dagger would die. But their captive, the wyfe who commands Fènnù, would die with them."

Mary went silent, her eyes wide. She would be remembering Miss Rees.

My guilt from that day had lost its fire, the way all grief cools into the black iron of mourning, but now it burst hot in my chest. "I do not know if it is right. Should it be done?"

Mary stepped back. "You cannot ask me!"

"I must. I need a mind I trust. You are not infected with a thousand years of vengeful wyves butchering enemies."

"Lizzy, this is beyond me. I am sworn to do no harm." She cast a desperate look around the yard. Hunting for Georgiana. "Are you saying this evacuation is hopeless? Will we die if you let them live?"

The answer was on my tongue, short and blunt. I held it back. Speaking would force my hand.

Seeking an alternative, or just to delay, I closed my eyes and reached out again to that spot of oily black.

Think as our enemies do. They expect Yuánchi to defend us; that is the sole reason we would shelter at Pemberley. So they do not fear a battle between Yuánchi and Fènnù. They know they will win.

An old memory surged, even more vivid—did that mean Fènnù was nearer? Honorable teacher, stiff with age, white-haired as snow, spoke: "Attack where your enemy is unprepared. Appear where you are unexpected. Fall like a thunderbolt."

Destroying the cave was the unexpected attack. Our enemy could not know that I sensed dosed wyves. But I would murder an innocent woman.

Consider if you must, but prepare as well. Only a coward lets indecision force their choice. *Yuánchi, fly to the lake. Be ready.* I felt wind rush over his scales as he turned in the sky.

Mary's voice came, abrupt and urgent. "Lizzy, I have realized that you cannot do this. The dagger must not be destroyed. That is what I wished to discuss. We need all three items to heal the fracture. Our enemies hunt for the items, too. That is why they stole Queen Mary's pendant. They seek power more deadly than what Fènnù provides. But the queen tricked them. She tricked all of history."

I understood her words, but it was the passion in her voice—the shining illumination of her life—that made me decide. Whatever punishment I earned, I would accept. "I do not want you to die, Mary. Or Darcy, or your beloved Georgiana. Besides, your books will be gone if I do nothing. Then how would you solve these puzzles?"

Yuánchi reached the lake. I compared his position to the black tendril of control. Yes, the cave.

But the tendril had thinned. Weakened. Was it vulnerable? I tried to break it like I would the influence of a lesser wyfe, but the essence of the black dragon anchored both ends, stronger than I.

Still, it was unquestionably wavering. Diminishing in a quickening, fluttering pulse. "They are losing control. The venom is wearing off, or... I think the wyfe is weakening. She may be dying." Selfish, perfidious relief filled me.

More vivid yet, another memory overtook me. My father cross-legged opposite me. He was a powerful man, thick through his swordsman's arms and chest, honed in intellect, rich with wisdom.

The tip of his brush rose from the paper. He had inked: "The pinnacle of skill is to subdue your enemy without battle."

This was the guidance I sought.

Yuánchi, can you delay Fènnù? You must protect yourself. She is controlled, so she will attack. But we need only a few minutes.

I can.

I opened my eyes. Darcy and Georgiana were rushing up. I smiled in relief. "We have a chance. Yuánchi need only delay their attack. The wyfe controlling Fènnù is weakening. She will not last much longer."

Concealed by my smile, I left a mental finger stretched out, resting on that tendril of control. Testing it. If it did not weaken soon—or if it strengthened—I was prepared. Then death would fall like a thunderbolt.

VENOM

EMMA

The path had never faltered. It might spread and fade while crossing a large log or curl in a generous half-circle to skirt a fall of rocks, but always in the distance, it led onward.

This, however, was unquestionably a fork. I could guess north well enough because the morning sun shone between the puffs of clouds, but even that did not help—north was ahead, but that was an unclimbable peak. The path split east and west around it.

Released from their endless plod, my knees shook. The trance that carried me through the night had ended at the meadow. Since then, I had drunk from a stream to relieve my parched throat, and my clothes were warm enough while I moved, but my body was spent. If I sat, I doubted I could stand again.

The forest itself did not frighten me. It was aged and restful, its hunters skilled at avoiding clumsy humans. But I could not keep walking without food. And a change of weather—a freezing night, or even a wetting from a shower— would be deadly.

"I wish to go home," I said. I had taken to complaining to the mysterious wyvern, even though he had moved definitively to his rest. If he had ever been present. "Or simply to *find* someone." There were supposed to be Britons guarding the estate. They seemed to do a poor job.

Walk, or your knees will buckle for good. More light showed through the branches to the left, so I took one step that way, wincing at a sore ankle and a blistered heel, then another.

The path rounded the side of the hill. The trees fell away. A crystal lake spread below me, more than a half-mile across. On the far side, a stream cascaded to the shore, and a road wound among sweeping, natural gardens. Pemberley House.

"Found!" I shouted, then the scene vanished in a watery blur while my sobs escaped. I let that finish, then I picked my way along the increasingly scraggly path as it descended the hill face.

As the lake's stony shore drew close, the path widened into a shelf. I smelled woodsmoke and, incredibly, the delectable aroma of frying sausage. My stomach growled loudly.

A thin stream of sooty smoke rose from an opening in the hillside. It was broader than a door, the rock floor trampled with muddy bootprints.

I called in, "Are you at home?"

"Is that Miss Woodhouse?" a gentleman said behind me, so near that I would have jumped if I had the strength. "What on earth has happened to you?"

Weary and very confused, I turned to Mr. Tinsdale. He wore immaculate hunting dress in forest brown, the waistcoat snug around his barrel chest. One thick hand carried a paper-wrapped package.

Mr. Tinsdale. Here. I tried to assemble a response. I had heard snippets of conversation between Lord Wellington and the Darcys. This man was a traitor. Lord Wellington was searching for him in...

"Are you not in London?" I said, feeling I should report that.

"Unfortunately, this business requires my presence." His palm pushed his coat aside to stroke the hilt of a long, sheathed dagger at his belt.

Behind him, a red-coated officer stepped from the trees, then uniformed soldiers with muskets. Saviors. But no. The captain stopped respectfully behind Mr. Tinsdale, waiting for orders.

Mr. Tinsdale smiled broadly. "Would you like something to eat?" Unwanted tears filled my eyes, and I nodded. He pointed to the cave entrance. After a hopeless pause—the other option was running, which was ludicrous—I limped in.

It widened inside, a wandering passageway with rock walls like puddled custard, so smooth they gleamed. Ridges of rock dangled stone icicles like fangs. Firelight flickered beyond a bend.

Mr. Tinsdale continued pleasantly, "I would say you look like something the cat dragged in, but that would insult dead mice. Though, I feel I should have expected you. You show up with a certain regularity."

His hand grabbed my upper arm, stopping me amid a clutter of gear on the floor. A small, open chest held medicinal bottles of powders and liquids. A bucket of water sat by a soot-stained kettle and a brace of pistols. The rest was a shapeless pile covered by a blanket.

Mr. Tinsdale rustled his paper package. "Our sortie to Pemberley has faced unexpected shortfalls. But good leaders adapt. My men have been stopping carriages. Here is our latest, whimsical acquisition..." He smiled and dangled a scone a few mocking inches in front of my nose.

The mockery did not bother me. I took the scone with shaking fingers and cradled it in both hands. The first bite was fresh and tender and tasted of currants, and it was the most delicious thing I had ever eaten. I closed my eyes and took another bite, savoring it and pretending I was saved.

Finally, the voices around me broke my fantasy. An American man was speaking, his vowels even more drawled than their usual accent.

"...she made the link fine, but she fights when I give her orders. That's the problem with fresh ones. Don't know how to be obedient. She didn't bear the last dose well. The full dose is going to kill her. Then what'll we do?" A finger jabbed my belly. "Not like *this* mess is one of your fancy English ladies."

"Oh, but she is," Mr. Tinsdale said. "Are you there, Miss Woodhouse?" Thick fingers seized my jaw, and I opened my eyes in fright. Mr. Tinsdale smiled beneath his curled mustache. "Providence blesses our cause. If she has sent you, you must have value." Steering my face as if I were an animal, he dragged me past the corner.

Harriet lay slumped on the floor, her eyes closed, her chest heaving. I pulled free and knelt by her. Her wrists were tied, but I could hold her fingers. One palm was sticky with dried blood.

Mr. Tinsdale squatted, an imposing bulk beside me. "Your friend is another prize from the local traffic, but better than breakfast. She is our fresh stock."

"Wyvestock," the American grunted, baring his teeth in a grin.

Mr. Tinsdale patted me on the shoulder. "I thank *you*, though. Without your tiresome advocacy for Miss Smith, I would never have spent valuable venom on an African. Still, she has endured. Perhaps it is her animal strength. Our London wyfe did not last five minutes." He jerked his thumb toward the blanket-covered pile we had passed.

Like he was a nightmare, a fantasy of the miasma, I pushed him from my mind. "Harriet. I am here." She moaned, her eyelids fluttering. Her fingers twitched in mine.

"Good. You have roused her," Mr. Tinsdale said. He turned to the American. "No more waiting. Give her the full dose. If she dies, she dies."

I kicked and clawed, but Mr. Tinsdale dragged me away while the American uncorked a glass bottle. An odor of sour orange and bitter almond burned my nostrils. The crawler venom Lizzy had described.

"I invented her affinity!" I cried. "She will never survive. Use me! I am a great wyfe!"

"Stop," Mr. Tinsdale said. His hands pulled me around to face him. His mockery had become a cold threat. "How do you know of great wyves?"

"I am one. I am the great wyfe of healing."

"You?" he scoffed. "Frivolous Miss Woodhouse who dresses like the morning sun at balls? *You* are one of the chosen three? *You* can wield the great song?"

I had no idea what that meant. "I swear it."

"That would be providence indeed," he whispered. "Or a lie for a friend. You will have your chance." He raised his voice. "Proceed."

I shouted "No!" and fought and thrashed, but Mr. Tinsdale held me easily. With cold-blooded precision, the American poured a measure of the venom between Harriet's lips. Her throat convulsed while he sealed the bottle away. Then he held out his hand to Mr. Tinsdale, waiting.

Mr. Tinsdale drew the black dagger from its sheath. He fondled it, watching the firelight on the serrations. "*This* is true power, sweeter for the irony of being wielded through the inferior sex. Not even the Emperor can match this. This shall be the scepter of my rule." Reluctant as a miser surrendering coin, he passed it to the American, who pushed the hilt between Harriet's bound hands. She cried out at the touch, her back arching while he tied her palms around the dagger with a leather thong.

The American thrust his face obscenely close to Harriet's, his peculiar hat brim nestling in her hair. He began whispering.

"See his skill?" Mr. Tinsdale said admiringly. "He *whispers*. There are ten thousand slave masters in the world. They break a hundred thousand slaves. A million. But to enslave the mind is a rare skill. Opium and venom and cocoa leaves, then fear and pain, balanced just so…"

Harriet's hands began to shake in an uncontrolled, violent palsy. Her head jerked, banging the rock. Her breath shortened to violent, choked gasps.

The American leaned back on his heels, clicking his tongue with dissatisfaction. "She's got command. She sent the orders. This one's stronger than that last one. But once they get to shaking like this..." He shook his head. "She's going quick. Not gonna last long."

I was hanging from Mr. Tinsdale's hands, weak and panting. In my despair —at last—I saw how this fable was written. The wyvern had foreseen it all. This was the third life to save. My sister, who fled because I was mindlessly cruel and who suffered because I told lies she never wished, needed me.

"Let me touch her," I said. The wyvern's pure, golden gift stirred within me. "I can save her. You will see. I can heal her."

RUT AND ROCK

LIZZY

I stood on the front steps of Pemberley House, watching. The young princess was aiding her grandfather, the king, into a coach. The prince and a handful of his retinue milled outside another. They were so slow. Mrs. Reynolds had packed Nessy off with Lucy five minutes ago.

Mary strode up beside me. "Coaches can be seen from the air. The grooms are saddling every horse. We should ride to one of the Briton villages. The forest will screen us."

"Take Georgiana and go," I said. "Do not wait for me."

Mary gave a scoffing laugh and set her feet. "We will all go together." Softer, she added, "Are you able to ride?"

"I am very well. Every color shines and is extraordinarily pure. I have noticed a pattern to this disease. Before it rages back, the world turns to transcendence. For a time, every edge becomes the finest etching. Every stone becomes a jewel." The effort of speaking made a burning twinge climb my spine. "Is that normal?"

Mary took my hand, her fingers very tight. "Yes."

Darcy burst into view, galloping his gray stallion flat out along one of the narrow garden paths around the house. Five of the soldiers that guarded the royal family followed single file at a saner pace, all mounted on Pemberley horses.

His steed skidded to a gravel-spraying halt before the stairs where I stood. Darcy had a pistol and sword on his belt, and a hunting gun strapped to the saddle. He shouted to be heard over the clamor. "We are going to the cave."

I ran down the steps. "You must not!"

He dismounted, the tails of his morning coat swirling, his boots landing as I reached him. He pulled me against him. "We must reclaim the dagger. If their wyfe loses control of Fènnù, they will attempt to flee. And if she keeps control, our lives depend on taking it from them."

The first was true. The second was not, but he did not know my plan.

"Send the soldiers," I said. "You do not need to go."

"I know every rut and rock of those hills. We need speed. I am leading their best riders." His head lowered so our faces were close. "Elizabeth, this is my duty. I will not shirk it."

I reached with my mind, testing the black tether of the dosed wyfe's control. Weaker. Not yet broken.

"Love," I said, "do not approach the cave. Not until I send a signal."

"What signal?"

"I will have Yuánchi fly to the cave mouth. When he flies away, you can approach."

"Very well."

"If you recover the dagger, destroy it. Promise me."

Mary was a few steps away, far enough to be polite, but I knew she heard. She stiffened at my words but did not speak.

Darcy was grave and serious. At last, he nodded, then when I took a breath, his finger sealed my lips, stopping my next words. He spoke instead. "Do not say goodbye. Just know I love you." He mounted the saddle in one swift motion and thundered down the road, the soldiers behind.

"You did not tell him why he should not approach," Mary said behind me. When I did not answer, she continued, "I am not so dull that I fail to guess why you stand, watching and waiting."

"I promised to defend Pemberley." Standing high to watch a field of battle had summoned a hundred years of ancient calm. "Our plans are made. Our orders dispatched. The path of this battle is now determined by our enemy."

The winter roads were damp, so there was no dust to reveal the horses. I caught glimpses through the winter-thinned trees until they cut from the road to circuit the lake. That shore was broken with ridges and cliffs, so they would ride in the forest, hidden. Safer than here. How fast could Darcy circle the lake? Ten minutes.

Yuánchi hid in the skies above me, his circuits never the same twice. Only the silver trace of our binding revealed him. Not once had he shown himself to ordinary senses. Not a flicker of shadow. Not a wingtip.

Like a sunrise, golden radiance filled my mind. This was a force in the world of draca, unfamiliar and pure.

I shut my eyes, concentrating.

The black tether of the dosed wyfe had weakened to a flutter, pathetic as a dying bird. Now it surged, drawing taut like a rope anchored to the sky. The oily black churned and thickened, sucking in the golden purity I had sensed and corrupting it to evil.

This was new and strange. But that did not matter.

Yuánchi, I thought. *Fly to the cave.*

I have not seen Fènnù. She could be near.

We are not fighting her. We will free her. I will show you how. May I share your vision?

Beneath my closed lids, a fog of cloud appeared, streaming fast as he descended. The fog vanished to reveal the lake, colored cold and looking round as a huge wheel when viewed from so high.

My human ears heard the servants' excited shouts as they spotted Yuánchi. Already his eyes had fixed on the cave mouth. At least I chose this before Darcy approached near enough to be in danger.

The view through Yuánchi's eyes jolted crazily. His silver binding yanked desperately at my heart. Then his full senses slammed into me, blowing my fragile human perceptions aside like a leaf.

I was plummeting, driven down by colossal strength, my wings frozen with numbing black and crushed to my sides. The underside of Fènnù's black wing flashed past my eyes, then the black scales of her side. Pain exploded as her claws tore me, cutting scale and muscle, but her grip was turning me also, purposefully, a spider turning a helpless fly.

The turning stopped with a massive foot before my face. The claws spread and struck. My eyes tore away.

Then there was not even the refuge of blackness. Sight became shrieking hues of pain, and I was falling, falling.

47

WYFE OF HEALING

EMMA

Harriet moaned, her head cradled in my lap.

When I had laid my fingers on the sides of her neck, the poisons in her body became vivid, a stench of corruption filling my nostrils —a filth that strangled her nerves and froze her heart. Then the golden radiance of the wyvern had poured through me to strengthen her. To fend off death.

But her blood was still flooded with vile toxin. There were other injuries, too. Her back was bloodied, her ankle bruised. I let the radiance flow, but cautiously, strengthening only her breath and heart. I needed a reserve to cure Lizzy—how much was impossible to know, but if I spent it all, I would be trading one life for another.

My effort was like trickling water into a raging fire. Did I dare try to remove the poisons, instead of just fending them off...

Harriet's eyes roved beneath her eyelids. The dagger tied in her bound hands twitched. "I will slay the devil..."

"It is a dream," I whispered.

The American shoved me to the floor and hauled Harriet to sitting with a grunt, then slung her over his shoulder like a bag of grain.

"I must stay with her!" I cried.

"Then come," Mr. Tinsdale said. He hauled my hand roughly, his face ruddy with excitement. "You have done it!"

He dragged me out of the cave, carelessly kicking through the gear on the floor. My elbow scraped the rock, tearing cloth as he pushed me out into the day. When he looked up, his face lit with triumph.

Higher than the hilltops, trailing a thick column of night-black smoke, a confused tangle of wings and limbs fell from the sky. The wings were both scarlet and black—the dragons, grappling in midair. They broke apart, Fènnù's wings spreading smoothly as she banked away, but Yuánchi continued to tumble, staining the air with thinning coal-black coils. At last, his wings opened, awkward and bent, and his fall angled into a curved, blind plunge toward Pemberley House. He fell short, an unchecked crash into the forest that felled trees. The sound reached us seconds later, a massive shattering of wood muted by distance.

Wind pummeled me, driving my dirty skirt out like a flag, and Fènnù landed in the lake shallows in front of us. Inky drops rained from the edges of her wings. Where they struck the lake water, black fog curled. Hissing ice congealed.

Her massive head swung toward Harriet, lying at the American's feet. Mr. Tinsdale recoiled, shoving me in front of him like a shield. "Is she controlled?"

"The darkie has her locked tight," the American said, staring boldly up at the dragon. "That lady of yours did some trick. She's gonna last a while more."

The shred of hope I had gained by helping Harriet turned sour. This was the purpose of his whispers—to bring down Yuánchi. I looked at the flattened stretch of trees. Unmoving scarlet was visible amongst the scattered trunks, but I sensed a living presence. Not dead.

"You have made me a king," Mr. Tinsdale crooned, his breath hot on my ear. Then he shouted, "Destroy the house. Raze the forests. Kill everyone."

The American bent and whispered.

LIZZY

THROUGH THE SEETHING PAIN, I heard Mary's voice, intent and focused. "Lizzy, come back. It was not you who fell. Your binding—" A broken bone grated as a wing twitched, and her voice drowned in torment, then returned "... follow the song."

Music teased the threads of my mangled thoughts apart—a woman's voice and the piping harmonies of a chorus of flutes. My tangle of senses separated. The violent tremors of my silver binding stilled. The shattering pain distanced.

I opened my eyes. Mary was leaning over me, her gaze intent behind her spectacles. Georgiana knelt beside her, singing softly, tears on her cheeks. All around us, small song draca were perched, singing a peculiar chorus. One even sat on Mary's shoulder, peering down as intently as Mary.

"Songs," I muttered, my voice raw in my throat. Had I screamed?

Mary brushed at the draca on her shoulder. He flicked his wings to land on the ground. "Stay still. You have had a shock."

I pushed her aside, forcing my shaking body onto my feet. Her arm caught me as I swayed. Nausea climbed my throat, then became a hot needle in my spine and skull. *Not now.* I blinked hard, fighting the glares. "Where is he?" but already I was following the silver line of our binding to where Mary pointed wordlessly.

Fifty yards below us, there were trees broken and scattered, upended earth, and scarlet.

I am coming, I thought, pulling free of Mary to run, ignoring the pain from each jarring step. I smashed through brush and ivy, sparse from the cold, then passed a snapped tree. The stump was stained with golden blood, and I slowed to a terrified stumble.

Yuánchi's flank was heaving like an agonized bellows. I approached his shoulder, trying not to tread on his torn wing. His neck lifted, and his head reached for me, swaying and blind. His face was a ruin, his beautiful eyes gone. Edges of jet-black bone showed from the wet sockets.

I grabbed his jaw, pulling my forehead against his muzzle, feeling the heat of his scales. "You will heal! I will care for you."

Elizabeth Darcy Bennet. I must go into the water. I must go deep and sleep the centuries to heal.

"No," I whispered. "It is all my fault. I should have sent you away. Kept you safe."

You are a great wyfe. It is I who leave. I who failed. His body shifted, a huge leg scrabbling at the ground. I felt the agony of broken bones, the weakness of lost blood. *I must get to the water. Move back, so I can stand.*

I backed away and met Mary struggling through the brush toward us. "Mary, we must give him room."

"Lizzy, we need to go. It is not safe."

"*Leave* him? Are you mad?"

In answer, Mary pointed across the lake. A black-winged shape stretched wide on the far shore.

I had forgotten. The battle was not done. "How long was I unconscious?"

Mary's forehead furrowed. "Five minutes. Or six."

"Darcy is almost at the cave. We still have a chance."

"He will have turned back!" Mary protested.

"No. Seeing this will only make him drive harder." Thick branches were snapping as Yuánchi forced himself upright, one foot half-raised like a lame horse, his wings unable to mesh properly. But he was moving. The heavy bones that drove the bulk of each wing were intact.

I thought, *Can you fly to the water?*

His head hunted one way, then another. *Where is the water?*

That answer tore me. His magnificent vision, lost. But I steeled my mind. Be strong as a draca. *The lake is downhill from us. Once you rise, it is one long glide. You are almost as high as Pemberley House.*

He fumbled his feet among the fallen branches, turning downhill. A hanging wingtip struck a tree, and fresh pain blazed in my mind. *I cannot rise blind in these trees.*

"Mary, I have a plan," I said. "You will not like it."

She watched me. "Suspense will not make me like it more."

"I will ride Yuánchi down to the lake. He is too injured to heal. He must go into the water and sleep. If he shares my vision, he will see well enough to fly."

"Fènnù will kill you both."

"She will not attack him while I am riding."

"You do not know that! She is commanded by the dagger."

"I am her wyfe of war. And while Yuánchi flies, our enemies will ignore other targets. Darcy and those soldiers will have time to take the dagger." I produced a smile, ignoring the blazing pain between my temples. "It is a perfect plan. But you must help me mount. It is too high to reach alone."

Abruptly, she hugged me. "You are a most remarkable sister."

"I am sure we are tied. But hurry."

At Yuánchi's shoulder, awkwardly, she made a step of her hands the way grooms sometimes help a gentleman. That lifted me enough to grab hold of one of the knobby neck ridges, then I scrambled for purchase while she pushed at my feet and I pulled my skirts aside. Finally, with a last shove from below, I threw a foot over his neck and slid into place.

It was different from a saddle. Closer; I felt the heat of his body, and the scales caught at my clothing if pulled the wrong way. But it was secure enough if there were no acrobatics.

Across the lake, Fènnù rose into the air. I thought, *Share my vision. We must rise now.*

I threw my mind open and felt his presence. Odd features drew my attention—the broken branches and downed trees around us, but also the clouds, then the bare treetops downslope as I judged winds.

What has happened to your eyes? he thought. *They are worse.*

Even in this clouded light, haloes were skittering. Shapeless, dark blurs pulsed around dark spots.

"I told you. I am ill. Go!"

Yuánchi picked through the fallen logs and broken stumps, then took two running steps off a small prominence and spread his wings. For a moment we were falling, then wobbling weight returned. Wind grew. I had no goggles this time. I squinted, not willing to loosen a hand to shield my eyes.

Despite all the horrors and my surging illness, being in the air again was a thrill. Our speed increased, and the ride smoothed. I barely managed three breaths before we swept over the last of the trees and glided over the lake.

Too soon.

Yuánchi, can you see... I stopped that thought, ashamed. *I am sorry. Darcy hunts our enemies. Can you stay aloft longer? Any delay will help him.*

In answer, Yuánchi's wings began a halting stroke. The thick, leading bones of his inner wing segments were intact, but one wingtip hung like a broken tent, and he tucked the other for balance. We climbed in a feeble curve.

I craned and spotted Fènnù, much higher. I closed my eyes. Her mind was locked in the grip of the dagger. I stretched my senses toward her. *Fènnù. I am here.*

Open your eyes! Yuánchi's voice shouted in my head. I snapped my eyes open as a colossal black mass flashed past. Her wake shook us.

I was right, I thought. *She did not strike. We can delay her.* I watched her bank effortlessly, already over the hills. She was so fast. We were flapping along like a wounded pigeon while a hawk circled.

With a graceful flip, she turned ahead of us. Facing us. The distance closed faster than my land-based perception could comprehend. Her wings blurred and darkened. My vision? No, her wake was turning to a churning storm cloud...

Her jaws opened and black surged, obscuring her, roaring toward us.

Hold firm! Yuánchi shouted in my mind, then his wings folded, hiding the sky, wrapping me in a cage of shadowed scarlet. Unsupported, we fell like a stone. Thunder exploded and the last traces of light vanished. The air chilled, turned frigid, became searing cold. We tumbled, and I slipped sideways, my face and shoulder striking Yuánchi's furled wing. The scales burned. Terrified, I scrambled for a neck knob and dragged myself back. The skin of my cheek pulled, frozen to his wing, then tore free.

Shadowy light returned at the creases of his wings. The interior of his wings was frosted and motionless. Still we fell, then with a crunching spray of broken ice, his wings spread, catching us in a glide barely above the lake's choppy waves.

Wet warmth was running over my cheek and blowing away in the wind, but I felt nothing. Too terrified to feel pain.

This is enough of your plan, Yuánchi thought. *I will drive her back, then set you down.*

I had never heard anger in his voice before.

His wings pushed hard, new rips flapping in the wind as he lifted us.

EMMA

THE CAPTAIN STRODE to Mr. Tinsdale and pointed. "Sir, riders are approaching."

Several hundred yards away, six horses were picking their way down the rough hill. They moved slowly, but when they reached the lakeshore, they could gallop the rest of the way. Even here, I recognized Mr. Darcy's tall form in the saddle of his gray steed as he guided it, skidding, down the scree. The others had the red coats of soldiers.

Mr. Tinsdale looked up at the flying dragons, assessing. "Take your men. Stop them." The captain barked commands, and they mounted and rode out onto the lakeshore. His nine men against Mr. Darcy's six.

The dragons had clashed in dark thunder over the lake. Now they were approaching each other again, but Yuánchi was flying poorly, slow and level, like a lumbering carriage, not an agile draca. Wounded.

Then I saw the figure clinging at the base of his neck, skirts flapping and hair knocked loose by the wind. Lizzy was riding him. The strength I had given Harriet would kill them both.

Harriet was on the ground a few steps from me. The American crouched by her, whispering in her ear and watching the sky.

The world lit with glaring, brilliant gold light. Mr. Tinsdale dropped my arms and cried out, his hands over his eyes.

In that blinding glare, I threw myself down by Harriet and clutched her hands. Her heart was stuttering again, her lungs spasming. Every instinct screamed to help, but I ignored that, finding the poisons swirling in her flesh, then pouring in the gold purity—feeling how similar it was to the gold radiance filling the sky—to melt them away.

The blazing golden illumination faded. A crash of thunder hit us. A second later, a heavy boot kicked me away from Harriet.

"Keep her away," the American said as Mr. Tinsdale yanked me to my feet, my ribs throbbing where his boot hit. The American kneeled by Harriet, and her eyes opened weakly. He cursed. "Now I got to dose her again." He pulled a vial from his pocket, leaned close, then shrieked and reeled back. Blood ran from a cut that crossed his forehead and the bridge of his nose.

Weakly, Harriet waved the dagger tied between her hands. The American swore violently, then stomped her wrists to the ground with his boot. He pried the dagger free. "Goddam blackies. You'll pay for that." He spat on the dagger in his hand.

"Stop!" a voice commanded. Mr. Knightley, in muddy and torn day dress, stood on the path.

"Mr. Knightley!" I cried. "You found us!"

"Miss Woodhouse," he acknowledged, his eyes on the American and the dagger. "I saw you take the north path. I followed, or tried to follow. I became peculiarly lost."

"They have pistols in that cave." I pointed.

"Shut your mouth," Mr. Tinsdale snapped, cranking my arm painfully and dragging me back a step. He shouted at the American, "What are you waiting for? Kill him!"

Mr. Knightley had taken two cautious steps to stand between us and the cave mouth. In a rush, the American attacked him, the dagger flashing in a wicked, underhand strike—a strike that stopped short, his wrist caught in Mr. Knightley's hand. Mr. Knightley's other hand grabbed the back of the American's neck, locking their faces close while his elbow jammed the American's shoulder at a painful angle. Their pose held, rigid as a statue, and the American began to strain, blood running from the cut Harriet had given him.

Mr. Knightley watched him with cold disdain. "My father taught me to fight," he pronounced softly. "He was a gentleman, and a gentleman duels with pistol or sword. But he also honored his roots. A slave must fight without weapons. In his memory, I teach his skills to those who have been stripped of freedom."

"Goddam darkies," the American gasped. The point of the dagger quivered, barely an inch from Mr. Knightley's waistcoat. "Not worth the chains I'll put on you."

"An English gentleman does not wear chains," Mr. Knightley corrected. "No innocent person should suffer that abomination. Drop the dagger. I have no desire to fight a wounded man."

"He is a slaver!" Harriet croaked hoarsely from the ground. "He killed all those wyves."

Mr. Knightley's grip must have tightened because the two men's faces drew close, the American's chin jerking as he struggled. Mr. Knightley whispered, "My error. You are not a man at all." He shifted, sudden as lightning, and his arm wrapped the American's neck. I looked away as a thick, wet snap sounded, and the American fell limp to the ground.

Mr. Knightley retrieved the dagger from the ground. He turned it, curious, and said idly, "Mr. Tinsdale. You have wandered from your false parliament of traitors and sycophants."

Wind was growing, whipping the trees, and a flood of shadow crossed us as a huge, scarlet shape swept low in the sky. An even larger black shape followed—the soft glide of two fliers in tandem, not the press of pursuit.

As the dragons glided away, Mr. Tinsdale threw me hard to the ground. His running steps faded.

I crouched there on aching hands and knees, staring at my dirty, scraped fingers. Relief for my rescue fought with a new panic. The miasma was pooling under each stone.

I staggered to my feet, smoothing my skirt by touch, averting my eyes from my ruin of clothes. I fumbled in my reticule for my gloves and drew them on, then held them up, finding the symmetry of the pristine lace and trying not to see the dirt beneath.

"Help has arrived," Mr. Knightley said from where he crouched by Harriet. "Let us go down." On the narrow shore below us, Mr. Darcy and his soldiers were mounted on horses. Mr. Tinsdale's soldiers were seated on the stones in a small, slump-shouldered huddle—surrendered, likely after Yuánchi overflew them.

"Should you not catch Mr. Tinsdale?" I said, looking at the path behind me.

"He is just a man. This time, let us get the dagger to safety." Mr. Knightley tied the sheath to his waist and inserted the dagger. He lifted Harriet, cradling her in his arms. "She cannot walk on this ankle."

I ran to her. "I am sorry I could not cure your ankle. I needed strength to help Lizzy. But it is only sprained." Harriet clutched my hand weakly, but her smile was strong.

We scrambled down the slope to the shore, met partway by two of the soldiers. I ran to Mr. Darcy, who was watching the dragons.

"Call your wyfe," I cried. "I can heal her."

His expression became wondering, then he clasped my arms in unrestrained joy. The lake was fringed with ice, but he splashed out calf-deep like an eager boy, waving his arms hugely.

"Your mother's wyvern gave me a great gift…" I began, then trailed off.

I no longer felt the golden glow. But it could not be lost. The wyvern promised.

48

SOARING

LIZZY

I felt the dagger's influence break. Fènnù's mind came free—still damaged, still seeking for me, but calming as the dagger's commands for violence faded.

Yuánchi and I flew past Darcy's soldiers on the shore. They were a blur. We circled the lake twice more while I tried to get a better glimpse. But my vision darkened until I could barely tell water from land.

Even whipped by the cold air, my face and neck were burning and slick with perspiration. And I was burned more truly. Splashes of black breath had penetrated Yuánchi's shield through tears in his wings. Ragged holes were cut in my clothes, the skin beneath blistering.

Elizabeth Darcy Bennet. I must go into the deep.

I know.

Our senses were merged. I felt his unimaginable strength, at last exhausted. I felt the wind on his shredded wings. Drops of golden blood trailed in the air like a rain of jewels. At least his pain was no burden. My own illness outshone it.

That harmony made my choice easy. *I am coming with you.*

That is human foolishness. Return to your life.

My life is finished. Darcy told me not to say goodbye. I wish him to remember me as I was then, not nurse me through a handful of wretched hours.

Yuánchi did not reply. Silently, we glided around a quarter of the lakeshore.

I leaned closer, touching my cheek to one of the smooth, scarlet knobs on his neck. *We saved England together. Perhaps it will not fade like a dream. Perhaps you will wake and find it flourishing.*

The stone beach by the cave passed below, a burning, vague glare.

I hugged his neck tight. *Remember me.*

EMMA

AGAIN, Yuánchi passed over us, so low that I saw Lizzy clearly. Mr. Darcy shouted this time, waving hard, and Yuánchi turned at last, sweeping out over the center of the lake. He soared up, higher and higher, then his wings folded around Lizzy like sheltering hands. He fell, a scarlet spear, and vanished in a colossal tower of spray.

Horrified cries and exclamations came from the soldiers. Harriet was sitting on the rocks beside me, and she gasped, "No!"

Mr. Darcy rushed into the lake, tearing off his coat, throwing his boots aside. He plunged into the water and swam, his powerful strokes meeting the cresting wave rolling from Yuánchi's fall.

Mr. Knightley had taken off his own coat, but he was looking around the shore. "He cannot swim that far. The water is freezing cold. Is there a boat?"

There was nothing, of course. Pemberley lake was pristine and natural. One of the soldiers set out after Mr. Darcy, but he returned after fifty feet, shivering and defeated.

Silently, we gathered at the shore edge, watching the long swim until Mr. Darcy reached the center of the lake. He dove and vanished. It seemed a full minute before his head appeared, alone. The soldiers swore when they saw that, and Harriet, propped up to stand with Mr. Knightley, began to sob.

Mr. Darcy dove again. I counted my breaths this time. There were a dozen before his head reappeared, alone.

"Call him back," I said. Mr. Knightley waved and called, but Mr. Darcy dove again. Grief was tearing my heart, but again I counted breaths. Twenty. Thirty. Still nothing.

I felt in my reticule and found the precious tea for Nessy. I passed it to Harriet and said, "Keep that safe," then I waded into the lake. The water was a shock, numbing my feet in a step. The shelf was shallow at first, then dropped. Twenty yards out, it lapped my chest, and my ribs clenched.

When Mr. Darcy's head reemerged. I shouted and waved, and he began to swim back. I breathed a gasp of relief, and finally, tears of grief ran from my eyes.

He splashed up beside me and stood, the water high on his waist. He bent in two, gasping, staggering in the water while he fought for air. His hands were blue, his arms shaking. He lost his balance and fell, choking, submerged.

I caught his arm, pulling him up. "Come to shore. There is nothing more to do."

The water trembled as Fènnù swept over us. She crossed the center of the lake, her wingstrokes slow as a dirge. She turned at the far shore and crossed a second time, then a third. A mournful call sounded, then she drove upward and away, rising toward the farthest hills.

Mr. Darcy was staring at me with mad eyes, water streaming from his soaked hair. "The waters of Pemberley are a curse. They took my mother. They take my wyfe."

"Come back," I said. "I implore you."

I reached for him, but he pushed me away, then turned to the depths of the lake and cried, "Here lies Elizabeth, my Juliet, and her brilliance makes this tomb a brave arena full of wit. My love, my wyfe, why art thou sunk so far? Shall I believe that red and greedy dragon binds thee here in dark to be his paramour?" He waded deeper. "For fear of that I stay with thee, and never from his grasping lair, depart again. Here, here, will I drown my bitter loss."

I was struggling to catch him, and finally I caught his sleeve. "Mr. Darcy. Stop." He strode on, pulling me behind him. My toes scrambled on the slippery rocks as the water reached my chin, then the bottom fell away and my full head ducked, my soaked clothes dragging me down. I floundered, fighting panic, unsure even where the surface was. I had never been in water deeper than my shoulders.

A pair of hands seized my waist. Desperate, I grabbed around Mr. Darcy's neck and hung, coughing, while he waded into shallower water. Then, gently but insistently, he pushed me to arm's length.

"You cannot do this," I gasped. My body was shuddering uncontrollably. "You have a sister to protect. Do not abandon her. There is nothing worse than being abandoned." He watched me steadily, then backed toward the depths. I cried, "Your mother's wyvern promised I would save a third life today. Do you not see? It is you I am to save!"

He stopped, his eyes amazed.

Water sloshed as Mr. Knightley splashed up beside me. His arm steadied mine, and when the heat of his fingers sent a tremor through my frame, he pulled me against his side. It was like leaning against a gloriously warm stove.

He extended his hand to Mr. Darcy. "The lady is cold. We should accompany her to shore. Please."

Mr. Knightley waited, his offered hand steady, neither demanding nor conceding. Mr. Darcy's wondering, pained gaze found me again, then he gripped Mr. Knightley's hand, and we waded back.

Ashore, the soldiers shed their coats and waistcoats, toweling the cold water off us. They wrapped me in layer after layer. Under it all, I hugged my gloved hands, counting by touch the soggy lines of lace.

Mr. Knightley, his wet coat discarded, approached Mr. Darcy. Wordlessly, he offered the sheathed dagger.

Mr. Darcy drew the black blade, weighed it once in his palm, then turned and threw it—a tremendous, violent, savage throw. The dagger spun, glinting and soaring through the air before it plunked into the water, distant and deep.

49

HANDSOME AND WELL

EMMA

"Miss Woodhouse?" Lucy's voice said softly from the guest room door.

I smiled at her. "Good afternoon, Lucy. Has there been a letter?" My reply from Hartfield was overdue.

Nine weeks had passed since that terrible loss on the lake. I was still a guest at Pemberley. I was afraid to leave—worried by Mr. Darcy's plunges into despair and trapped by my own hidden dependence.

"No letter, madam," she answered. "It is nothing like that. I was only dusting Mrs. Darcy's things, and..." Her words hitched, then she burst into sobs. I held her, awkward at first while the miasma gleamed in the corners, but Lucy was just a child who needed care, so it retreated.

"Harriet will visit soon," I told her when she quieted. "Would you join us? She was cross with me last time, so I am a little nervous about it."

She sniffed. "Did you do something wrong?"

"Not that I intended," I said, honestly. "But I am still learning to be a good sister."

We went down and found Harriet arriving, but with Mr. Knightley as well, and my pulse fluttered. After the tragedy, he had postponed his travel to the occupied south, but he had not been to Pemberley for weeks.

When we were seated, I asked Harriet, "Are you established in Lambton?"

"Quite established. I have a pretty room all to myself, and nicer than my old room at Mrs. Goddard's. Mr. Knightley negotiated a stay of six months." He had assisted her, as a lady could not sign a contract of lease. "Then, if this mad war is done, I should like to teach at the Martin school. It would be exciting to live in London."

She sparkled with enthusiasm, so I gave her fingers a pat. "I am happy for you."

I had been visiting the Lambton school twice a week, accompanying Nessy to her classes. Nessy always dashed ahead the instant the coach door opened, so I would enter afterward and watch from the back, admiring Harriet's competent demeanor and trying not to see the chalk on her sleeves.

Still, if Harriet was determined to go to London... "I am sure Mr. Darcy would host you at Chathford. You would look very fine coming and going each day." Harriet shook her head. This was like our last argument, so I tried a fresh approach. "You are a gentleman's daughter. You must support your claim to that station. There will be plenty of people who take pleasure in degrading you."

"I feel only affection for Mr. Woodhouse. No insult will take that from me." She gave me a warm smile. "And they cannot degrade my love for you, Emma. But Mr. Darcy has closed Chathford. I do not think he will reopen it."

Harriet and Lucy went, chatting comfortably, to find the other ladies. Mr. Knightley and I were left alone to wait. He had dressed with particular care today. Every button and seam of his charcoal calling dress was perfect.

He touched a black ribbon dangling from the mantle. "Pemberley is a house of mourning. You have no such duty. You should return to your life."

"I would mourn at Hartfield, also."

Mr. Knightley snorted. "Darcy wanders these halls like a tall, dark mop."

That image was so perfect that I laughed. "He is only a mop on his bad days. But Georgiana will make him cut his hair."

"What if life drew you out?" More softly, he said, "What if a proper life were offered to you?"

I imagined him admiring a neighbor's orchard from his little room in Chelsea. A gentleman musician could use a proper life. But Mr. Knightley faced one barrier in society already. He should not be ridiculed for a wyfe who failed to bind and who stared at loose threads.

The benefit of being known as a selfish and thoughtless creature is that no one suspects you have other motives. I smoothed the black silk of my gown and did not meet his eyes. "There is nothing improper about my life."

"No, of course not." He sighed. "You look handsome and well."

I swallowed against a swell of feelings, but I knew this was best.

LOCH BAIRN

MARY

M*ary Bennet's journal, 4th day of February, 1813:*

My pen catches on the paper, the tip roughened and split. These tracings blotch and skip, betraying the clefts in my thoughts and the hurt in my heart.

Dearest Lizzy. For all your Artemisia bravery, I never thought you could fall. You seemed destined to forge bolts and witticisms until you tottered about, surrounded by irreverent grandchildren and doted upon by all. Not least your younger sister who, shy and envious, never found words to express her adoration.

You and Papa would both mock a house embalmed in mourning. I have not your gift to rouse others from despair, though time slowly serves. But I must rouse myself, for when you sank, fate assigned purpose to me.

The breaking of Fênnù's mind—called 'the fracture' by draca—unleashed more than a mad dragon. Before that day, thirty years before the Christian era, there is no record of foul crawlers, those poisonous vermin called 'draca bane.' The influence of their venom upon draca and wyves are hints of their importance. Others lie in Georgiana's vision of the swelling storm. So, I must breach the shroud of Pemberley and go forth.

I put aside my pen. Nine weeks. Lizzy would laugh at me. Why do you wait? Pemberley's edition of *Debrett's Dracal Lineage* was old, the frontispiece stamped 1805, but my interest was old as well. I flipped to the page for "Wyves of Surrey." Emma's maternal line was prominent; her grandmother bound the 1764 wyvern. But it was the introductory passage, "Lore and Myth," that my ribbon marked:

> *As is common, Surrey's regional folklore revolves around an ancient wyfe attributed with supernatural powers and wisdom. Inevitably, these tales are kin to myths of fairies and demons, but the Surrey mythology is unusual for its mundanity. Rather than miracles, it celebrates a 1557 royal commission by Queen Mary I to investigate a unique magical object—an amulet of dragon scale.*
>
> *No corroborating record exists in the royal archives, so this most cherished achievement of the 'the Witch of Woodhouse' must be gently placed in the book of fable.*

I had asked Emma, of course. Was there an heirloom on her father's side? An amulet or necklace? She shook her head: Nothing.

Fang, scale, and claw. The first was sunk in the unsoundable depths of Pemberley lake. The second had passed through Surrey. I had no hint of the third item, the claw, but if Mary Tudor's thieving knights found two, why not three?

There was a knock at the open library door. Mrs. Reynolds, visibly disturbed, said, "Miss Bennet. If I may interrupt?"

"Yes?"

"Lord Wellington has called." Her wrinkled fingers fretted. "I gather he wrote to inform Mr. Darcy that he would visit, but the master neglected to tell me. Mr. Darcy chooses not to see him, and Miss Darcy is out, walking for how long I do not know. Lord Wellington is an old family friend, so I thought... I feel *you* are a proper mistress of Pemberley, madam, if you would greet him?"

That tribute from this dedicated woman, so dear to Georgiana, squeezed my heart between childish gratitude and a fear of exposure I could never truly banish.

We went down to the west sitting room. Lord Wellington's hair had grayed at the base of his temples. After a silence, he said, "So Darcy will not see me."

"I gather not," I said.

"Do you blame me also?"

"No. But neither am I eager to discover what stratagem brings you to our door."

"Is Pemberley your home, now?"

To evade that, I said, "I am soon to depart. How goes the war?"

"Brutally. It has descended to the slog of attrition. Both sides dig graves to bury the prodigal waste. The remnants of our navy sail again, but Tinsdale rules the coast of Kent and all of Sussex, Hampshire, and South West England. The treason he preaches sprouts in the north like far-flung seeds, so our line of battle judders and retreats, undermined by deceit and betrayal." He shook his head. "The American slave states have mobilized to a war economy. Chained slaves are building warships. Their sailors ride on timbers bloodied before their first battle."

This from a man who unflaggingly supported the West Indies trade through his entire career. "I would think the paragon of England's military establishment was inured to blood."

"Less and less, as I watch the world," he said. My jibes always fell short against him. He added, "Fury was sighted in Derbyshire."

"And in Scotland. And in Wales. You have wasted a trip."

He gave a slight smile. "I think she is drawn here."

"I have not seen her."

"Then perhaps you are not the great wyfe she seeks."

Bitterness roiled my breast. "Stop your tricks. Leave our family be. If you skirted blame for my sister's death, it was by blind fate, not innocence. Fight your war with cannon and men. The dagger is lost, and Fènnù is broken. I will not let you torment Georgiana with futile schemes."

He stood with a sigh. "Miss Bennet, I dearly wish I had a scheme. But I did not intend to press myself upon you. I bid you good day." He bowed. "Know that, every day, I mourn your sister."

Frustrated by his visit, I braved the drizzle and trod Georgiana's favorite path. I found her, the rain sparkling on the pearly fairness of her complexion, her slim figure, clothed in black twill, bending graceful as a poplar in the squalling gusts.

We were met at the entrance by Lucy and Harriet, who had come with Mr. Knightley, so, a little soggy, we rushed to the sunroom for a reunion of smiling embraces and even laughs.

At last, Mr. Knightley turned serious and asked Georgiana, "How are you managing?"

"I am sad, but well enough. It is my brother for whom I worry." She took my hand with a smile, and my heart skipped. Firmly, she said, "Mary and I have each other."

Emma was taking turns between talking with us and giving Nessy a lesson in watercolor painting. Nessy was a fiend for the gardens, so this was Emma's bribe to bring her in from the rain.

I watched Emma advise Nessy's work. Once, no black thread touched Emma. Now, she was draped in ebony lace and jet buttons, a carbon ink engraving save for the stray locks of gold below her cap. Her fine wardrobe was courtesy of Pemberley's seamstress.

Nessy, satisfied with her painting, put down the brush and came to give Mr. Knightley a hug. She invited him to tour the paths. "The rain is no bother, and it is mysterious here! There is magic, I *am* sure. Aunt Emma says you walked the wyvern trail?"

"I am not sure of that," he answered, smiling. "I went searching for Miss Woodhouse. But it was a long and strange path."

"It *was* magic, then," Nessy decided.

"Knightley!" came Mr. Darcy's surprised voice from the doorway as he entered. They shook hands, then clasped arms for a long time.

We took seats, Emma in a chair that Lizzy had favored, which set my teeth on edge. She removed her gloves, and my eyes narrowed. I had seen this before. Soon, in a careless moment, her finger would brush Mr. Darcy's hand. The bitter part of me wished to accuse her of flirtation—then I could hate her—but she did not smile or simper. There were no longing looks or fatuous compliments. Emma was a perfect guest in mourning. If I were honest, my frustration was that she helped. On Mr. Darcy's worst days, when his half-lidded eyes stared like lifeless pits, she could draw him out with news of a Pemberley farmer or of Nessy's bafflement at a quirk of school. But honesty did not satisfy my heart, which resented any light diminishing the shadow of absent Lizzy.

Emma's fixations were evident today. Her gaze had snared on her sleeve. That tickled my mind. There was some oversight in my thoughts. I closed my eyes to see what would flow. Glimpses of our family's journal, Loch bairn. I had not read it since Jane was ill. Why that?

Mr. Knightley drew me back with a question about my planned trip. I explained: "Jane's child is due soon. I must ensure she is not draped with leeches or other idiocy by a male doctor. And a birth is a restorative wonder. I will enjoy that."

Nessy, who was scuffing her feet, rolled her eyes. Dull Aunt Mary ranked far below charming Aunt Emma who played games, gave sweets, and found magic wyverns.

"We might travel to Longbourn together," Mr. Knightley suggested to me. "Even in Hertfordshire, there are ruffians and scoundrels encouraged by the malice of the south."

"Will you travel to Brighton?" Emma asked him, concerned.

"My preparations are complete. I must."

"Be careful," she said, and if I were to accuse someone of longing looks it would be the two of them, separated by eight feet of fine rug and a tangle of sensibilities and pride I could not begin to unravel. Nor, apparently, could they. Emma added, "You could look in at Hartfield. The mail seems very poor. I have written to my maid twice and not had a reply. It is not like Surrey has fallen to the slavers. I know Hartfield would shelter you well. Just smile and say you are my friend. I would like that."

"I will travel through Surrey, so we shall see."

That made me consider. I must visit London, but also Surrey, and maybe go farther. Mr. Knightley's clandestine network in the occupied south might be useful.

It became time for Mr. Knightley to go. Mr. Darcy had sat straight in his chair, hardly speaking. That reminded me of his long-ago visits to Longbourn where he stared, speechless, at oblivious Lizzy. But this cause was not so happy.

We rose, and Emma said, "May we all hold hands? Who knows when we shall be together again." We gathered in serious but smiling silence, our fingers a messy tumble at the center. It was charming and sincere, and I knew Emma's ungloved finger would touch Mr. Darcy's.

THE NEXT MORNING, Georgiana and I stood arm-in-arm on the shore of Pemberley lake. The rain had turned to snow in the night, and the hill's oaks and ash were black-limbed skeletons dusted with white. But that was a morbid illusion. Their dark meditation held dormant life and the promise of flowering growth.

Two weeks after the funeral, nine sculptors had queued at Pemberley's door. Mr. Darcy handed them a pose study of Lizzy sketched by Georgiana last summer. Then the Darcy gallery became a studio ringing with hammer on chisel while Mr. Darcy prowled, scowling and critiquing every stroke.

A month later, I went down one morning and found the sculptors gone. A likeness had been chosen, and the artists dismissed. I discovered the rejected statues hidden in an overgrown corner of the garden, a verdant gallery filled with obscured aspects of Lizzy. Doubtless Mr. Darcy could not bring himself to dispose of them.

The chosen statue was moved by Mr. Darcy and two footmen to this place at the lakeshore. The stone was silvery and copper-infused: granite of the local cliffs. Lizzy's head and shoulders were fully formed, though unpolished— granite was a hard stone. Her torso and legs were a mere suggestion of rushing motion. On a buried plinth, she faced the shore, the lake lapping at a trailing heel as if she were stepping from the waves.

Facing this memorial, I wiped a wet eye, then bent to straighten a bouquet of crocuses, purple and white. "The Britons brought these. Spring has come early to the hills."

Georgiana caressed Lizzy's stone hair. "Pemberley cares for her wyves." She sniffed, then scanned the sky. "I thought Lord Wellington would stay for this."

"He would have, but I told him that Fènnù does not come here."

Her sapphire eyes widened. "You lied to him!"

"A wound heals best undisturbed. His war does not belong with us."

Georgiana slipped her arm back through mine. "Emma sent Mr. Knightley away." I made an uncaring noise, and Georgiana arched an eyebrow. "Mary! Is it the clothes? Has she surpassed your wardrobe of black?"

"*Hers* are bought by your brother," I muttered.

"You do understand that *her* selfish brother keeps all her money?"

I had not known that.

Georgiana hugged my arm tight. "Emma has helped Fitz. And you must see that she and Mr. Knightley care for each other."

I would not surrender that easily. "I see that he falls at her feet."

Georgiana answered in the cadence of a song. "He loves her, and she loves him. Now they are parting, which makes me sad, though I know they will meet again. But you will not lose Mr. Knightley. He admires you. The world *sees* you, Mary. And I see you and am yours forever."

A lifetime of sisterly teasing left me suspicious of effervescence. "Is this a campaign so I fall at her feet as well?"

"Of course not. Only... we *are* the great wyves. We should be united." She lifted my wrist to her lips for a fleeting kiss.

Impulsively, I leaned and kissed her lips. I intended a chaste touch in this place of remembrance, but she pressed back, and my breath caught. Her lip balm, beeswax and peppermint, tingled.

Lizzy would not mind. She would just smile and study the sky.

"Do you trust Pemberley at last?" Georgiana whispered.

"I should not."

"Will you be civil to Emma, at least?" I gave a grudging nod, and she smiled. "Good, because here she is."

"I fear I have intruded," Emma's voice called behind me.

Georgiana's eyes had lit with amusement. Outmaneuvered, I answered, "You are welcome."

Emma came up, dressed in surprisingly sensible walking clothes. She made a respectful curtsy to Lizzy's sculpture. "I sometimes visit to talk with her. To imagine her advice. I am worried about a choice I made." She folded her hands, freed of the fixations I had noticed yesterday. "But I know I am right."

I tugged my arm free of Georgiana and found that was solely so I could cross my arms and scowl. *Be civil.* I tapped my fingers on my sleeve, seeking a topic. "Do you still sense Yuánchi?"

"In a way," she said vaguely.

She and Yuánchi had been destined to bind. But fate decreed this harsher path.

I gestured to the three of us. "Georgiana said we are the great wyves. But not truly." I met Georgiana's questioning gaze. "You are the wyfe of song. I am redundant."

"No," Emma said. "You are joined. Can you not tell?" She took off her gloves and offered her palms. Georgiana took one. Uneasy, I took the other, then held Georgiana's hand so we formed a triangle.

I expected a show of effort—Lizzy had always concentrated to invoke her powers—but Emma smiled sunnily. "There is the most beautiful blue glow of binding between you. When I first saw it, I fancied that you had bound each other. But that was silly. You cannot bind without a draca. It is... a shared promise of binding. But even as a promise, it is bright. When you bind, it will be a marvel."

Georgiana gave me an enchanted grin. I sensed something too, but what it was, other than love, I could not say.

With a quick-drawn breath, Emma turned to the western hills. One rounded crest seemed to rise and darken, then Fènnù's silhouette soared over the summit. She sped downslope, too distant to hear, but the treetops in her wake shook like grass in a squall. An airy rumble reached us as she skimmed the waves, so low that her claws cut the water and tossed spray twenty feet high. Then her wings stroked, lifting her like a wild swan.

"She will pass twice more," I said, for that pattern had never altered.

She banked and crossed again, then flapped a long, curved path around the valley's periphery to begin her third pass from the far shore.

Precisely from the far shore. Her shape hung pendulous above the water, swelling.

"She is coming here," Georgiana observed, her voice a little high. "Is that usual?"

"No," I admitted.

The rumble became thunder, and her monstrous bulk filled our eyes before she veered, wings flaring. A torrent of wind and spray pummeled the shore forty yards beside us, but my skirts only fluttered as I brushed blown locks from my eyes.

Fènnù settled, broad chest toward us, gravel creaking beneath her claws, her wings held half-spread and her shoulders hunched, a posture ungainly and uneasy like a wounded bird. Her head tilted one way and another, studying us. Her slit nostrils gaped like chimneys for each bellowing breath. Venomous drops leaked from the sores on her jaw and wings, and an astringent scent prickled.

"Goodness, she is very big," Georgiana said tensely. "Why did she land? I thought she sought Yuánchi. Or the dagger."

"Do not worry," I said, summoning courage. "I have spoken with her before. Spoken *to* her, at least."

"*When?*"

"When Lizzy and I flew to London."

"Were you going to tell me?"

"A great deal happened after."

Emma's face was uplifted and raptured. "She hurts. She fears us, or... no, she remembers fear. Her mind skitters like breaking glass."

"Lizzy wanted me to understand her," I said. "To help her. I should approach."

"No!" Georgiana locked my wrist in both hands. "Mary, she is not a book to puzzle through."

With a feathery flutter, a shining blue song draca landed by my foot. Another plopped down a yard in front. A third, the bold one that had followed from London, found my shoulder, his ebony claws pricking through layers of cloth. These arrivals no longer surprised me, although I did not know why they came.

They all watched Fènnù, curious but no worse than that.

"They would not come if there were danger," I said, not sure that was true, and eased Georgiana's fingers loose. Encouraged by woodwind cheeps, I took a step, then another, but, heart pounding, my knees balked at a third. Awe had overpowered my resolve.

Perhaps a respectful distance was wise.

"Do you recall our meeting?" I called out. "You sought my sister. But she is lost."

Fènnù stepped forward. The impact of her foot rattled pebbles under my toes and sent ripples across the lake. She towered, a behemoth that exceeded the sky.

Georgiana's fingers, slim and strong, meshed with my hand. Emma's grip, gentle but certain, took my other. Georgiana hummed a melody, and in my mind's eye, the musical counterpoint to her song assembled—

I saw three great wyves crowned in shining auras of gold. Their clothes were ancient styles that celebrated wisdom and rank. They stood on a lakeshore—not Pemberley lake, but like enough to dredge this memory from the sea of past lives.

The first wyfe's outstretched arm held a gleaming black dagger. The second's raised hand held an amulet that shimmered scarlet. The third stood simply, her empty hands spread and welcoming.

They brought glorious song, then drowned in black and death.

REALITY RETURNED IN JUDDERING STEPS. I had fallen hard to my knees; my shins were bruised from the rocks. The oily dampness of half-dried tears clung to my jaw.

The three tiny song draca were poking in crevices and puddles. Bored. Fènnù was gone.

Georgiana's palms cradled my cheeks. "Mary?"

"I am myself," I said. "Did you see?"

"Yes," she whispered. "Three wyves."

"It was their attempt to heal the song. Their failure." I committed the vision to memory—the wyves' clothes, their hair and complexion, the shape of the lake and color of the foliage, my glimpse of the amulet, and... that *song*. "They had only two items. That is why they failed. The wyfe of war held the dagger, and the wyfe of healing held the amulet. But the wyfe of song had nothing. They had not found the claw."

"I saw their bindings," Emma said in a wondering voice. "One shone with the scarlet of Yuánchi. One held the beautiful blue you two share, radiant as a sun. But the third, the wyfe who held the dagger, was unbound. *That* is why they failed. The wyverns told me over and over that a wyfe must bind for strength."

The three of us traded uncertain looks. Whatever inadequacy doomed those wyves, our preparation was worse. The bravest of us was lost, and the dagger with her. And, despite the glimmer that joined Georgiana and me, none of us were bound.

But Emma's words filled my mind's eye with swirling pages. Passages coalesced, and I realized my error.

I pushed to my feet and grasped Emma's shoulders. "You feel the scarlet of Yuánchi's binding. That strength is why you are healthy at Pemberley."

"This is no secret," she said, but her hazel eyes were wary.

"That is why you *touch* Mr. Darcy! To harvest that strength."

Trapped in my grip, she had to fumble blindly to tug her gloves from her reticule. "I am... Mary, I know it is improper... I mean no harm. I hide it so he is not shamed."

I hugged her, which earned an astonished yelp, then I splashed into the shallows of the lake, the chill ferocious around my ankles. "When Jane had binding sickness, we pored through old lore. There have always been widowed wyves who hold their bound draca—a few, at least. But *only* wyves. Draca bind through the wyfe. No widowed husband can hold a binding."

Motion on the path to Pemberley house caught my gaze. A tall rider on a gray horse was exiting the switchbacks to the lake. Mr. Darcy had seen Fènnù and ridden to us.

The sanctum of Pemberley lake stretched before me, and I knew why Fènnù came. She waited for her sleeping wyfe to wake. Whether her vigil would last days or centuries I could not say, but today I shouted, "Lizzy is alive!"

End of Book 2
the story will conclude
in Book 3 of Jane Austen Fantasy

THANK you for reading *Emma's Dragon*. I always write bonus fiction for mail list subscribers, but this time I got carried away and wrote a short novella, *Emma in Highbury*. It's a cozy read (we've had enough tension) set at Emma's home a few years before *Emma's Dragon*.

If you'd like the free ebook, which also has deleted scenes and other notes, please sign up for news at mverant.com/join. The only news I send is book announcements, so you'll receive about one email per year.

I'd be very appreciative if you take a moment to rate or review *Emma's Dragon*. Reader reviews are crucial for a book's success, and they help other readers find stories they enjoy.

Find out more about me and my books at mverant.com or follow me on Bluesky @mverant.com

May you be bound with love.

M. Verant

AUSTEN'S EMMA, RACE IN THE REGENCY, AND OCD

AN AFTERWORD

Occasionally, I'm asked: Why mess with Jane Austen? Why not write these books as stand-alone fantasy?

The short answer is that I love Austen, so this is my homage to an innovative writer and her beloved characters. In fact... why *not* include Austen? I enjoy imagining how Austen's stories would change in this altered world.

That reimagining drives the first book, *Miss Bennet's Dragon*, as it retells Austen's *Pride and Prejudice*. There are twists (draca, the occasional death), but the original story arc holds until, stretched by draca and a world at war, we thunder into a dramatically different end.

Retelling another Austen novel was not an option for book 2. When book 1 finishes, Lizzy has bound Yuánchi, and the English military wants him. I could hardly abandon Lizzy's story. Still, there was room for more Austen. But which novel? *Persuasion* is too introspective and delicate; it deserves its own world. *Sense and Sensibilities* would be fun, but it's a lot like P&P. However, for an edgier, darker, middle-of-trilogy volume... *Emma*, welcome aboard! And although *Emma's Dragon* is not a retelling, a great deal of Austen's *Emma* is threaded in these pages—and remains for book 3, as Emma's story is unfinished.

Why pick Emma as a character? She's well-intentioned and caring. She's privileged and overconfident—so overconfident that, in Austen's novel, she thoughtlessly ruins her friend Harriet's life not once but twice. She's superficial, introspective, annoying, charming, manipulative, sweet... the list is endless. She is Austen's most complex heroine.

My portrayal of Emma began with a question: What if Emma had not married before her father died? Chapter 16 (Away from Mayfair) and 20 (Call me Emma) show Emma begging her brother-in-law John for funds and freedom. In 1813 England, the dangers facing Emma would be very real, including being locked in an asylum. That was a tried-and-true solution for male relatives when an unmarried heiress refused to surrender her funds. After all, a gentleman has to pay his gambling debts somehow.

Emma's hallucinations and her obsession with clothes show obsessive-compulsive disorder, a debilitating mental illness (nothing like our casual jokes of "I'm so OCD! My spice rack is alphabetized!"). Emma's condition is a magical malady with unrealistic aspects, but when possible I've tried to portray a severe form of OCD sometimes called "Pure OCD." Rose Bretécher's autobiographical book, *Pure*, is a moving account of this.

Emma's self-centered project to elevate Harriet in society reminds me of white savior complex, which is why Harriet is Black in this novel, and why Knightley's rebuke of Emma in chapter 41 (Box Hall) includes those concepts. However, the modern white savior concept fits Regency society only so far. Emma's project to elevate Harriet is more about class than race, reflecting England's restrictive class hierarchy.

A Black Harriet requires other changes. In Austen's *Emma*, Harriet is a meek dishrag who worships Emma. With Emma white and Harriet Black, that dynamic would be cringeworthy. My Harriet has more backbone.

Knightley, a Black gentleman, adds Regency London's more sophisticated perspective on race. Records from the 1810s (books, articles, court records) veer between offensively dated and remarkably progressive. There was racism, but many Regency social norms would fit neatly in a 21st century liberal society. For example, the Regency's polite designation of race was "white" or "black"; other than capitalization, many newspaper articles from the time meet modern style guidelines for race.

Other history is surprising to a modern reader. Slaves were free once they set foot in England, yet slaves visited England with their owners, then departed with them, returning to their slave status. Then, like now, barriers of economics and education enabled exploitation. If you're curious, I recommend Mary Prince's biography, the harrowing story of how she, a West Indies slave, attained her freedom in England.

Mr. Knightley is loosely inspired by a real Afro-European violinist of that time, George Bridgetower, a performer Beethoven so admired that he dedicated a sonata to him (before their angry falling out). Articles in *The Times* mention Black gentlemen, and mixed-race marriages, although unusual, were accepted in liberal society. Even without *Bridgerton*-style colorblind casting, Emma and Knightley's romance is quite possible.

Having said that, I'm a novelist, not a historian. I take liberties with history for storytelling, and I make mistakes. The errors are my fault.

If you'd like to dive deeper into the book, sign up for my mail list and download the free companion ebook. That includes the *Emma in Highbury* novella, notes about Mary's choice of music and poetry for the Aria ceremony, and lots more. Sign up at mverant.com/join. Thank you again for reading.

ACKNOWLEDGMENTS

Emma's Dragon would have been impossible without the help of my wife, who has a remarkable tolerance for hearing me ramble about plot before offering her excellent advice. Equally important were the friends, fans, and colleagues who beta read the book. I owe an extra thank-you to those who read the distressingly dark first draft!

Critique groups were invaluable. Our tiny four-person CWC gang has unfailingly traded cross-genre excerpts for years, and the East Bay Science Fiction and Fantasy Writers is a fabulous group supporting many writers (worldwide since our meetings went virtual). I attended the Milford Writers' Conference to critique *Tiger Seed*, a different project, but the positive writing energy powered me through the last pages of *Emma's Dragon*.

Some locales stand out. With COVID restrictions easing, we visited the fascinating Chelsea physic garden. Thanks to Pippa, our guide, who cheerfully provided bonus Regency details after the main tour. I enjoyed touring Apsley House, the Duke of Wellington's home in London, which documents his personal life and close friendships with women (an influence on book 3). Lastly, the National Museum of African American History and Culture in Washington, D.C. is a must-see. That soul-wrenching history informed Knightley's family backstory.

Finally, my thanks to two Regency authors: Jane Austen, a crafter of timeless stories, and Mary Shelley, who inspires Mary Bennet's character and the voice of Mary's journal.

ABOUT THE AUTHOR

M. Verant writes noblebright fantasy where good eventually triumphs and worthy people fall in love. His latest work is *Dragons of the Great Wyves*, which completes the award-winning Jane Austen Fantasy trilogy. Next project is likely *Tiger Seed*, a contemporary fantasy rooted in ancient Indus history. He's active in the writing community, moderating the East Bay Science Fiction and Fantasy Writers and serving on the SFWA Independent Authors Committee. In spare moments, he collects Jane Austen paraphernalia and two-legged dragons while dodging wild turkeys in the San Francisco Bay Area.

BY M. VERANT

Thrillers

Power in the Age of Lies

Jane Austen Fantasy

Miss Bennet's Dragon

Emma's Dragon

Dragons of the Great Wyves

www.ingramcontent.com/pod-product-compliance
Lightning Source LLC
Chambersburg PA
CBHW032142190726
48290CB00005BB/1360